WINDMASTER'S BANE

"HOLDS THE READER SPELLBOUND!
ENCHANTING!"
Fantasy Review

FIRESHAPER'S DOOM

"EVEN BETTER!
YOU'VE GOT ANOTHER WINNER HERE!"
Katherine Kurtz

TOM DEITZ

"GIVES EVERY INDICATION
OF HAVING SEVERAL MORE EQUALLY
IMPRESSIVE TALES UP HIS SLEEVE.
FEW WRITERS MATCH PERSONAL CRISIS
WITH EPIC CONFLICT AS EFFECTIVELY."
Dragon

THE GRYPHON KING

TOM DEITZ

AVON BOOKS  NEW YORK

THE GRYPHON KING is an original publication of Avon Books. This work has never before appeared in book form. This work is a novel. Any similarity to actual persons or events is purely coincidental.

AVON BOOKS
A division of
The Hearst Corporation
105 Madison Avenue
New York, New York 10016

First Avon Books Printing: June 1989

AVON TRADEMARK REG. U.S. PAT. OFF. AND IN OTHER COUNTRIES, MARCA REGISTRADA, HECHO EN U.S.A.

Printed in the U.S.A.

K-R 10 9 8 7 6 5 4 3 2 1

for
Mike, who survived Park Hall,
Barb, who braved the library,
and
Brad, who got the double whammy

Acknowledgments

Denver Adams and Michael Bishop
Mary Ellen Brooks and Jack Dominey
Jim Dunning and "Mama Celia"
Midge Easterling and J. Larry Gulley
E. Gilbert Head and Margaret Dowdle Head
Sylvia Hillyard and Arthur Hinds
Jacquie Houston and Cathryn Farebrother Jackson
D. J. Jackson and Rick Johnson
James Kibler and Adele Leone
Chris Miller and John Monk
Klon Newell and Robert Owen
William Provost and Vickie R. Sharp
Barbara Strickland and Brad Strickland
and . . .
all the folk of Athens, Georgia,
—past or present, real or feigned—
who may find themselves reflected hereinafter

Author's Note

Though most of this novel is set in the very real city of Athens, Georgia, it should not be assumed that an exact correspondence exists between any persons, places, or institutions and those herein depicted. The author's craft often dictates that primary reality be blurred or reconfigured—sometimes for the sake of freedom *of* expression, sometimes for the sake of freedom *from* litigation. For this reason, those inclined to close inspection will note that no such building as Friedman Hall currently exists on the University of Georgia campus and that certain agencies have been uprooted from their present precincts and relocated elsewhere. The drama department and rare book library, in particular, bear no relation to their actual staff or situation.

Nor has reality modification been confined to the university campus. Toombs Avenue does not figure on any map of Athens I have seen, for instance; and there is no such emporium as Tennis Bird Shorts. Similarly, the site I have chosen for Scarboro Faire is, as best I can determine, presently a patch of scrub forest with no designs afoot for its elevation into anything more evocative. And finally, though some major characters have names common—even prominent—in the area, no direct analogy to any actual persons, living or dead, is intended.

Thomas F. Deitz
November 1988

Prologue: Precaution

(Ripon, North Yorkshire, England— Early March)

Professor Charles Bowman-Smith, who had until the previous summer occupied the Hollingsworth Chair of Comparative Religion at the College of Ripon and York St. John, had suddenly found himself wishing he had time to occupy even a footstool. The packers had arrived in the middle of breakfast, and he had been scurrying about in his robe and slippers ever since, attending to the details incumbent upon simultaneously preparing his massive library for overseas shipment and the remainder of his possessions for an imminent move to Morecambe, all in a frantic haste that left him quite breathless. He should have had hours yet to sort through the shelves in the surrounding study, but he was obviously not going to get them.

No time for sitting around today, he told himself, much less for the sort of wistful contemplation with which he liked to fill his mornings. Sixty years seemed like such a

3

little while when you looked back on them—sixty years probing wicca covens and voodoo cultists, foot-washing Baptists and Holy Rollers, not to mention that New Age foolishness.

New Age indeed! *Old* age was his problem now. Bowman-Smith sighed and propped his bony octogenarian body against a doorjamb, oblivious to the nip of chill breeze sneaking in from the adjoining vestibule where the packers were running in and out the front door. Something tickled his nostrils, and he sneezed, then wrinkled his nose at the faint odor of mildew insinuating itself into air already thick with dust roused from ancient slumber.

And of course it would *be raining,* he added to himself, directing a frown through mullioned panes at the steady late-winter drizzle that had apparently soured the packers as well. Having to fill crate after wooden crate with books, pad the crannies with crumpled newspaper, then wrap the whole mess with metal strapping and protective plastic sheeting and tote the beastly heavy things out to a mismatched pair of Transits was enough to foul anyone's spirits. And these fellows were no exception.

They were a dubious lot at best: local lads he'd recruited at the Black Bull with a promise of more pay than he could really manage—at least until the cheque for his library arrived from across the water. He could hear the young infidels now, scraping and thudding about as they cleared the four big cases in the hallway.

A sharp screech tortured his ears, and he grimaced, certain someone had dragged a crate across a stretch of polished oak flooring. A heavy thump followed, then another and another, each louder and more nerve-racking than the one before. The floor trembled beneath his slippers, and he thought he caught the heart-stopping sound of paper ripping. Coarse guffaws ensued; and Bowman-Smith ground his teeth on the stem of his empty briarwood. Gad, what a bunch of heathens.

One lad was *not* dubious, however, and he was an odd lot in more than that. He was an American, for one thing: a

solid, handsome, dark-haired fellow a little younger than
the others. True, he spoke mostly in interjections; but his
sharp eyes, nimble fingers, and bouncing steps told of a
zest for life and learning that was absent in his companions. That boy had actually seemed interested in some of
Bowman-Smith's books, and had even shown some reverence for the valuable first editions he was loading into
crates addressed to:

REED-GILLESPIE RARE BOOK AND MANUSCRIPT LIBRARY
UNIVERSITY OF GEORGIA
ATHENS, GEORGIA 30602
USA

Idly Bowman-Smith pondered what the University of
Georgia might want with his lifetime's hoardings, though
he knew they had already bought several other private British libraries. His old friend A. L. Rowse, for one, had sent
them veritable lorryloads of British local history, and they
had a number of important theological collections as well.

"Wondering about it doesn't get the work done," he
muttered, then sighed and began scanning the shelves to
the left of the doorway. This was the material he was most
uncertain about, the section on the occult arts: Albertus
Magnus and Montague Sommers: Hugh Hohman's *Long-
Lost Friend;* Dr. Dee's *Conversations with Some Spirits*
(would the university want that? he wondered—they already had Rowse's copy); Judge Keith Hilary Pursuivant's
Vampyricon and *The Unknown that Terrifies;* Pratt's *Perse-
cution of the Tennessee Witches.* . . . The list went on and
on. His gaze wandered down to the next shelf: more of the
same, and bound bibliographies listing others.

What did it matter, he decided, it was all nonsense anyway: let 'em take the bundle. He had already sent a few
choice volumes to his son's place in Morecambe, and most
of the remainder he could get in modern paperback editions. For the rest, he doubted he would really miss them.
It was his watercolors that called to him now; he desper-

ately wanted to do an illustrated version of "Barbara Allen" for his great-granddaughter's birthday.

A troubled frown creased his forehead as he gave the shelves a second going-over. Nonsense or not, these books were old and fragile. He dared not trust them to the packers' none-too-tender mercies: far too many of their spines would rip off if ill handled; others might fall away to powder. He'd unshelve them himself, then watch every move while they were crated—preferably by the American.

Loading his arms, Bowman-Smith carried some of the sturdier items to the walnut table that graced the middle of the chamber. A second batch followed, then a dozen or so more. His joints began to ache, his breathing to grow labored.

Eventually, though, the shelves were empty: every precious volume stacked upon the table—except one.

That one.

It stood alone now, high on a shelf dusted into scallops by time and neglect. Though it had been in the family since 1511, there was nothing really special about its appearance —if you were used to incunabula. The flaking leather spine, thick oak boards, and heavy brass clasps spanning sturdy rag paper were all typical of the period—1490— when it had been published. Nor were its contents unusual; it was a standard copy of St. Augustine's *City of God*.

Yet something about it had always disturbed him, made him reluctant to touch it, hesitant even to gaze on its bog-brown binding. His late wife had never opened it, saying it gave her the willies; his son had run screaming when as a child he had caught Bowman-Smith nervously prowling its ragged pages. "It was watching me," the five year old had told him. "I felt like it wanted to eat me." Bowman-Smith understood perfectly. He had never shown it to either of the next two generations. By slow degrees he had allowed himself to forget it.

That was rather peculiar, too, now he thought of it; such hints of the paranormal usually attracted him, skeptic though he was. Well, he wouldn't put it off any longer; as soon as he had got reestablished, he'd make it his first priority. He was still a scholar, after all; he needed to understand, to analyze such illogical feelings.

Maybe it was simply the book's age that troubled him. It *was* a major Bowman-Smith heirloom, and perhaps he had a subliminal fear of damaging it. But he had other volumes equally old, equally valuable, that he did not hesitate to lay before the occasional curious visitor; yet he had never done anything of the sort with *that* book, nor felt inclined to.

Could his aversion possibly lie in the epoch the book represented, when God *was* in his heaven, and the flames of Hell licked close beneath one's feet; and Death with his grinning skull-face and grim scythe haunted every dark corner of the world. Maybe that was it—religion was fine when it was remote from you, a quaint aberration from another age. But the man who had written *that* book had *believed,* and through it Bowman-Smith could actually share in that belief. He had handled other old books before, of course: books centuries older. But his own past had not met him then; not *his* ancestral God or Devil.

But what was he going to *do* with the bloody thing?

The Americans could not have it—not, at any rate, until he made up his mind what caused such bizarre reactions. Better put it out of the way in the bedroom so there would be no confusion. And he should move the sword that went with it; wouldn't do for the two of them to get separated—though why he thought that he couldn't say.

Still puzzling over his decision, he padded to an adjacent cabinet, unlatched it, and reached inside. Knobby roughness met his fingers: the wire-wound leather and bright-gilded brass hilt of a well-used antique broadsword. Late fourteenth century, tradition said that weapon was, though he'd never got around to having it authenticated. In any event, the sword, like the book, had been in his family for generations; and in its own way was easily as disturbing. Should he check it one more time?

He slid the blade from its leather scabbard and flourished it, filled anew with the curiously youthful exultation that grasping it somehow instilled in him, then paused; held his breath for an instant, waiting.

For *sometimes* touching the sword invoked a terrible sense of foreboding. On those occasions—and they were mercifully few and unpredictable, and this was evidently not one—the weapon seemed to vibrate in his hand: a curious low-pitched thrum that unnerved and confounded and fascinated him. And, he suddenly realized, this was yet another irrationality he had never found time to follow up on. *Two* atypical memory lapses, now, and a troublesome concession to superstition.

Frowning, Bowman-Smith stared at the weapon for a troubled moment longer. As he sheathed it a broken hilt wire snagged his finger, bringing forth a tiny bead of scarlet. He swore absently, considered affixing a Band-Aid, but decided against it. Instead, he laid the sword on the table beside the mounded volumes, shuffled back to the empty shelves, and reached for *that* book—no sense making two trips, after all. It was heavier than he recalled, and as he strained to lift it, he felt something twitch in his rib cage. His breath caught. *Dammit, old son, you've pulled something.*

It twitched again.

And then the twitches became white-hot pain that clamped around his heart and squeezed, then yielded first to fear, next to resignation, and finally to a startled joy that seeped into his mind like dark still water and drowned him utterly.

In the outer room one of the packers jerked upright, glanced sideways at his fellows.

"'ey, you blokes 'ear somethin' fallin' hin there? Somethin' 'eavy-like?"

"'Tweren't nothin'; prob'ly just the ol' bloke knockin' things over."

"Yeah, man, but he *might* of fallen. He could be, like, hurt, y'know."

"So *you* check on 'im, Yank."

"Yeah, *Yank*, see wot the ol' bloke's up to."

And so it was that the American boy found Professor Charles Bowman-Smith lying dead on his study floor beside an eight-foot table mounded two feet deep in books. It was he who told the disbelieving others, he who called the doctor and the police, and he who presumed to finish Bowman-Smith's packing for him, by removing the single remaining book from the shelf (as the old man had obviously meant to do), then secreting it in the bottom of one of the crates beside the sword he had already put there.

Two days later, Professor Charles Bowman-Smith was buried in a private cemetery near Fountains Abbey. The American boy—who'd had headaches and troublesome dreams for a couple of days, and remembered very little about the packing—had gone back to his regular job at the pottery. And the Bowman-Smith Collection was on its way to the University of Georgia.

PART I

Chapter I: Pilgrimage

(Athens, Georgia—April 2)

"You can always find somebody stranger than you are in Athens," Jay Madison's girlfriend had told him. "A place of inspired craziness," was his roommate's equally apt observation. "Oz Upon The Oconee," his musician friend Piper had styled it. And now, eyeing the outlandish figure trundling through the Friday morning South Lumpkin Street traffic, Jay was more than ever inclined to agree with them.

The Green Rug Man, folks called this particular aberration, because of the rectangle of lime-colored shag the fellow wore serape style across his narrow shoulders. That he usually accompanied it with a battered top hat, scruffy jeans embroidered with calculus formulae, and a fringed black leather vest—and was inevitably perched atop a rickety unicycle—generally garnered little more acknowledgment than an elevated eyebrow.

But it could hardly be otherwise, Jay concluded. For

Athens, Georgia, was a college town, and its very nature (to quote from one of his old sociology papers) "set a pattern of subtly enhanced animation: a pound-and-pulse of energy born of new bodies, new freedom—even, sometimes, newfound knowledge—each seeking expression and equilibrium." That was a bullshitty way of describing the student mentality, he now admitted, but it was nevertheless accurate. Freshman year sowed the seeds of incipient lunacy; the next three weeded and watered them; by the time grad school rolled around, they were ready to put forth their strange flowers.

And despite his twenty-three years, Jay was right up there with the best of them as far as lunacy was concerned. For Jason Marcus Madison was filled with a keen-edged impatience that—along with Lloyd Cole's frenetic "Perfect Skin" booming on the Monarch's cassette player—set his head bobbing and his long fingers tapping the steering wheel so fast it attracted giggles two cars over.

Dread and anticipation were what did it. First the bad part: a long-delayed thesis conference with the Elf (as he called his youthful major professor and sometime sadistic taskmaster, Dr. Peter Girvan Sparks), then two hours of Old Norse seminar. But after that things would get better, 'cause then he would get to see his sweetie.

Though it had only been an hour since he had left her bed, Jay couldn't help but grin when he thought of her: Dahlia Cobb—rich (relative to him, anyway), gorgeous (by any standard), talented (was there ever a doubt?) daughter of an Atlanta judge and a female Athens attorney. Those were the basics, yet they did her no justice. Drama major, art minor; slender, blue-eyed, brunette: again, only words that could apply to hundreds on the University of Georgia campus. Trilingual, omnivorous poetry reader, former artist's model, sometime New Wave singer: that was getting closer.

His lady: that was the heart of the matter. She was Jay's first true love, and he was an incurable romantic. He knew

it, accepted it, played it to the hilt at every opportunity—
and was about to embark on another indulgence. This afternoon was Dal's first public performance as Lady Macbeth, even if it was technically an open dress rehearsal,
and he didn't want to miss a second. The play was one of
his favorites, too. He almost couldn't stand the anticipation.

But attendance at one of Dal's shows demanded precise
preparations. He patted a cubical bulge in the pocket of his
black leather jacket; good, that part of his surprise was still
in there. He would give it to her before the performance—
if he could connect with the other half. It was time, he
supposed, to call in the heavy artillery; time to ring up
good old Scotto. Then four hours to go, plus or minus,
until the Ritual started.

If there were no more complications . . .

He sniffled liquidly. Speaking of complications, this in-
fernal cold was another; along with the rainy weather that
had begot it. It had held off so far this morning, but Jay
doubted his luck would continue.

And indeed it did not, for scarcely five minutes later—
just as he eased the Monarch's grimy black bulk into its
parking space beside the railroad tracks—a single vast
drop of water cog-wheeled onto the windshield. It was followed by an ambush of others.

Rain washed Athens, Georgia, then: washed College
Square with its bright, turn-of-the-century storefronts;
washed the columned mansions of Historic Cobbham and
Prince and Milledge avenues; washed Georgia Square Mall
and the strip of fast-food restaurants and car dealers along
the Atlanta Highway; washed the old bricks and wide
decks of the mill at O'Malley's, and the gaudy garage door
facade of the Rockfish Palace, and the matte black cavern
of the Uptown Lounge. Washed the University of Georgia's Greek revival chapel and art deco Memorial Hall and
the modern, angled slabs of the art building. And washed
the futuristic black marble and mirror glass cube of the
drama department's brand-new showpiece, Friedman Hall,

which stood on a sloping hillside that two years before had been Jackson Street Cemetery.

It also washed away most of Jay's humor.

He sighed, slapped an *Athens Observer* atop his spiky dark hair, and began the long soggy trudge up the steep steps beside Friedman. There was a silver Corvette parked behind it, he noted through rain-streaked lenses. And that was *all* he needed.

Robert Inman Tolar (who *drove* that silver Corvette) wasn't at all certain when he had got in the habit of reading other people's correspondence. It was not a good thing to do, he knew, but somehow he could not seem to help himself. He had started with magazines; it was easy to spot them in the other boxes ranked around his in the drama department office. They'd stay there for days sometimes: unnoticed, unread—especially when their intended recipients were on sabbatical or out of town. One day he'd simply grown tired of waiting and snatched a *Theater Arts* when old half-blind Ms. Marx, the department secretary, wasn't looking. He'd given it a quick once-over for an hour or so, then sneaked it back when she was on her break, and no one was ever the wiser.

That was how it had begun. But from magazines Rob had graduated to campus mail: yellow envelopes that were not usually sealed, or if so, were frequently secured only with hoary cellophane. He'd learned some interesting things that way—things involving promotions and tenure and departmental infighting. Then he'd gone on to full-fledged letters—not often, only when they promised some particularly useful tidbit about one of the faculty or a fellow teaching assistant. It was easy enough: just tear into the item, scan the contents, then scrawl "opened by mistake" on the envelope and clumsily reseal it. All that was required was that he be careful not to pull the deception on the same person too many times close together.

This morning, however, he was disappointed. There were neither letters nor magazines in any of the boxes adjoining his in the Friedman Hall office—unless you counted *Research Reporter* or *Columns,* UGA's biweekly staff newsletter, which everybody got. Nor was there anything else of interest. He checked his own box, found a couple of deadly dull memos about when mid-term grades were due, the expected personal copies of *Columns* and *R.R.* And a catalog from Carolina Mountain University Press. Ah, well, if he couldn't get scandal and sedition, he'd take anything he could flip through in his office for the few minutes before his nine o'clock survey.

Mail in hand, Rob sauntered out into a high-arched hallway where floor-to-ceiling windows alternated with identical mirrors to show him first the sudden spring downpour, then his own bright reflection: six-one and lean-bodied with short, dark hair and blue-gray eyes. Not bad, he admitted, but he stopped looking after the third repetition because he thought he had seen a particular someone at the end of the corridor. Medium tall, sleek black hair, slim body in black leotard, man's gray suit jacket, and India skirt—could it be . . . ?

No. As he drew nearer the face that looked coyly over a padded shoulder at him was not the one he had hoped for: not his number one Object of Desire, the Fabulous Dahlia Cobb. The unknown girl flashed a tentative smile, but Rob only glowered scornfully back. The smile faded abruptly, and the girl stiffened and turned away. Rob did smile then but only because he had felt the tingle of power. Fear or admiration, jealousy, even love, all were his to conjure at a moment's notice; and all were equally potent weapons to command. That girl had received only the tiniest taste of his arsenal. If he had chosen the right combination of grins and glances and casual conversation, he could have had her for his bed by eleven; he would have bet his life on it. His current squeeze, Erin Stillwell, had been almost that easy a conquest.

He was still smiling as he pounded down two flights of black marble stairs and entered another arching corridor. Third door to the right, and he entered the cramped cubbyhole his department had decided was sufficient for a mere grad student—even a first-string Phudder like himself.

Rob poured himself a steaming mug from the Mr. Coffee atop the filing cabinet and settled back in the chair. Nothing in *Columns*, of course, except the usual lists of tenure recipients and . . . He turned the page.

"Shit!" he spat as he saw the photograph at the top of the right-hand column. Dark eyes stared out at him—dark eyes beneath darker brows that almost met, near-black hair cut short and high tech; high cheekbones, good strong nose; a face that might have been a younger version of his own had not the cheeks and chin been softer, the lips fuller and turned up in a smug, quirky smile Rob could not have copied had he wished to. His scowl deepened as he scanned the caption underneath: *Jay Madison Wins Bishop Prize with Essay on Yukio Mishima.* "So little bro's won another one, huh?" he muttered. "Yeah, sure, and five hundred bucks, too. Probably blow it all romancing his lady."

Rob crumpled the paper in disgust. *That* was something he didn't want to think about: his scrawny half brother and the Fabulous Dahlia Cobb going at it. He'd even heard rumors of marriage—as if the naive little twerp could afford to maintain the world-wise Miss Cobb in the manner to which she was accustomed. She was much more Rob's kind of lady. That she'd adamantly resisted his advances for over three years—ever since they'd had a class together when she was still an undergraduate—simply made her that much more desirable. And if he could also steal her away from his brother, that would be even better. He glanced at the picture again, thought of the two of them together. It made him want to vomit.

His mood soured, Rob scanned the other publications. *Research Reporter* had some stuff on biomass. *Yawn.* There was a copy of the summer quarter registration schedule. *Yawn, yawn.* He tossed them all in the trash, picked up the CMU Press catalog, and flipped aimlessly through the pages.

His expression brightened as he scanned the full-page advertisement for the latest volume in CMU's Celtic Stud-

ies series. He read it again to make certain it actually said
what casual inspection had indicated. A smile curled across
his features.

Wait'll baby brother sees this! he crowed silently. *Won't
that little bastard be surprised!*

And bastard was just the word for him, too: Mom had
already been carrying Marcus Madison's child when the
divorce papers were filed which ended her marriage to the
nearly psychotic 'Lanta Carpets heir, Arthur Tolar. In spite
of a few raised eyebrows, the courts had decided she was
by far the best parent for both children, and Rob's dad had
been strongly advised not to contest the ruling; it would be
bad for the corporate image—and besides, everyone knew
Arthur had married beneath himself.

Rob had been a canny three-year-old at the time, but
Dad had made sure his son never forgot who his *real* father
was by setting up an astonishing trust fund, the interest on
which was redeemable in fractions starting on Rob's eigh-
teenth birthday, and meanwhile sending him birthday and
Christmas checks that were more than the poor woman
made in a month. She had moved the lot of them to Blairs-
ville, Georgia, where she had begun dabbling in real estate, and Dad had died five years later of cirrhosis of the
liver. By then, though, Rob had been hopelessly spoiled
and had conceived a thorough and abiding hatred for his
younger brother, whom he identified as the cause of his
vanished prosperity, trust fund notwithstanding. Their next
nine years together had seen an escalation of rivalries, and
college had only decreased the frequency of their clashes.
Jay's award had just one-upped him again, but Rob already
knew an effective counter.

He rummaged in his desk for an X-Acto knife and freed
his newfound bombshell. He composed a quick note,
folded the ad inside it, stuffed them both in a campus mail
envelope, addressed it to Jason Marcus Madison, Department of English, Park Hall, and trotted upstairs just as the
student mail boy was picking up the morning's haul.

"This has gotta get there today," Rob stated flatly. "Will

it make it—or am I gonna have to run it over myself?"

The skinny mail boy frowned at him, looking surly under black brows almost hidden beneath a mop of curly brown hair. "Prob'ly not today," he drawled sullenly.

Rob glared back, but then remembered something he'd seen on the bulletin board downstairs, and his eyes took on a sly glitter. He stared at Ms. Marx, who, perhaps feeling the weight of that inspection, looked fearfully up at him.

"Today's the dress rehearsal, isn't it?" Rob purred. "Of *Mac*— of the Scottish Play," he corrected, though he was already cursing himself for acknowledging the ridiculous theater superstition that proclaimed it to be very bad luck to name *Macbeth* while a production was actually in progress.

"Certainly," Ms. Marx replied. "Says so right here on the calendar: 'Friday, 12:00 to 3:00. Main auditorium reserved for dress rehearsal of *M*—. Clarke Central and Cedar Shoals high schools—eleventh and twelfth grades— will be attending.'"

"How nice for them," Rob replied absently, imagining the look of despair soon to cross his half-brother's guileless features. Dahlia Cobb was in that play, and if Dal was in it, Jay would certainly be there, because he *never* missed one of her performances.

Rob grinned fiendishly, then looked back at the fidgeting mail boy. "You can run on now," he told the kid. "This is so bad I think I'd better deliver it in person."

Two buildings away, the still-damp object of Rob's machinations had just about had as much of Old Norse masculine *a*-stem nouns as he could stomach. It was not that the instructor was bad. Considering the subject matter, Dr. William Provost was a model of lively enthusiasm. Nor was the work particularly difficult, given that there was a whole lot of memorization involved, mostly of the dreaded declension. It was simply that Jay had received some encouraging news from the Elf right before class and was practically about to burst to tell Dahlia, *still* had the Ritual of Preparation to contend with, and so far hadn't heard from Scotto.

He glanced at his watch and for the tenth time that period tried to figure out if he could actually execute the entire Ritual and still make Dal's debut in time. *If* class didn't run over, *if* Dr. P. didn't take forever to make the next assignment, *if* Slowtongue Harold ever finished his labored declining of *vegr*, so the rest of them could get on with theirs. If—if—if—Jay was thrall to a bunch of conjunctions.

"Harmr, harm, harms, harmi," someone muttered behind him—probably Mary Balin; she'd started two days late and hadn't caught up yet.

Jay sniffed and looked at his watch again; saw four become five, wished it were zero, and ground his teeth slowly together. *Hurry, hurr, hurris, hurri . . .*

Eleven forty-nine finally became eleven fifty, the period ended, and Jay did not so much as pause to jot down Monday's assignment before he was out the door. He had exactly ten minutes in which to dash down the stairs, check the department office to see if the Elf had left anything there for him to work on, then execute a quick costume change in his basement office. All that remained then was to zip over to Friedman in time to deliver both his news and the surprise before claiming his accustomed place in front row center.

That was how it was *supposed* to work; but it all depended on whether his roommate, Scott Gresham, had deigned to pick up the particular special Something Jay had frantically phoned him about earlier that morning and whether he had found Jay's spare key and left that same Numinous Object in Jay's office.

Possessed (as Scott often told him) of more enthusiasm than discretion, Jay simply ignored the last two steps and leapt for the second floor landing, narrowly missing a startled freshman. As it was, Jay impacted a little harder than he had expected, and his backpack sailed up to thwack him on the back of the head. For the fourth time that morning he cursed the mass of master's thesis that hung entombed there like some misdirected albatross. *"The Secret Common-Wealth"* and Yeats's Faerie: Folklore in a Faithless Age" had never seemed so vast, so unwieldy, so—in spite of being four-fifths finished in rough draft—far from completion.

"And damn you too," Jay whispered, catching the startled boy's curse as he shouldered through the doorway. Maybe he should just forget the mail. Except that the Elf had a way of needing things done yesterday, which meant that *any* advance warning was useful.

But luck was not with Jay forty seconds later when he ventured into the offices of the English, comp. lit., classics, and linguistics departments.

The Elf had indeed been there, for Jay's wooden cubby was crammed to overflowing with printout which he recognized as the first draft of Sparks's next scholarly opus, an annotated edition of T. H. White's *The Once and Future King*. The single word "ABSTRACT" was scrawled across a yellow Post-It stuck on the top sheet. Someone cleared her throat behind him, and he looked around into the sad gray eyes of Mrs. Bowen, Dr. Sparks's personal secretary. "I think he wants it ready when he gets back from Chicago on Tuesday," she said quietly.

"Tuesday?" Jay muttered, then, "Sneaky bastard!" He sighed and flipped through the pile of paper. It wasn't as long as he had first thought, roughly ninety pages. If he was lucky he could go to the play and still get through a solid chunk before six, when he had to pick up Piper at the rare book library and haul him way the hell out in the country to band practice. He wished his friend would get his ancient Harley running, 'cause he was getting tired of having to play chauffeur.

Brow still furrowed in irritation, Jay stuffed the manuscript in his pack and darted to his office. An elbow stab on the light switch revealed a tiny sanctum sanctorum almost as severe as a monk's cell. Only a Myra Buchanan portrait of Dahlia done in ink on Japanese paper and a black-and-white rag rug (a present from LaWanda the juju woman) gave the spare cube any sparkle.

Jay dumped the pile of manuscript in the center of his desk, ripped off his backpack, and started stripping. In less than ten seconds he was down to black bikini briefs and beginning the transformation. Another sneeze, a check of the time, and he reached for the trousers of the black tuxedo that hung on the wall beside him. The boiled shirt that went with it was also black. But so was every other item in his wardrobe.

It was an affectation, he knew, but harmless—except, perhaps, in the high heat of August. But even then, he always dressed in black—Byronic black, Edgar Allan Poe black, ninja black, light black, dark black, lawyer's heart black—he had names for the subtlest variant. The important was that there be no other color—except perhaps a glint of silver or gold or maybe a delicate patterning in white or gray or crimson. It had even earned him a nickname: Black Jay Madison.

The tux itself was another eccentricity: even the most tradition-bound of Southern gentlemen had long since ceased dressing for the theater (at least the university sort on a Friday afternoon). Yet Jay insisted on wearing full formal attire for each of Dal's performances, and he had not missed one in the almost year they'd been dating. It was simply a habit—initially another manifestation of his romantic streak—but now his friends had come to expect it, and he hated to disappoint them.

Fully dressed a moment later, Jay snagged his mirror-shades (a third idiosyncrasy: he did not like just anybody to see his eyes because he said one's soul could make embarrassing declarations from there, and his was both talkative and tactless). Those windows of vulnerability safely obscured, he retrieved the Surprise and looked around for that which Scott was supposed to have delivered.

It wasn't there. Naturally.

Jay had already opened his mouth to call down curses on the thoughtless and unreliable head of Walter Scott

Gresham III, when the door snapped open and he whirled around to come eye-to-mustache with the intended object of his invective—rather squishy about the sneakers and frayed-hem Levi's but flashing his white teeth like the proverbial Tennessee 'possum.

Scott grinned wider and thrust a single black silk rose (custom ordered complete with thorns and perfume) into Jay's clutching fingers.

"Thought I'd forgot, didn't you, boy?" Scott drawled in his Foghorn Leghorn impression. "Thought ol' Scotto wouldn't come through for you, I betcha! Well, have I ever failed you, *boy?* I say, I say, have I ever *failed* you?" He stabbed a red and black umbrella into the corner trash can, then flicked a lock of curly blond hair out of his eyes as he flopped his long, rangy body against the door frame.

Jay glared at his roommate. "You *almost* made me blow the Ritual, boyo," he snapped. "Hell does not know the torments I'd have inflicted on you and you neglected to bring me this precious posy." He stuffed the rose in his buttonhole.

"If you ever get me outta bed on any such fool quest again, it'll be *me* talkin' about torments," Scott shot back, and reached over to adjust Jay's velvet bow tie.

"But it wasn't *ready* when I went by earlier," Jay objected. "And I couldn't afford to cut class 'cause of Provost's blessed pop quizes!"

"Some gentleman *you* are, sir, to set mere academia ahead of your lady," Scott snorted. "Should have given 'em more notice."

"But all those bloody Norse paradigms have plumb addled my poor simple thinker," Jay protested.

Scott regarded him skeptically. "More likely all that vino you've been kickin' back over at Miss Dally's lately. Or maybe just too much of ol' Miss Dally herself. Too much *sex-yul inner-course* destroys brain cells, y' know. So which is it, kiddo? When you gonna start warmin' your own lonesome bunkbed again?"

Jay grinned smugly and adjusted his hematite cuff links.

"Been helping Dal with her lines, Scotto. Had 'em tattooed in braille all over my body, and single-spaced on my p—"

"Jason!"

"You're the one who stands around naked while Myra Buchanan draws pictures of you!"

Scott's tanned cheeks darkened.

"Got a session today, too, don't you?"

The blush expanded to the hairline.

Jay nodded triumphantly. "I thought so." He snagged Scott's umbrella from the trash can and pushed by him into the hallway. "Hey, look, roomie, be a good chap and fold up my clothes, how 'bout it?"

Scott stared after him in confusion. "Hey, that's *my* um—" he began, then, "Goddamn it, Jason—"

"Feets don't fail me now," Jay tossed back cheerily, then was beyond further hearing.

North campus quad was a rain-shrouded parkland of lawns and oak trees surrounded by neat, one or two story brick buildings, mostly dating from the mid-nineteenth century. Roughly halfway across it, Jay felt a small pang of guilt over the stolen umbrella. Scotto was a damned good guy when you got down to it. Not just anyone could put up with Black Jay Madison on a day-to-day basis; it took somebody with a lot of tolerance and a good level head—like a lanky geology major from Tellico Plains, Tennessee.

Or like the Fabulous Dahlia Cobb: sweet Dal, perfect Dal, brilliant, beautiful, wonderful Dal. Dal the very essence of all good fortune—who would soon be his forever, if things went according to his liking. *If* he ever got nerve enough to ask her. (Another of those insidious *ifs*.)

He splashed across Jackson Street, and Friedman Hall's cantilevered facade loomed before him: a black marble cube on which the masks of tragedy and comedy peered forth as inlaid stainless steel outlines ten feet high. Jay sprinted up the wide marble stairs two at a time.

Once inside, he was engulfed by a horde of giggling, fidgeting teens. He strained to check the doors into the main auditorium, saw dark-kilted ushers still handing out programs there, then stowed the umbrella and ducked to the right to fling himself down yet another stairway.

Thirty seconds later, he emerged into the precurtain chaos backstage. Frazzle-faced stage crew were everywhere, mixing incongruously with actors and actresses in jewel-toned medieval costumes. Here a girl was sorting out weapons; there a boy adjusted Duncan's flowing mustache while his companion filled blood bags for the climatic battle. A clank of metal on metal was Macbeth trying to scratch in too-snug armor.

And there, by the row of pine boughs that would become Birnam Wood in the final act, was the Fabulous Dahlia Cobb herself, just as he had hoped to find her: eyes closed, breast rising and falling slowly as she went through the breathing exercises she always did to calm herself before a performance.

She looked magnificent: imperious and regal. Her short, jet black hair (dyed at his suggestion back in November) was at the moment obscured by a blood red wimple, and her slender body by a long, tight-sleeved robe of burgundy velvet dotted with tiny golden skulls. Her slightly pointed features had been powdered to a deathlike pallor, and her full lips were almost purple. Swatches of dark rouge accentuated her high cheekbones. All in all, she looked every inch Lady Macbeth—schemer, murderess, Machiavellian *par excellance*.

Jay froze, spellbound. That was *his* lady, his alone. After all this time, he still could not believe his luck at having actually won her. Men aplenty had tried, men smarter, richer, handsomer than he—men, in fact, like his wretched half brother—but somehow his poor, simple self had triumphed. Once he had dared ask Dal what made him so special. "Honesty," she had told him flatly, "and maybe a touch of magic."

Well, he had no idea what else he would be *except* honest—and if he had any magic, he sure didn't know where to find it, in spite of her pet name for him, Witchboy, from

Richardson's *Dark of the Moon,* in which she had played
Barbara Allen.

But Dahlia, now—*she* was magic incarnate.

And magical beings deserved very special surprises.

Jay ducked behind a convenient curtain, reached into his
jacket pocket, and pulled out the small cube that bulged
there; then flipped it open to reveal a pair of pierced earrings in the form of inch-long silver daggers. Three tiny
tear-shaped garnets depended by an almost invisible chain
from each point. He had commissioned them from their
jeweler friend, Charles Wiley; Lady Macbeth's instruments
of mayhem.

A quick glance around the curtain showed him that Dal
was still psyching, so he withdrew the earrings and jabbed
the golden points on their backs into the black rose's stem
just below the bulging calyx, where they glittered like tiny
lost stars against the tuxedo's inky satin. He squared his
shoulders then, and crept toward her.

Dal's closed eyelids never fluttered. An arm's length in
front of her, Jay withdrew the flower and wafted it gently
beneath her nostrils, then drew it delicately along the
smooth curve of her jawline.

Her eyes popped open, blinked thrice in consternation.
Jay could see her trying to shift mental gears between the
shrewish noblewoman she was about to become and the
capricious, outrageous girl who was his joy.

"I'm late," he apologized. "Sorry." He placed the flower
gently in her fingers.

Dal blinked again, her mouth rounding as she focused
on the blossom. "Good lord, Jason," she whispered, "so
this is why you sneaked off so early this morning!" Her
eyes grew even wider as she noticed that which glittered
just below the calyx. "And are those *daggers* I see before
me?" She laughed, then paused, suddenly serious. "You
really shouldn't have, you know. I don't even want to think
about what these cost you."

"Myra Buchanan's hubcaps," Jay said promptly.

"Jason!"

"My firstborn male child?" he suggested.

"Don't *I* have some say in that matter?" Dal shot back, grinning wickedly. "Unless you—"

"You *know* better."

Dal suppressed a giggle.

"Actually," Jay confessed, "I spent the Bishop money."

Dal smiled and shook her head, then cocked an inquiring eyebrow. "So spill the news, Witchboy. *Something's* obviously happened, it's written all over your face. Let me guess: the Elf had a breakthrough suggestion."

Jay blinked back surprise. He'd mentioned his appointment with Sparks so casually, he didn't think Dal had noticed. "Oh, the *thesis,*" he replied, drawing it out for effect. "Well, he was appallingly nonplussed by the whole thing. Simply shook his head, took a draw on that clay pipe of his, and told me that doubtless I had neglected to put out cream for my brownies so they had inflicted me with a case of researcher's block."

Dal folded her arms and regarded him imperiously. "Well, *did* you?"

Jay stared back at her. "Wha?"

"Forget the cream, of course."

Jay's mouth twitched sideways in his lopsided smirk, but he forced himself to be serious. "I wish it was that easy," he whispered. "But, no; he just told me to take a couple of weeks off and see what turned up. Said if nothing came to me by the end of the month then we'd both start to worry. I don't *have* to finish it this quarter—though obviously I'd like to."

Dal's brow wrinkled in perplexity. "Yeah, bet if you don't finish now, it'll mess up your plans for graduation— Oh shit!"

"What's the matter?"

She tapped the tip of his nose with a black-lacquered fingernail. "Dad'll just love it if he finds out you're not gonna graduate."

"Does he have to find out?"

"Of course he will; he'll be at commencement."

"Well, the old goat'll just have to live with it!"

"Jay!"

"I'm just quoting you, my love. *But as I was saying:* there's some good news as well. Seems Sparks has run into a glitch with his book, so he can use me into the summer. He's got me an extension on my assistantship and everything, even a little extra—which means, while I'd have to enroll an extra quarter, I wouldn't have to rush to finish the thesis, and I wouldn't have to worry about job hunting for a while longer, either."

"Oh, Jay, that's wonderful!" Dal cried, throwing her arms around him and kissing him firmly on the left cheek.

Jay blushed, as he always did when Dal showed affection in public. "Got any cream at your house?" he asked suddenly.

"Regular, sour, whipped, or half and half?"

"How about Bailey's Irish?"

Dal smiled knowingly. "Ah, but you'll be having your brownies *drunk* if you offer them that stuff!"

"More likely we'd find Piper curled up on the doorstep with a blissful smile on his face."

Dal's laughter was cut short by the blinking of the backstage lights that signaled two minutes to curtain.

Jay bowed chivalrously and backed away. "Break a leg," he called. "Just think, in another three days you'll be done with old *Macbeth*."

Dal's face froze, and every trace of warmth had vanished from her features.

Jay felt his stomach flip-flop as the enormity of what he had said dawned on him. He swallowed nervously.

"Shit!" Dal snapped. "Dammit, Jay, you know what you just did, don't you?"

Jay rolled his eyes. "Double shit," he muttered. "Yeah, I know. Bad luck to name this particular play while it's in production. But I did, and I have, and I'm sorry." His words sounded more sarcastic than he intended, but the sudden mood shift had caught him off guard. Sometimes, he thought, Dal took her major a little too seriously.

"Very bad luck," Dal replied stiffly.

"Want me to go through the bloody ritual? Go outside, turn around three times, and ask to be readmitted?"

Dal's expression softened only slightly. "Well, *maybe* the curse won't find us. *Maybe* you were referring to the character, not the play. *Maybe* old Willie's ghost'll see it that way and forgive you."

"I hope so," Jay muttered, frustrated by Dal's sudden coolness. "I sure don't need to weird out my good fortune."

The auditorium lights were already fading when Jay finally made it back there. He took a program from the tall shadow shape to his left and paused to remove his shades and let his eyes adjust to the darkness.

"No kind word for your dear brother, Jason?" a low voice whispered from the gloom immediately behind him.

Jay spun around, faced the taller silhouette there. "Drat it, Robby, you scared the crap out of me," he rasped. "What the hell are *you* doing here?"

"All things are possible when you've got connections. But I guess it's a good thing I didn't let the word out, 'cause I'm certain you'd have made other plans."

Jay tensed and wished for the millionth time he was six inches taller. "Give me a break, man; you know I'm not scared of you."

"I hope not," Rob said smoothly, "'cause then I wouldn't have the challenge of . . . altering your attitude. But look, baby bro: truce for now. I just found a little item of particular significance to your academic future." He thrust an ochre envelope into Jay's free hand. "Better go find your seat now, kiddo. Enjoy the show—if you still can."

The house lights dimmed abruptly to almost full dark; Rob melted back into the shadows; and Jay had little choice but to fumble to his front row seat, wondering why he suddenly felt such a strong affinity with Banquo.

* * *

A kettledrum rumbled, then segued into silence. The gray velvet curtain ascended, revealing a dimly lit stage swathed with fish nets and adrift with dry ice fog amidst which ragged figures hitched and shuffled to the breathy music of a wooden flute and the patter of a muffled bodhran. The unruly teens giggled apprehensively, but Jay scarcely noticed—he was still staring at the campus mail envelope. His wicked half brother (Dal always added the "wicked") never had any more to do with him than he could help, unless, in fact, it was something unhelpful; and Jay doubted this was any exception. The last missive from Robby had contained another triumphant review of one of his productions, on which Robby had scribbled, "And how, may I ask, are *you* doing?"

Jay had countered with a copy of Dr. Kibler's comments on his latest Edgar Allan Poe paper, which described his prose as "clear, lucid, and enjoyable," and concluded by calling it the best student paper he had ever seen. Jay had derived some satisfaction from that, but the hurt had not been lessened. It would be nice if his older brother liked him.

Not that Jay liked Robby any better, though he hardly had any choice. It was hard to like someone who continually rubbed your nose in crap—especially expensive crap, as Robby had been doing since the trust fund kicked in at eighteen. There was the Camaro big brother had bought himself as a high school graduation present, and the Trans Am for his bachelor's. For his M.A. he had rewarded himself with a silver Corvette. Jay didn't want to think what the doctorate might bring, but he suspected it began with either a *P* or *F* (and not for Ford). And those were just the cars; never mind the clothes or the trips to Europe, Mexico or Japan.

And neither Mom's failed first marriage nor Robby's dad's subsequent drinking was in any way Jay's doing. *I'm just sort of a symbol for him, I guess. He can't let himself hate Mom, so he turns it all on me.* Add to that the fact that Jay had beaten him out for Dal after Rob's three years of trying, and you had a perfect recipe for disaster.

Jay wondered if he should even bother with the envelope until after the show—and knew he would be unable to enjoy the show if he didn't. He steeled himself and slipped a nail under the closure.

Inside was a single white square of Georgia bond paper folded around a smaller piece of expensive cream-colored rag. The larger sheet bore a printed message in Robby's careful hand: "Lo, it is written that great minds think alike. Too bad yours didn't think faster."

Jay crumpled the note and flung it under his seat. He was almost tempted to trash its fellow too, but curiosity got the better of him. Reluctantly he unfolded the item.

It was a page neatly excised from one of those fancy catalogs academic presses were forever sending around.

Then Jay saw the first line of type, and his heart did a double thump. For set out there in naked print was the one thing he had most dreaded since beginning his thesis. *Yeats's Faerie* and *The Secret Common-Wealth, Faithlessness and Folklore,* it said. *By Gregory Jackson Waldron. (Carolina Mountain University Press, 357 Pages).*

Jay swallowed twice before he finally got up nerve enough to read the accompanying commentary: *A detailed study of the Perilous Realm as set forth in the poetry and drama of William Butler Yeats, here contrasted to the traditional view first presented in Rev. Robert Kirk's seminal study of Scottish fairy-lore, and how each reflects on the prevailing spirit of the age. Ten years in the writing, Waldron provides the most in-depth exploration so far of . . .*

Jay could not go on.

"In other words," he whispered to nobody, "somebody just blew hell out of my goddamn thesis."

On stage Macbeth cast a murderous eye toward his former comrade. Jay knew just how they felt. Both of them.

Chapter II: Toys in the Attic

It was two forty-five in the afternoon and still raining like a son of a bitch all over Athens and nobody wanted to do anything except curl up and sleep, except for James Morrison Murphy, who—on his way to his student job at the rare book library—was in the closest thing to heaven he could imagine. For James Morrison Murphy (Piper to the Toombs Avenue Mafia) was the only person currently alive in Christendom who actually preferred rainy weather.

And he did, too: drizzle, scattered showers, thunderstorms, typhoons—all these were his glory. Needless to say, all his friends had some tale to tell about his peculiar preference, and he was resigned to hearing them over and over.

Jay's favorite (which Piper had caught him recounting just the day before) involved the time young Mr. Madison had been awakened at about 2:00 A.M. by the sound of a downpour against the roof of the Toombs Avenue house. Suddenly he'd heard strange noises coming from outside, had glanced out the back window—and seen wiry little Piper stark naked in the middle of the backyard happily soaping himself all over and singing, "Lily, Rosemary, and the Jack of Hearts" at the top of his lungs and in no particular key—exactly as if he were in the world's largest shower.

Jay had roused Scott, who had alerted Piper's live-in squeeze, LaWanda, who had gone downstairs and collected Myra Jane Buchanan and her across-the-hall neighbors, Small, Medium, and Large. The whole lot of them had crept up behind the backyard fence, and then, just as Piper reached the line about the Hanging Judge being drunk, they had all switched on their flashlights. Piper had stared for a puzzled moment at the unlikely tableau of seven grown people in bathrobes and bumbershoots, each with his or her mouth wide open in amazement as they stared at him in his lathery altogether. And had simply kept on singing. He had followed his performance with a deep and profound bow in response to his friends' rousing applause—and then thoroughly hugged each voyeur in turn. The whole thing had almost turned into a mud-wrestling bout. Jay's bunny slippers had never been the same afterward.

So it was that Piper alone of all the folk on north campus that soggy afternoon cast a disparaging eye toward that vaguest of thinnings in the eastern clouds which could indicate that the afternoon might *not* be a total washout. If the sun came out, Piper's excellent mood would be ruined —although a brief clearing spell might be useful just about six, so Jay wouldn't be too grouchy when he came to take him to practice. That much, at least, he could manage. But now, gazing eastward again, he felt it was too late already; somehow he had acquired a subtle misgiving.

Thus is was no surprise for him to learn upon his arrival at work that even the indoor part of this nice gloomy day was about to be spoiled—by having to help unload, unpack, and reshelve an entire truckload of books that had just arrived.

Piper gazed down at the immaculate white linen performing shirt he had chosen along with his Royal Stewart plaid pants, to advertise the impending debut of his new band, and sighed. Moving packing crates was sweaty work—not at all good for handmade white linen shirts.

And unfortunately, there was no elevator.

He looked at Thin Greg, the one other student worker who had unwisely shown up in time to join the impression gang.

And then he looked inside the large van which had backed up beside the loading dock, and sighed again.

For inside, from wooden floor to metal ceiling, was roughly seventy-five boxes labeled the Bowman-Smith Collection. It appeared to have come from England.

Thin Greg returned Piper's despairing stare and rolled his soulful eyes. "Many, many trips, *Kemo-sabe,*" he said, unbuttoning his cuffs. "Many, many trips."

Still clad in his tuxedo, now soaked thanks to whoever had stolen Scott's umbrella from the theatre, Jay had been pacing the steaming downtown sidewalks for over an hour, trying to burn off his rage. Trying, more to the point, to keep from doing something *really* stupid like carving Robby an extra asshole, say, or maybe firebombing his office. And trying, most of all, to figure out what to do about the shattered remains of his future.

What he needed to do was talk to somebody. Dal was the obvious first choice, but she'd been flying so high after *Macbeth* it just hadn't seemed right to bring her down. She'd noticed something was wrong, of course, and had apologized immediately, attributing Jay's mood to her pre-curtain burst of temper. But he'd only kissed her, said all was forgiven, then as quickly as possible had made his apologies and bowed out. After all, there *was* a pile of manuscript waiting to be abstracted back in his office.

But the abstracting hadn't gotten done, nor did he care

if it ever did. Both his luck and his muse had abandoned him, and for the first time in recorded history none of his close friends were available, either. LaWanda was busy getting ready for the dinner shift at Snelling Dining Hall; Piper had been warned about having too many visitors, so he was a no-no; and when he'd stopped by Barnett's Newsstand to see if his roommate was still at his day job, Midge had told him Scott was off that afternoon—a geology lab or whatever. Which left Myra, who just might be painting in her newly opened studio-cum-frame shop across College Avenue. And Scott would be there later; he'd admitted to having to pose for her today.

Feeling a glimmer of hope, Jay sprinted across College and bounded up a narrow staircase that opened directly onto the sidewalk. A thick oak and glass door to the right of the second floor landing bore the calligraphed sign, BU-CHANAN GRAPHICS AND FRAMING. It also bore a scrawled note that read "gone to snag some brew, back at 5:30."

"Must be nice to set your own hours." Then Jay hesitated. Myra had a tendency to close up when she was involved with a painting, but she might see him. There was one way to find out for certain.

Three short knocks, two long, then three more short ones: he rapped out the secret combination.

No reply.

He pounded again, until his knuckles hurt.

Still no answer.

"Shit," he muttered finally and stomped back down the long flight. "Maybe somebody'll be at home." As he cranked his car, Pink Floyd's "Another Brick in the Wall" came on the radio, he sneezed three times in succession, and the clouds released an ominous sprinkle.

Somebody had been home, all right: Scott—grouchy as a pit bull over having his umbrella stolen (he, too, had gotten soaked,) and in no mood to provide comfort to an inconsiderate roommate, whatever crisis might have befallen him. He hadn't approved of Rob's method, of course;

Jay had got that much out of him. But the whole encounter had left such a bad taste in Jay's mouth he wasn't at all certain he should even bother telling Piper about his calamity, and indeed was still debating when he reached the flight of concrete steps that led up to the Reed-Gillespie Rare Book and Manuscript Library.

In spite of his shades, he squinted as a stray beam of watery sunlight struck the new brass letters above the entrance. A year ago they would have read GEORGIA MUSEUM OF ART. But the new art museum had finally been completed, and that had allowed the rare book department to move into these more spacious quarters.

But how much should he tell Piper? His number two buddy was so sensitive to everybody else's troubles that Jay feared his news would weird out his friend entirely. Probably just ought to sit on it until after his band's performance that evening—put up a front in the meantime.

Still undecided, Jay slumped into Reed-Gillespie's sprawling outer lobby and wandered toward the reception kiosk in the center, receiving a grunted acknowledgment from the skinny blond guy on duty there. Jay was a known, if begrudgingly tolerated, fixture of the department, as were all the Toombs Avenue Mafia.

Blondie gave a vague nod of permission, and Jay pulled open one of the heavy glass doors and entered the reading room.

He stared morosely around the windowless chamber. Once an art gallery, the large room was partly lit by a frosted Plexiglas skylight which at that moment allowed only a dull gloom to fall on the thick gray carpet, maroon-upholstered chairs, and long walnut reading tables. A series of glass-fronted display cases lined the paneled walls, most displaying a selection of curios from the Eugene Black Collection: things like an autographed portrait of Haile Selassie in a silver frame, or an ebony African goddess.

Jay was staring at a foot-tall Egyptian pharaoh carved

out of ivory when Piper came up behind him and pinched him on the fanny.

"Christ, you look wired, man," Piper said in his soft Savannah accent, when Jay had scraped himself off the ceiling. "What's happening?"

"Uh, nothing, really," Jay lied. "Little problem with the thesis; needs a touch more work than I'd anticipated." He shrugged, then noticed the state of Piper's clothing.

The white linen shirt now bore black smudges all across the front, and the bright plaid pants showed a large rip in one leg. "So what've *you* been up to all day?" Jay asked, forcing himself to cock an eyebrow. "Wannie'll have a fit when she sees the shirt."

"Oh, Jason, Jason!" Piper cried wretchedly, wringing his shirttail with both hands and gazing at the carpet. "I'm afraid you're right; I'm afraid my Wannie-girl'll beat me when she finds out." He looked up then, and grinned winsomely.

"And it's not even my *fault,* man. Got in a shipment from Merry Olde just as I arrived and spent all afternoon hauling the stuff upstairs."

Despite his mood, Jay's eyes narrowed with sudden interest. "What *kind* of stuff?"

"Books, man. Old, old books. Books to break your heart to look at—and your back when you lug about a million of 'em up a couple of levels!" He paused. "Hey, look, man; we've still got 'bout a dozen or so to open; wanta hop up and see 'em? I don't think Ms. D. would be bothered."

Jay sighed listlessly. "Whatever."

Piper led the way through another glass door at the side of the room and down a long narrow corridor lined with offices. Jay was conscious of treading on sacred ground, of a sort. The vast unwashed did not generally get to enter Reed-Gillespie's nether regions.

Up a steep, narrow staircase, and they emerged into second floor back, which housed most of the actual rare book stacks, as well as a small holding area for incoming material. Jay found himself playing follow the leader around the mass of splintered crates, scattered newspaper, and strips of metal strapping that littered the blue linoleum floor.

Marlyn DeRenne, an attractive, black-haired woman of about forty, was squatting by a crate calmly removing dusty tomes and wiping them with a rag before passing them on to a sturdy girl who was carefully arranging them on a series of metal shelves hung from a nearby wall. She looked up and smiled at Jay, but went on with her unpacking.

Jay wandered over and stooped to examine one of the shipping labels. He stared at it for a moment, then took off his shades. *"Good lord,"* he whispered, "do you know *whose* stuff this is? Bowman-friggin'-Smith! I didn't know you guys were getting this! Hey, wanta change occupations?"

"We could *use* an extra body right now," Ms. DeRenne noted with a touch of irritation. "Piper doesn't appear to be using his at the moment."

A sudden realization struck Jay. "But...I thought Bowman-Smith was dead. Didn't I read that somewhere?"

"He is," Ms. DeRenne acknowledged. "He was packing this very material when he died. Heart attack, I think it was."

Piper skirted around to stand behind Ms. DeRenne and peer absently over her shoulder. "I thought I'd let old Black Jay watch us pop one of these 'fore I vanish, okay?"

Ms. DeRenne sighed wearily, stood up, and without a word handed Piper the strap cutters. "Be my guest. I've had enough bending and squatting."

Piper nodded thanks and made a show of choosing just the right box, finally settling on crate 22, because of its fearful symmetry, he told them. Clicking the snippers with a theatrical flourish, he knelt beside it.

Clip-sproing. A metal strap narrowly missed Jay's cheek as it whipped past him. He leapt backwards, startled.

"*Jesus*, Piper, watch it! That could have snagged an eyeball!"

"Sorry, man."

Its fellow followed, then Piper eased the heavy lid aside. Jay caught a whiff of some indefinable smell: bitter and sharp and unpleasant. For a moment he felt light-headed—as though his whole memory had vanished. Then his nose prickled, he sneezed, and the sensation disappeared.

He started to mention the peculiar occurrence, but his attention was drawn inside the crate where Piper was already brushing aside a layer of crumpled newspaper to reveal the glossy covers of modern British best sellers. These he also cleared away, obviously disappointed.

Below them rested a stack of much older folios in crumbly vellum bindings, which proved to be obscure eighteenth-century bibliographies of works with mostly Latin titles. But below those . . .

"Oh-ho!" Jay cried, stretching an arm past Piper, then remembering himself and snatching it back at the last moment.

Piper was not so hesitant. He reached in with both hands and dragged out a long, cross-hilted sword with brass quillons and pommel and a leather and wire wrapped grip, the blade masked by a brown leather scabbard. He held it for a moment, squinting at it distrustfully, then passed it to Jay who took it with considerably more reverence.

"Scott'll crap purple cowbells when he hears about this," Jay exclaimed, then remembered who else was present, and found his ears burning. "We've got a friend who's seriously into weapons," he added by way of apology. "Used to be in a medieval re-creation group. He could probably tell you all about this—" He paused, staring at the shrouded blade. It had a very pleasant heft to it. Evidently it was a really first-class weapon.

"Has it got a label?" Ms. DeRenne inquired, frowning. "This material's all supposed to be labeled."

Jay looked around. "Negative. No labels."

"There's supposed to be an inventory," Ms. DeRenne insisted. "I don't think we were supposed to get weapons." She turned and strode away, high heels clicking.

Jay grinned at Piper and closed his hand on the hilt; started to slide the blade from the scabbard (which looked in remarkably good condition); then gasped and paused, staring. Energy was flowing into him! Energy and—there was no other word for it—joy. He felt wonderful: super-charged, ready to run a marathon; ready to begin a new thesis, even—or two or three. Ready to—

The flow of energy ceased abruptly—but the odor he had noted earlier was back with a vengeance: the bitter, metallic smell he now recognized as hot metal.

Jay's gaze shifted to the shining pommel, half expecting to see it glowing red, but it remained unaltered, though the odor had become stronger. He sneezed again, then sniffed once more. The odor was gone, and there was no further sign of the elation. Had he even felt it? he wondered. *Lord*, that was strange. He shifted his hold, carefully avoiding a barb of loose hilt-wire, and shook his head. His fantasies had simply got the better of him.

But his desire to look at the blade still persisted. Not bothering to ask permission, Jay grasped the hilt with his right hand and drew the blade clear. The cold steel glittered in the dead air for a moment, unexpectedly bright. Bright as it had glittered in the open air of other ages, Jay thought, as he stared down the clean line of the edge, turning it this way and that.

Something flashed; an anomalous sparkle maybe three inches from the gleaming quillons. Steadying the hilt within his armpit, he ran a tentative finger lightly along the edge. Careful . . . careful . . .

Then: "Ouch—motherfucker-*drat*-it!"

Piper's brow wrinkled in concern. "Cut yourself?"

Jay slammed the sword back in the scabbard and stuffed the wounded digit into his mouth, nodding. "Damn . . . hell . . . No, blast it, I think I got a splinter."

"A metal splinter? Oh, Christ, man!" Piper cried. "You could get tetanus!"

Jay snatched his hand away from Piper's questing fingers. "I told you it was nothing!"

He stowed the sword on a nearby table and took quick stock of the damage. A small sliver was embedded in the flesh of his index finger. Nothing to worry about, though; the pain was already subsiding. Once he got home he could dig it out with a needle. But it had been a very peculiar sort of pain, for it had seemed, for the merest instant, to have flashed outward along his nerves to shock his entire body with an icy, razor-edged agony that was yet so similar to the sudden burst of ecstasy that he had nearly cried out for joy at its return. But then it was gone again, almost too soon to register.

"Hey, Jason, look here!"

Jay joined Piper by the crate.

At the bottom of the crate occupying almost a third of the lowest layer, was a book: a large, dark-brown volume, bound in plain but very thick wooden boards and leather spine. A pair of brass clasps still tautened leather straps across the fore edge.

"Looks *old*," Piper said. "You wanta do the honors?"

Jay hefted the book out and laid it on an unopened crate. Filled with a strange impatience he could scarce control, he released the clasps with shaking fingers and swung back the heavy cover.

It appeared to be a very early printed work, with thick Gothic type and assorted woodcuts. Jay scanned the title page, reading aloud to himself: *"De civitate Dei cum commento Thomas Valois et Nicolai Triuet*—that'd be *The City of God, with commentary by Thomas Valois and Nicholas Triuet*. It's Saint Augustine! Saint Augustine's *City of God!"*

"Is that the date? Fourteen-ninety?" Piper asked, pointing.

"Yeah, I think so."

Ms. DeRenne had returned empty-handed and glanced

at it over his shoulder. "You know, I think we've already got one of these—same edition too. Does it say where that one was printed? Oh yes, there it is: Basle, Switzerland."

A buzzer sounded at some remote distance.

Jay and Piper looked at each other in surprise, then sniggered self-consciously when they realized they both had started.

"Better put that away and take off," Ms. DeRenne told them. "It's closing time."

Piper looked at his watch. "Christ, man—I got so interested, I nearly overstayed!" He closed the book and picked it up to shelve it—but as he turned, he struck his toe against a protruding crate top and sprawled forward, arms flailing.

The book went flying.

Jay grabbed for Piper—

Ms. DeRenne grabbed for the St. Augustine—

Jay was successful.

Ms. DeRenne, unfortunately, was not.

A five-hundred-year-old incunabulum hit the hard linoleum with a sickening crack. The back cover snapped upward at an angle far beyond its previous range of flexion.

Jay was instantly on his knees to retrieve it.

As Ms. DeRenne took it from him, the back cover ripped the rest of the way off and clattered again to the floor.

No, not the *entire* back cover, Jay discovered when he looked, for a thick piece of wood was still loosely attached to the endpaper. What had fallen was only the *outside* of the cover. It had been some kind of laminate: two pieces of wood glued together.

Jay looked down at the fragment and gasped.

Along with the square of wood, there were a dozen or so sheets of heavy white paper covered with tightly spaced writing. He picked them up and studied them intently.

"Now this is interesting," he said. "Look at this—the back board was hollow. These pages must have been hidden inside." He turned the bit of board around so that they could see the square place that had been chiseled in the solid wood just large enough to hold the pages. A quick check showed a similar cavity in the attached portion.

"Wonder what *those* were doing in there," Ms. DeRenne said.

Jay handed her the ragged sheets and looked on impatiently as she scanned them. "Hard to tell the time period," she said finally, "but it looks medieval or early Renaissance. We'd have to get an expert to check for certain."

"But what does it *say?*" Piper asked.

"It looks," Ms. DeRenne said, "like a play."

The buzzer sounded again.

Ms. DeRenne raised expressively arched eyebrows. "Sorry, boys, but we really *do* have to close—security system kicks in and locks the doors automatically." She retrieved both book and binding and carried them toward the shelves.

"But what about the manuscript?" Jay called. "It's gotta be important."

"It *is* important," she replied. "But I won't be able to find out anything until tomorrow."

A third buzzer.

Piper tugged at Jay's sleeve. "Jason, come on!"

"Yeah, sure."

Jay followed Piper down the stairs through the lobby, and into the waning afternoon. The sun was shining fitfully, but as soon as they stepped outside, thunder rumbled in the west.

Piper's mood brightened immediately, but Jay discovered that he was scowling for no obvious reason, given what he had witnessed. For a few minutes, it had made him forget his thesis.

"Now there's an idea," he mused. "If it *is* a play, maybe I could do a thesis on that!"

"What happened to the one you were doing?"

"Oh, crap, Piperman," Jay sighed. "I didn't want to tell you till later."

"Tell me what?"

Thunder rumbled again, louder, and the wind picked up; the air felt suddenly electric with the promise of impending lightning.

"Jason?"

"Well, you see, Piper, it's like this . . ."

"Don't talk with your mouth full, man."

Jay jerked his hand down and stared at it. Quite unaware of what he was doing, he had been nibbling his punctured finger.

Chapter III: Dance This Mess Around

Fifteen minutes was long enough for anyone to remain frozen in snarling silence, Scott decided. Besides, his jaw muscles were tiring. Maybe he should risk it . . . "And another thing I meant to tell you," he began tentatively. "Young Jason got some *serious* bad news today, but I'm not sure I ought to—"

"Whatever it was, *you're* about to get worse," Myra Buchanan warned. "You talked *right* as I was getting ready to draw your mouth. Act like you're seriously pissed."

Scott gritted his teeth and twisted his lips as far away from them as he could, hoping it didn't make him look too much like a bad Billy Idol imitation. He allowed himself the luxury of a wistful eyeroll, but tried not to move his glowering eyebrows; Myra'd just call him down again. Being a naked barbarian was more work than most folks suspected.

His wandering gaze focused briefly on a small spider that was working its way down from the grimy skylight which dominated the studio portion of BUCHANAN GRAPHICS AND FRAMING. It fell another six inches. One more slide and it would just about be on her noggin. Should he tell her? he wondered. Nah, a little dose of alarm was good for the soul.

Myra frowned at her drawing board, wrinkled her stubby, freckled nose, and applied what appeared to be three diagonal slashes across the piece of illustration board she had taped there, then twisted her mouth in disgust. Scott watched her arm flexing in precise analog to the curl of her lips. The spider dropped another two inches.

The stereo whirred and clicked and started the soundtrack to *Conan the Barbarian* for the fourth time that afternoon. The thundering drums and blaring horns made a darker counterpoint to the pounding of the rain on the roof. The plastic drip bucket in the corner was half full.

Myra put down the pencil and leaned back, wiping her small, neat hands on the oversized man's dress shirt she used for a smock, then ran a hand through the untidy mop of wheat blonde hair rubber-banded atop her head like a furry fountain. "It's okay, you can move now."

"I was beginnin' to wonder." Scott sighed, lowering his cheap replica sword. "I was beginnin' to think I wasn't gonna get to tell you there's a spider glowerin' at you from right above your topknot."

Myra raised a pale eyebrow at the venturesome arachnid. Calmly she took a scrap of paper and raised it gently beneath the creature until the dangling legs were touching. Then she crossed to the window and shook the spider delicately into the window box.

"Very tender," Scott said. "Now can I put my clothes on?"

Myra propped a hand on her hip. "Well, if you must," she replied wistfully. "I suppose you'll be wanting your pay?"

Scott grinned and snatched his skivvies off the arm of

the faded red velvet sofa. "I tell you what, girl, this modelin' business is hard damn work."

Myra grinned back. "Yeah, I seem to recall the first time I got you to take your clothes off it was *real* hard—work."

A pair of holey jeans quickly covered the skivvies. Scott turned red. *"Don't* remind me."

Myra's brown eyes twinkled. "Oh, but it's such fun to see guys blush."

"It's also fun for 'em to get paid."

"Spoilsport," Myra sighed. "Heineken okay?"

"Whatever you've got the most of."

As Myra pranced into the studio's tiny back room where she kept a small refrigerator and a hot plate, Scott pulled on his yellow T-Shirt. DO IT IN CHAIN MAIL, the caption demanded; he had, too—for a while. Not anymore, though; the shirt was another reminder of his Creative Anachronist days.

It had been a couple of years ago. A girl he'd met had belonged to the local chapter. Before he knew it, she'd dressed him in tights and tunic and had him sitting at mock medieval banquets. Not long after that, he'd found himself on a tourney field fighting for her honor in barrel helm and handmade mail. He'd even got moderately good at thrashing around with a rattan-and-duct tape sword. Had won quite a few fights, made lots of friends, established something of a name for himself as Bryan of Scotia.

The fight he had *not* won was with the lady, who found someone else and trashed him like spoilt wine. No longer able to abide her presence, he'd left the society. And now the lady was gone, moved away. Scott wondered why he'd never rejoined. The memories were still too painful, he guessed. Still, this kind of posing set his blood to stirring. Maybe he ought to drop by a meeting and see if there was still anyone there he knew—or who knew him.

He ambled over to the drawing board and stared down at the nearly completed sketch. It was him, all right, every six-foot, one-seventy-five bit of him—though why Myra thought anybody would be roaming around the frozen North naked except for a sword was anybody's guess. She hadn't even drawn him a scabbard.

The soft thump of the fridge closing reached him, followed by the clink of glass and the *snap-hiss* of bottles being opened. He turned to look at the series of pegboard panels Myra used to display her illustrations.

There were lots of scientific ones, since that was a prime source of income—mostly detailed renderings of internal organs, fish, or birds *(scads* of birds). But the ones he liked best were the fantasy illos. His own face gazed back at him from more than one of those. And there was Dahlia and Piper, but in no place either of them had ever been; Myra stole her backgrounds out of *National Geographic* or else made them up. She had even used one of Scott's spelunking pictures.

Here Scott faced a golden dragon, there Piper was portrayed as Chaucer's miller complete with bagpipes. And there was the first one she had done of Jay. She'd taken one look at him and screamed *"Cuchalain!"* and the next thing the poor boy knew she had limed his hair with white theatrical hair spray, painted blue spirals all over him (including the underwear he'd blushingly refused to shed), and done him as the flighty Irish hero in full battle frenzy. His thick dark hair, pale skin, and wiry, muscular body had been perfect.

And right in the middle of the whole bright array was a framed reproduction of the single sci-fi illustration Myra'd sold professionally: a black-and-white interior for *Analog,* showing her younger brother as an android calmly unscrewing his hand, while a couple of his hometown cronies looked on in amazement. Scott bent closer to study it more carefully.

Something cold pressed against the back of his neck.

"God*damn,* woman, what're you *doin'?"*

"Your pay, sir."

Scott whirled around and took the mug that Myra offered him. A thin layer of frost was still visible around the top and on the handle. She clicked her own mug against his. "You started to say something about Jay?"

Scott slumped into the couch. "Right. Well, to put it bluntly: Jay's had his thesis blown to hell and back."

"Shit! What happened?"

Scott told her what Jay had said before he'd left the house to pick up Piper.

"You're right, that sounds just like Robby," Myra said when he had finished. "Where's that s.o.b. get off, anyway? What'd Jay ever do to him?"

"You *know* the answer to that, my girl: nothin', 'cept bein' born." He pounded the dusty cushion. "God, I'd like to beat the shit out of that fucker!"

"You and me both. The guy's simply got no conscience."

Scott paused, bit his lower lip. "Yeah, and I really *should* have shown Jay more sympathy this afternoon when he told me. Oh, we talked about it some, but I was still pissed at him over this mornin'. And it's not like Jay often does things like make me chase a black rose or swipe my umbrella in the middle of a downpour. I mean, hell—when Lori ditched me in Savannah, Jay left Athens at midnight in a blindin' rainstorm, picked me up in the lobby of the DeSoto Hilton, then plied me with coffee and pep talk all the way home—and still got me back to Athens in time for my nine A.M. midterm. Guy'd been plannin' an all-nighter that time, too, and missed it and flubbed his own midterm all 'cause of me. And now I can't even cut him enough slack to make myself available for him when he's in trouble? God, what a son of a bitch I am."

"Any idea where he's got to?"

"Probably gone back to Dal's."

"She know about this?"

Scott shrugged. "Jay hadn't told her when I saw him, which is probably just as well, 'cause I saw her this afternoon, and she told me the judge has really been on her case about him lately."

"The judge is *always* on her case about him."

"Good point. But anyway, the whole thing's startin' to get to me. I mean, I love the guy like a goddamn brother, but sometimes I get so friggin' sick and tired of havin' to cover for him all the time I could just *strangle* him. Sometimes he's the superserious scholar, so pompous nobody can stand him; and then other times he's just got no sense of responsibility at all. I mean, the guy had his thesis blown to East Jesus, but is he bothered about that? Hell no, he's pissed at his brother for tellin' him. It's that kind of weird-ass fucked-up priority that gets to me. Sometimes I just don't understand him."

"Yeah, but he *is* your friend; that's the bottom line. He's all of our friend, whatever his obsessions."

"True."

"And we both jumped on Robby, if you noticed."

"Yeah, but—"

A series of loud knocks rattled the glass in the door of the adjacent frame shop. Myra padded off to answer it, leaving Scott alone in the studio. From the sound of the voices drifting back from the next room, Scott gathered that someone had come by with a rush job to try to foist off on her. Lord knew she needed the work: quitting grad school to open a business was a damned risky venture, though it was succeeding so far. Fall would mark Buchanan Graphics's first anniversary.

Scott wandered over to the wide front window and surveyed College Avenue below. The rain had stopped again, and the hot dog venders and the little old Salvation Army lady had both emerged from under the green-striped awnings. Around them a steady file of well-dressed business people on their way home from work were mingling with an equal number of students in search of an evening meal. Many wore jeans; a few were more trendily attired. One or two looked like they were hoping to be mistaken for members of one of the scores of ephemeral bands that sought to follow the B-52s and R.E.M. to fame and fortune on MTV.

His gaze shifted to the ramshackle bookcase beside the

window. An unfamiliar volume proved to be a new book on hiking trails in north Georgia. It struck him that he should get a copy for Jay, to cheer him up. Jay was fond of spending breaks and holidays bumming around in the woods, and the book would also serve as a reminder of how they had met three years ago.

Scott had been hiking the Appalachian Trail between Franks Gap and Unicoi, expecting to spend the night in one of the lean-tos along the way. When, around four o'clock, a horrendous storm had arisen, he had soldiered on. After all, he had nowhere else to go. Half an hour later he had reached his prechosen campsite—only to find it occupied by a very surprised Jay Madison calmly cooking an early supper. Jay had offered him shelter, food, beer, and too-small dry clothes and he had gratefully accepted them all, spent the night, and the two of them had gone on together the next morning. Somewhere in there they had discovered that they both went to the University of Georgia. Jay had just lost a roommate, so had Scott. They appeared to get on tolerably well. The rest, as they say, had been history.

It had been a real stroke of luck for Jay, too; because through Scott, Jay had met Myra Buchanan, and through Myra, the Fabulous Dahlia Cobb when she returned from a year in Paris the following spring.

"Hey, Scott, look here!" Myra called, returning to the studio. She was accompanied by a short, long-haired man with a rolled-up bundle of what were probably posters tucked under his arm. The guy looked at least thirty-five— an unreconstructed hippie with dirty blond hair tied back in a scraggly ponytail. He wore faded jeans with the requisite holes in both knees and a new black T-shirt neatly silk-screened with a court jester's head in brilliant white. The bells on the foolscap had been picked out in gold. A semi-circular logo in Gothic lettering beneath the leering face read SCARBORO FAIRE, and below that in smaller letters: EAST GEORGIA'S OWN RENAISSANCE FESTIVAL.

"Thought you might want to see one of these," Myra said, unrolling one of the sheets and shoving it at Scott.

"Piece of hurry-up I got handed yesterday morning. Just came back from the printers. Not too bad for a quickie, huh? Wants to know if he can put one up at the newsstand."

It was a copy of the T-shirt design, only printed in red on pink. And it gave more information: the fair would be starting May first, less than a month away. Music and crafts, it promised; artisans and theater; flesh and fowl and beer. It would be located in a strip of unused forest between U.S. 78 and 29—a little way beyond Bogart, four or five miles west of town.

"Yeah, go ahead and stick it in the window," Scott replied absently. "Tell Midge I said it was okay. She don't like it, she can always take it down."

"Right-on, man," the fellow said. "Hey, thanks."

"Carry on," Scott called to the hippie's back, as Myra escorted him out.

He stared at the jester's face and made a mental note to tell Jay about it. That was just the sort of off-the-wall thing he would want to know about. And Dal might also be intrigued—they were both interested in the Middle Ages, though Scott had never managed to get either of them to more than a couple of SCA events. Too idealistic, Jay had said, all chiefs and no Indians.

"Going to the hoot?" Myra asked when she returned.

"Yeah, guess I better. Gonna be late, though; gotta put in an appearance at the bookstore. And you?"

She nodded. "And I'll give Dal a call and be sure she brings along young Mr. Madison."

"Good idea. Probably be good to keep an eye on him." He paused. "Hey, look, Myra, you'll probably see him first, so would you mind not tellin' him about this Scarboro Faire thingie? I'd kinda like to surprise him."

"Assuagement of guilt, huh? Sure thing."

"'Preciate it."

Myra noticed the hiking book in Scott's hand. "You can have that if you like. Did some of the maps in there. Guy left me a whole bunch of freebies."

"Hey, thanks."

She indicated his half-empty mug. "Want another?"

"Can't, gotta get to work."

When Myra had gone, Scott opened the book and wrote a brief inscription on the flyleaf: "To my favorite thoughtless, asshole roomie, from another of like kind. May our trails always run together."

"Take *that*, Robby Tolar," Jay cried, as he stabbed another toothpick into the man-shaped effigy he and Myra had constructed out of cottage fries and parsley. Five other toothpicks already bristled there, reminding Jay of the ten of swords of the tarot, the one LaWanda always referred to as "I am nailed to the beach."

"And *that*," added Dal as she inserted her second.

Myra and Jay contributed another apiece: "And *that*, and *that*."

"And *this*," put in LaWanda Gilmore as she extinguished her cigarette with an elegantly vicious twist in the center of the manikin's stomach. A veritable dragon's hoard of cheap golden bracelets clinked on her dusky arm.

"Does it have extra power when a juju woman does it?" Jay wondered. He stared at LaWanda speculatively, and for some reason, found himself wondering exactly when he had lost his sniffles. "Hey, you didn't put a mojo on my honker, did you?"

LaWanda smiled sweetly but did not reply. Instead, she cocked her head, listening. On the low platform that served Sparky's Seafood Café as a stage, Mad Tom Hundley of Just Thrid was concluding the forty-fifth verse of "Bend Over, Greek Sailor." "That's the dirtiest song I *ever* heard." She giggled.

Jay gave vent to a giggle of his own, then cleared his throat self-consciously and resumed glowering at the table. After all, he *was* supposed to be sulking.

But at least he wasn't hungry anymore; none of them could possibly be. Four plates piled high with shrimp tails, oyster shells, and potato remnants were proof enough of that; not to mention six empty bottles of Guinness (with three more still in process), and finally and most sadly, the two bottles of Perrier which were all his friends had seen fit to allow him.

And it was really hard to stay depressed when you were sitting next to someone like Dal—especially when she was wearing white jeans and a gold puff-and-slash doublet she'd "borrowed" from the costume shop.

Myra gave the figure oversized eyes made of olive slices—and crossed them.

Jay sniggered, caught himself again.

Dal slipped the black silk rose from behind her ear and tickled his chin with it.

He was finding it hard to keep a straight face.

She poked him in the ribs. "Something *funny*, Witch-boy?"

Myra crossed her eyes at exactly the right moment.

Jay broke up.

Dal joined him.

Jay collapsed against her, tears rolling from his eyes.

"Ho, folks, what's up with old Black Jay, here?" came Piper's coastal drawl from across the planter-filled half wall behind them. Jay felt a hand clamp down on the top of his head. "I thought you folks were supposed to be givin' my man Jason serious adult advice about his future. Me, I'd advise he sell everything and hit the road. Become a full-time vagabond."

"A man of the road," Myra echoed. "Now there's an original notion."

"On the run," Dahlia added, wiping her eyes.

"Under the gun."

"With his back up against the wall."

"Yeah, Piperman, how come *you* never use neat, original lyrics like that?" Jay asked slyly. "I mean all this stuff about selkies and ravens and wolves and blowing up important monuments with gelignite's all well and good, but don't you think it's gotten to be just a wee bit *predictable* lately?"

"It's squeeze your head till your brain pops out, we'll do, laddie," Piper countered in the pseudo-Scots accent he used onstage. "Ole Piperman'll use yer lungs for bellows and yer bright eyes for buttons on me jacket."

"Have a seat," Dal offered. "When're you guys playing?"

Piper squeezed his narrow body into the equally narrow space beside LaWanda and snaked a hand around her to quickly cup an unguarded breast, then whipped it back again and gazed innocently skyward, looked as guileless as the Savannah choirboy he had once been. Jay wondered what LaWanda's hand was doing under the table. Piper's suddenly lifted eyebrows gave him a pretty good notion.

"*Yes*, Piper?" LaWanda prompted calmly.

"Ahem . . . well, as to that, we're next. Any requests?"

"'Finnegan's Wake'"—that was Myra's inevitable suggestion.

"That one you got from Rob Greenway about the food, you know, the sorta kinky one."

"Nothing too morbid."

"No," Jay said slowly, "but I could really get into a good kick-ass fighting song. 'Follow Me Up to Carlow' or 'Shield Wall,' or something."

"I think we can manage that." Piper glanced over his shoulder at the tall, lanky fellow who had just entered and was unpacking a worn-looking fiddle. "Well, looks like the rest of the laddies're here. Gotta run, gotta split, gotta hit the road."

"Et cetera, et cetera, et cetera," Myra finished when he had departed.

Just Thrid concluded the fifty-eighth verse (they added one per concert; this one involved two tom cats, a pumpkin, and circumcision), and wound up in a flourish of kazoos and cymbals.

The applause was overwhelming.

In the ensuing confusion a tired-looking Scott, newly escaped from his night job at a local used bookstore, scooted into the seat Piper had just vacated. "So, Ms. La-

Wanda, ma'am," he drawled, sidling up to her, "what'd yo' feller ever decide to call his band, anyhow?"

LaWanda lit a cigarette and allowed the smoke to spiral ceilingward before she blew it away. She regarded Scott coolly from under the black bandana confining her dreadlocks. "That we will know when they announce it," she said slowly

"Touché," Scott said. "But seriously, Wannie . . ."

"I have no idea."

"Tell me about it," Myra said. "I felt like an idiot making up posters saying 'Morry Murphy's New Band.'"

Scott started to say something further but froze with his mouth open when the announcer's microphone, which had been hissing softly in the background, suddenly made a rude-sounding blatt and fell silent.

"Ladies and gentlemen," the portly announcer's shaky voice boomed a moment later, followed by a blur of feedback, three exploratory runs of fiddle, one of penny whistle, and a buzz of bagpipe chanter. "Ladies and gentlemen; here at Sparky's new Friday Night Hoot we're proud to bring you the Athens debut of a great new band in the fine old tradition of Blackwater and Doctor Paddy and"—the announcer (not the usual one) consulted his notes and raised a quizzical eyebrow—*"The Pogues . . . ?* Hell, *they've* never been to Athens!"

"It says 'in the tradition of,'" Piper stage-whispered to the befuddled MC.

"Whatever," the big guy went on. "Anyway, let's all give a big hand for Eidolon!"

Piper let go with a howl of bagpipes, and Barry Knight with a surprise buzz of rock guitar, then there was a thunder of drums like men going to war and a tickle of fiddle, and somehow the whole thing coalesced into Gary Moore's "Over the Hills and Far Away," which became by slow degrees a traditional rendition of "Scotland the Brave" then segued into the plaintive "Green Fields of France," with Piper swapping the war pipes for Uillean pipes on the fly and taking over on the mournful vocals.

"Not too bad." Jay nodded at LaWanda, who was keeping time on the table with her Guinness. "Not too bad for a white boy, eh, Wannie?"

LaWanda nodded back and grinned broadly. "Why do you think I picked 'im, sweetums?"

"And we're gonna end this set with some real fightin' music for a buddy of mine," Piper was saying, "a good buddy who got some real bad news today and wants to hear a fightin' tune. This one is"—he held the pause for effect —"a fine old Irish jiggin' song called . . . 'Sunday, Bloody Sunday.'"

And so it was: U2's rock anthem, somewhat strange with fiddle and pipes thrown in but with the familiar beat undoubtedly present, and Piper's vocals sounding every bit as angst ridden as Bono's.

"C'mon, Jay, let's dance," Myra cried, nudging his foot under the table. "Dal doesn't mind, do you, Dal?"

"Go with my blessings." Dal laughed, poking him in the ribs. "*Go!* Do you good!"

Jay shook his head in protest but Dal slid out of the booth and grabbed his arm. "Come on, I know you're dying to."

He grimaced in resignation and eased out of his seat, whereupon Myra dragged him into the open area before the stage. Tables framed the perimeter, but there was still space for the sort of impromptu high jinks the music encouraged. Myra began to buck dance, arms swinging, legs pistoning up and down, knees lifting higher and higher, occasionally raising one leg and letting the other switch from side to side as she kept time with the other: *shuffle, toe, stomp; shuffle, toe, stomp . . .*

Jay's specialty was jigging. A year and a half ago Scott had dragged him to an SCA revel, and he had picked up a simple one. Myra had tried to teach him to buck-dance, but somehow it always kept turning back into a jig. He had eventually begun to derive a perverse pleasure from doing traditional dances to rock songs.

Both intensity and tempo increased, and Jay let his

pent-up anger and frustration find an outlet in the violence
of his movements. This was better than sitting home taking
verbal potshots at Robby; this way he could stomp the floor
as hard as he wanted. *Take that, Robby Tolar,* he thought.
And that . . . (stomp, stomp).

The third impact threw him off balance. He glanced
sideways, caught Piper's eye, and grinned. Piper gave him
a quick thumbs-up without losing a note. Jay reciprocated.
"Make it looonger," he mouthed. Piper nodded, and the
band began to break into improvisations. Somewhere in the
middle they found another tune, lost it, then commenced
another one that Jay did not recognize—but by then it had
ceased to matter. It had a lot of fiddle in it, and a lot of
penny whistle, and just kept getting faster and faster. Jay
could hardly keep up with it, but didn't want it ever to
finish.

The tempo picked up another fraction.

Jay really turned it on, then. Sweat poured off him. He
flung away his jacket, unbuttoned his shirt. *Left, right, left
right . . .*

Faster and faster; bow sawing as fast as the arm could
swing it; fingers a blur on the penny whistle. *Apart, together . . .*

Drums and cymbals and pipes, impossibly fast. *Left-
rightleftrightaparttogether . . .*

A crescendo—*stompstomp*—over.

Jay sagged onto Myra's shoulder and had to be led off
the floor, as the appreciative crowd went crazy with
whoops and foot pounding.

"Well," said Dal when he returned, "I hope you feel
better now. You guys had the floor bouncing so hard Wannie had to go to the rest room. Shook the pee plumb out of
her."

"I feel," Jay panted, wiggling his eyebrows like Grou-
cho Marx, "I *feeeeel* like I would like to take a long, hot
shower with a very attractive lady—and then explore some
options."

Dal grinned and licked Jay's ear, and he had just begun

to return the favor when Piper slapped him on the shoulder and squatted down beside him. "Hey, man! I ain't *never* seen that kinda dancin'!"

Jay wiped his sweat-streaked face with a napkin. "Jesus, Piper," he gasped, "what the hell *was* that you were playin' there at the end? 'Bout wore my bloody legs off! Damn, that was a weird-ass number."

Piper was practically glowing with pleasure. "Oh, that was just a little item called 'King of the Fairies.' Got it off a Horselips album. You ought to hear *them* do it!"

"Which ones? Them or *Them?*"

"Huh?"

"You know, Those Ones: the Fair Folk, the elves, the Sidhe, or whatever."

"But you really *did* like it?" Piper asked hopefully.

Jay suppressed a desire to reach down and pet him. "Yeah, really, really good. Best thing I've heard from any of your bands. Any idea where Horselips got it?"

Piper shook his shaggy head. "No idea, man. From the form, I'd guess it's Irish. But beyond that—who knows? Hey, who *is* the King of the Fairies, anyway?"

"My old roommate?" Scott suggested.

Jay ignored him. "Good question. Depends on when you're talking about, I think, and where. There're three or four alleged fairy kingdoms I can think of; one of 'em's even supposedly in America—Tir-Nan-Og, they call it: the Land of the Young. People with the second sight are supposed to have seen it. Even some folks up my way, so they say."

"But what about the *Irish* one?" Piper persisted. "Who's the king of *their* fairies?"

Jay looked thoughtful. "Finvarra, I think. I read the lineage when I was working on the late, lamented thesis. Lugh Samildanach is supposed to be the High King over here. It's Arawn in Wales; and I don't know who in England or Scotland."

Piper regarded him seriously. "Hey, you don't *believe* in that stuff, do you, man?"

Jay shook his head. *"I* don't, but a lot of people used to."

"But Jay—" Piper began.

Jay's expression clouded. "Uh, look, Piper, usually I love talkin' about this, but it's hittin' kinda close to home at the moment, if you know what I mean. Like a lot of this was in the thesis, and you *know* what an open wound that is."

Piper looked worried. "Sorry, man." Then his face brightened. "Oh, and by the way," he added to the group in general, "did anybody tell you all about the Renaissance fair?"

"What Renaissance fair?" Dal practically shouted.

"Yeah, what Renaissance fair?" LaWanda echoed, having just returned.

Piper grinned foolishly, a smirk, of scarce-contained excitement.

"Oh no you don't!" Scott exclaimed. "That's *my* news." He reached into his backpack and smacked a poster on the table in front of Jay.

"May be *your* news," Piper shot back, "but *I'm* gonna be playing!"

"Oh yeah?" Jay cried, slapping him on the back again. "Hey, that's great! When'd you find *that* out?"

"Right before the show." Piper giggled, unable to restrain himself. "One of their folks was here for setup, and he told me they were looking for local folk musicians to play weekends at a Renaissance festival. Hell of a nice guy, too. Bought us a round and everything."

"Back to the fair, Piper," Dal urged, looking up from the poster. "Know anything else about it? Think it'll be any good? I've always wanted to go to one."

Piper looked offended. "With J. Morry Murphy there, how could it *help* but be excellent? Well, actually, the folks *look* for real, anyway; said they were gonna use as many of us artsy types as possible—take advantage of the university community."

Dal nodded. "What about drama? Don't they usually have a lot of that?"

"Gonna have a *bunch* of theaters."

"Shit," Dal snorted. "I'd give my left—well, my left *whatever*—to be involved with something like that. Oh, Jesus, just think of it: live street theater, theater in the open like it used to be, maybe even on moveable stages like in the old cycle plays, oh lordy, lordy!" She took Piper by the arm. "Any idea who's coordinating?"

"I know *one,* I bet," Jay muttered glumly.

Dal screwed up her face in disgust. "Yeah, right. God, I hope *he* doesn't get his slimy fingers on it. Maybe he's already too busy with his dissertation project; maybe he won't have time."

Jay shook his head. "Oh, come on, Dal; you know as well as I do that with a specialty in medieval drama on the one hand and a Renaissance fair on the other and him knowing your fondness for open-air theater on the third, I don't see how he could help but stick his nose in. That combination'd attract him like shit draws flies."

"More like flies draw shit," LaWanda observed.

Jay laughed with the rest of them. But his body shook with an unexpected shiver.

Chapter IV: Deep Sleep

"Be back in a minute, love," Dal murmured. "I know just what you need to finish things."

Jay felt her lips brush the back of his head, then heard the soft whisper of her bare feet across the thick white carpet as she padded back to the bathroom. *I am a lucky man,* he thought, *to have such a marvelous lady.*

Dark head pillowed by his folded arms, Jay lay face-down and naked on a pile of sheepskin rugs. Quickly fading toward slumber, he was listening to the dreamy hiss of waves and the tinkle of soft harp music of Alan Stivell's "Ys" drifting along on the stereo. A pale blue radiance from the globes in the front parking lot was the room's only illumination. The important thing was that they could see each other: sleek blue-silver shapes caressed with shadows of a darker blue that made their bodies look strange and ethereal.

They'd showered together: hot water first to ease tension; then cold to make their bodies tingle; then warm again, this time with all lights extinguished. They'd spent a long time there in the steamy dark, slowly soaping each other, simply touching: feeling smooth skin glide and shiver beneath the brush of lips and fingers. He'd hugged her to him, but not for the usual reason. No, he'd just wanted to hold her, to be close to her—to be close to *somebody* long enough to have a good cry over his shattered future. It had only taken a moment; that was all it needed—just a chance to drop his barriers and commence the healing. Dal understood and simply let him have his time, holding him quietly until the sobs had ended. That was why he loved her—one of a thousand reasons.

Had it only been a year? No, not even that—their first anniversary was still almost a month away.

They had met at one of Myra's parties—a welcome-home bash for her junior college partner-in-crime, Dahlia. Jay had arrived late, but had recognized Dal from some of Myra's paintings even before they'd been introduced. It was hard not to notice someone who looked like Dahlia Cobb, especially when she was dressed from head to foot in *his* color leather and had blonde hair with emerald accents. He'd caught a fragment of her conversation and couldn't help but interrupt: "Excuse me, but who were you talking about?" She had been talking about Robby, about what a sneak he was, without any idea that Jay and he were related. "Just this asshole we know," Dal had responded. "This guy named Robby Tolar." Jay had volunteered the fact that he was kin to the person in question, and had watched Dal become flustered, then angry, and finally realize the humor of the situation when Myra had explained to her that *this* was the guy she'd been writing her about for the last nine months—the one who'd posed for Cuchulain. In an attempt to recover her equilibrium, Dal had said something about having gone to Young Harris College, which was near Jay's hometown, though he'd gone to Mactyrie Junior. That had degenerated into a round of *do you knows and did you evers*. Somehow they had wound up at the Taco Stand, and that was how the whole thing started.

He had a very good idea where he wanted it to end, too; as soon as he got up nerve enough to ask her. He closed his eyes, faded further, almost dreaming. . . .

The sound of Dal's returning footsteps rescued him from slumber. She knelt beside him and Jay felt a thin line of moisture trickle across his skin. "Baby oil for my baby." Dal's voice was low and sultry. Gently but firmly she began to knead his shoulders.

"Jesus, oh Jesus, oh Jesus!" Jay sighed, flopping his head over so that he could watch her out of the corner of his eye, though all he could see was a curve of silvery thigh.

"Witchboy, oh Witchboy, oh Witchboy!" Dal echoed as she slowly worked her fingers into the hollow of his spine. "What am I gonna do with you?"

"Don't call me that," Jay muttered sleepily. "I've seen the play, remember, and I don't think we're very good analogues."

"Oh?"

"Yeah, 'cause that guy abandoned his sweetie, re-member? Course it was after she betrayed him."

"Not of her own volition," Dal noted.

"Whatever. There's nothing magic about me, anyway, and I don't ever plan to abandon you, no matter what you do. *You*, on the other hand, have truly sorcerous fingers."

Dahlia bent over and kissed him on the nape of the neck, then resumed the massage. "Have you decided what you're gonna do about your thesis yet?" she asked softly. "It's all well and good to be pissed at Rob for acting like a jerk about it, but I'm sure you know that's not the real problem. In fact, in a nasty sort of way he did you a favor."

Jay sighed. "I know, and that just makes it worse. I suppose the first thing I oughta do is tell Sparks, see if he has any useful suggestions. But I guess the bottom line is that I'll just have to write off a couple quarters' work, come up with a new topic, and start over. It's not like I've got people lined up with job offers or anything."

"I'd hire you—just for your body."

"Sweet girl."

Dal poured a second line of oil below the first. "Just remember one thing, Jay Madison: you're smarter than anybody I know. What've you got to do, in the last analysis? Come up with an original idea, read a bunch of books, and write a hundred pages. I bet nobody's ever done one on folklore motifs in *Dark of the Moon,* or even in The Scottish Play, for that matter. *I* could almost write one on that!"

"Why don't you?" Jay mumbled drowsily. "And I'll sign my name to it."

"Don't tempt me. But seriously, you could do it on—oh, I don't know—Appalachian folklore in contemporary drama, or some such. Use *Dark, Foxfire,* whatever. Being a north Georgia boy and all, you'd have a hand up on everybody else. Or—" She paused.

"Yes?"

"I've got it! You could do it on that play you told me about; the one you and Piper discovered."

"Actually, I've already considered it, sort of. But there'd be procedural problems."

"Such as?"

"Permission, for one thing. The library can be mighty persnickity about stuff like that. And what's to keep some hotshot drama or English prof from swooping down on it like a duck on a June bug? Besides, medieval drama's not really my thing—not something I'd want to live with for as long as I'd need to, anyway."

Dal dug her fingernails into his sides. *"Jason!"*

"I wasn't talking about *actors* in medieval drama, my love, I was talking about the stuff itself. It's a lot more entertaining to watch than it is to study. But the bottom line is that I'm just too lazy or too burned out or something. I'd have to read all the other medieval plays and all the scholarship. Shoot, I bet half of it's not even available in this country. I'd have to go through bleedin' interlibrary loan, or else to the Folger, and that'd take even longer." He paused, then chuckled.

"And what's funny—besides this cute little dimple?"

"Oh, nothing—it's just that here we are in this romantic setting getting our nerve endings sensitized, and all we can talk about is bloody English literature."

"But that's what I was trying to do, Witchboy." She laughed. "Trying to get you relaxed enough to think rationally—to start your mind working in positive, creative ways." She halted the massage just short of Jay's buttocks and snuggled down beside him, ran a hand along his stubbly jawline.

He opened a drowsy eye, then took the hand in his own and gently kissed each knuckle. "God, you're a wonder, Dal. A blessed wonder. All things to all men—and I've got you all to myself." He started chuckling again.

"What's funny now?"

"You're one thing Rob'll *never* master."

"I hope so," Dal replied seriously. "Now roll over, I want to do your tummy."

"My what?"

"Your *tummy,* foolish boy; do you have any *other* suggestions?"

The muffled patter of rain on the roof awakened Jay. He dragged his eyelids open and glanced at his watch: five-thirty. Good, another couple of hours before he had to get going. Another couple of hours to lie beneath Dal's cool satin sheets and feel her smooth, supple body next to his.

The tempo of the rainfall quickened. It almost had a beat to it, he noticed—and a vaguely familiar one, too. Somehow a tune wrapped around that rhythm, and Jay discovered that "King of the Fairies" was running through his head. He could almost hear the quick-sawing fiddle, the frantic scream of the whistle. And with that strange, savage melody haunting him, he let his lids once more drift downward.

A warm breeze swished through the half-open balcony door and touched his naked thigh, caressed his arms, tickled across his belly. He thought of tropical lands . . . the desert . . . being with Dal in the darkness of a desert night. . . .

But it was a cold dream he awakened into. At first he was aware only of a bone-biting chill and a floating sensation and a sense of dreadful urgency which would not focus.

The dream took him, drowned him, spat him up. . . .

He was not himself, but an Outsider, viewing what transpired from a distance. He could feel the cold in his toes and fingers as his shadow-self tracked across a wintry landscape of night-frozen hills and leafless forests. Here and there a tiny clearing had been scraped from the wild and gave shelter to a few acres of fields that now showed only unlikely stubble. The houses looked poor: low stone walls and steep roofs of rat-gnawed thatch. Starlight glittered on snow that pressed in heavy, threatening layers atop the roofing.

Ahead was a larger house of rough-cut stone with—wonder of wonders—one or two windows that bore real glass. He looked at it curiously—suddenly was inside.

The interior was dark and reeked of smoke and unwashed bodies. A blackened fire pit in the center showed a few flickers of flame amid ashes, but the cold seemed to pool upon the floor in an almost visible layer like blue-white fog. Jay looked for his feet but could not find them. He was still an Observer.

But then he *was* there, or rather was there and had become another person. He was curled up in bed—if you could honor the rough, prickly sack of hay beneath a pile of lice-ridden blankets with such a term. More blankets lay atop him, and beside him a fat woman snored loudly, her back warm against his, chubby arms wrapped around their latest offspring. Three more slept in the opposite corner, all boys. He could hear their gentle snoring. Their breaths trickled like ghosts into the frigid chamber.

There came a knock on the door.

Or *was* it on the door? Even in the dream the room seemed to have gone strange: Jay was aware that the man whose body he shared sensed that strangeness as well, as if he were himself operating at one remove. *A dreamer dreams a dreamer,* he decided.

Once more the knock; loud enough to wake the dead.

Yet only he seemed to hear it. The woman slept on. The children—even Harry, the lightest sleeper of them all—did not so much as grunt or wiggle.

A thunder of noise, the door shook, the metal hinges rattled.

No use for it, then, Jay thought without realizing they were no longer quite *his* thoughts. *'Tis even colder without than within, I reckon; and I'd not have it said Edward the smith turned away a traveler on a freezin' night.*

Edward slid wearily out of bed and threw a cloak around his hulking shoulders in spite of the fact that he'd gone to bed fully clothed. His big feet whispered amid the rushes strewn across the raw earth floor. He opened the door.

A tall man-shape stood there, cut out against the starlight. Some great lord, Edward reckoned, until he saw the fire in the man's blue eyes, the sparkle of snow in hair of impossible blackness, the richness of black fur and black silk and black velvet studded with silver.

"I will not ask you for shelter," the man told him in a voice which bore the lilt of the northland. "But nevertheless I have need of you."

"But what need has any man but a roof and a fire on such a bleak night as this?" Edward asked him courteously.

"I understand you are good with a blade, Edward the smith of Ripon."

Edward's glance met the eyes of the stranger. "Some say that I am."

"*Some* say that you can take off a man's head with a single blow," the stranger continued.

"Some say that," Edward acknowledged.

The man's eyes glittered in the starlight. "Is it true?"

"Aye . . . sometimes."

A smile of satisfaction curved the stranger's lips. "That is enough, then. I have need of a man who can take a head off with one blow."

Edward eyed him askance. "This seems a strange time for such an offer," he said. "Surely it could at least wait till morning."

The stranger's eyes flashed. "Indeed it cannot! I have searched Alban already and found no one, nor in Erin or Cymru. If the Land of the Angles proves fruitless, I fear I must press on to Norvald."

"You must have been traveling some time then," Edward said carefully, having decided the stranger, however rich, was also crazy.

"Since midnight I have journeyed," the man replied.

A nervous laugh. "Ah, yes, a fine jest. But come in and warm yourself, or go away. I have to be about early."

"I could make this hall warm for the rest of the winter," the man told him. "I could make it so that no wind *ever* enters, that no warmth *ever* leaves—unless you will it."

"Do you take me for a fool?" Edward retorted. "No man can accomplish such marvels."

"I have not *said* I was a man."

"That I'd believe," Edward replied after a moment.

The stranger's eyes glittered more brightly. "Will you do my work then? If not for yourself, for the sake of your family? Your third son will take a fatal chill this night if he does not get warmth, and quickly."

Edward stiffened where he stood, clenched his fists. "Do not threaten—"

"I only prophesy."

Edward stared at the ground, but finally his shoulders sagged. "I'll come with you," he said slowly. "But first I'd have proof of the bargain."

The man nodded and raised his right hand. It was glowing like iron steeped in forge fire. A dagger appeared in his other hand. He pierced a finger, drew blood, touched a single drop to an oak roof beam. Fire brushed the wall, thrust into the thatching. Edward gasped, stretched a hand toward the stranger who only smiled and pointed inside.

His whole dwelling was burning. Blue flame crackled from every stone and timber, from bench and bed and table, yet nowhere did anything blacken. As Edward watched, the fires faded. The room was warm as an oven.

"You have your proof now, Edward of Ripon, and a drop of my blood to seal it. There is no more time for excuses."

"But tell me, is it far we must travel? The woman—"

"It is far and far, but have no fear of distance."

"I trust you have a fine sharp sword for me? Mine is old and dented."

The stranger smiled a cold, thin smile. "Your own sword is of iron, which is all I require."

Edward turned away from the stranger, crossed to the cupboard where he kept his sword. He took it out, spared a look toward his sleeping wife, and joined the stranger in the dooryard.

It took a moment for him to find the man, for he seemed at one with the winter night: snow lit white flame on his clothes and hair the way the stars burned bright in the sky.

"Edward?" his wife's voice echoed faintly.

But he found he could not answer.

"Edward . . ."

"Jay? *Jay!*"

Jay dragged himself awake. Lord, what a dream. A chill shook him and he looked down, saw the goose bumps stippling his body in the wan morning light. He was *shivering,* when he should have been sheened with sweat.

"Jay, what's wrong, you look white as this sheet—"

"Dal!" Jay cried. *"Goddamn,* what a dream!" He

opened his eyes, blinked a moment, for the dream seemed
on the verge of returning.

"You sure you're all right?"

Jay pulled the sheet closer. "I . . . sure I am. But jeez—
all that talk about the Renaissance fair last night must have
got to me. I mean, I was dreaming the real Middle Ages—
the Middle Ages like it was, not like folks *imagine* it. It
was gloomy and bad smelling and itchy and so cold it'd
freeze your blood!"

Dal laid a hand on Jay's shoulder and studied his face
curiously, but then flinched away. "Christ, Jay," Dal cried.
"You're like *ice*."

Jay shivered and ran a hand over his chest and
shoulders, rubbing until some warmth began to return.

"Never had a dream like that before, Dal—so goddamn
real."

"Too much seafood too late, maybe?"

Jay shrugged. "Maybe. But, Jesus, Dal—do you suppose I've medievalized my mind? I mean between my
blessed thesis and the Old Norse class and you in—the
Scottish Play—and finding that manuscript and Piper and
Scott going on about the fair . . ."

"Actually, that sounds reasonable," Dal told him. "I'm
sure I was dreaming in iambic pentameter while I was
learning lines."

Jay tried to smile, but another shiver wracked him. "I
just can't get over how real it was, Dal. It was more real
than any dream I've ever had."

"Evidently," Dal agreed. "You're still quaking." She
snaked an arm around his waist and began brushing her
fingers lightly up and down his belly, then hugged him
close to her. Jay could feel the firmness of her breasts
against his shoulder blades.

"I bet I can warm you up real quick," she whispered.
Her lips brushed his nape, then his earlobe. And when her
hand began to slide downward, he gasped—and bit on his
finger.

PART II

Chapter V: Pretty Persuasion

(April 5)

"Damn, I hate rain," Rob muttered to Erin Stillwell, whose white-clad long-legged body lounged beside him in the Corvette's other red leather bucket—more chipper than anyone had a right to be at such an ungodly hour on a stormy Monday morning.

A scowl darkened Erin's pale, heart-shaped face. "But we *need* rain, Robby; the drought's a long way from over. Don't be so goddamn selfish."

"Could have picked some other time," Rob snapped, flipping the wipers on to high. Ahead of him parts of South Lumpkin Street were flooding. The right-hand lane would be under six inches of water on the steeper part ahead, and he knew what six inches of water could do to Goodyear Gatorbacks—like cause them to aquaplane.

Rob glanced into the rearview mirror and changed lanes; then—since Erin seemed disinclined to respond to his complaint—reached over to turn up the volume on the radio. WUOG-FM was still playing classical; maybe that would improve his mood. He cursed himself for accepting a second period class. Eight-forty was too early for any reasonable person to be awake. Certainly too early for him to be fully functional—especially after only one cup of coffee.

He'd been up almost all night grading papers from his survey class, but even with Erin's help, it had taken longer than expected. She'd let him sleep as late as she'd dared (he'd dozed off on the sofa), then prodded him in the ribs, stuck a cup of coffee in his hand and told him to march.

And march he had, muttering imprecations upon his own conscientiousness all the way. There were times when a reputation for next-day service on student papers was more trouble than it was worth in end of the quarter evaluations.

A larger puddle appeared, lapping into the center lane. Almost before Rob knew it he was on the brakes and in it; holding his breath, feeling his back tires start to slip sideways before the antilock system took over. Damn thing still wasn't working right, either. That was the trouble with the 'Vette: damn thing always needed fixing. Hell, that was the trouble with his *life*: it never seemed to work quite right, either. And one source of a whole lot of trouble lately was the present company. Erin had her sights on him; that was obvious from the way she'd begun talking about commitment and similar unpleasant things. He still had uses for her, but if she didn't watch it . . .

"Hey, slow it down just a little."

"Yeah, right. Brakes're screwed up's all. Where'd you need off?" he added, though he already knew her answer.

"Bottom of Baxter's fine. I've got an umbrella."

"I can take you on in, if you want me to."

Erin managed a strained smile. "I swear, Robby Tolar, you are the biggest mess of contradictions in one body I *ever* saw. A real Southern gentleman one minute and the biggest asshole in Georgia the next."

Rob fixed her with a steely glare. *"Watch it!"*

It was as if a wall of ice slammed down between them. *"You're* the one who needs to watch it, mister," she retorted, "and I'm not just talking about me. There's a dark side to you I don't think I very much care for."

"Would you like me to let you out right here?"

Blue eyes flashed fire. "Would you like me to open one of your very expensive doors into traffic?"

Rob forced himself to relax and made it a point to chuckle. "I guess you just proved your case, didn't you?" He pitched his voice to sound light and casual with just a touch of contrition.

"I doubt it," Erin replied under her breath, as she reached into the foot well for her purse and backpack.

Ahead was the intersection of South Lumpkin and Baxter streets. To the left the three high-rise dorms marched up Baxter Hill; to the right, beyond a sprawl of parking lots, lay the University Bookstore and Tate Student Center. A little further on loomed the blocky backside of the old fine arts building, lately usurped by the journalism school's film division.

The light obligingly turned red—the first thing that had gone right all morning. Rob hoped the street-wide puddle at the bottom of the hill was not so deep that the car would drown out. As he plowed into the water, a plume of spray arched across the sidewalk to soak a pair of luckless Tri-Delts.

Erin opened the door and looked out over a muddy, fast-moving stream almost up to the door sill, then paused, fumbling for her umbrella. The look she gave Rob mingled anger with disappointment.

"I did *not* do that on purpose," Rob said quickly.

"You have no right to make anyone else's life more difficult," Erin replied. "You know what I mean—and who." She stepped into the water and slammed the door.

The light turned green, and Rob accelerated away, half a mind to try to splash her. He presumed she was referring to Jay, though he hadn't told her about their little encounter on Friday. Just to be sure, though, he set his psyche to checking out several of his other insecurities. He had a bunch of problems besides a healthy dislike for his younger brother, but they weren't the sort of hang-ups most twenty-six-year-old grad students had.

Not by a frigging long shot.

He had success, relatively speaking, money by the buckets from his trust fund (though it never impressed Dal, who wasn't hurting either). There was the car, the nice apartment which he did not have to share except by his own volition. Good grades, too, and academic honors. But the trouble was that they had all come too easily. He needed risk, excitement, something to stir his blood. And he needed it almost constantly—which Erin hadn't figured out yet.

The things most people had to deal with as a matter of survival were no problem for him. That was why he forced himself to go beyond, to play as close to the edge as possible: the business with reading other people's mail, for instance, or sexual experimentation at a time when AIDS had his buddies scared practically celibate. Even occasional dabbling with drugs—which he took as much to see what lay beyond the limits as for any other reason.

A part of him hated that dark twin—the dangerous alter ego he sometimes called the Angel of Death. But he realized that without it, he'd be just another T.A. in the drama department of an unremarkable Southern university; another fairly tall, fairly nice-looking guy striding around stage self-consciously, always careful to project, always careful not to turn his back to the audience, always standing up straight unless his role demanded something different.

Sometimes, though, he wished he *could* turn his back, not only on the crowds but also on the whole fucking world. He'd go off to L.A. or somewhere—spend his days drifting along in a sort of dreamy stupor in pastel rooms draped with pale, thin fabric dramatically lit by indirect lighting, with Jan Hammer music playing softly on hidden

Japanese speakers. Yeah, that could be real enticing.

As for his nights...he would spend *those* at the movies, drinking up hour after hour of celluloid fancies until he lost touch with his own dreams entirely. And then it would all transfigure: the room would become a box. The fabric: spiderwebs. And he would be an empty husk stuck there forever, having passed from life to death without notice.

Getting melodramatic, kid, he told himself. *Can't even get to L.A. until I finish my friggin' degree.* That was one of the few conditions laid on the trust fund: he had to pursue a doctorate at Dear Old Dad's alma mater. There was no time limit, nor did time really matter; he wouldn't get the whole bundle until he was thirty anyway.

He had chosen drama his first year at Georgia because it looked easy, only to discover that he had quite a knack for it—acting, set design, costuming, lighting.... In the years that followed, the siren Theater had by slow degrees laid him in thrall, and as he had added directing to his repertoire, her strange, sweet song had also directed him. The controller and the controlled: somehow Rob was both.

His craft controlled him, but he controlled other people, whether onstage or in real life; he set up situations, then stood back and watched what happened. His last encounter with Jay had been like that, but drama was like that too: a set of situations to which people reacted, only Rob got to decide their reactions. He could take a sweet young thing straight from Oral Roberts U. and cast her in *Who's Afraid of Virginia Woolf?* and make her spout obscenities; or take the biggest whore on campus and have her portray St. Joan. As director, he was good. Brilliant, some said, because he pushed the limits.

But wasn't life itself drama? "All the world's a stage" and all that crap? For a moment, the windshield become a TV screen filled with speeding cars and faceless people all wet and in a hurry. For that same protracted instant Rob felt as if he could simply let go of the controls and everything would keep going on Cruise. That there would be no

sickening crunch of fiberglass against flesh or concrete or
metal.

Fool, he thought. *Gotta get some coffee in you* real
quick.

Maybe he should just trash it all—get an old pickup
truck or something. Now that might be an idea, something
to make the real world more immediate: something that
rattled, that had wind blowing in around the doors, that
you had to manhandle to get around a turn, that you had to
have real good coordination to shift 'cause the gears had no
synchros.

Maybe Dahlia would even like that. He imagined himself pulling up behind Friedman Hall at just the right time,
and Dahlia looking puzzled, then breaking into that daz-
zling smile of hers when she saw him and realized he had
dropped his pretentions. . . . Dal running to him, climbing
in the cab with him . . .

Except that Dahlia *never* smiled at him. She never did
anything to him, with him, or for him—if she could avoid
it. Her smiles were reserved for his brother. But someday
he'd get Dal in a show. Someday, she'd be his to master.

The rain had slackened by the time Rob snaked the
'Vette around beside Baldwin Hall and key-carded his way
into the faculty/staff lot behind Friedman. He looked
straight at the mirror-glass wall as he entered, saw first the
reflection of the few remaining oaks behind him, then once
again was drawn to his vitreous doppleganger. Rather like
Kevin Costner, he thought, or maybe a young Alex Cord.
A glance at his watch made him wince: he was almost late,
would barely have time for a cup of wretched departmental
coffee and a Vendo honey bun before he had to start teaching. But first, he'd see what the mail offered.

It hadn't come in yet.

Rob spent an hour talking to the brain dead about Mar-
lowe.

Class ended, and it was time to check again—but first
he had to drop off some papers downstairs. He hurried
along the hallway, then paused when he came to his office.

Someone had left him a message.

Rob ripped the note off the door and scratched his head in consternation. "See me *as soon as possible*," the neat typing read. "I found something interesting in my box this morning." The initialed signature bore Dr. McLaren's familiar back and forth flourish.

His heart flip-flopped as he read the last line over: surely his major prof hadn't guessed what he'd been up to with the mail (not that he had anything on her, yet, and damn her to perdition for it, too). And he hoped it wasn't about his eternally delayed dissertation project; they'd been hassling over *that* for at least the last three quarters.

It wasn't really like Dr. McLaren to send messages this way, though. Usually when the old gal wanted to see him, she simply left a note in his box or else called him. But this summons had been affixed to his door by one of her famous steel pushpins. It was all getting stranger and stranger.

What *did* she want? Though they both maintained a veneer of pleasant civility, she liked him about as little as he liked her, he suspected. She made no bones about pointing up his failings, sparing no quarter in her assessments. On the other hand, she respected both his talent and imagination—and had told him as much with the same scrupulous honesty she criticized his methods. She was also the foremost authority on pre-Shakespearean drama in the Southeast, and Rob could not imagine allying himself with anyone lesser. Fortunately for him, where academics were concerned, Dr. California Montana McLaren was the soul of fair play and discretion.

But her sudden command performance made him wonder.

Thus it was that before he was ready, Rob found himself standing in the elevator with two cups of coffee, brewed from his personal stash of custom-blended Colombian. McLaren had a weakness for coffee, and at this point he was willing to do almost anything to hedge his bets, because once he pushed Up, there would be no turning back;

for good or ill, he would be committed. The elevator opened directly opposite McLaren's office, and she *always* left the door open. And so it proved to be.

Rob did not like the way Dr. McLaren stared at him over her gold-rimmed spectacles. It was one of her standard mannerisms, but there was something different about it today: a sort of hungry intensity like a black widow spider contemplating her mate.

He frowned, still framed in the doorway, unable to place the discrepancy.

McLaren leaned back in her wheelchair and adjusted a pillow behind the small of her back. "I see you got my note," she said. The tires of her wheelchair squeaked on the tile floor as she spun it around, then motioned him to the Chair, which he grudgingly accepted.

As gray and severely unpadded as she was, the Chair stood firmly against the wall directly in front of her desk. Scooting it forward was not allowed, nor was tipping it back. California McLaren liked to retain both distance and decorum. None of this buddy-buddy/chum-chum stuff for her; strictly teacher/pupil, that was how she liked it.

Rob smiled and slid a cup of coffee onto her desk. She wheeled herself forward and took it in a clawlike hand but did not thank him, though a ghost of smile played briefly about her lips after the first sip. Abruptly she set down the cup, stuck a hand into her briefcase, and pulled out a large sheet of heavy pink paper. "Have you, by chance, seen one of these?"

Rob studied the paper. On it was a jester's face. Below it was the legend SCARBORO FAIRE.

"So we've got a new Renaissance festival," he said noncommittally. "Well that's nice. We'll have to give it a go some weekend—just for giggles."

McLaren's eyes twinkled dangerously. She did not look amused. "What I had in mind was for *you* to give it a go. *Every* weekend."

Rob's eyes narrowed with suspicion. *"Oh?"*

"Have you ever been to one of these things?"

"Once or twice. Went to the one out in 'Frisco when I was a freshman. Lots of drama. Played mostly for laughs, though."

"For laughs, huh? Comedy's as valid as tragedy, boy; and sometimes there's a fine line between them. Don't you ever forget that. And each is made more potent by the presence of the other."

"I meant—"

She silenced him with a sweep of her hand. "So you don't think much of that sort of theater, huh? Well, do you think *you* could do it? Stage a play at a Renaissance fair?"

Rob shifted uneasily in the Chair. He did not look at her. "Well, if you're talking about the light stuff," he began uneasily, "I'm not certain. Comedy's not really my thing."

"Then maybe it's time you *made* it your thing!"

He glared back at her, crossed his legs, and folded his arms across his stomach. "Okay, enough fencing. What're you getting at?"

"Just this," McLaren replied calmly. "A close friend of my son is one of the backers of this wingding. He's arranged all of it: got a long-term lease on a tract of land just past Bogart. He put in a road last December and has about a hundred and fifty good old boys out there right now building booths and walls and God only knows what else in what I hope won't be a vain attempt at recreating a Renaissance village. They'll get it done, but it remains to be seen how well," she added a moment later, with heavy sarcasm.

"And . . . ?"

"He's also rounded up a good bunch of artisans, got a hold of some medieval reenactment groups for local color and jousting. And he's arranged for four separate theaters and got commitments for all of them. One's to do straight farce with a lot of audience participation; one's a sort of day-by-day medieval soap opera thing I wouldn't touch with a ten-foot pole; one's a showcase for various college and local amateur groups and will be doing modern compositions with medieval subject matter: *Becket, The Lion in Winter,* that kind of stuff. But they want to have one to do authentic medieval and Renaissance drama: miracle plays, moralities, St. George and the Dragon, Robin Hood, you name it. Sword dances, possibly, maybe even something as recent as the pre-Shakespearean farces like *Ralph Roister Doister*."

"So what do you want me to do?"

"You still don't have a dissertation project, do you?"

"Well, I thought we'd agreed I was going to work on that Chaucer into drama idea. That's what I've been researching, anyway."

"We had not agreed, as I recall. No. I want you to work on *this*. My son needs the help, and I promised him."

"A full show in less than a *month?* You have *got* to be kidding. I'd have to abandon my other work entirely."

"I never kid, Robert, you should know that; and *you* should consider it a challenge. Besides, there are ways around it."

"For instance?"

"You did the *Wakefield Mystery Cycle* last December; use that to start off with to save time; you should at least be able to salvage some props and costumes. You'd only have to come up with one or two short pieces to go with it, initially; though I'll expect you to retire it as the season progresses and you add new stuff—including, needless to say, some light material. You'll be coordinator; the Faire can lend you some actors who don't have classes if you can't reassemble the cast you used for *Wakefield*. Direct if you want to, act if you must, bring the show off in top shape and on time, that's the bottom line. Oughta be simple for the best student in this department. Besides, I've already told them you'll do it."

"You *what?*" Rob leapt to his feet, not knowing whether to be flattered or pissed as hell.

"Sit down, Robert."

"You must be kidding."

"Sit down!"

"I don't like this," he muttered, ignoring her command

as he stalked toward the door. "You're manipulating me—and I don't *like* being manipulated!"

"Have you checked your mail today, Robert?"

Rob went instantly rigid.

"Uh, no, actually," he stammered, reluctantly resuming his seat. "Well, just when I came in, but not since then."

McLaren's eyes sparkled. "Then you haven't seen *The Red and Black?*"

Rob shook his head. "Any reason I should have?"

McLaren handed him a copy of the campus newspaper. "Fourth page, bottom right."

Rob opened the paper and saw:

UNKNOWN PLAY DISCOVERED

The manuscript of a previously unknown Renaissance play was discovered Friday at the Reed-Gillespie Rare Book and Manuscript Library.

The manuscript—probably a folk or morality play—was discovered among books belonging to the late Professor Charles Bowman-Smith of the College of Ripon and York St. John, in England. The library had recently acquired his unique theology collection, and library staffers were unpacking it when they discovered the play.

Richard Johnson of UGA's art department has estimated its date at about 1500, pending further authentication of paper and ink samples.

"This discovery is particularly significant," said Dr. John Schleifer of the English department, "because handwritten manuscripts of dramatic material are virtually unknown from this period."

Noted drama professor Dr. California McLaren will oversee translation and possible publication of the text.

There was more, detailing how the manuscript had been found sandwiched inside the hollow endboards of a copy of St. Augustine's *City of God,* but Rob barely scanned it. He took a deep breath, folded the newspaper, and looked at Dr. McLaren. "Well, *that's* certainly interesting."

McLaren nodded firmly, her mouth a thin line but her eyes twinkling. "I thought you'd say that."

"Why didn't you tell me earlier?"

"I like surprises, and I thought you'd get a charge out of reading it in *The Red and Black*. And to be honest, I've only barely had a chance to look at the thing, what with that dratted Dixie Drama Workshop. It was discovered Friday afternoon, but they couldn't get hold of me until nearly 3:00 P.M. Saturday. Needless to say I rushed right over, but only had time for a quick scan before their damned alarm started honking. I knew right away, though, that it was unique, nor did I waste any time getting permission to edit it, though I had to mess up some people's Sunday in the process. Monteagle's already been up here complaining that I bypassed him. I did, too."

"Couldn't it be a fake?"

McLaren shook her head. "Paper, ink, handwriting's all the genuine article. I called just now and checked."

"But how do you know it's unique?"

"Because I've read everything there is from that period, including every word of Ordish, Sharp, Helm, and Chambers, and seen most of 'em performed. This one's different. Not very long, either, no more than ten or twelve pages. But it's much more overtly pagan.

"How so?"

"Because it includes the resurrection of the Devil."

Rob's eyes brightened. "Oh yeah?"

"Apparently. On the surface it's a standard man tempted by Satan plot, the old 'All the kingdoms of the world' routine. But halfway through it metamorphoses; picks up some elements from the St. George plays, which is to say there's a combat and somebody's defeated—in this case, the Devil—by beheading. But this time the St. George figure is also killed, and when the doctor comes in at the end to work the traditional healing, not only is St. George healed but also the Devil!"

"That *does* sound different," Rob hedged. "I'd like to take a look at it when I get the chance."

A sudden smile cracked McLaren's features, and he knew the trap had been sprung. "Good—because you're going to get to."

"Oh?"

McLaren nodded. "First of all, I want you to be the good boy you can be when it pleases you and trot over to the library and bring me a copy of the manuscript they just called me and said they had ready. I need to go ahead and start on it if we're going to be done with it in time."

An uneasy feeling developed in the pit of Rob's stomach. "In time for what?"

McLaren's lips stretched wider than he'd ever seen them, and the corners lifted alarmingly—exactly like a gambler about to trump somebody's aces. "Why, for you to put on at Scarboro, of course! I would have thought that would be obvious."

Rob shook his head vigorously, though he had already begun considering the advantages. "I haven't even said I'm doing it yet!"

The old lady slapped the metal desk top with an open palm. "The *hell* you're not!" Then, more softly: "Just think, boy. Here's your chance to put on a play for the first time in maybe five hundred years. I'll do a quick translation—good enough for you to work from, anyway, and you can take it from there. Oh, go ahead and rehearse whatever else you want, but leave room for this. It'll be the climax of my career and another step up from obscurity for you."

Rob bit back a scathing retort. "Then why don't *you* oversee the production?"

"Because I don't want to go flossying through woods and rough terrain in this dratted wheelchair to deal with the little varmints. Age and infirmity do bring their inconveniences, after all. You, however, have no such limitations."

"No, but I wasn't planning on making like Robin Hood

all summer, either. Besides, I can't afford the time."

"Sure you can."

Rob twisted around to scowl at her. "Okay, so when am I gonna get a text to work from? If I don't get something number-one pronto, it won't do either of us any good."

"I should have a rough done by—oh, Thursday or Friday. You can read it over, and we can talk more about it then."

Rob had a good idea that it might be much longer than that before he felt compelled to even speak to her again though he had to admit she had made him an intriguing proposition. He turned and stomped out of the office.

"Oh, and Robert," McLaren called sweetly after him in that irritating way she had of affixing zingers to his departing back. *"Don't* forget to pick up those copies for me, hear? I don't think I can rely on the mail. They'll be sealed with tape, by the way. *Scotch* tape."

Rob nodded stiffly.

Bitch he mouthed as he stomped out of the office.

"Most certainly," McLaren's voice acknowledged behind him. She followed him to the door in her chair. "Oh, and one *more* thing, Robert," she added as he entered the elevator.

Rob whirled around as the door began to close. "Yeah? What is it?"

"You haven't noticed anything *strange* about the mail, lately, have you? I know for a fact *I* have."

Chapter VI: Nip It in the Bud

If I drop these dratted things, I'm just gonna walk off and leave 'em, Dal thought, as she staggered through the gray marble lobby of the main library with books piled from chin to belt buckle. For the last two hours she'd been trudging back and forth between the third floor and the seventh, all the while cursing the lack of consideration on the part of her instructors that had resulted in papers coming due the following Monday in both Stage Costume III and Italian for Actors.

At the moment, however, she had a more pressing problem: her arms were about to give out on her. She paused at the automatic glass doors, waiting. *Okay, guys, any day now.* One of her hands slipped a fraction.

The doors showed no signs of moving.

Swearing softly, she turned and backed through them, and cursed once more as the handle snagged a pocket of the black leather vest she wore over white shirt and Levi's.

"Hey, preeetty señorita, wanta seee some dirty *peec-tures?*" Jay whined in a mock-Mexican accent as he popped out from behind one of the six square concrete columns that supported the pediment. Then, "Good lord, girl, let me help you."

A heavy sigh signaled her assent. "Just what I need: a knight in scruffy black denim to save me. These mothers are heavy!"

Jay relieved her of most of the books and glanced down at his black jeans, tank top, Frye boots, and jacket. "I call this particular shade coal-miner Stygian."

"Shoot, and I thought it was midnight Michelin radial."

"Nah, that's got a blue cast to it and holds the road better."

Dal laughed as she stuffed the remaining volumes under her arm and swooped down upon the large stack of the latest *Red and Black* piled by the doorway. "Ah-ha," she crowed, snatching a copy, "supposed to have a review of my show in it."

Jay raised a quizzical eyebrow. "What good's a review when the play's already over?"

Dal started to say that it should be obvious, then remembered how miserable poor Jay had been at the Saturday and Sunday performances, which he had nevertheless dutifully attended. He'd broken with tradition, though, and switched to solid white, both for his tux and a second silk rose token—to try and fool the Luck Lords, he had told her. She almost hadn't known him when he'd snuck in backstage. "Yeah, well, you know the *R and B,*" she managed finally, "always a dollar short and a day late. But at least we get some recognition—and some feedback."

"I'll feed on your back any time." Jay laughed, making snapping motions with his teeth in her direction.

"Not now, piranha breath." She giggled, fending him off with the newspaper.

Jay looked crestfallen. "Okay, so let's have a look at it."

"Let's get these books to the car first," Dal replied, as

she started down the short flight of steps. In spite of the frivolous persona Jay had adopted, she was certain he was still fretting over his thesis—and probably would be for a good while longer. She'd have to treat him with more than usual caution—which was hard when you had your own problems. Of course when he came on like this, all bubbly and full of foolishness, it was easy to forget everything else, easy to recall why she loved him. Still, she'd have to watch herself, not let her frustration with her papers get misdirected.

"Have you had lunch yet?" she asked. She'd have bet a stack of Bibles that he hadn't. That no-time-for-breakfast fretfulness was all over him.

Jay shook his head.

"Oh, good, then we can do this thing up right: lunch and Bloody Marys at O'Malley's. I'll buy, and then we can sit out on the deck, and you can read the review to me, and I'll pretend you're a famous *New York Times* critic."

"Sounds good to me." Jay chuckled, wiggling his eyebrows behind his shades. "Especially the bloody part."

Once a large cotton mill, the vast brick mass of O'Malley's straddled a branch of the Oconee River. Around the entrance and along a corner of the back side, a sprawl of decks had been added, rather like mushrooms shelving an oak stump, Dal thought. It was early afternoon, and the lunch crowd had mostly left but the Greek invasion at happy hour had yet to arrive, so when Dal led the way onto the back deck, she and Jay found themselves alone with the birds and the lizards.

Though the sky was still thunderous, the sun had broken out and was quickly drying the thick boards. Mockingbirds sang along the riverbanks, their warbles a counterpoint to the sparkling burble of the water where it washed among hulking gray stones, fifteen feet below. Trees and bushes towered on either side, and except for the distant hiss of traffic and the occasional honking of horns, the illusion of solitude was uncanny.

Dal flopped down on one of the board benches that ran around the weathered railing. She took a long draw of her drink and helped herself to a handful of chips and a bite of hot turkey sandwich. Even without looking at him, she could feel Jay's eyes upon her and felt herself start to color, marveling anew at the seemingly limitless extent of his adoration, even after nearly a year together. "Okay," she sighed, "let me have it."

"Huh? Oh." Jay sorted quickly through the paper. "Ah-ha! There's not much, I'm afraid, and it's all on page three. But there is an excellent picture of you, my proud beauty, apparently up to no good."

Dal reached for it automatically. "Let's see. No, wait—" She yanked her hand back. "Read the article first."

Jay cleared his throat and began: "'William Shake-speare may be dead and buried, but Dahlia Cobb brings his bloodiest play back to vigorous life. A standout production by the UGA drama department, well directed by Eleanor Pritchett, the highlight of the show was Dahlia Cobb's portrayal of the scheming Lady Macbeth. A first year graduate student in drama, Miss Cobb takes to this role like it was written for her, giving it a power and immediacy too often lacking in academic productions. One word from her, and you forget she's a student. Two words and you believe she's a murderess. And this is not to sell short the other actors. As the ambitious Thane of Cawdor who heeds a witches' prophecy, betrays his friends, and gains a throne, Owen Montgomery is . . .'" Jay paused in mid sentence. "Here, you read the rest, I just want to sit here and watch you. You turn such pretty colors when you're being flattered."

Dal growled and snatched the paper. For a moment she sat quietly, scanning the lines.

"Well, that was nice," she said finally. "Very nice indeed." She flipped the page, chuckled over Bloom County, then felt her eye drawn to a headline of the bottom right corner. "Hey, did you see this? There's an article here about that manuscript you found."

"Oh really?" Jay replied. "Now *that's* interesting. Of course they've not been in touch with *me* or anything," he added sullenly, "and I *did* find the bloody thing. But—"

Dal surveyed the article, only half hearing him, but then her eyes widened. "Oh, shit, Jay," she cried. "You really had better take a look. I think somebody's beaten you to it."

Jay's nose twitched in irritation. "But I told you, I don't want to do a thesis on it. I just want your basic recognition. I mean it really would make a good story. . . ."

"That's good, 'cause it looks like writing on it may not be an option any longer."

Jay retrieved the paper and started reading.

"Well, fiddle," he said, when he had finished. "It's just like I figured. Word gets out and some drama prof's already got her hands all over it. It'd be nice if they'd at least *asked* if I wanted a crack at it."

"I thought you said you weren't interested."

"I'm not; I'd just like to have had first refusal."

A darker realization dawned on Dal. "Double shit! Jay, do you know who Dr. McLaren is?"

A shrug. "In a general way. Why?"

Dal took a deep, ragged breath. "She's Robby's major professor."

"Oh lord," Jay moaned, "and if Robby gets hold of it . . . and finds out I discovered it, I'll *never* hear the end of it. He'll be rubbing it in forever!"

Dal reached out and took Jay's hand. "But even if he does, just remember one thing, Witchboy."

"What's that?"

"It's *you* I love, not some stuck-up scholar."

Jay grinned. "Now *I've* got a question."

"And what might that be?"

"Well, uh . . . Who kisses better—me or the traitor king of Scotland?"

Dal regarded him slyly. "Hard to say."

"Dal!"

"Get that celery stick out of your ear, Witchboy, and you can refresh my memory!"

"Oh lord, Dal," said Mitchell W. Tolliver later that afternoon, "I've got a case of opening night jitters—and we don't open for over a month yet."

Dal looked up at him from the year-old copy of *Time* she was reading and smiled sympathetically. Standing in front of one of the floor-to-ceiling windows that comprised most of one wall of Friedman Hall's graduate lounge, with sunbeams slashing through the cloudy sky behind him to cast his lean, muscular body into shadow, Mitch looked a lot like Jay. She suppressed an urge to call him Witchboy, just to see what would happen, then chuckled. Mitch was a nice guy, but he had none of Jay's reckless magic; just a gentle, boyish enthusiasm that—under the light control of young Dr. Harvell—had made him perfect for the lead role in the upcoming children's theater production of *Peter Pan*.

"Well, I happen to know someone who's got some vodka stashed down in their office, if you think that'll help," Dal volunteered. "If you want to we could—"

"Can't!" Mitch shot back too loudly. "Got a test in half an hour."

Dal regarded him steadily. "Then you oughta be studying for that, 'stead of worrying about opening night."

"Easy for you to say!" Mitch cried, exploding into a mass of wildly fidgeting limbs. *"You've* done this kind of thing before. This is *my* first big role."

"They're all big roles, Mitch."

"But there's just so much to remember," the poor boy went on obliviously, "lines, cues, effects. That damn flying harness—"

"A-ha, I *knew* it! I *figured* it'd come down to that."

Mitch looked as if he might cry. "Well, jeez, Dal. It's the climax of the whole first act, and it's not even gone right *once*. I don't want the thrilling finale to suddenly turn into slapstick on me. Fantasy, yes; farce, no way! Uh-uh."

"Then you're in the wrong business, my man," came a deeper voice from just outside the door. "'Cause it's up to *you* to see that it doesn't. Think Burton would've let something like that bother him?"

Dal frowned but did not look up.

"I *ain't* Burton," Mitch spat, as Robert Tolar sauntered into the lounge.

"I *know,*" Rob replied with quiet sarcasm. "I thought I heard you saying something about having a test. Maybe you should spend the next little while studying for it."

Mitch's darting glance flickererd nervously between Dal and Rob. Finally he could stand it no longer and dashed out. "S-see you, Dal," he called from the hallway.

Dal's frown became a full-fledged scowl. "Well, *that* wasn't very nice—though I don't suppose I should expect any better."

Rob sat down across the low coffee table from her, and Dal offered mental sacrifices of gratitude to whatever deity's intervention had made her choose a chair with arms high enough to preclude him sitting any closer.

"Yeah, well, I need to work on that, I guess," Rob replied casually, though Dal was not for a minute deluded. "Somehow things like that just slip out. But," he added, "it's such fun to see them hopping."

"Teasing's one thing," Dal told him flatly. "Torture's another."

Rob raised innocent eyebrows. "And which do you suppose that was?"

"I'd prefer to think it teasing," Dal snapped, "except that you liked it far too much, and poor Mitch far too little."

Rob shrugged noncommittally. "It's true, though, whichever way you want to look at it. Guy's gonna be an actor, he's gotta learn to cover regardless of what happens. Accidents do occur, and he's gotta be ready."

"Yeah, but he doesn't need anything to decrease his

confidence right now. All we need's for him to nerve himself into the hospital."

Rob looked thoughtful. "Good point. Maybe I'll chase him down and apologize."

"He'd probably run if he saw you coming."

A ghost of wry smile. "Indeed!"

"I wouldn't blame him, either."

Rob stared her straight in the eyes. "I don't see you running."

Dal returned that stare. "I wouldn't give you the satisfaction."

Rob's eyes twinkled dangerously. "Now, Dal, you know I'm not *that* bad."

"Oh yeah? I know what you did to Jay."

An eyebrow lifted in amusement. "Which time?"

Dal threw down the magazine. "You know perfectly well what I mean: that circus with the article that blew his thesis to hell!"

"And what *should* I have done? Let him go on until he'd finished the damned thing and *then* find out? I'd *really* have been an asshole then."

"You could have been more civil about it. There's absolutely no excuse for such snottiness. I mean, what'd Jay ever do to *you?*"

"He was born."

"So were you—regrettably."

Rob sighed, almost seemed to slump down in his chair. When he spoke again, his voice had become much quieter, which put Dal even more on guard. "Okay. I'll be perfectly frank with you, Dal." He paused to take a deep breath—for effect, she thought. "I love my mom, and I loved my dad—what I remember of him—and I suppose I would have loved Jay if he'd been their son. But when Mom got pregnant by that other guy, and Mom and Dad's marriage fell apart, it was just too much. Jay, by his very conception, destroyed my happiness."

"But you were only—what?—three or four when they divorced. Surely you can't remember that much about it.

And anyway, you know it's not *Jay's* fault. Why not hate your mother? That'd make more sense. Or your dad, for that matter. He was fooling around too, wasn't he? Wasn't that what caused the split during which she met Jay's father?"

"If I hated Mom, that'd—I don't know—be disrespectful of Dad's memory. I couldn't stand that. But look, Dal, this is *not* what I came here for. I don't need a lecture on family relations."

"No, you need a shrink."

"Uh, yeah, maybe I do. But right now I've come to lay it on the line. I've got a proposition that, if we can bury our differences, could be beneficial to both of us."

Dal regarded him doubtfully. "Indeed?"

"Look, you heard anything about this Scarboro Faire thing yet?"

"As a matter of fact, yes."

Rob nodded. "Okay, good. Well, there are gonna be a bunch of theaters and one of 'em's doing straight medieval drama. A small group of representative short works—I'm not certain how many, but there'll be a rotation. But the point is, I'm in charge—and directing."

Dal ignored his last remark. "Which works?"

"Wakefield, to start with, though I'm planning to phase it out as other pieces come on line; probably a couple of St. George plays; *Everyman,* maybe; possibly *Ralph Roister Doister* or *Gammar Gurton's Needle*. And," he added after a suitably dramatic pause, "that new play they just discovered at the library."

Dal felt her heart skip a beat. *Oh Christ,* she thought, *so that's it. Why me, Lord, why me?* In spite of her best efforts, her face showed a spark of interest.

Rob noticed the change. "I need someone with your rapport with the public, Dal, someone who knows what they're doing, who's easy with early period drama. You'd be perfect! Besides, think of the challenge: you'd be bringing something to life that's been dead for five hundred years."

She eyed him narrowly. "I'd have to be in all of them? Learn how many plays?"

"Oh, maybe only one or two to start with: short ones. It'd be an ensemble. And anyway, didn't you do *Second Shepherd* at Young Harris before you came down here?"

" 'Fraid so."

"Okay, well, see? That one ought to be a piece of cake."

Dal stared at the chipped edge of the coffee table in silence.

"So? You want to be my leading lady?"

"I don't know," she whispered.

Rob stood up and wiped his hands on his thighs. "Okay, I don't need an answer now, but you *will* think about it, right? Look at it this way: you'd be doing the one thing you love most in the world, and I'd have the best actress in the department. We'd both come out winners."

"You're overlooking one thing."

"Which is?"

"The fact that I can't stand you." She locked gazes with him for a long moment.

Rob returned her stare. "I can overlook it if you can."

"I can't."

"Are you thinking about what's good for you or what's good for Jay?"

Dal's eyes flashed sudden fire. "What's good for me *is* good for Jay—and vice versa. Same goes for bad."

Rob sighed and strode toward the door. "I really need to know by Friday at the absolute latest. I've got a second choice already lined up. But I just wanted you to know you were my first. It never hurts to ask for what you want."

"Be careful what you ask for, though, you may get it."

Rob's face brightened. "Does that mean you might do it?"

"It means that if I do you might wish I hadn't."

"Oh ho!"

"Yeah," Dal replied with a saccharine smile. "There's always a chance I could stand up on opening day and tell the whole world what a screaming asshole you really are!"

Rob surprised her by laughing. "That's what I like about you, Dal! You're dangerous. I *love* danger!"

"I think you'd better leave."

"I'll put a list of readings in your box."

"Get *out*, Robby."

He did. But the things he had said remained with her.

Dal stared absently at the rough wood paneling that lined the booths of Yudy's Sandwich Shop. Across from her, LaWanda was absorbed with the final bite of a Philly steak sandwich. This was Miss Gilmore's one free week-day evening. Their meeting was a sort of ritual.

"So what's it gonna be?" LaWanda asked finally. She withdrew a pack of cigarettes from the frayed pocket of the red silk man's smoking jacket she was wearing. Her dread-locks had been swapped for closely spaced cornrows.

"I just don't know," Dahlia replied, shaking her head.

"Well, you're gonna have to tell Mr. Jason sooner or later, even if you don't accept Robby's offer." She took a sip of Killians Red and waited for Dahlia's reaction.

Dal twitched her nose thoughtfully. "No, I don't have to tell Jay about the offer. He'd simply go off on another tirade, which—justified or not—would serve no useful purpose. Last weekend was plenty, let me tell you."

LaWanda nodded but did not look convinced. "Well, that's the truth, I guess. But I still think you oughta level. Jay's a big boy; he can take it."

Dal rolled her eyes. "Sometimes I wonder. Jay's older than me in years, but in a lot of ways I'm older than he is. Sometimes I wonder why I put up with him."

"I'd assume it's 'cause you love him."

Dal took a deep breath. "Do I, Wannie? I *think* I do, that's for sure. There's something special about him, a sort of innocence or something I can't resist. Oh, he puts on a lot, but you always know where you stand with him. I guess what I'm trying to say is there's no falseness. Pre-tention and self-delusion, yes, but nothing truly artificial."

"If he likes you, he likes you. . . ."

"Yeah, and if he loves you, he loves you—heart and soul and body. It's hard not to fall for that kind of devotion. But sometimes I think we might both love each other for the wrong reasons: him 'cause I represent some impossible ideal, and me 'cause—no, I won't say it."

"Yes you will. You'll feel better."

Another deep breath. "Sometimes I think maybe I hooked up with him partly as a way to thumb my nose at Robby—though I suppose you could suspect the same thing about Jay. Or maybe I just like the novelty of being idolized. Or maybe—"

LaWanda shook her head. *"Wrong.* You're rationalizing!"

"I may be about to hurt somebody I care for. Maybe I'm just trying to build some distance."

"Dal—"

"It's scary being this important to somebody, Wannie, scary as hell."

"I know it is, girl. But you're gettin' off the subject. Why, exactly, don't you want to tell Jason?"

"Like I said: because he's been through so much angst lately and is just now starting to get his act together. I don't want to fire him up again. If you want to know the truth, part of me would like to be a healer, try to patch things up between him and Rob. Maybe then Rob would leave me alone. 'Course I wouldn't want either of them to know it."

"Anything else?"

Dal shook her head. "No, not really. I guess I just doubt that he could handle it."

LaWanda laid a hand on the forearm Dal had draped across the table between them. "Don't *ever* doubt Mr. Jason. He just sloughs off on you because he knows he can get away with it, and you know yourself that you let 'im. Put his back to the wall, that boy'll come through okay. You mother him too much."

"I agree with you," Dal sighed as she stole one of La-Wanda's cigarettes—mostly to fidget with. "That is, I'd agree if it was anything *else* we were talking about. But we're dealing with twenty-odd years of hatred, here."

"We're also talking about trust. You trusting Jay to be strong. And him trusting you. How you gonna find out how things really stand if you don't test him? You were strong for him when he needed you. Now he's gotta be strong for you when you need him to, 'cause if you do accept Robby's offer, you're gonna have to have somebody to let your hair down to. Jay'd be the perfect person 'cause you both know the truth about Robby."

"Maybe. But don't forget that I don't like Rob quite independently of the way he treats Jay. If I'd never heard of Jay Madison I'd still be leary of letting Rob Tolar direct me. I'm not even *that* keen on his project, now that I've thought about it a little."

"Wrong again!" LaWanda snorted. "You'd give . . . certain parts of your anatomy to do the kind of thing he's doing. Face it girl, it's decision time: are you gonna go with what's definitely best for you in the long term—intellectually, if not emotionally—and at that, it's only for what? two-three months max and it's over, but you've still got the experience. Or are you gonna go with what *might* be good for you in the short term, and cop out on the both of you in the bargain?"

Dal shrugged uncertainly. "I *think,*" she said carefully, "that I'm not gonna do it. I've gotta catch up on my classes now that *Macbeth*'s done, for one thing."

"That's an excuse, and you know it."

Dal smiled ruefully. "Yeah, it is."

"So you've got—what? A week, more or less?"

"Less. Rob says he wants me for *The Second Shepherd's Play* because I've done it before, but he also says he can save rehearsing that for last. He left me a list of possible other works, though, and told me to start reading them over."

"And have you?"

"Haven't even looked at it."

"Sound's like your mind's made up; no *think* about it."

"I guess so—but, God, Wannie, I still wonder if I should even tell poor Jay that he asked me."

LaWanda threw up her hands in resignation. "Well, *I* still think you ought to, and *I* still think he can handle it. But," she added with a dry chuckle, "I'd make mighty sure there's no sharp objects or valuable breakables in the room!"

"What about Jay's heart?" Dal asked sadly.

"What about it?"

"That I should even consider."

"That, my girl, will have to be your decision."

Dal nodded and picked up her handbag. "I'll tell him, then," she sighed. "But in my own good time. Right now, I guess I'd better break the sad news to Robby."

Chapter VII: Dirty Back Road

(April 6)

"I'm sorry I wasn't here for you, Jason," said Dr. Peter Girvan Sparks, "but maybe it was better that you couldn't reach me when you found out about your thesis. I might have helped trash your brother and got fired for my trouble, and then where would we be? I must say the guy doesn't impress me."

Jay smiled wanly. "Thanks for the support, sir."

"I really do think it was for the best, though," Sparks added.

Jay's eyes narrowed. He was tired of being told that, even if he was beginning to accept it. "How so?"

The Elf took a puff from his long clay pipe (a gift from Jay), and directed his green-eyed gaze toward the ceiling. "Well, to be perfectly honest," he began, "I never really *liked* your old topic. What you had was fine, but it really was too broad a subject for the narrow confines of a thesis.

Now granted, you did a good job condensing *The Secret Common-Wealth,* but even the most basic discussion really would require at least a hundred pages to do it justice, and that much more to lay out the groundwork on Yeats: two hundred pages right there and you've barely started. It would be more appropriate for a dissertation."

"Then why'd you let me get so far with it?"

"Because you were doing a perfectly acceptable job. That you'd taken on more work than you really needed to didn't seem relevant, considering what *most* students get by with these days. Overachievement's definitely preferable to the alternative; 'Man's reach should exceed his grasp,' and that sort of thing. Which is not to say there weren't problems—besides the length. For one thing, you . . ."

Jay rearranged himself in his chair and tried not to show his increasing irritation as the Elf began one of his famous Drones. Sparks was easy to underestimate: his slender body, nearly beardless face, and youthfully pointed features (which were collectively the source of his appellation) disguised a mind that was sharp as a platinum razor and a tongue that could be even sharper.

Still, Jay had no one to blame but himself, at least not for this Tuesday afternoon audience. What with one thing and another he had only gotten a fraction of the T.H. White manuscript abstracted. Since he was usually very reliable about such assignments, he had felt he owed Sparks an explanation. He had stated his case, and now Sparks was returning the favor. That he only caught about one word in seven scarcely seemed to matter.

Four days had passed since Rob's untimely revelation, and he still hadn't thought up a new topic. The whole problem was keeping him so wired he could barely dress himself, never mind abstract, pay attention to Provost, or memorize declensions. He had already blown one pop test. His solution to it all had been to spend a lot of time napping.

But with sleep came the dreams: none so vivid as Friday's but similar enough to be disturbing. Mostly they consisted of half-formed images of wintry landscapes and frosted stone that had as their common thread a terrible sense of deadly purpose, of a mission begun but not accomplished. Not his thesis: something much more ancient.

He hoped he wasn't about to go bonkers.

But he need something to work on, some direction, and he needed it as soon as possible. He had hoped the Elf might suggest something.

The Drone rolled on to what was obviously a well-reasoned and elegantly phrased resolution, then ended so suddenly that the silence made Jay jerk upright.

The Elf took a draw from the pipe and grinned disarmingly. "Oh, come now, Jason, relax. Though I have been known to nibble upon the odd student, I'm in no mood to sample *your* overstressed person. It's a long way to the end of the quarter. What're you in such a hurry for?"

"Well for one thing," Jay replied, "I've still got Dal's old man to worry about. I'd . . . I'd sort of like to ask her to get married, but I'd like to have my degree before I do that. That way he might think just a little better of me. Besides, I've got to finish the blessed thing sometime!"

"And you truly have no notions?"

"Nothing that sets my blood on fire." A pause, then, "Well, that's not really true. Some of my friends are after me to work on that play manuscript I sort of discovered."

"You mean that medieval morality play—Bowman-Smith Codex? Actually, that's not a bad idea. You could do a critical edition. You'd have to read all the other extant examples, but that shouldn't be too difficult. Discuss sources, do a fair translation, gloss any interesting words and phrases. Then compare the analogues. Piece of cake . . . of course publication might be another matter, if you chose to pursue it."

"Right," Jay replied quickly. "Dr. McLaren's already got that part sewed up—translation and publication, anyway. Read it in the paper."

Sparks gnawed thoughtfully on his pipe stem. "Yes,

that's true. But as long as you did your own version without reference to her work, I think you'd be on safe ground —at least as far as a thesis is concerned."

Jay shook his head. "I've already been burned once by duplicating someone else's research. I don't want to risk it again."

"Tell you what," Sparks said, "let me think on it. I'll get on the horn to McLaren and see what she says. Meanwhile, I'd advise you to sit tight and keep thinking."

Jay sighed. He would get nothing more useful out of Sparks that day. "I'll do that, sir."

"Oh, and Jason?"

"Sir?"

"You are, of course, aware that there's a reason for all this ill fortune."

"Well," Jay began, "I did say *Macbeth* out loud at the wrong time."

The Elf shook his head. "Oh no, Jason, it's much worse than that."

"Worse . . . ?"

The Elf smiled sadly. "I understand you've been shamelessly neglecting your brownies.

Jay tried not to betray his exasperation at the ancient joke. Sometimes he got the idea that Sparks really believed in brownies. Maybe he should ride by his house and look for a saucer of milk on the back porch stoop. Maybe he should even empty it and leave doll-sized footprints nearby.

"I'll . . . I'll try to do better, sir," he finally stammered. "May I go now?"

A smoke ring and another shrug. "If it pleases you."

Jay nodded silently and stood.

"Take care, Jason. And—"

"I know: don't forget to leave out cream for my brownies."

Jay was wondering why he had even bothered talking to Sparks, since their discussion had ended exactly as he had expected, when a pair of figures leapt from the shadows of one of the blind arcades near the Park Hall cupola and clamped their hands on his elbows.

Jay skidded to a halt and glanced around to see Piper and LaWanda.

LaWanda bent close and whispered, gravel voiced, "Yer bein' *kidnapped*, young fella."

To which Piper added, "Aye, it's a shanghaiin' and a waylayin' we're up to. An' if ever I seen man in need of either, it's you."

Jay examined his companions more closely, then chuckled. "And if ever I seen man *or* woman more in need of the funny farm, it's *you* guys!"

They could say little to dispute his point. LaWanda was thrashing about in tight black jeans, knee boots, and vest over Piper's recently soiled performing shirt. She'd tied a red bandana around her head buccaneer-style, and wore immense golden hoop earrings. The effect was not that different from the way Jay habitually dressed, but there was just enough exaggeration to set the ensemble flirting with costume.

Piper, on the other hand, was wearing last year's designer fatigues (bought used, ripped off at the knees, and frayed); one of LaWanda's paisley scarves for a sash; and a yellow and blue tie-dyed tank top. He had a stuffed parrot duct taped to one shoulder and a cardboard hat from some Long John Silver's promotion atop his mass of curly brown hair.

"And where am I being shanghaied *to*?" Jay asked.

"Why, the sea, of course," cried LaWanda.

"Actually," Piper corrected, "we thought we'd take you to Bogart."

Athens, like most cities of northeastern Georgia, seemed determined to draw as close as possible to Atlanta, sixty miles to the west. To this end, a finger of it had extended beyond the city limits, pointing along the Atlanta Highway in a several-mile strip of fast-food restaurants, motels, car dealers, and—just beyond the newly completed bypass—Georgia Square Mall. The excrescence's westernmost limit was marked by a Pepsi-Cola bottling plant, the half circle of bogus standing stones that identified Stonehenge subdivision, and a brand-new Buick–Pontiac place. Just beyond them, the limited access four-lane of U.S. 78 broke off to the left and headed more sharply west, first through Monroe, then through Loganville and Snellville to Atlanta.

But right up ahead there was Bogart.

The twofold claims to fame of Bogart, Georgia (besides its name, which everyone seemed to find humorous, and a general tendency to defy the slickness of Athens) were Athena Carpet Mills where you could get cheap carpeting, and an overblown rep as a speed trap.

It was a strip town, with a few streets paralleling the main highway and several more intersecting them at right angles for a half mile or so. Houses were strewn about largely at random, and there was only a block or so of two-storybuildings that might loosely be termed a business district.

"Actually, we lied," Piper called over his shoulder from the front seat of LaWanda's ancient yellow Pinto. "We're not taking you *to* Bogart, exactly; we're taking you *through* Bogart."

"Well, that's a relief," Jay muttered from where he was scrunched up in the back. "I was beginning to fear for your minds, if you thought you could go be-bopping around out here in those getups."

"Shoot, I came out here in my bra and half slip after *Rocky Horror* one time," LaWanda confided. "'Course I *know* better now."

Jay nodded ironically. "Of course."

"Actually," she continued, "we thought we'd check out this Scarboro Faire doohickey. Hey, here's our turn!"

"Jesus, Wannie!" Jay protested, as LaWanda jerked the wheel hard left and swung onto a narrow road between two derelict houses.

They bounced and wove and skittered and slid along a gravel road that snaked between overhung branches, pirouetted around one final turn, and found themselves facing a formidable-looking gate lashed together from utility poles and hay thatching. A cardboard sign promised PARKING, with an arrow pointing to the left. Below it someone had tacked on an adendum: NO ADMITTANCE EXCEPT ON REAL BUSINESS.

"I *have* real business," said Piper, patting his hip pocket. "Folks gave me their card and told me to come out and case the joint."

LaWanda parked the Pinto and they followed the main road into the forest. It was really only a track now, though the ground was waffled with the tire marks of heavy equipment where it was not littered with flat mud blocks fallen from a bulldozer's cleats.

They walked for almost a quarter of a mile before construction sounds reached their ears: hammers and electric hand tools, men shouting and swearing.

One final quick jog between a pair of thick oak trees, and they were there.

A convincing simulacrum of a Renaissance city gate reared up before them, wrought of cinder blocks and plaster and topped with phoney concrete battlements. Across the arching entranceway hung a large wooden sign on which SCARBORO FAIRE had been penciled in spiky Gothic script. On the ground directly beneath it a tanned young man in midriffless T-shirt, cutoff jeans, and Makin' Bacon cap was absently mixing paint with one splattered hand and scratching his bare belly with the other. He nodded at them as they passed.

"Jeez," LaWanda cried, obviously impressed, "I think this thing might actually happen."

Scarboro Faire occupied what had until lately been a good-sized tract of scrub forest. It was bounded on one side by a shallow stream, while a high screen of utility poles lathed with rough-sawn boards formed a substantial part of the other. An open square near the gate was flanked with small booths, where plywood and two-by-fours were being transformed into half-timbering by judicious application of white and brown paint. Workmen were everywhere, mostly shirtless local types given to slogan caps and beer bellies. Large numbers of them were occupied in cutting scrollwork shapes out of plywood or fabricating dummy crenelations from the same material. Efforts had been made to preserve as many trees as possible, especially hardwoods, so that in places it really did look like a Renaissance village peeking out of the forest primeval.

Jay decided, after they had completed most of a circuit, that the grounds were shaped roughly like a bird's foot. They'd entered at the back claw, and four more paths (making for a very strange fowl) forked off to either side around the middle. At the end of each path was a theater.

One resembled a small castle; another was a mere shaded platform framed by two-by-sixes from which sheets of canvas were evidently to be hung. The third—the leftmost—was more impressive. Six feet off the ground at least, its backboard towered two stories higher. It too was made mostly of utility poles and rough lumber, but the effect was not unlike reconstructions Jay had seen of the Globe Theater, except that there were no outside walls on three sides.

And the fourth, the one to right-center . . .

The fourth was flanked by round concrete towers large enough to contain rest rooms on their lower level. Jay led the way through a gap in the high wooden gate and inside to where arcs of low benches made of split tree trunks sloped down to a simple wooden platform about three feet high, behind which stood an unpainted canvas backdrop. A complexity of wooden scaffolding to either side hinted at on-going construction, though no workmen were evident at the moment. At the left a cinder block wall made a substantial barrier, but to the right (which bordered the forest) a screen of heavy-grade canvas was all that was deemed necessary.

"Wanta go for a closer look?" Piper suggested.

Since there was no one around to stop them, they sauntered up to the stage. A sudden madness struck Jay, and he
scrambled up the steps and bounded across the unfinished
plywood. LaWanda and Piper took seats in the front row.

Though Jay had never acted in his life, he was a ham at
heart. At a loss for anything else to perform, he resorted to
Edgar Allan Poe's "The Raven." His voice quickly shifted
into W.C. Fields and Mae West, which had LaWanda practically rolling in the aisle as Jay's Fields voice whined,
"'Sir,' said I, 'or madam, truly your forgiveness I im-
plore . . .'"

He had got through the third recurrence of "Nevermore"
(which he always did as Miss West) when the sound of
footsteps backstage stopped him. He glanced around, saw
a heretofore closed flap of fabric to the left rear flip open.

And recognized the unmistakeable form of his brother.

It was difficult to say who froze more quickly or who
straightened his back and squared his shoulders sooner.

Since he could scarcely retreat without losing face, Jay
stood his ground while Rob strode forward until they were
no more than a yard apart. "A bit far afield, aren't you,
little brother?"

Jay shrugged. "I could make the same observation."

Rob's eyes narrowed just a fraction. "Except that *I'm*
where I'm supposed to be. What's *your* excuse?"

"He's, like, with me," Piper interrupted, bounding up
on the stage. "I'm part of this wingding too."

"Lord preserve us!" Rob snorted. "All this place needs
is a crazy Irishman. I suppose you're gonna be caterwaul-
ing morning, noon, and night?"

Piper drew himself up to his full five-foot-seven.
"What's it to you?"

Rob glanced at Jay and cocked an eyebrow. "Does he
always resort to hostility?"

Jay's eyes flashed. "Only when provoked."

Apparently feeling outnumbered, Rob took a deep
breath and smiled uncertainly. "Well, how're *you* doing?"

Jay wasn't fooled for a minute. "Okay, I reckon," he replied with calculated unconcern.

The lips curled slyly. "How's the thesis?"

Jay's head snapped up, and his eyes locked with his brother's. "Oh, I have a new topic," he lied, never faltering. "*Much* more challenging. Any progress on the dissertation?"

Rob gestured around him. "You're looking at it."

It was Jay's turn to lift an eyebrow. "*This* is your dissertation?"

Rob nodded, grinning smugly. "Dissertation *project*, actually. Writing it up's just a technicality."

"Hmmm." Jay was impressed. Maybe if he played it cool, he could still turn this aside from disaster. "Let's see," he began, counting his fingers, "you'll be doing *Everyman*, right? And a couple of earlier works. St. George plays, maybe?"

"*The Wakefield Cycle*, or *Second Shepherd*, anyway. But I'm doing something new, too. Something that's not been done in about five hundred years. Perhaps you read about it in the paper?"

The words hit Jay like a hammer blow. "You're *what*?"

Rob studied him carefully. "I take it you *have* heard of it?"

"He's doing his thesis on it," Piper inserted, then "Ooops!" He clapped a hand over his mouth as both La-Wanda and Jay glared at him. Rob's eyes widened with fury.

"The *hell* you are, you little bastard! That play's mine!"

"From what I hear, it's McLaren's," Jay shot back, abandoning all pretense of civility. And then so quickly it surprised even himself: "But it so happens that I *am* doing a critical edition."

Rob's eyes were blazing. "You use one *word* of my text, you're a dead man!"

Jay folded his arms defiantly. "I wouldn't think of it. I'd prefer a *correct* translation."

"McLaren's translating."

Jay nodded derisive agreement. "I'm sure you won't leave it alone, though; you never can. You'll add your own touches till the original's obscured entirely. Might as well write 'Fucked up by Robby Tolar' on the program and be done with it!"

"Shut up!"

Fists clenched, Jay took a step forward, only to feel two pairs of hands grab his arms and drag him back—Piper and Wannie, he assumed, though all he could see was Rob's face turning redder by the instant. It always came to this when they met: two usually rational human beings just getting more and more irrational.

"Get the hell off my stage!" Rob shouted.

"My pleasure!" Jay retorted.

Their voices were beginning to draw a crowd. A foreman-type separated himself from the sea of caps and wandered toward them. "Oh, there you are, Mr. Tolar," he said, seeming oblivious to the altercation—though he looked sharply at the other three students. "I need to talk to you about them movable panels you ordered."

"We'd better go," LaWanda said, smiling smugly at Rob, as Jay allowed her to draw him away.

"Stay off my turf, punk," Rob gritted under his breath. He spun around and marched off toward the foreman.

"Bastard!" LaWanda hissed.

"Asshole!" Piper added.

"To which I should add son of a bitch, except that would impugn my poor lady mother," Jay finished, as they left. "But it's true anyway."

"He's got nerve."

"Balls, girl, balls."

"But Jay's got balls too." LaWanda grinned, cuffing Jay on the shoulder. "Hey, way to go, guy! Facing down the prick on his own territory!"

"Yeah, but Jesus God, Piper, why'd you have to blurt that out about me working on the play? I've told you before, I don't want to, and now you've given me no choice."

"Just being helpful," Piper began brightly, but when he saw Jay's troubled expression he laid an arm across Jay's shoulders. "Sorry, man. Tell you what, when we get home I'll let you kick my butt for me."

"Piper?" Jay grumbled.

"Yeah?"

"Just shut up!"

By the time they had returned to the car, Jay was in no mood for conversation. Although the day was sunny, a cloud had fallen across them. Even the irrepressible Piper had finally figured out the extent of his faux pas, and was busy guilt-tripping himself.

Jay wedged himself into the back of the Pinto. "By God, I'll show him," he muttered. "I *will* do the bloody Bowman-Smith Codex, Robby and McLaren be damned. I'll get the fucking thing in print before he even gets it onstage. Hell, if I had a copy I'd start right now!"

Piper's face brightened. "Well *that's* no problem." He reached under his seat and pulled out a manilla envelope. "Just so happens that I had to do a copy for ole Ms. McLaren herself, and—well—it just seemed like a good idea at the time to do an extra. Just in case, y'know?"

"And you just *happened* to have it with you?" Jay snorted. "Yeah, sure. You guys had this whole thing worked out in advance, didn't you?" He snatched the envelope.

"It seemed the right thing to do at the time," LaWanda admitted.

"Uh-huh. Seems like I've heard those words before." He glared at LaWanda. "You knew Robby was gonna be out here, didn't you?"

"Uh-uh," Piper said. "You gotta *trust* the juju woman, she had a *feelin'* about this, she told me so—"

"Bullshit! I bet Dal's in on it, too! I bet she knew the whole thing and was just afraid to tell me 'cause of what I might do. Shit, I bet that asshole's already been after her about this."

"Jay—"

Jay grabbed the back of LaWanda's seat. "Has he, Wan-nie? Has Robby been after my woman?"

LaWanda jammed on the brakes and twisted around in place. "All right, Mr. Jason, *stop it!*"

Jay started to reply, but bit back his words. "Oh, never *mind*," he growled. "Just forget it."

Piper and LaWanda exchanged glances but said nothing further.

Jay bit his lip and stared blankly out the window for a moment, then picked up the envelope and slid out the pages. It was the first time he had really looked at the manuscript, and he was surprised to discover that he could make out most of the words despite the crabbed handwrit-ing. Unconsciously he began reading aloud, his voice growing stronger by the moment. He reveled in it, joyed in the sounds, in the rhythmic power of the ancient words. He lost all track of time.

A pattering sounded against the roof, and he glanced up, surprised to find it was raining since the sun had been shining only moments before. Piper's face—visible in the rearview mirror—was ecstatic. "Well, at least *somebody's* happy," Jay muttered and looked back at the dense script, distantly aware of rain falling harder and harder. Only a few more lines to go . . .

"Damn!" LaWanda's curse roused him from his concen-tration just as he finished, which was probably just as well as he was beginning to feel a touch queasy.

"What?"

"Oh, I've missed a turn somewhere and wound up on a friggin' logging road or something. But I swear I don't know how!"

"Probably just vee'd the wrong way," Piper suggested. "Roads don't always look the same going out as coming in 'em."

"Yeah, but this road hasn't been used in a long time. I don't like this."

It was true. The trees had grown very close of a sudden, their gnarled limbs dragging small-leaved twigs across the little car's roof. To make matters worse, the engine was beginning to hiccough. Jay peered between the front buckets and saw that the way ahead was becoming a mere track, by equal turns mud, moss, and bracken. And the trees had become very dark indeed. He had never seen such a close growth of timber—nor, come to think of it, trees exactly like these. They resembled live oaks, and something like Spanish moss was hanging from their branches, but he didn't think live oaks grew this far north, and he knew that Spanish moss didn't.

The car continued to bounce and sputter along, though LaWanda had slowed to a crawl. Every now and then Jay felt the back end slip sideways in the mud. The rain was falling much harder, too. He wondered how LaWanda could see at all through the gray smear of windshield.

The ferns grew closer as well; and once there was a hideous scraping along the side of the car. Tatters of mist rose up around them.

LaWanda stopped the car and threw up her hands in disgust. "Now I *know* we're lost."

"Can we back out?" Jay asked hopefully.

"You're kiddin'," LaWanda snapped. "I can't even see out the *windshield,* and it's got wipers!"

A stronger wind set the leaves thrashing, flogging against the windshield as though they sought to claw through. Through the drizzle and the foliage Jay could make out a patch of sky. LaWanda frowned and inched the car forward.

"Want me to drive?" Piper volunteered.

"Not on your life." She leaned forward, squinting into the rain and leaves. The tires were often spinning now. Eventually they started up a gentle slope: more spinning more frantically—but far less forward progress.

Abruptly the car stumbled to a halt.

LaWanda yanked up the hand brake and turned off the ignition. "Well, guys, this is it. Who's up for pushing?"

"You could *always* back up," Jay repeated.

"The hell you say! I ain't backin' up through no jungle!"

And looking backwards, Jay could barely see any sign of the road they had traveled. Then he noticed something more disturbing.

"I hate to tell you guys this," he said slowly, "but I have just *got* to pee."

LaWanda cast her gaze skyward in mute resignation. "Christ-on-a-crutch, white boy—*now?* I mean, here we sit in the middle of East Jesus and you tell me you gotta whiz?"

"Actually," Piper said ruefully, "I have to pee too."

LaWanda sighed. "I'd better check under the hood, I reckon. Might've shaken a plug wire loose."

Piper got out, and Jay followed him on the same side. LaWanda found her door blocked by a tree trunk, so she had to scrunch her way across the transmission hump. Jay heard the rusty groan of the hood hinges as he and Piper pushed aside low branches and proceeded back down the road about twenty feet. By unspoken consent they chose opposite sides of the trail and unzipped.

"Hey, look here, Jay," Piper called after a moment.

"I've seen it *before,* Piper. Mine's still bigger."

"No, man, look at the *road.*"

Jay secured his fly and turned around. "What about it?"

"We *did* just come this way, didn't we?"

"Far as I know."

"Then shouldn't there be tire tracks?"

Jay stared at the mossy ground between them. "You'd think so, wouldn't you? But maybe with the ground so wet, and the moss so thick and all . . ."

Piper reached down to prod the spongy turf. "Hey, it *is* thick, ain't it? Real gooshy. I oughta take some back for Myra's moss garden." A pause, then, "Wow, listen to the quiet!"

Jay did. It *was* quiet. Deadly quiet. The rain had stopped, though he had not noticed exactly when. Already the ground was steaming—the Pinto was practically shrouded with the stuff. Sunlight filtered in beams through gaps in the small, thick leaves. The world looked newborn: light glittered from droplets everywhere. A small, bright green bird hovered by Piper's head and began to sing.

"Hey, what kinda bird *is* that?"

Piper jerked his head around, startling the creature, so that it flew away before he had a chance to focus. "Parakeet, I reckon. Looked like one, anyway."

"What would a parakeet be doing out here? And wasn't there something weird about its legs?"

"Search me, man. I don't even know what *we're* doing out here."

"Do parakeets sing?"

"Plants are *my* thing, O Black One; not budgies."

Jay gestured at the trees around them. "These *are* live oaks, right?" he asked, remembering Piper's horticultural period—what was it—two majors ago?

"Dunno, man. I should have said *ornamental* plants. I could snag a sample and check it out, though."

"Whatever," Jay replied and started back up the hill. "Let's see if Wannie's got the car fixed."

She had, though it was running but fitfully, and Jay and Piper found themselves faced with the unpleasant prospect of getting the car unstuck and pushing it up the hill.

"You really *are* gonna have to back up, girl," Jay began, then shook his head. "No, tell you what: let's at least see how much further we're gonna have to go, and *then* decide."

LaWanda nodded. "Good idea."

"As soon as it quits raining."

"Oh Christ, here it comes again!"

Jay and LaWanda dived for the car, but Jay had to go back out and fetch Piper who was just standing there getting wetter.

"You're a crazy man," LaWanda chided, when Piper had finally been dragged back inside.

The rain enclosed the car in a shroud of gray and a grumbling roar that evoked both threat and comfort.

"Wish I had some dope," Piper said.

"So do I," LaWanda agreed.

"I've got some," Jay volunteered, digging in his back-pack.

The next several minutes passed quickly, as Jay's stash proved surprisingly potent, leaving them all feeling mellow.

But outside it was raining harder. The world became a blur of grayish green as water sheeted off the windshield with so much force they could see nothing beyond it.

And then everything turned solid white as lightning struck a tree right in front of them. A white noise boom shattered their hearing; and the scent of ozone filled the air. Through a break in the madness, Jay saw a massive limb rip loose and smash through the screening branches to slam the earth not five feet from the Pinto's front bumper.

Abruptly it was over: the rain slowed to a drizzle, then stopped. There was no more lightning and only a distant growl of thunder that quickly receded. Blue sky broke out above them.

Piper and Jay climbed out and looked around tentatively, neither quite believing what had happened: the fury of the storm come so sudden, then so quickly vanished. Already the air was clearing: clean and fresh as a summer morning.

Jay shrugged his confusion and stuck out his lower lip in bemusement, a gesture Piper echoed precisely.

"After you," Jay said, bowing gracefully to let Piper go on ahead. Together they dragged the limb out of the way.

Beyond was open air and twenty feet of hill remaining: too steep for them to push an enmired car up. But when LaWanda restarted the Pinto its back tires caught instantly, and—aided by a touch of male muscle—managed to scoot the remaining distance with little trouble.

Piper and Jay climbed in at the top, and they all sighed in relief as they saw the way open ahead of them. A final handlike splay of mist-wrapped oak leaves brushed the side, and they were skittering down a wider dirt road between open fields beyond which showed a gray line of highway. Behind them loomed a dark line of pines.

"What time is it?" LaWanda asked. "I gotta get back to work dinner."

"Two-thirty," Jay said. "Best we boogie."

"But that's when we left," Piper noted. "Left the fair, I mean."

"Who knows?" Jay said, staring at his wristwatch curiously. "Can't trust these cheapo imports." He shook it and looked more closely. "Well, crap, my LCDs have done died on me. All they're showing is 18:88."

"Well then we really *should* boogie. We're almost to the highway. Which way, man?"

"Ho," said Piper as they paused at the edge of the pavement. "I think this is seventy-eight."

"You sure?"

"You worry too much, Mr. Jason."

Jay did not reply, but as the road bent right toward the city, he glanced once more toward the line of dark pines now far behind them. *Funny,* he thought. *I could have sworn there was nothing but hardwoods.*

Interlude One

The beast was sleeping.

It was the hottest part of the day and it usually slept then, for the bluish light hurt its raptor eyes, the hot stone burned its tender foot pads, and there was rarely anything awake then worth eating. Half a thousand years it had lived in that land, but yet was not accustomed, though Master had promised to fix that—long ago, before he had vanished.

The glare of too-bright sunlight slashed black shadows across the jumble of white rocky shelves on which it was resting. The stone grew hotter, and it twitched irritably, stretched a taloned forefoot across a smudge of moss to brush cliff-shadowed bracken. A neck feather ruffled in the breeze.

Something disturbed it, then; something awoke it. Something was calling.

* * *

Cathal the wingless male gryphon raised his head and
gazed about the rocky outcrop, squinting golden eagle eyes
against the glare, while feathered ears sorted wind songs in
the mountains around him. He blinked, once, twice, then
rose stiffly, his eagle-clawed front half responding first as
he lifted his head and shoulders on massive legs thick as an
ostrich's. The leonine hindquarters followed. He opened
his beak, thrust out his forked tongue, and tasted the noon-
day breezes; then flexed his mighty back and armored
limbs, setting joint-lights chasing the shadows.

And from out of nowhere came the Calling. Not heard,
not felt, simply *being*.

The gryphon blinked three more times, troubled by the
not-sounds that thrummed in his brain. He paced a circle,
surveyed the horizons, seeing life everywhere, but never
the source of the Call, which by the moment became more
insistent.

His heart speeded up, beating faster and faster as though
it would rip itself from his body and follow that unspoken
summons. And a sort of itchy twitching had appeared in
his stomach—rather, he thought, like a tickle.

He relaxed. *That* was the problem: something he had
eaten had just found out it was dying. He was sleepy, well-
fed, too tired to think. Maybe if he followed the Call for a
moment, it would let him return to his dreaming. He
yawned once more, copper beak gaping wide enough to
swallow a man's head—and turned loose his body to
wander.

He had come into a forest, Cathal realized a short while
later, though he could not recall how he had got there. But
up ahead a light rain was falling. A curious thing, that: like
a silver curtain spilling pale striations in the ether. It moved
toward him, glittering enticingly among the trees and
flowers. And where it lapped across one, that thing would
then fade and shimmer. He wondered about that too; for he
was certain that was not natural, yet the Call was stronger

there: a constant almost-torment, as his heart beat nigh to exploding.

Almost without thinking, he gathered his haunches and sprang into the sheet of silver.

A tingle shook him, he wanted to turn back, but his body would no longer obey him. The Call was still with him, though; and with it now was another, stronger and not so unfocused. *Cathal!* that new Caller whispered, spreading soothing thoughts across his terror. A touch lighter than even a shadow ruffled his feathers. He thought he remembered it, put forth his own thought in answer: *Master?*

Only in part. I am Watcher.

Watcher . . . ?

Watcher's thought bored into him. *Come to me, come now, come hither; come help me, come make me stronger.*

There was another shimmer ahead, a brighter one, a *golden* one, beyond which he could see more of the forest.

Cathal went that way, felt the first Call grow stronger, only this time Watcher went with him.

He was there, his head through the threshold. Raindrops tickled his feathers.

But . . . but something was wrong!

First Call was fading.

The forest twisted and blurred. Trees doubled, then vanished and reappeared and vanished again, like a ripple smashed on a shoreline. Even the raindrops had left him.

Watcher? Cathal screamed. *What has happened?*

An unspoken howl of anguish answered him, then words strained and unclear: *Too long I slept, then too long I waited, and now the World Wall has once more risen . . . But soon the Call will come again—and this time we will both act more quickly.*

And with that Watcher fell silent.

Cathal leapt once more through the silver.

Chapter VIII: Party Out of Bounds

(April 9)

Scott reached up to grab a handful of Ruffles from a wicker basket someone was passing by with, ate the three largest, and took a swig from the plastic cup of draft Kirin he had stashed between his legs on the next porch step down. "What I can't figure out," he said, "is how we wound up hosting the cast party for a play none of us had anything to do with except Dahlia."

"I think—" Jay began, but was drowned out by the resumption of music in the hallway behind them—La-Wanda's rendition of the B-52s' "Private Idaho." He could hear the windows rattling on the low notes and feel the floorboards rise and fall beneath the stamping feet of a score of dancers.

"I say," he tried again, shouting into Scott's ear, "I say, I *think* it's 'cause we've got the biggest backyard, the mos' laid-back bunch of housemates, and the neighbors least

likely to call the con-stab-u-lar-y—'cept that they did anyway. 'Sides, this way the whole lot of us c'n be here.
Otherwise, it'd just've been me 'n' her 'n' a bunch of
drama geeks off in some spiffy restaurant."

"Yeah," Scott replied, flopping a brotherly arm across
Jay's shoulders. "And I think the fact that Wannie brought
her band for free didn't hurt, either."

"Actu'lly, m'brother, the band brought itself, Wannie
was here already. She *lives* here, don' forget."

Scott pushed Jay away and studied him (a little crookedly) at arm's length. "Are you drunk?" he asked, frowning. "I don't want to have to play drunk doctor." ·

"Aw, Scotto, why not?" Jay replied, laying it on thick,
when all he actually felt was a middling buzz.

Scott showed his impressive teeth in a friendly snarl.
"Come on, guy," he snorted, "let's go see what the other
fools're doin'."

Jay stood, stretched, and gave Scott a hand up when the
taller boy paused to retrieve his beer.

"Law, what fools these mortals be," Scott intoned.

"Careful, my man," Jay warned, "that's Mr. Willie his
own bad self you're spouting. Can't have you poaching on
my turf."

"Unfortunately, geologists are *not* given to quotability,"
Scott replied.

"'You will observe by these remains—'" Jay began to
recite a bit of doggerel about the alleged two-brainedness
of certain of the ornithischian dinosaurs.

Scott clapped one hand over Jay's mouth and steered
him inside with the other.

The party had long since ceased to be a blowout for the
Macbeth cast and crew. LaWanda's band, Save the Feet for
Last, had taken over the wide central hallway and most of
the living room of Myra's apartment, having been forced to
move off the front porch half an hour earlier because of a
firm reminder about noise ordinances from Athens's Fin-
est. Now they were cooking again, filling the whole downstairs with an incredible, if slightly off-key, din. Just then

they were trying to fake their way through "Safety Dance," with little success.

Jay was trying to figure out whether or not the tall, hawk-faced fellow talking to Dal in the corner was in fact Pete Buck of R.E.M. when Piper popped out of the open door across the hall (where Small, Medium, and Large lived), and dragged him inside.

"What th' hell're you doin', Piper?" Jay growled. "I think that's Pete—"

"Taste this," Piper cried, as he thrust a cup of transparent liquid into Jay's hand.

Jay took a sip, opened his eyes very wide, and took another, much larger one. "God bless *America,* Piperman," he sputtered. "This is grade-A, top-of-the-line, the Lord Jesus's own number one *moonshine!"*

Piper nodded smugly, looking inordinately pleased with himself. "Straight from the hills of Savannah."

"There *are* no hills in Savannah, Piper."

"Wrong-o. There *weren't* any hills there, but guy I got this from accidentally spilled some and—*poof*—there they were, good as any you got in Union County."

"We got *mountains* in Union—"

"What *about* Union County?" somebody interrupted from the hallway.

A lanky grad student peered owlishly in. Jay recognized him as one of Scott's geology department buddies. He had apparently corralled Scott just outside. "Oh Lord," Jay sighed, exchanging glances with his roommate, "I thought we had your crowd quarantined upstairs talking about plate tectonics."

"I *had* to get out," he moaned. "Bobbo started off about erosion patterns on Ayers Rock, and I just couldn't take it anymore. I mean the guy's a hard rocker, for God's sake, and there he goes on about sandstone. Next thing you know, it'll be fossils. I mean, what's a guy to do to preserve the purity of his discipline?"

"I take it you're a hard rocker?"

"I'll just *bet* he is," cooed a dark-haired girl, possibly

one of the drama crew, as she came up behind him. She eyed him speculatively. "I'll bet I can make his rocks *real* hard."

The guy turned red, and Jay, Piper, and Scott made themselves scarce as the girl took the dumbfounded geologist in hand and dragged him toward the stairs.

"Better go after 'em," Scott told Piper. "They'll be exploring horizontal stratification in your sheets any minute."

"Let 'em," Piper said. "Looks like it'd do him good."

On their way out, they stuck their head in Myra's back room, to discover her showing some of her paintings to an interested group of the art crowd. Jay wondered how many of them she'd talk out of their unconventional clothes in the next few weeks.

Outside once more, they paused on the porch. Jay craned his neck into the largely empty backyard. Several of the big candles and Japanese lanterns they'd put there earlier had gone out, but the remainder were casting such eerie shadows around the hedged-in enclosure that it looked more like Halloween than early April. The now-empty Kirin keg sat forlorn and deserted in its tub of melting ice on one side, while on the other an amorous couple was practicing their art in the cast iron loveseat. Near the driveway a small group of Anachronists was examining lengths of rattan lashed atop an old Datsun station wagon. A dark-haired figure slumped next to the steps closer in was quietly mumbling yet more new verses to "Bend Over, Greek Sailor"—Jay recognized him as Mad Tom Hundley, the lead singer for Just Thrid. The girl curled up in his arms looked shockingly young. Jay wondered where she had come from.

"Did I tell you I finally got up enough nerve to drop by their meetin' last night?" Scott asked. "And guess who was there? *That* guy! Managed to convince me to come by fighter practice on Sunday, too."

"You're gonna let yourself get dragged back in yet,

pal," Jay warned, then added, looking at Mad Tom, "Well, at least he ought to add some spice to their chorister's guild. But who is that child with him? Don't tell me she's —*shit fire!*"

Jay yelped and spun around, clutching his bottom.

—And confronted a wickedly grinning Dal holding a long and glittery sewing needle poised between her thumb and forefinger.

"Did I ever tell you," she whispered, "that you've got a simply irresistible hiney?"

"Last week," Jay replied instantly.

Dal jabbed the needle into the fleshy leaf of a nearby jade plant, slid her hands into Jay's front pockets, and started working her fingers inwards in the most provocative manner conceivable. "Well then, did I ever tell you that you've got an *amazing*—"

"Don't say it!" Jay cried, shooting panicked glances at Piper and Scott who were observing the proceedings with considerable interest.

"He does not!" Piper avowed with conviction.

Jay cast his gaze skyward in resignation as Piper wiggled his eyebrows at him, plucked the needle from the plant, kissed it apologetically, and stalked off, muttering, "Oh, Wannie, Wannie, yo' fine black fanny's in trouble!"

Scott mirrored Jay's expression. "Well, it looks like you two've got matters well in hand. Maybe I'll go watch Wannie vivisect Piper. Keep your ears poised for a screech to end all screeches."

"Just tryin' to help her with the upper part of her range," Piper shot back, as Scott followed him inside.

Myra stuck her head out of her back hall door as Scott passed. "Yo, Scotto. You know anybody sober? We need somebody to make a booze run."

"You've got the wrong guy, then." He motioned over his shoulder—"Ask Dal. She looks to be in decent shape —if Jay doesn't knock her up in the next five minutes. They're the only people I know can have sex back to back with their flies closed."

Myra smiled and marched onto the back porch. "Dal, my girl," she announced. "I need you to perform a great service: I need you to get some more liquor."

In her old house on Dearing Street half a mile away, California Montana McLaren poured herself another cup of bitter black coffee and wheeled herself through her bedroom and into the tiny office cubicle she had added to one side. The wheelchair's rubber tires squeaked as she turned the corner and positioned herself in front of her desk. She had one more page to key into the Kaypro and the transcription would be finished. It had not been difficult; most of the words had been essentially modern English. She'd regularized the spelling a bit, smoothed out the syntax for contemporary ears, and disposed of as many archaisms as she could; it never paid to overestimate the intellectual level of an audience. Basically, though, she thought it was a sound rendition.

But it was also damned peculiar. Though she was more than usually aware of the pagan roots that underlay many medieval folk plays (including some of the moralities), this one was a couple of hundred years closer to those roots than any she had seen before, and commensurately more perverse. The names were typical, for instance: Biblical names or the names of saints—only the characters didn't act like saints. And McLaren had the peculiar feeling that the names used were not the proper ones, that something older, stronger, darker lurked just beneath the surface. Even the sentence structure was a little skewed: at times it appeared to be forcing itself into patterns of rhyme and rhythm that did not seem native to English.

But it would be a joy to see it performed, despite the hassle of getting out to the site for the opening performance. Only for her son would she do such a thing. And perhaps for Robert, though she'd die before she'd let him know it.

Twenty minutes later she had finished the remaining page. She checked the beginning of the file one final time to be certain the whole play was still there (it wasn't, always, given the pitfalls of absentminded saves), and gave it a last going-over to check spelling and punctuation. Eventually satisfied that the text was as free of errors as she could make it, she called up the print menu, turned on the printer, and—once the machine was clattering happily away—trundled off to the kitchen for her nightcap.

It was one of the many rituals that ordered her existence: a half-inch of Irish Mist added to her last cup of Maragor Bold to smooth out both the drink and her nerves. A blueberry Danish joined it.

Back in the office, McLaren watched as the printer scrolled out the pages. When it had thumped to a stop and she had turned it off, she tore off the edges and settled herself to proofreading.

It was satisfying to know she was the first person in several hundred years to read what she was holding. Robert would be the second, then the kids who would act it. That was it. Dr. Sparks had been after her to let one of his students work on it, but she'd told him he was crazy if he thought she'd consent to that. This was *her* baby, hers and Robert's.

The words swam before her eyes, their accents and rhythms crying out to her. Some of the scansion still wasn't working. Maybe if she could hear it in its proper format . . .

She took a large swallow of coffee and set her mind to roaming. Getting into the drift, she called it. First she imagined herself onstage—striding about with strength and conviction, not bound to the hideous chair. She knew that women were not generally allowed onstage until after Shakespeare's time, but that had no bearing on her fancy. In her mind she saw herself in a flowing gown of red velvet, cut in a deep vee across her breasts (high firm breasts, like she'd had as a girl). She was Juliet and Ophelia and Cleopatra and Cordelia.

Then she pictured a site where the play would likely have been performed: a town square paved with cobbles, narrow streets feeding in on every side, high buildings smeared with new whitewash between their ancient timbers; the stench of horse droppings and open sewers. She saw the townswomen: sturdy matrons in drab clothing trying to look stylish, their dingy, yellowing linen proof of inadequate sanitation.

And ahead of her a wagon rolled into the square—a wagon maybe thirty feet long and drawn by a quartet of oxen: at least three stories high it was, with Heaven a golden sun at the top and Hell belching sulphurous fumes below. A man pranced on the stage and began declaiming: "'I am called Satan, I'm Lord of this World...'"

She glanced at her page, began to read aloud, imagining herself that man: the Devil, bright in motley and red tights, pitchfork in hand, enormous codpiece poking brazenly out before him like a challenge as he reveled in his power. "'All the kingdoms of the world,' he cackled, 'All the worlds are mine!'"

She was really getting into it now: immersing herself in the sheer, joyful wonder of the words.

"'In man's strength is the power; in his blood is the cure...'"

Somewhere along the way she realized that she was thirsty, but when she reached for her coffee, she discovered to her horror that her tongue would not stop moving.

Oh my God! her mind screamed. *What's happening?* She tried to halt it, tried to raise her hands to her lips, but they would not obey. Yet her tongue blundered on—as if the words passed from eye to mouth on an automatic circuit she could do nothing to terminate.

She tried to drag her eyes away from the page but could not, tried to shut them and failed. A dreadful prickling crept into her extremities, as though her whole body had been asleep and suddenly was wakening. Even the dead nerves in her legs came horribly, painfully alive. She felt —almost—as if she could stand. Almost as if she could walk again.

No! This wasn't happening; this wasn't real! But still the words raced onward.

All at once she found herself standing, feet braced apart. Of themselves, her hands curled into fists and came together as if they gripped some phantom weapon which they then began to flourish.

And then the last word was sliding off her tongue. She almost hated to see it end.

But the tingling in her nerves increased, starting in her fingers and toes. And that tingling became pain, and that pain a burning agony, racing inward, filling her with its fury.

She knew what would happen, knew in some unaccountable way that something was loose in the world—something she herself had summoned. Was it the Devil? she wondered, as agony seared through her. *There* is *no Devil*, she answered herself. Her vision glazed with red. She felt like a glass poured too full, like a balloon too taut with air. Comfortable at first, then stretched ever tighter within a net of pain until all became agony and it exploded.

The last two things she saw were the flashing green light of the Kaypro's patient cursor, and shining in the window beside it lights of a dimmer, yellower cast that looked like the aloof, piercing eyes of some vast and silent raptor.

Chapter IX: Fifty-three Miles West of Venus

Dal was beginning to wish she'd asked someone to come with her on the beer run. It hadn't seemed like a big deal at the time—just a quick zip down the tail end of Milledge to a certain store she knew that could be persuaded to stay open a wee bit past the usual midnight closing. The guy on graveyard there had once shared a class with her, so she'd called and asked him to hold a couple of cases of Bud.

Only she'd forgotten she had virtually no cash and had used her last check that afternoon, so she'd stopped by an instant banker, to find it empty and had made a mad dash home to get more checks.

The upshot of it all was that she had wasted over an hour on piddly stuff; the party was most likely winding down by now, with her having missed a good chunk of it; and Jay had probably passed out already.

But she still had to get back; folks were relying on her. Except even that was a problem because, as she had discovered a moment before, she was running out of gas.

The needle wasn't moving at all, and her Prelude had already stumbled once when she'd been forced to brake quickly for a traffic light. She'd managed to nurse it another few blocks—to Five Points Chevron—to find it closed and press on in disgust, her options quickly narrowing to convenience stores—except that none of them *were* particularly convenient, and she didn't think she had enough gas to look for one anyway. To be honest, she didn't know if she could even make it the two miles to Jay's. But if she was going to get stranded, it would damned well be there or as close to there as she could manage, and the beer in the trunk could just *get* warm; that was how you were supposed to drink it anyway.

The light at the corner of Baxter and Milledge turned red, and she held her breath as she coasted up to it, cursing the delay. There were intersections you could creep through late at night and ones you couldn't, and this was one of the latter.

So she sat and idled and glared at the fuel gauge and tried to convince herself that the needle had space to travel.

The light changed.

She eased down on the gas.

The car coughed and quit.

She turned the key.

It caught, hesitated, then stumbled forward.

She got the Prelude another three blocks before it conked out entirely. Completely devoid of power steering and brakes, she managed to coast into one of the side streets between a pair of elegantly columned houses.

"Well, shit," she said, as she considered her choices. She'd have to call the party, she supposed, and get someone to come and get her—but there didn't seem to be a pay phone close by. She eyed the houses speculatively. One had been converted to a real estate office, the other was a mortuary. Neither looked occupied, though she imagined someone was on duty in the latter. Maybe she could borrow their phone.

She scowled. That wasn't a very attractive idea. And in any event, one of her classmates, Celia Broxxon, had a room in a rambling old mansion on the next corner down; she could see one of its gingerbreaded gables from where she was sitting. Dal checked the Prelude's locks, dashed off a note saying the car would be retrieved as soon as possible, and climbed out. A twist of cool breeze brushed her face, and she shivered, then pulled her denim jacket tightly around her shoulders and began to jog.

A moment later she pounded around the unruly, man-tall hedge that shielded Celia's backyard and driveway from the sidewalk—and was engulfed by near-total darkness. Her heart flip-flopped at the sudden change, the abrupt cessation of light and noise. She had never liked this place, especially not at night; it was too sheltered, too remote from its Victorian neighbors. And now the yard light was out, and there was no sign of Celia's old green Valiant, which meant that her friend probably wasn't home. Certainly no lights were on inside.

Christ, it's like a dungeon in here, she thought, glancing around at the dark foliage. *She really should at least turn on the porch light*.

Still, considering the condition of Celia's car, it wouldn't hurt to make sure. Casting one final glance at the looming foliage, Dal squared her shoulders and marched up to the rear stoop, then paused and looked around. Lordy Jesus, she was jumpy. She knocked three times, paused, then knocked again, and waited.

And wished she hadn't, because the silence was suddenly broken by a rustling in the thick bushes that angled out behind her from the side of the house.

Already wired to the hilt, Dal spun around, instantly wary.

Nothing.

She peered into the leafy gloom beyond the driveway.

Zip.

A violent chill swept over her body.

The rustle again. Something *was* out there.

Okay, one more time, then we boogie. She knocked harder; banged until her knuckles hurt.

Still no answer, though somewhere a cat howled and spat. She laughed giddily. That was probably what she'd heard—she hoped.

Rustle rustle rustle.

She turned and scanned the bushes once more, feeling the small hairs rise up on her arms.

Rustle rustle rustle rustle rustle.

To hell with this! Fifty feet to the street, fifty more to the corner, and I'm clear. A block more up to the mortuary, and maybe I will *call from there*.

She glanced at her watch: almost one-fifteen. It looked like she was just gonna have to risk it. Jay's place was only five blocks down Milledge Avenue and three more down Toombs. If she jogged down the better lit side of Milledge, she should be safe. If she could get that far.

Shut up, girl; get rational.

Ears alert for any sound, eyes darting anxiously into the gloom, Dal began to walk very slowly back toward the gap in the hedge that gave onto the sidewalk.

Rustle rustle PAD.

Hands at guard, she whirled around in a complete circle.

Nothing.

No, not quite: a flash of shadow this time by the corner of the porch, and with it a strong animal musk that nearly made her sneeze. Maybe somebody's pet skunk was loose.

To hell with it.

Suddenly she was running—clearing the bristling mass of hedge and reentering the light, then swinging around toward the main thoroughfare, Adidas slapping loud against the pavement. Light was growing around her now, puddling beneath her feet, stretching her shadow long before her like a crazily twisting black animal.

The mortuary now? Nah, she still wasn't that desperate.

There were any number of things that could make rustling noises in the bushes. She slowed a fraction, trying to force herself to be reasonable, wondering just what it was that had made her so jumpy.

A quick survey of the street showed no obvious threats, so she jogged on, reached the corner and turned right down Milledge. Though her heart was still thumping like a drum, she forced herself to slow down there, to assume an aura of quiet self-confidence. Would-be assailants tended to home in on fear, and she was determined to appear unafraid.

But something was following her—she was sure of it. There was a subtle difference in the feel of the air, in sounds too faint for her ears that yet registered on her subconscious that told her so. She remembered as a girl walking home from Girl Scout meetings after having read one of Ivan Sanderson's books on Bigfoot, and being scared shitless by every crouching bush and ill-lit stump she saw along the way. She felt like that now.

She stumbled to a halt, glanced over her shoulder, saw nothing unusual—except, perhaps, a shape that dodged into the shadow well between two streetlights about fifty yards behind her.

Better speed it up a little.

Another half block.

—A thump and a swishing sound; she spun full around, just in time to see something large and dark momentarily sail over the good-sized hedge a couple of houses back. There were some people in the Dearing Street area who kept peacocks; maybe it had been one of them. But could peacocks fly? Or had it been something leaping—a large dog, perhaps?

Still not quite running, though she more and more felt like it, Dal made it to Broad Street. Only three blocks further this way, then three more to the right. She sprinted across the four lanes and through a gas station's deserted forecourt.

This was the older end of Milledge now, going away from the university into a section of vacant lots and crum-

bling turn-of-the-century houses many of which were
slowly metamorphosing into the nicely restored offices of
various professionals.

Unfortunately, that meant there were more trees as well,
which meant more gloom and vulnerability, as the heavy
masses of new leaves dampened the pale glare of the
streetlights and cast the sidewalk into a deeper darkness.
Dal found herself glancing back more often, thought once
she heard an avian shriek, but shrugged it off. She passed
the vacant lot where a brace of Tudor houses had once
stood and thought about cutting through, but just as she
started, she heard a sound like air ripping and the resumption of the *pad pad pad* behind her. She squinted into the
gloom, thought she could make out a large shape slinking
along maybe forty yards back, largely obscured by a tree
trunk.

It was one of the hardest things Dal had ever done: to
turn and walk away from what ever it was. Only one thing
sustained her: that every step brought her closer to security,
closer to Jay.

RunDal-runDal-runDal-run—her mind set words to her
panic.

Somehow she made it to Toombs, turned down it. The
nearest house was still a block away. If she could just make
it that far . . .

RunDalrunDalrunDalrun—as panic hovered nearer.

Pad/scrape-pad/scrape-pad/scrape-pad . . . Faster.

Rationality left her—she ran.

The footfalls became a rasping scramble, and in spite of
herself, Dal glanced over her shoulder to see a gold-dark
shape streaking toward her no more than thirty yards away:
cat shape, it looked like, but moving too fast to see clearly
in the limb-broken shadows. Like a lion, maybe, except
that wasn't right either, because she would have sworn
whatever it was had a feathery mane, a strangely narrow
skull, and bare forelegs.

Jay's house was close now, just at the end of the next
block.

Runrunrunrunrun . . .

Before she knew it she had leapt off the sidewalk, was hurling herself across the intersecting street—

A horn blared almost on top of her, its raucous note blending with her scream as she threw herself aside, hit the pavement, and kept on rolling. A car swished by, narrowly missing her.

Brakes squealed; the car slid to a halt.

Jesus, girl, just get yourself run over while you're at it. She stood up and dusted herself off, apparently intact.

A power window whirred down, and a worried-looking teenage boy stared out at her. "Hey, 're you okay?"

Dal nodded shakily. "Think so."

"Hey look, sorry, lady," the boy went on quickly. "But you, like, just showed up out of nowhere. I was, like, lookin' at that big cat and didn't see you!"

"Cat?" Dal panted, trying to catch her breath.

The boy nodded vigorously, eyes wide. *"Yeah!* Almost hit it. All I seen was yellow eyes in my headlights and somethin' big an' catlike stretched out behind it."

"Didn't feel no thump, though," mumbled the red-haired boy in the passenger seat. "Didn't hit nothin', don't reckon."

"Might've scraped it," the driver allowed.

"Look guys," Dal burst out, "I'm a little weirded out here—think you could give me a ride down the block?"

"Sure thing, lady, just let me check out the car. I still think I might've hit whatever it was. *Damn* big cat, looked like. Maybe even a lion or somethin'."

Dal joined him at the front of the late model Cutlass. She felt suddenly light-headed. It had all been *too* strange; maybe she'd had more to drink than she thought. Too much excitement, too late an hour, too much pressure from over-due papers: her mind had played tricks on her.

Only—that would mean these guys' minds were fooling around with them too, which didn't seem likely. It was quickly becoming more than she could handle.

Partly to calm herself, she glanced down at the Olds's

egg-crate grill. Nothing odd there, no damage—No, wait!
—a couple of long, golden feathers were stuck into one of
the plastic rectangles. Impulsively, she tugged them loose
and stared at them, then dropped them abruptly. They were
as hot as fire! And as she watched, they began to melt
away upon the wind.

The driver shrugged. "Well, can't *find* nothin', but I
swear I thought it happened. Oh well, hop in—where is it
you need to get to?"

Dal slid into the front seat beside the two boys, and only
then realized she was shaking.

A moment later they dropped her off at 414 Toombs
Avenue. A drop of rain brushed her face, and she looked
up into the sky. Another drop, then another, then a torrent
as the heavens unloaded.

"All I need," she muttered as she dashed up the steps,
then "Where *is* everybody?"

The house was silent.

Gone an hour and everybody vanishes.

It was true—and probably her fault for not getting the
beer back sooner. Fair-weather friends, for certain.

Dal stumbled into the front hall, kicking aside empty
beer cans, gazing across the mounds of detritus.

The shaking grew worse, and she hugged herself.
Maybe the backyard; maybe someone's still there.

Nothing but sheeting rain.

Something caught her eye: a bottle of vodka half buried
in a pile of trash next to the door frame. It was nearly full.

She snagged it, raised it to her lips impulsively, and
drank until her throat felt like fire.

Another chill, as she made her way upstairs, and another as she crawled in bed with an unconscious Jay.

Her last memory was of thunder.

Her last thought was *so much for footprints*.

Then the darkness fell on her.

Rob stood in the doorway of his bedroom in 8 Rebelwood Villa and stared down at Erin's sleeping body. The

sheets had slipped off when he'd gotten up a moment before to take a leak, and now she sprawled across the middle of the bed in all her pale naked glory. He remembered the feel of her, the taste of her skin, the thrill of his flesh thrust deep into her. But though he'd had sex with Erin's body, his mind had made love to Dahlia.

He continued to stare at the sleeping girl, but now his imagination was taking over, transforming her part by part into Dal.

The Fabulous Miss Cobb would be taller: five-foot-seven. He knew that as he knew all her measurements: because he had looked them up in the files in the costume shop. The rest he knew partly from memory, partly from speculation.

Dal's legs would be more slender; and likewise her arms and hands, her nails tapered and neatly polished with that sinister black lacquer he found so enticing. And her hips would be thinner, with a trace of the arc of hipbone visible where Erin showed only a curve of soft (a tad *too* soft) flesh. Her breasts would be smaller as well, their nipples dark, as he had seen when he'd managed a glimpse down Dal's blouse one happy morning.

He felt his groin tighten. Maybe he'd go over there and take Erin in his arms, and they'd do it *his* way: in the dark—and he could give full vent to his fantasies.

He started forward.

Thump!

Startled, he whirled around. A flick of a switch and a shaft of golden light slanted over his shoulder to stretch a long rectangle on the living room carpet.

Thump. Scratch.

Rob strained his hearing. The sound had come from in there. He glanced around for something with which to wrap his nakedness, then decided it didn't matter. Probably wasn't anything—a cat or a wayward 'possum, maybe. He had heard a similar noise once and had checked the front window, the one that was half underground, and had come face-to-face with the biggest, grayest 'possum he'd ever seen grinning at him from six inches away.

He would keep the lights off so as not to startle it, then just ease the drapes aside and find out once and for all.

If it *was* a 'possum, why he'd just turn the lights on real quick and run outside and yell *boo* and scare the be-jesus out of it and have a giggle. And if it wasn't . . .

Thump.

Not alone this time: there was a sort of scrabbling sound with it, like the chickens used to make on the back porch of his grandmother's house in Union County.

The dark hair on his arms prickled for no clear reason, even as his balls began a quick ascent toward his stomach. *Dammit, man, what's your problem?*

He reached the beige drapes and knelt, keeping his body parallel to the doorway, then raised the lower edge of the heavy fabric a couple of inches, his face barely a foot above the floor. Whatever it was, he'd see it eye to eye.

Or, he told himself, *if it's something I'd see eye to eye standing up, I'd rather see its feet first.*

He raised the curtain higher, thought he saw a dark shape leap across the backyard. But before his eyes could focus, it was gone, one with the line of trees that marked the property boundary.

Wonder what that was?

His gaze was drawn to something on the concrete patio. A cigar stub, it looked like. Maybe there had been a burglar and that big dog or whatever it was had frightened him off. Maybe . . .

Still kneeling, Rob eased to the right and flipped the latch that unlocked the doors, then reached down to remove the board he had stuffed in the runners to prevent their being jimmied.

A rumbling hiss of heavy glass and metal, and he stepped out onto the concrete slab.

Cold air hit him, making him shiver. He knelt beside the cigar, then picked it up. It was warm, not surprisingly, and damp. Only—only the *color* was wrong, now he looked at it, and it felt far too smooth. He stood up, brought it into the light.

—And screamed.

It was not a cigar, but a *finger*—the tip of a slender human finger! A young man's, it appeared, from the smoothness of the skin, the hardness of the muscles.

He screamed again—for the finger had stirred in his palm.

Rob shook his hand reflexively to fling the ghastly thing away. But when he stared at it once more, the awful object was still there, only now it seemed to have lodged between his thumb and forefinger. Indeed, it seemed fixed there, as if it had *grown* there, as if—

Pain filled his hand, and his fingers twitched in spasm —all five. And then the new one began to rotate, drilling a hole next to his thumb.

Rob tried to scream once more, but his mouth froze— for images were rushing into his brain: images slamming straight into his mind without pausing at his eyes. It was as if he dreamed while waking, as if fifty—a hundred— movies unfurled themselves in his head. He knew things, saw towers and palaces, strangely clad warriors, beasts from his wildest fantasies. He fought battles, loved women, ate feasts—and did it over and over. His mind felt as if it were on fire, as if it had been filled to overflowing.

One last time he tried to scream, but his jaws were still locked, tight. He closed his eyes and sank against the brick wall, feeling the rough bricks rip blood from the crests of his shoulders.

Then the memories began to seep in. And as they found places among his own, they seemed to vanish. He felt suddenly sleepy, yet uncannily alive.

But mostly sleepy. . .

Sometime later Rob awakened to find himself naked and shivering on his back patio. His shoulders hurt terribly, as did his head—and his right hand. He squinted with the pain. What had happened? He remembered coming outside, looking for something, picking something up, standing to look at it more closely. But then what? He seemed to recall a dizziness. Was that it? He'd been sleepier than he'd realized, had stood up too quickly, lost his balance, and fallen against the wall.

He shrugged and padded back inside, wiping his hand absently on the curtains as he passed. It felt dirty, and he found himself counting fingers—finding, naturally, the accustomed four. He thought of grabbing a fast shower, but then glanced through the bedroom door and caught sight of the sleeping Erin.

Unbidden, Dal's image came to him once more, imposing itself upon the sleeping girl. It was so vivid, he could almost see her. He stepped closer, then turned and shut the door. Finally entombed in shadows, he stumbled to the bed, touched Erin's arm. She groaned and rolled over. "Again?" she mumbled.

"Yeah, again." Rob grinned into the darkness.

And again and again and again that night, as Robert Tolar, who was no longer alone in his own mind, enjoyed the new strength that had somehow awakened.

But not even a dream marked it in the morning.

Interlude Two

...A light and a glitter and a weaving of patterns and the colors of sky and fire—like one of those colored glass windows that had once been in favor in the Lands of Men spinning and spinning endlessly. Except the panes of *this* window were faceted gemstones, and they sparked and glowed as they twirled, and gave off beams of silver and copper, of garnet the color of burning and sapphire the shade of the sea. . . .

...Spinning at once in every dimension, with every color shifting faster than even his strange, skewed senses could follow, so that nothing existed for certain but a flicker of colors and light, in the center of which Colin floated no longer in pain.

Half a thousand years had passed since Colin mac Angus had felt pain of any consequence, and that had been enough and more than enough to last him.

Now there was only peace and serenity, broken but rarely by some unfocused, lazy recollection of a precious thing lost and not recovered.

I dream, Colin thought, except it was not a dream because he could never awaken no matter how he tried, or at least not of his own volition. And if he *had* awakened, what would that accomplish? He had no body anymore, not since the Silver Cord had been severed. No present, no certain future; ah, but the past . . .

Something stirred Colin's dreaming. . . .

He roused himself, reached beyond the shell of his thought and his memory. A shadow-touch from the World Without, it had felt like; or a warning call from the Watch-self he had set there to mind the sun and the Tracks and the seasons.

A Time must be coming, he thought, as he sent his consciousness questing. It was rare that such a thing happened: that *any* three Worlds should line up and spin for a while together. Not for nearly five hundred human years had it happened, and that Time, his plan had been thwarted.

Still, if this *were* a Time come round again, it was half of what might bring his freedom.

But only half: a Time was no good without some tool through which to function—someone Outside to order the words and bind the blood and empower the Calling.

He touched Watcher, took that splinter-soul back within him, and it spoke to him, and he listened.

It *was* Time. Watcher had sensed a chance and used two years' worth of hoarded Power to stop an old human's heartbeat and blur the mind of a boy. He had been watching ever since, sorting minds, waiting. One had come close, one with Power—but that one had been wrong in all the ways Colin needed. Not all had been in vain at that encounter, though: Watcher had seen a chance to free the Wish-Words and had done so. Shortly after had come the Call, and Watcher had grown stronger, and Cathal, too, had been summoned. Even the World Walls had faded. But it had been too soon, the Wish-Words read while in motion. He would have to beware of such things, horde such rogue Power and let it focus while he held off that which would answer—until the Time arrived.

Another Call, then, much more recently: a woman so rich with unsuspected Power it had killed her when the Wish-Words awoke it. The search had begun in truth, at that: the girl first, aglow with the strength they needed, but then the iron thing had come, and she had eluded his agent. It was good, though; because in her mind Cathal had at last seen the new master of the Wish-Words: one strong enough to be useful, yet weak enough to be their servant.

Chapter X: Begin the Begin

(April 11)

The saddest sound in the world, Rob thought, *is the noise the first spadeful of dirt makes sliding off the top of a coffin*. That dry, rattly hiss always evoked visions of desperate fingernails clawing unyielding metal: a final echo of a soul's efforts to cling to its mortal existence.

Jay would appreciate that image, he suspected; it was one like Edgar Allan Poe would have used, and even as a boy Jay had adored Mr. Poe. Good thing little bro wasn't here, 'cause there was no way he'd not be thinking about "The Black Cat" or "The Premature Burial."

And it's apparently a contagious affliction, Rob added to himself. *Now the little twit's got* me *doing it!*

He shuddered in the afternoon coolness. A breeze had twisted its way through splayed leaves of oak and poplar to taunt him where he stood; halfway up a low knoll in the middle of Oconee Hills Cemetery. Winter was gone—officially—but sometimes its camp followers took their own sweet time leaving, even in the supposedly sunny South. Athens had known snow in April.

Hunching his shoulders against the wind, Rob turned away from the grave side, trying to put as much distance as he could between himself and the dull green tent beneath which a cluster of black-dressed family still sat in numb silence beside the marble headstone carved with the words:

CALIFORNIA MONTANA MCLAREN
GONE GENTLY INTO THAT GOOD NIGHT

That was a laugh. If the rumors he'd heard were correct, the old gal had either had a heart attack, a stroke, or—just possibly—electrocuted herself at the word processor. The coroner hadn't been certain, but no autopsy had been ordered; her son hadn't wanted one.

There he was now: a youngish, red-haired fellow, who wore his black suit as though he didn't often wear one of any kind. Rob hadn't met him, nor did he want to. Funerals were for the family. So he had lurked in the background: close enough for decorum's sake but not so near as to catch the minister's mumblings. *Hollow words, anyway,* he thought.

Sounds reached him: the low mumble of the crowd beginning to disperse. A woman began to shriek hysterically: McLaren's mother, he thought.

Another drift of breeze brushed Rob's face, and he hunched his shoulders more and continued up the hill—but by then the hair on his neck had begun to prickle. In some uncanny way he knew that someone was watching him.

He turned, scanned the dark line of trees at the crest of the rise beyond the grave site, saw two black-clad figures there, almost invisible among the trunks and bushes. Even eighty yards away Rob recognized them as Jay and Dahlia. As he watched, Jay extended his hand and let something— probably a handful of earth—trickle to the ground. Dal chose a flower from a bouquet she'd been holding and dropped it as well. *Such a touching gesture.* He'd wondered where Dal was, had figured she'd want to be at the funeral—but she'd been giving him such a wide berth since she'd turned down his Scarboro offer (by one-word letter), he'd decided she had wimped out for fear of confrontation.

Jay touched Dal's shoulder and pointed in Rob's direction. Dal nodded and folded her arms in that way which accompanied her sourest expression of displeasure.

Disgusted himself, Rob turned and continued walking. He had gone scarcely ten paces when he heard footsteps on the pathway behind him: expensive-sounding shoes slapping hard and fast on concrete.

"You there, wait up . . ."

Rob spun around, glowering. "You talking to me?"

The man skidded to an awkward halt, panting lightly. He was shorter than Rob—comfortably so. Rob could easily look down on the bald spot within the fringe of longish brown hair that hinted at a past at once wilder and more laid-back than the frantic fellow he now confronted.

"Yeah, I guess," the man said. "If you're Mr. Robert Tolar."

Rob simply stared at him, volunteering nothing.

"Well, *are* you?"

"As a matter of fact, yes," Rob snapped. He was determined to give no quarter to this interruption, not when he was trying to puzzle out what was up with Dal. Was she really so pissed she wouldn't even come near him?

Relief softened the man's earnest features. "Good!" he cried. "Oh, I oughta introduce myself, I guess—" He stuck out a pudgy hand. "I'm Rodney Carnes, Ms. McLaren's son's lawyer. He gave me something to pass on to you."

"Why didn't he do it himself?" Rob replied, and could have kicked himself. *Well, hell, man: the guy's just lost his mother. Last thing he needs is one more piece of hassle when he's got to deal with a funeral.*

The lawyer twitched his nose at him. "Do I really have to answer that? You look like a bright young fellow."

Rob sighed as he followed the lawyer up the walk toward the nearest parking lot. "Yeah, well, sorry about that. I've got a tongue that sometimes thinks it's God, I reckon."

"That woman thought you were God, too, Mr. Tolar; but I think it would have killed her ten times over to actually admit it. I've heard her talk about you, though; seen stuff about you in the paper. Never met you, though—obviously."

Hope he's a contract lawyer, not a courtroom shyster. He's too scattered to ever do any good in a trial. "So what's this you want to give me?"

"Just some papers McLaren's son told me to hand over to you. Said you'd know what to do with 'em."

"Papers?"

"Papers. Got 'em in my car. Ah, here we are."

They had reached the parking lot at the top of the hill. Rob glanced around impatiently, wondering what had happened to Dal and Jay, but could find no sign of them, though he thought he could see Dal's Prelude down the lot a way. Or maybe not; there were a lot of Preludes in Athens.

Rodney reached into his Thunderbird to snag a shiny new briefcase. "Ah, yes, here we are," he said, pulling out a large manilla envelope and handing it to Rob. "There's a letter with it."

Rob took the envelope and opened it. Inside was a sheaf of computer printout. Atop the first page was a note in a wobbly, unfamiliar hand which read:

Dear Mr. Tolar:

We have never met, but my mother spoke very highly of you. First of all, I want to thank you for helping out my friend with his Scarboro project; it means a lot to him, and I know your involvement meant a lot to Mom. I'm writing you this letter because I've got the time now and may not get a chance to catch you at the funeral, and I know time is of the essence. Enclosed is what Mom was working on when she passed on: it's the final draft of that play you and her were going to put on at the fair—as final as there'll ever be, anyway. I'm sorry she'll miss it. I'm sorry I'll miss it too, but I've got business in Oregon and have to rush off right after the funeral. I'm also sorry you have to get this third hand, but I know she'd have wanted you to continue working on this, and since I'm her executor, I want you to just go on like you would have.

Yours in haste. I promise I'll be in touch when I'm more together.

Dakota McLaren

P.S. Yeah, some name, huh? Well, Mom always liked to spread the luck around. Said a name with character would help make you one. Maybe it did for her. Didn't work for me, though.

Cheers.

P.P.S. Monteagle's literary executor except this.

Rob closed the folder and looked back at the lawyer. The man shrugged and smiled uncertainly.

"You read this?"

Carnes nodded.

"And all this is legal? With the university, I mean?"

"As far as I can tell, since it was all her work, though copyright's not my strong suit. I tell you what, I'll—"

A dark shape shadowed the yellow folder.

"Is that what I think it might be?" a sharp voice spat. It was Rob's department head, the brittle and bewhiskered Dr. Vaughn Monteagle.

"Dr. Monteagle," Rob acknowledged, trying not to let his face betray him. "I didn't see you there."

"Didn't look then," Monteagle snorted.

Rob went on guard. Monteagle didn't like him at all, and more than once McLaren had had to intercede between himself and the fiery drama department head who had his own tightly regimented ideas about policies and procedures. Rob wished he knew some dirt from the man's mail, but Monteagle was either remarkably scrupulous, remarkably devious, or both. He thus had not one bit of leverage on the old fart.

"So what can I do for you?" Rob hedged.

"Answer my question. Is that the manuscript McLaren was working on?"

"As a matter of fact, yes," Rob replied, not daring to lie in the presence of the lawyer.

"So she wanted you to have it, huh?"

"That's what the note from her son indicated."

"So *he* wants you to have it, then? That's a pretty tenuous claim, since the primary source is the property of the university, she worked on it on university time, and you're using university staff and facilities to put on what is essentially a money-making project for an off-campus institution." He eyed the lawyer speculatively, but Carnes remained silent, looking flustered and a wee bit fearful.

Rob stood his ground. "I thought she had that cleared."

"Dean rubber-stamped it to shut her up. *I* never approved it."

"Do we really have anything to talk about then, since the dean's already approved? She *wanted* me to have it; I've got it in writing right here."

"Too damn bad!" Monteagle exploded. "That woman was an important scholar, and I'll be blessed if I'm gonna have her last work fall into the hands of any hack who thinks he knows scenery from highway signs!"

"If it's that big a deal, then I hope you know my brother's working on it too."

"I'll worry about that in due time," Monteagle shot back. "Right now my concern's seeing that a piece of valuable scholarship doesn't get turned to mush by a snot-nosed kid."

"I can do you a Xerox, if you'd like," Rob suggested.

"I'd rather have the manuscript—*now,* if you don't mind."

"I've got a show due in three weeks, Dr. Monteagle. I

can't spare the thing even a day. I was supposed to have the whole text two days ago as it is. I'm already that far behind."

Monteagle thrust out his hand. *"Give it to me."*

"No!"

Though Rob's reply had been as cold and forceful as he could make it, he felt alive with fury. He was on dangerous ground: Monteagle could take the manuscript, probably had every right to, letter or no—and would glory in just such an excuse to snatch the whole fucking Scarboro project away from him. But Rob wouldn't let him; it was *his* play now, *his* project. The other parts were already coming alive under his direction. Flat lines of text were acquiring three-dimensional bodies, words now had voices. Stage directions were coalescing into an elaborate choreography.

"What did you say?" Monteagle whispered icily.

Rob glared at him. "I said *no.*"

And with that Monteagle snatched the envelope from Rob's hands and stalked away.

"Bring that back here!" Rob screamed.

"Over my dead body," Monteagle growled, not slowing.

Rob was speechless with rage. He felt it bubbling up inside, a hard core of hate and anger that grew hotter and hotter with every step Monteagle took. He *had* to do something. A darkness welled up in him, overpowering him, leaving him adrift in a dreamy limbo.

"Stop!" he heard himself shout—and it was as if with that one word, all the hatred, all the anger he felt burned into his brain and from there set fire to his tongue and fled outward.

And Monteagle *did* stop—frozen exactly in mid stride.

Rob felt the hair rise up on his neck. *God, what have I done?*

But then another voice was there, telling him to seize the moment and ask questions later. He strode down to Monteagle, came around to face him, waved a hand before the man's staring eyes, then plucked the manuscript from the nerveless fingers and tucked it inside his jacket.

Monteagle's eyes were blazing, his lips working in silent fury. Finally he struggled free of whatever paralysis had gripped him.

"What did you *do?*" he demanded shakily.

"Do?" Rob responded, strangely calm. "Why, *nothing*. What makes you ask that?"

"The manuscript . . ."

A flicker of returning anger lit Rob's eyes, a focusing of whatever power he had used before. He locked gazes with the old man.

"You mean the one you just *gave* me?" he whispered softly. "The one *no one's* allowed to work on except me?"

Monteagle's eyes glazed for an instant, then he was staring blankly at Rob—staring and blinking and shaking his head.

"Rob . . . dammit, I was going to ask you something, but I'll be damned if I know what it was now."

"You were congratulating me on a good job with the Renaissance fair," Rob supplied quickly.

Monteagle frowned. "I *was?*"

Rob smiled. "Yeah—and I appreciate it."

Monteagle turned away, muttering to himself, and Rob wandered back up the path to where an incredulous Rodney Carnes was still staring. Rob fixed him with a steely glare. "And *you* didn't see any of this either!" he hissed, watching in silent satisfaction as the lawyer's face blanked for a moment, then resumed its former helpful eagerness. Then: "So you'll check on the copyright for me?"

Carnes blinked and swallowed. "Uh, yeah, sure. Shouldn't be any problem."

Rob stuck out his hand. "Thanks a bunch. Nice to have met you."

As quickly as he could without running, Rob made his way to the 'Vette. He paused with his hand on the door handle and shook his head, suddenly so dizzy he felt as if he might vomit. Reality was a-whirl. Had he or had he not done what he thought he had: used his own strength of will to stop a man in his tracks—and make him forget an entire conversation? And had he done the same thing to another? Surely not. Surely the whole thing had been a misapprehension. But he had the manuscript and the project, and that was sufficient.

Or was it? Hadn't he also felt a touch of some new thing within him? Something that felt very much like raw, unadulterated *power?*

He thought he had. He also thought he liked it.

PART III

Chapter XI: Through with You

(April 28)

It's amazing the difference three weeks can make, Rob thought, as he eased himself down atop one of the long split logs that comprised the seats of the Morrisman's Men. Unfortunately, and in spite of his persistent pleas, one of the differences those weeks had *not* made was in the choice of names for his theater. He'd tried to explain to the Scarboro entertainment coordinator that names like So-and-so's Men were essentially post-Renaissance—Elizabethan and later; whereas morrismen, which he supposed was meant to evoke Morris dancers, had flourished long before then. Morrisman's Men, therefore, reeked of a clumsy commercial ineptitude that offended his scholarly aspect to the hollow. And it was hard to pronounce in the bargain.

Rob checked his watch and glanced over his shoulder. More of the log seats fanned out behind him in a quarter circle which was split into three wedge-shaped segments

by two aisles. The gentle slope led uphill to the gate
proper, where a pair of imposing concrete towers, lately
plastered and recently roofed with thatch atop tar paper
over plywood, gleamed in the early afternoon sunlight.
The right-hand one as he looked at them marked a terminus
of a crenelated block wall the other end of which butted
right up to the stage. When the naked flag poles atop their
turrets gained bright pennons in another two days, the illusion would be complete. They'd put a saucy ticket wench
behind one of the ground level windows, and the show
would be on.

And speaking of shows . . . He twisted further around,
saw the line of tall, stretched-canvas panels that connected
the stage and the left-hand tower to mark that boundary of
the Faire. The panels obscured a handsome stand of pine
trees (to which some of them were nailed), but what made
that barrier special, indeed made it almost a show of its
own, was that the individual sections were even then being
decorated by a team of chattering student artists who were
busy transferring blown-up portions of the Limbourg
Brothers' *Trés Riche Heures* to the canvas with latex house
paint and acrylic. There had been some discussion of having the art done off site, but it had been decided that doing
it at the Faire would allow the artisans to tune into the
subtle creative vibrations that resonated throughout the
park. And the work was better for it.

The rest of the place seemed to be coming along equally
well. Scarboro looked for the first time less like a devel-
oper's nightmare and more like a genuine Renaissance village. Workmen crawled here and there upon the structures,
but at this distance Rob could easily squint his eyes and
transform their khakis, work shirts, and Caterpillar caps
into homespun breeches, woolen tunics, and linen coifs.
Their colorful profanity would need very little alteration.

All in all, things were right on schedule.

Rob hoped he would be as ready. It was already
Wednesday, the Faire opened on Saturday, and there were
still too many things to do. He needed to work on acoustics

and makeup, approve lighting, sound effects. Devise a contingency plan for sudden downpours . . .

He checked hs watch again and glanced up at the fixed simulacrum of a portable medieval stage that was the heart and soul of the Morrisman. Four feet off the ground it stood, with a gaping, red-lipped Hell mouth on rollers to the right, and above it all a golden sun-in-splendour slowly rotating in God's azure Heaven. A movement to his left caught his eyes and he nodded to Barney, his stage manager, saw Barn nod back and give him a thumbs-up, which he acknowledged.

The musicians were the first to enter: three men and a woman prancing out from the wings to the right. They wore cutoffs and Scarboro Faire T-shirts at the moment, but the shortest had managed to appropriate a jester's cap from somewhere, and all three had painted large red circles on their cheeks. One man was playing a shiny new lute, the remaining two tootling on penny whistles, while the woman beat time on a small hand drum.

Grinning foolishly and walking in exaggerated, bow-legged steps, they strutted to the middle of the stage and announced themselves first as the Morrismen's Man, then as the Morrisman's Men, and finally as the Morrisperson's Woman—at which point the girl was stared at speculatively by the other three, one of whom tried to lift her nonexistent skirt.

What followed was a dance: a lively number full of acrobatics and general foolishness intended to relax the audience and set the mood for what would come after.

Next came one of the funnier miracle plays—the *Second Shepherd's Play* from the *Wakefield Cycle*. Rob was holding one about the henpecked Noah in reserve in case the audience didn't take to this one or his actors showed signs of boredom.

Another dance interlude followed, then a very short Robin Hood play, and then another dance.

And then *his* play—his for certain, now that McLaren was dead. (Monteagle hadn't said a word about it since their encounter at the funeral, either; though Rob knew there was a reason for that—a reason that scared the crap out of him whenever he thought about it.)

Not that Rob had adhered slavishly to the old lady's text. He'd changed a few things and made a fair number of innovations. He was noted for pressing the limits, after all, and one of those limits was about to be tested.

The musicians were back onstage, cavorting in the center, but unbeknownst to them, the Hell mouth had begun to sneak up behind them (rolled by a quartet of brawny lads who would be dressed as demons in performance). As soon as it was right at their backs, a jet of fire was supposed to spurt out and scorch their backsides—but the system wasn't working yet. At this point, the flames of Hell consisted of a skinny, shirtless fellow with a squirt gun. With luck they'd take care of that tomorrow.

The musicians reacted with appropriate surprise, however, grabbing their bottoms and capering about as they glanced nervously around—all except the whistle player, who did not move.

The Hell mouth gaped. Sulfurous fumes billowed forth (a roll of burning toilet paper), a stench of rotten eggs permeated the air (the genuine article). The musicians held their noses in disgust—except the whistler, who was so absorbed in an increasingly complex series of fingerings that nothing could distract him.

The woman tugged at him, then the men, then the woman again, dragging him either way, but he stood his ground.

More fumes emerged; a red light filled the gaping mouth. Kettledrums rumbled offstage (causing the drummer girl to stare at her own small instrument in dismay).

Finally the cacophony reached a fever pitch, and the Devil leaped out, clad from head to foot in the traditional skintight red costume (one of the few that was finished), horns brightly gilded, forked tail flopping behind. She brandished a pitchfork and ran forward, breasts bouncing gently beneath the bright, slick fabric.

Rob smiled. *That* was this show's innovation: having Erin play the Devil. And she was marvelous, stalking evilly about the stage as the unsuspecting musician tootled on. Eventually she sneaked up behind him and poked him with her pitchfork, sending him leaping into the air, then chased him three frantic laps around the stage before cornering him at stage right.

Finally the poor fellow escaped through the fabric panels at the rear—dragged there by the deliberately obvious hands of his prior accomplices.

The Devil turned abruptly serious, strode across the platform, arrogant in her power.

"'I am called Satan; I'm the Lord of this World,'" she began, flashing her teeth and drawing her tail lasciviously between her legs.

"'I've more power in one finger than a king or an earl . . .'"

Rob could feel himself grinning as he watched her; as the spell of the play unfolded before him. His whole cast was marvelous—students and pros alike. But using Erin as the Devil had been a masterstroke. Not only did it allow him to provide one more female role than was usual, but it gave the powers of evil a new, more seductive slant, as they were brought to bear on the wandering shepherd boy who had just happened in and was about to be offered all the kingdoms of the world.

Good, they were maintaining just the right balance between camp and serious, the various segments each benefiting by the juxtaposition of conflicting emotions. Thus, when the poor shepherd found himself betrayed and bereft, Rob nearly wept; when St. George finally appeared onstage wielding his great broadsword, elation made him feel he would burst. When St. George stepped on Satan's tail, making the Lord of Evil squirm and bellow, Rob laughed out loud.

And when it was over, he stood, applauded, and leapt onstage to congratulate his ensemble.

Erin was the first to reach him, stretching up to plant a

kiss on his cheek, just as Roger the lutist slapped him on the back. "Good job, Rodg," he cried, glancing all around at his folks. Erin kissed him again.

"Good job, Gene, Susan, Lonnie. You too, Dal," he added absently in the direction of the kiss.

"Dal?"

Rob's breath caught in his throat. Had he actually said that to Erin?

"You goddamn asshole!"

He jerked around, his face ablaze with embarrassment. "Oh, jeez, Erin, I'm sorry," he finally croaked, "I meant . . ."

"You were thinking about Dal," Erin snapped. "You're *always* thinking about Dal. You think I don't know? Hell, everybody in the fucking place knows you're obsessed with her."

"Erin, I . . ."

"Don't say a word. Don't say another fucking word, I've had enough of you. I should have known better. Hell, I knew you were after her when I met you, but I thought that poor little old Erin Stillwell could make you forget her. But I guess I was blinder and stupider than I thought, 'cause I thought that when we first did it and you mumbled her name, you were just remembering sometime when you two were a pair, but then I found out you'd never made it with her 'cause she wouldn't give you the time of day. And you know what? I'm not either! You can *have* your goddamn play! And you can take this goddamn Devil's rag and stick it up your fucking ass!"

She ripped the tail from her costume, threw it as Rob's feet, then whirled about and stomped away.

Rob stood speechless, taken completely off guard, and with so many people around it was impossible for him to think clearly. He was at once so shocked, so pissed, and so mortified that he found himself quite unable to speak. Erin didn't get mad often, but when she did . . . Jesus! But why did it have to be *now?*

"It's three days until we open, Erin . . ." he managed to shout at her departing back

Erin swirled haughtily around. "Tough *shit,* asshole," she screamed. "That's *just* the kind of goddamn self-centered trash I'd expect from you. All you care about's your goddamn play, your goddamn ego, your goddamn reviews, your goddamn place in the history of theater. Well, I'll teach you what your goddamn place in history is: as the biggest fucking asshole who ever lived!"

"Bitch," Rob spat. "You're nothing but a goddamn bitch!"

"Oh no, sonny," Erin shot back, as she paused on the threshold of the wings, "I'm the most God *blessed* woman in this whole fucking country, 'cause I've finally seen through you, and finally had sense enough to do what I should've done long ago. We're through, boyo, and I hope your little show rots in Hell!"

Rob could feel rage rising in him. It felt familiar, like that strange, anger-born power he had somehow used on Monteagle at McLaren's funeral. It *had* returned, he realized suddenly, awaiting only his summons. He thought of using it to recall Erin, to *make* her resume the role. But something stopped him, a kind of inner voice that insinuated words into his head. This was not the place, that voice warned; there were too many witnesses, too many potential questions. Erin was the wrong choice anyway.

Wrong choice for what?

Rob shuddered. The power itself was frightening enough, but throw secret voices into the bargain . . .

Except that another part of him liked it: the part that had tried a few times over the last few weeks to summon that power—tried and not succeeded. What awoke it? that part wanted to know. Anger maybe?

Not anger, the voice told him: *absolute desire. Anger is but the messenger.*

Messenger . . . ?

Silence. It was slipping away, leaving him with more questions than answers.

Abruptly, Rob found himself shouting. "Get out of here, all of you—*now!* Rehearsal's over. I'll see you tomorrow evening for dress rehearsal. I've gotta have some time to get my act together."

But he had already thought of a replacement, someone who would be absolutely perfect. And something told him that this time she just might listen.

"My *leg's* gettin' tired," Jay whined between clenched teeth as he shifted his pose to take some of the tension off his right thigh.

Crouched on the floor by his left foot, a bikini-clad La-Wanda shot out a finger and ran a razor-sharp nail down his bare calf, before returning to her former position.

She really does look like a cat, Jay thought, glancing down surreptitiously. *A very large cat—or a very small and sleek black panther.* He could imagine a long furry tail switching back and forth across the swatch of fake zebra fur she was crouched upon. Scott, poised directly before him with his sword drawn back and his shield up (and propped on a two-by-four duct-taped to the bottom) looked, by contrast, merely bored.

Perhaps he was.

It was four o'clock, and they'd been at this nearly an hour, between the initial poses and the assorted photography and lighting sessions, and for the last fifteen minutes or so, this carefully staged tableau. At least Myra hadn't tried to make them take *all* their clothes off this time, but the low-slung rabbit-fur loincloths she'd allowed him and Scott didn't leave much to the imagination. That Myra had thoughtfully provided him with a black one was not much comfort.

"My *leeeggg* hurts, Ms. Myra," Jay pleaded again. "Make it stop hurtin'. Kiss it and make it better!"

"I'll kiss it," LaWanda teased, "if you'll kiss my—"

"Not before *my* virgin ears!" Myra warned, laughing.

"Why, girl! You invented profanity."

"None of us would win any awards," Scott noted.

"I'm going to," Myra said with conviction, setting her pencil down and marching to a bin in the corner where she selected a three-foot sword from the assortment of foils, broom handles, maces, umbrellas, and other objects that bristled there. She started toward Jay, who twisted around to receive it.

"I didn't tell you to move."

Jay sighed and resumed his former pose, body braced on his right leg, left hand down and back, fingers outstretched dramatically, right arm extending horizontally at slightly above eye level to block the blow Scott had been about to deliver for what seemed like hours. Myra slipped the hilt into his fist and stepped back, eyeing her composition critically. She made minute adjustments to all three of them and returned to her drawing board.

"Draw fast," Jay cried. "I won't be able to hold this blessed thing like this very long."

"Don't *move*," Myra commanded. "Not a muscle, not an eyelash. You look at that sword and imagine the cold northern sun sparkling off it into your eyes—try to look just a little addled."

"That shouldn't be hard for him," LaWanda muttered.

"Not hardly," Scott echoed, eyes twinkling.

Jay ignored them and tried to act the assigned role. He stared at the blade, right at the point where Scott's downward blow would connect. His wrist and forearm were already beginning to ache, but he concentrated on sending the pain to another place. It was a yoga trick Dal had taught him.

Ah, that was better, the pain was easing. It was an attractive weapon, what with the ruddy afternoon light glittering along the edge, and all. And he could see the tiny pits that had been left on its surface when it had been forged: they nearly made patterns. He stared more intently, letting the whole world reduce to a sharp line of polished metal with a brass hilt . . .

A brass hilt? Where had he got that idea? This was a cheap Toledo replica, its hilt an intricacy of cast pot metal.

Scott would probably make Myra promise to redo both swords in the finished painting.

Jay resumed staring, let his eyes go slightly out of focus, fought off a sneak attack from the pain in his arm by centering on his breathing. The world became a series of lights and shadows in which the only constant was a gleam of steel in his hand—

And a brass hilt.

And the memory of a journey through cold and darkness, then light and forests, full of the sweet smell of growing things, with a flash of gold beneath the feet of a black horse that never seemed to tire, and before him, the broad shoulders of the stranger in black who had awakened him in the night.

But now, somehow, he stood in the center of a wide, embattled terrace, beyond which loomed something that looked by turns like a mountain and a vast, sprawling fortress ripped and fissured by countless ages. Wind whipped at him, bringing with it a sprinkling of fine blue snow, but he did not shiver, amazed as he was by what he saw ranged around the elaborate mosaic paving closer in.

What he saw was people—beautiful people with long, narrow faces and bright, glittering eyes and clothes that his own lord himself could never afford the least of. Every one of those folk was as tall as he was.

Directly in front of him a chained man was standing—if one dared call these folks men (and he was beginning to suspect the names by which some of his countrymen called them, though he preferred to think of them as devils). But if these folk were devils, this must be Hell—so why was he here? He did not think he was particularly sinful, and he certainly did not remember dying. Nevertheless, he appeared to have made a pact with the Evil One and now had come the accounting.

Why had he done it?

To keep his family warm, he told himself. He had sold his soul on a promise of a winter's warmth.

A word was spoken; the man knelt down before him. Edward moved to his side.

The man lifted his head proudly. The robe he shook back on his shoulders was of golden fur tipped with scarlet —the same shade as his red-gold hair.

The man Edward would kill.

Another man was beside him, the black-haired stranger who'd brought him here. But where was here? And how long had he been here? The man was wearing white now, but when had he changed? Hadn't they always been together?

Another word.

Edward looked down at his own body for the first time, saw that he wore black hose and black boots, and noted that while a black hood hid his face, no shirt obscured his muscular torso. Oil glinted there, but he did not recall when it had been applied, any more than he knew how he had acquired this darksome clothing or the gloves he was resting on the quillons of a broadsword—his good, serviceable broadsword. A tendril of smoke was drifting skyward from the point where its tip prodded the intricate stonework.

The word again: spoken? Or in his mind alone?

Taking a deep breath, he raised the sword above his head in a clean, two-handed arc, then slowly curved it down and around again to barely tap the victim's exposed neck. A strand of hair brushed it—and crisped and fell away as if the blade were fresh from the forge fire.

Edward's eyes widened. A chill pattered over his body.

Once more he raised the weapon.

And swung with his arms and back behind it.

He saw flesh part in a flash of flame; a bright gush of red spurt across the glittering pavement.

He did not hear the heavy thump that followed, nor the rumbling mutter of acclamation—because he had been distracted.

Even before he had lifted the weapon to wipe it clean, it had warmed in his hands—he could feel it even through the gloves. And for the tiniest of instants, it had felt as if someone had brushed one of those hands in passing.

He blinked—and found himself looking into the eyes of the man who had brought him there.

Blinked again—and looked into the worried brown eyes of Scott Gresham.

"What the hell are you *doin'*, roomie?" Scott's voice was sharp with concern. "Hey, talk to me, boyo."

Jay blinked a third time. What was going on? Scott and LaWanda and Myra were all gathered around him, doing something to his arm. He discovered that it was hurting.

Then he realized two other things: he was covered with sweat from the top of his head to the soles of his feet—and his arm seemed to have locked in the position he had been holding. There was no pain, but neither was there any other sensation.

But Myra found a point in the inside of his wrist and pressed it, and another in the vicinity of his armpit and pressed *that,* and he felt his muscles relax.

Scott slipped the hilt from his tingling fingers and helped him slump down on the dusty red sofa.

"Whew," Jay finally gasped. "Jesus, that was weird."

"What was?" Scott asked roughly. "What the hell's goin' on with you, Jason?"

"Going on?" Jay replied, confused and off guard. He hadn't told Scott about his previous dream. "Nothing's going on! I just went off on a daydream—got to playing around with some yoga stuff Dal taught me, and *poof,* there I was living a Technicolor vision of faraway places."

"Oh lord!" muttered LaWanda, "and you folks call *me* a juju woman!"

Scott ignored her. "What kind of faraway places, roomie?"

"Jay shook his head. "Can't say—I was an executioner, that's all I can remember. I'd been summoned from my own land to behead a man I thought was the Devil."

"And who did this summoning, may I ask?"

"I think," Jay said slowly, "it was the King of the Fairies."

"So is Monteagle still waffling on the permission?" Dal asked five hours later as she faced Jay over a large, expensive, and very highly seasoned dinner at Harry Bisset's New Orleans Café and Oyster Bar. A random shaft of moonlight slanted down from the skylight two stories above, turning the ferny hanging baskets in the roofed courtyard into balls of frothy silver-green fire. They were wearing identical black satin peasant shirts dusted with silver stars (first anniversary presents from Myra and La-Wanda), and each sported one of the dagger earrings. Hers had been the first serious question of the evening.

Jay took a sip of chablis and nodded. "Wish I could say even that much. Old bastard won't answer my letters or return my calls, or Sparks's either, which is why I've decided to try one more time to see him—tomorrow, come hell or high water."

Dal cocked her head. "What makes you think he'll see you this time?"

"I don't *care* whether or not he'll see *me*. I intend to see *him!* I'm running out of medieval plays to read, and I've already done a once-over on the available scholarship— I've got to start writing the bloody thing sometime. With McLaren dead and Sparks on my side, Monteagle ought to give in." He paused, took another sip. "I mean I'm not interested in publishing or anything—I told him as much in my last letter—which he ignored. But the blessed waiting is really starting to get to me, never mind that it's also a matter of honor now that I've told Robby I'm doing it. In fact, I've wondered if all the pressure hasn't, you know, kind of freaked me out a little lately."

"I *thought* you'd been acting a little stranger than usual." Dal chuckled, but then her expression turned serious. "Something else is bothering you, isn't it?"

Jay pretended a sudden interest in his dinner.

Dal regarded Jay levelly. "I thought we'd agreed on no

secrets: straight answers to straight questions."

Jay was still chewing his final mouthful of crawfish *étouffée*. He held up a finger to indicate it would be a moment before he could respond, and continued chewing, hoping the delay would buy him enough time to come up with an acceptable answer. Something *was* bothering him: he hadn't told Dal about the second dream yet and wasn't certain he wanted to now. He didn't want to lie to her; but he was afraid she would see how much the dreams really were bothering him and be after him to see a shrink, which was simply more hassle than he needed.

Besides, it was their anniversary, and he didn't want to get into anything heavy—except, perhaps, in bed a little later.

Dal twirled her goblet meaningfully. "I'm waiting, Jason."

Jay swallowed and pushed back from the small table. Doug Kershaw's rendition of the "Battle of New Orleans" came on the sound system. He hoped it wasn't an omen.

"Jason?"

"You *really* want to get into this?"

Dal nodded, her eyes never leaving him.

Jay grimaced and drained his goblet. "Okay, you asked for it. I had another one of those dreams."

"What dreams?"

"Those real vivid dreams, the medieval ones; you know, like I had over at your house after the hoot that night."

Dal's brow wrinkled. "So?"

"Same characters and *everything*."

"You're kidding!"

"Absolutely not."

"Want to tell me about it?"

Jay shifted uncomfortably. "No, but I guess I'd better."

"Well, that's interesting," Dal mused when he finished the story. "But it doesn't sound like anything to worry about. I mean, you *have* been absolutely inundated by things medieval for the last month or so—much longer, really, if you throw in related things like Scott's involvment in the SCA or Myra's fantasy paintings of your aborted thesis."

"Yeah," Jay agreed, "but normal people just don't have serial dreams. And *I've* certainly never had any. *That's* what scares me: I've been dreaming a series, a damned bloody *series*. It's like a blessed medieval murder mystery or something. Except that I'm there, I mean *really* there. I can recall every detail. I'm not *watching* Edward of Ripon, I *am* Edward of Ripon."

Dal stared at him. "You're kidding."

Jay shook his head. "Wish I was. I mean, look—most dreams you have, you just have 'em, and they fade away, even when you try to remember 'em. Sometimes you'll have a real neat one, and you wake up in the middle of the night and are just damn *sure* you're gonna recall it in the morning, but then morning comes and you reach for it, and it's gone."

Dal looked troubled. "But these aren't like that?"

"You got it. With these, I can close my eyes and see everything. I can tell you how many stones there are on the end walls of Edward's cottage, what color the blanket is, which boy's cheeks have the most freckles."

Dal bit her lips and folded her arms. "Do you know when you—Edward was born? Do you have his memory? Like in that Shirley MacLaine stuff?"

"No, I don't think so. I think it's—it's like I run on instinct. You know, like when you're a little buzzed or stoned or something, and you just live for the present, like you're watching a movie of your own life. Maybe if I dreamed him again and tried, I might be able to find his memories, but I'm not certain."

"Why don't you try it?"

"Try what?"

"To return to Edward, to make yourself dream about him."

"I dunno, Dal. Those dreams are pretty scary. And

speaking of scary, I haven't told you about the sword either."

"Sword? What sword?"

"The one Piper and me found in the Bowman-Smith Collection. I never told you the whole story. It was real neat—fourteenth century broadsword, I think—but it kind of weirded me out when I drew it—like it was filling me with energy and excitment. It really was a neat feeling." He paused. "Gee—I'd almost forgotten about that, so much has happened since."

"Forgotten—or suppressed?"

"Who knows? It *was* the day of the Great Thesis Disaster, so God only knows what's running around in my psyche these days."

Dal was pushing shrimp tails in circles with her fork, not looking at him. "Yeah, I know the feeling," she said finally.

Jay looked at her, startled.

"I've been holding something back, too, Jay."

"Oh yeah?"

Dal bit her upper lip. "Yeah. You remember the night of the party, when I ran out of gas and all?"

"Vaguely. I was pretty out of it by the time you got back."

"Yeah, and I was glad too, 'cause it meant you wouldn't notice anything funny about me."

"Funny?"

"I was scared shitless, Jay. Something followed me nearly all the way to your house—I think. At least it seemed real at the time, though most of what I remember now are just impressions of how I felt, not what I saw—or thought I saw. See, the problem is, I *had* been drinking when I left, and then I chugged a bunch of vodka when I got back, so I just don't know for certain how much was real and how much was the demon rum. I *do* know I was almost hit by a car; and I *do* know I got a ride from a couple of guys, and they also thought they saw something.

But by the time I got over my hangover, the whole thing just seemed too unreal."

Jay took a long breath. "And you didn't tell me?"

"I was afraid you wouldn't believe me."

"When have I not believed you?"

"Good point. But there are levels beyond which it's just not safe to push, even with you. People really do like to think the world's rational."

"Okay," Jay said slowly. "But you want to know something else, while we're talking about weird shit and all?"

Dal raised an eyebrow. "More true confessions?"

"Yeah, you could say that, I guess. You remember me telling you about Wannie and Piper kidnapping me to the Faire, and me and Piper and LaWanda getting lost?"

"When Piper put his foot in it about the play?"

"Yeah. Well . . . that's about it, except that the whole thing had a real weird feeling to it—the time we were lost, I mean. It's hard to explain, but it's like for just a moment we weren't quite in this world. And I swear to you, *swear* to you, Dal, that when we passed out of the woods we were under oak trees, but when I looked back, all I saw were pines."

"So you think . . . ?"

"I don't know what to think, and we *had* been smoking dope. But it's bloody weird."

"Think they're all connected?"

"Some of 'em might be, but I can't quite see how. Maybe if—"

"Excuse me," a smooth voice interrupted. Jay glanced over his shoulder to see one of the neatly clad waiters standing there.

The waiter ignored him and looked uncertainly at Dal. "Uh, would you be Miss Cobb?" he inquired.

Dal nodded. "Yep, that's me."

"You have a phone call. He says he's your father."

Dal rolled her eyes wearily. "Oh, Christ, what does *he* want, I wonder?"

"Only one way to find out," Jay muttered.

"Yeah, I reckon so." Dal slid out of the booth, leaving Jay to sit and fidget.

She was back a moment later, dinner check in hand. Her face was like thunder.

"Bad news?"

Dal nodded grimly. "The worst. The old fart's in town for some jurisprudence conference and wants to stay at my place tonight. Claims he wants to get to know me better, if you can believe that. More likely just doesn't want to pay for a motel."

Jay scowled. "Well, there goes the rest of the evening. So much for our wonderful first."

"Yeah," Dal grumbled, "and I guess I'd better get over there and let the old goat in. Good thing he doesn't have a key or we'd have walked in on him."

"Small comfort."

"We really do have to talk about . . . what we were talking about some more, though; maybe see if we can find some pattern."

"Tomorrow?"

"Lunch?"

Jay shook his head. "Negative. That's when I'm lowering the boom on Monteagle."

"Dinner, then?"

"If you can make it an early one; I've got to translate a chunk of *Hrafnkel's* friggin' *Saga*. My place okay?"

"You cooking?"

Jay smiled crookedly. "I'm always cooking."

"Foolish boy."

"Wonderful girl."

Dal reached over and took his hand, pressed it to her lips. "Oh Witchboy, Witchboy, I wish I could take you home with me."

Jay looked at her wistfully. "Can't I even zip by to tuck you in and wish you sweet dreams?"

Dal shook her head and stood up. "I don't think that would be too cool just now."

A worried frown creased Jay's brow for a moment. "No," he said at last, remembering. "I don't think it would be, either."

Chapter XII: What If We Give It Away?

(April 29)

Rob had been trying to catch up with Dal for almost a day now, and was beginning to get desperate.

It made no sense to call her; she had an unlisted number and probably filtered her calls through an answering machine. So he'd spent most of the previous evening zipping by her house every hour (it was only half a mile), but had always found her absent—until around 10:30, when she'd come cruising up with her daddy the judge in tow. That had *really* hacked him. Rob couldn't stand that sharp-tongued old curmudgeon.

Nor, apparently, could the troublesome power, for when Rob had thought of knocking on the door anyway and trying to hoodoo the geezer so he could see Dal solus, the dratted—*should* he call it power?—would not answer. Absolute desire was supposed to be the trigger, and he was certain he'd never wanted anything so badly in his life as he wanted Dal to save his ass with the Scarboro people. But the power, apparently, was not in agreement. He'd given up trying after that, but by then the whole evening had been wasted.

And now it was morning and Dal was still avoiding him. Rob did not suppose this, nor was it a symptom of paranoia; it was a fact—as real to him as the bright Thursday sky above Friedman Hall or the marble and mirror glass that sheathed it. She had evidently seen him lying in wait, too, and begun a game of avoidance and observation, correct enough in her assumption that he would not cancel a class he had to teach solely in order to detain her. She, on the other hand, had no obligations until eleven, so it had been easy enough for her to simply lurk in the shadows and watch until he had to give up and go about his business.

He'd searched for her later, first in the scenery shop where she liked to hang out, then in the office, then in the graduate lounge. Once he had even come face-to-face with her when an elevator door opened right in front of him and revealed her standing within, but he'd been so startled and she so quick on the CLOSE DOOR button that she'd escaped before he could wedge a hand in the slot.

Erin, by contrast, had been everywhere, giving him the coldest of shoulders; and where she was not she had apparently just passed, if the tide of dirty looks and furtive whisperings that ebbed and flowed through the halls behind him were any indication.

He was, of course, above all that.

But even the Fabulous Miss Cobb had to come to earth at some point. And so she did—in the costume shop right after her eleven o'clock seminar.

Rob found her there, alone except for a remarkably buxom dressmaker's dummy named Mrs. Brickbosom and a naked male department store mannequin called Eustace the Eunuch for obvious reasons.

He started in, then paused in the doorway, appreciating.

Dal was flopped back in a metal folding chair at one end of the bank of sewing machines, apparently absorbed in the new UGA Press collection of Steffan Nesheim's poetry.

She looked both captivated and captivating, though Rob wished she'd dispense with the basic black that had begun to monopolize her wardrobe. At the moment she was wearing jeans that looked suspiciously like Jay's and a black T-shirt which bore a cat's face picked out in subtle silver except for the mysterious green eyes. In deference to the NO SMOKING signs, she was chewing on a stick of beef jerky.

At least it's not Skoal or Redman, Rob observed, as he entered and clicked the door closed behind him.

"Son of a *bitch,*" Dal muttered as she twisted her head around.

Rob sat down on the machine next to her, conveniently blocking the most obvious escape route with a comradely arm draped across Mrs. Brickbosom's accommodating shoulder. He saw Dal stiffen and sighed. Why did she insist on making this harder than it needed to be? He really didn't want to have to use *other* means, unless he had to—if he even could.

Dal raised a defiant eyebrow and resumed gnawing on her jerky.

Rob ventured a thin smile. "I need a favor, Dal."

"I was afraid of that."

"I've not even stated my case yet, girl; can't you at least grant me that much courtesy?"

Dal leaned back and folded her arms. "Okay, spill it and get out of here."

Rob took a deep breath. "I guess you've heard about Erin . . . and our little misunderstanding yesterday."

"Who hasn't? Poor girl called me in tears just past midnight."

Rob tried his best to look chagrined. "Yeah—well, I was afraid of that. So you know why I'm here."

Dal's eyes narrowed. "I'll let you tell me anyway." Her smile showed less warmth than challenge.

Another deep breath. "Okay, cards on the table; I need you, Dal. You're the only person I know who's savvy enough to step in at the last minute and take over Erin's part. You know medieval drama; you were in *Second Shepherd* when you were at Young Harris, so that must still be pretty familiar. Most of the rest you can fake; the only hard part would be the new play, and even then there aren't many lines, just a lot of blocking. If it came down to it, you could even carry a script onstage. I've seen it done before. You could—"

"No."

"No?"

"No. *N-O*: The opposite of *yes*. An ancient and honorable word expressing negation."

Rob folded his arms in turn. "Oh, come on, Dal, give me a break. I know you don't like me, but think of it as a favor to the department. You're enough of a trouper to do that, aren't you? I can understand you not giving a damn if I fall on my ass, but do you want the whole department to fall on its collective and very visible ass in public?"

"I'm certain that someone else could be found who's willing to share your dream," Dal replied acidly. "And whatever other dubious perks association with you entails. Barring that, I'm certain Scarboro Faire could get along very nicely without you. I'm sure Piper'd be delighted to stand up on that stage and tootle away all day long."

"It could *not* go on without me," Rob shot back so sharply that Dal looked up in surprise.

"Okay, then, why not a delay until you get somebody else?"

Rob shook his head. "No, it has to be Saturday. The play has to open May first."

He started at that. Why had he said it so emphatically? He'd taken it as an article of faith, but he could wait a couple of weeks, couldn't he? Someone had already volunteered to step into Erin's role. With another week, that person could fill in. Three or four days might even be sufficient.

But something told him that was impossible, that same disturbing inner voice that had told him not to force Erin because she was not the right choice. He would see it done properly, though, or he would not see it done at all, and that meant doing it when it ought to be done: on Beltaine...

Now why did I call it that?

Dal was studying him carefully, trying to appear cool— but didn't part of her look scared too? Scared, and maybe just a little uncertain? Maybe she hadn't made up her mind yet. Perhaps with just the right strategy...

Dal broke his reverie. "What's so special about Saturday?"

"Not Saturday, Dal, *Beltaine:* May Day—which just happens to *be* on Saturday. That's when most of these things were traditionally performed. And there's good internal evidence that's true of this one."

Dal took a long ragged breath and stared at the floor. "Okay, Rob, I'll be straight with you: I would *love* to be in that play, okay? The period fascinates me, I'd like to have some part in Scarboro, and I'd like to help out the department. I'd also like to do something to help memorialize Dr. McLaren. And, God forgive me, you're a good director— when you can keep your ego out of it. But there's no way in hell I could stand being around you all the time, knowing that your mind was on my ass, not my performance. Knowing what you'd done to—"

"It's 'cause of Jay, isn't it?"

"Jay, *hell!*" Dal spat. "He's the least of my worries. What about what you just did to Erin, who's my friend, whom you just shafted by leading her on all these months? And believe me, she bloody well knows there's nothing to it on my side! And what about the way you treated poor Mitch, or the way you sucked up to McLaren and then made fun of her behind her back? Or..."

The catalog of slights and petty cruelties went on and on, and Rob found himself getting more and more impatient.

Dal stopped in mid sentence and glared at him. She'd been practically screaming.

His gaze locked with hers, and neither of them spoke for a long moment. He simply stared into her eyes. A man could get lost in those eyes, he thought. She wanted to do it, he was sure of that; her resolve, though stated in terms solid as marble, had a foundation of quicksand. He was tired of all this goddamn pussyfooting.

A flicker of power awakened in him, and that encouraged him. This was *his* play, by God, and he wasn't going to let Dahlia Cobb's scruples stand in the way of doing it up right and proper! It was both crux and capstone of his graduate career: get it done, write it up, you've got the degree; get the degree, you've got the rest of the trust fund; get the trust fund, you've got freedom. *Absolute desire*, huh? Suddenly he understood that. And with that understanding the flicker of power flared to burning life and overwhelmed him. Almost against his will he gave himself over.

"You will reconsider," he found himself saying. "You *will* be in my show."

Dal's eyes slid slowly out of focus. It was as if she were not looking at him, but beyond him.

"You *will* be in my play," he repeated.

Dal's cheeks puffed in thought. "Maybe I will." Her voice sounded as draggy as a record on a worn-out turntable.

"You know you want to—" that same distancing from himself. Whatever it was, the part of him that was running the show seemed to know what it wanted and how to achieve it.

"Yeah . . . I do."

"And anything that prevents you is the enemy."

"If . . . you . . . say so."

"That's what I say, my lady. First rehearsal's at eight tonight, on-site. You need a ride?"

Dal shook her head clumsily. "I'll be there."

"I'll look forward to it."

Abruptly the power was fading, but Rob thought he now knew how to revive it. It was just as the voice had said:

absolute desire focused and directed outward, but you *really* had to want something.

Next time will be easier, the voice informed him. *As time draws nigh, I grow stronger.*

Smiling, Rob reached out and patted Dal's hand. "I knew you wouldn't let me down, Miss Dahlia; you always were a trouper."

"Yeah, sure," Dal muttered distantly, as if she had just awakened.

"Take care, Dal," Rob whispered as he closed the door.

"I . . . will," Dal replied—and sat staring at her stick of jerky for a very long time thereafter.

"Look, Mr. Madison," Dr. Monteagle snapped, "I told you I didn't *get* any letters."

Jay's eyes narrowed. *"None?* I wrote you three times, and Dr. Sparks did twice. And we tried to call, but your secretary wouldn't put us through. She'd ask who we were, then say you were in conference when we told her. Same thing when I've been by. I'm not very old, Dr. Monteagle, but I think I can recognize a runaround."

Monteagle shook his lofty head. "I have only your word on that."

"Oh no you don't," Jay shot back triumphantly. "At least not on the letters; I've got copies of them. Xeroxes of every one I sent. I *always* keep copies." He flung a yellow manilla envelope down on Monteagle's expensive wooden desk.

It was not good to let himself get this angry, Jay knew, especially when he was trying to curry favor. But he'd already dealt with more drama department bureaucracy than he could stomach. Having to literally shove past Monteagle's secretary to get into his office had been bad enough—he hated being mean to little old ladies—but now the man himself was being even more recalcitrant. He didn't know how much longer he could stand it.

Monteagle glared back at him from under bushy gray

brows, but he took the envelope and scanned the contents. "This proves nothing."

Jay stared at him incredulously. "What do you mean it proves nothing? It proves I've done everything in my power to go through proper channels to get your permission to use the Bowman-Smith Codex. If I wanted to, I suppose I could go to the dean or the library. Maybe I ought to. The library gave McLaren permission, after all. It's *their* manuscript, in the last analysis."

"You may do what pleases you," Monteagle replied icily. "But remember that Dr. McLaren had written permission, and I'm her literary executor."

"We're not talking about her work," Jay said as calmly as he could, "we're talking about independent use of a primary source."

"We're talking about an arrogant and self-deluding twerp of a graduate student, if you ask me!" Monteagle snarled. "How dare you come into my office with such accusations!"

"Arrogant?" Jay cried, almost laughing at the absurdity. "Arrogant! My *brother's* in this department and you call *me* arrogant?"

"I'll call the campus police, if you're not out of here in one minute!"

Jay stood speechless, then turned and stomped to the door. "Just forget it, man," he gritted. "I don't know why I bothered. I've got my own copy of the bloody thing anyway! You're not the only person in the world with a lawyer—*or* with friends in the library!"

The door slammed behind him.

Monteagle slumped back in his chair, feeling a headache coming on. He'd had lots of them lately, beginning around the time of McLaren's funeral. And his memory had been getting worse and worse. Had that boy been right after all? *Had* he received those letters and simply forgotten them? And had he given some kind of word to the secretary to deny calls from that boy or Dr. Sparks? He barely knew the young English professor, but allowing for the cockiness of youth, thought fairly highly of him. So why wouldn't he want to speak to him? For that matter, what was *wrong* with letting the boy do a thesis on the Bowman-Smith Codex? Maybe he should call up Dr. Sparks and tell him he'd changed his mind. Maybe—

"Dr. Monteagle?" came a voice from the doorway.

Monteagle started, looked up, saw Robert Tolar standing there. Funny, he hadn't heard the door open. He frowned unconsciously. The headache was getting worse.

Rob was waiting politely, still in the outer office. "Can I come in, sir?"

The old man motioned him inside. Rob helped himself to the padded chair by the window. "Okay, what is it?" Monteagle grumbled.

Rob looked at him guilelessly. "Was that my brother I just saw in here?"

A tired shrug. "Said he was, but didn't have the same last name. Sure looked a whole lot like you."

Rob's jaw muscles hardened. "Yeah, so I've been told. He's only my half brother," he added. "So, what did he want?" There was a peculiar intensity to that question.

To his surprise, Monteagle found himself relating the whole encounter. Usually he told pushy young snot noses like Mr. Tolar to mind their own business, but something about Robert made him trust him, made him want to lay out the whole story.

"And you're sure he said he had his own copy?" Rob asked when Monteagle had finished.

Monteagle nodded. "He said, and I quote: 'You're not the only person in the world with a lawyer—*or* with friends in the library.'"

Rob looked puzzled, then his face lit with glee. "Piper!" he muttered. "James Morrison Murphy! I'll get that little son of a bitch, I swear I will."

"What . . . did you say?" Monteagle mumbled.

"Huh? Oh, nothing. I was just leaving. In fact," he added, fixing Monteagle with a penetrating stare. "I was *never* here—was I?"

Monteagle felt the headache return, worse than ever. A tiny part of his brain flipped over. He blinked, saw Robert Tolar standing at the doorway, smiling triumphantly. "Need something?" he asked.

Robert shook his head. "Just passing by and thought I'd bop in and say hi. I'm on my way to the library."

It would be nice to be a duck, Dal thought as she found herself once again approaching that segment of the southern edge of Memorial Park Lake a flock of those same creatures had long ago staked out as their own. Feeling considerably more herself than when Rob had left her, though still more than a little muddle-headed, she was on her fifth circuit—a good couple of miles now, but showing no signs of tiring, perhaps because she was not running laps (as many people did), but merely walking at her own strong, ground-eating pace.

Her nose twitched irritably as she had to break stride to hop an impudent white fellow who waddled out from behind a convenient bush and sauntered directly into her path. She suppressed an urge to kick his scuzzy wet fanny and vent her growing frustration.

It would be good to be a duck.

Because if you were a duck—or at least one of *these* ducks—all you had to worry about was whether the lake would freeze over, as it did perhaps once every five years, or whether some preadolescent boy might harbor ill will toward your tail feathers. Barring that, food was free, sex was for the taking, the clear air and wide world were all around you.

You did not have to worry about megalomaniacal grad students or oversensitive boyfriends or proper career moves or learning most of two plays and three dances in thirty-six hours.

Perhaps a dead duck would be most appropriate.

She rounded the lake's short western end, and picked up her pace along the northern side where a strip maybe fifteen feet wide separated the water from the parking lot.

What in the world had convinced her to commit herself to such foolishness? She'd had nothing to do with Rob for years, had sometimes gone to elaborate measures to avoid either taking a class with him or—God forbid—acting under his direction.

It had cost her, too: parts she had wanted, even a friend-ship or two had died a-borning because the other party was too buddy-buddy with Rob Tolar. And now she was going to let him direct her?

God, what a complex of emotions.

But logic said there'd be other opportunites. Shoot, there were three other theaters at Scarboro.

So what *was* so special about this show that she'd agreed to set aside all her misgivings and go for it?

She just didn't know. Logic had reared its head, and now she wanted to work all of it out that way—except that somehow her logic wasn't quite coming together; she couldn't tell facts from feelings. The whole thing had given her a strange sort of headache, too, making her feel dull and punchy, like she had back...where? Maybe if she started at the beginning...

It had been in the *costume* shop; she'd been reading, and then—

She blinked, tried to get her mind to focus. What was wrong with her, anyway? It had only been a couple of hours, yet already her memory had gone blurry.

Let's see: the costume shop. Right, and there *he* was, like Mephistopheles, reaching into his sleeve and drawing out marvel after marvel. And somehow he had produced the right one. There had been something different about him today, a fresh intensity, a sense of barely controlled power just beneath the surface. His words had been ordinary enough, but within them had lain a complex of emotions: threat, anger, entreaty—

She shook her head, strained her memory, trying to think through the muddle. It was damned mysterious.

In fact, that was *it:* there was a new quality of mystery about Rob that had seduced her subconscious, as if his old familiar asshole self now hid some new, secret persona that peeked out through his dark eyes and glittered in his white teeth and winked at her from the depths of that damnably disarming dimple.

She's put her finger on it. Her new fascination was no more than the simple desire to find out more about the shadow-self that Rob had manifested that morning.

And that was pretty stupid, she admitted. She'd been dreading telling Jay, but what was there to worry about? She'd still tell him—only she'd tell him something else as well: she'd tell him she *wasn't* going to do it. She'd say she had been stringing Rob along, and they'd both have a good chuckle. If Rob could be nasty, she could be nasty back.

She had reached the point on the southern shore where she had almost kicked the duck before. It was still there, eyeing her distrustfully from among the cattails. She fished in her pocket and pulled out a piece of baklava she'd bought for an afternoon snack, then knelt in the middle of the trail, unwrapped the packet, and offered the whole thing to the fowl.

"Oh Great God Quackus," she intoned. "I think I have solved my problem, and for your most honored assistance, I hereby offer you this pure and honorable sacrifice."

The duck looked at her, waddled slowly and majestically forward. Nibbled delicately at the end of the proffered morsel—

And very calmly bit the bejesus out of her hand right at the soft place between thumb and forefinger.

Sitting cross-legged on the floor between the flat folios and the uncatalogeds, Piper had just finished re-sorting the last year's worth of *The Atlanta Business Chronicle* for the third time that week when he heard heavy footsteps behind him. He sighed and glanced over his shoulder.

His immediate supervisor, Tony Vincent, was gazing down at him. He did not look happy.

"What's up?" Piper asked brightly, hoping Tony's grimness was not directed at him. Robby Tolar had just stormed in demanding an audience with Ms. DeRenne, and he'd heard his name mentioned in anger.

Tony sighed, "Boss needs to see you."

"Sure thing, man, just let me put these things up and wash my—"

"She said *now,* Piper."

Piper nodded. "Uh, yeah—sure thing, man." He stood and wiped his hands on his khaki fatigues.

Tony laid a hand on his shoulder as he passed, gave him a hard, friendly squeeze.

Piper looked up at him. "Bad news, huh?"

Tony shrugged. "Think it has to do with some Xeroxing you did that you shouldn't have that some department head complained about; Ms. D. sure doesn't look happy."

Dal thought Jay was going to have hysterics, he was laughing so hard. It was good to see him that way too, he'd been so wretchedly glum lately. She paused in her narrative of Rob's disgrace at Erin's tongue, and watched him: flopped back against the kitchen counter with a half-sliced bell pepper in one hand and a paring knife in the other, while tears ran down his cheeks.

"Serves him right," Jay panted as he abandoned the pepper and snagged a Heineken from the fridge. "Serves him bloody right." He offered her a brew, but she refused; she wanted her head clear for . . . For *what?* she wondered.

"Oh, but gee, I guess I really shouldn't be laughing," Jay said, "'cause poor Erin sure didn't sound happy when she called over here trying to find you. 'Course you warned her this would happen, too, didn't you?"

Dal nodded sadly. "Sure did," she sighed, "and Erin admits I was right. She's feeling better already just to be rid of the jerk. Her main concern was with losing control of herself and giving up the part."

"Yeah," Jay said, more subdued, "and it'll cause all kinds of problems, won't it? Like what's gonna happen with the play? I mean, doesn't this kind of blow it? I don't suppose Rob's found a replacement." He looked at Dal meaningfully and cocked an inquiring eyebrow.

Dal shifted uncomfortably and fished in her pocket for a cigarette.

"Well, has he?"

"Uh, not yet," she managed finally. "But I know he's done some hard looking."

Jay's eyes narrowed. "How hard? He's not been after you, has he?"

Dal took a deep breath and looked straight at him. "As a matter of fact, yes." (This was perfect. Now she could go into her second Robby story.)

"And what did you tell him?"

"Maybe I should start at the beginning."

"Maybe you should."

Dal didn't quite like his tone, but maybe she'd asked for it, and anyway, it really was a good story. "Okay," she began. "Well, I was sitting in the costume shop and Mrs. Brickbosom says to me, she says, 'Don't look now, Dal, my girl, but there's somebody a-sneakin' around by the door, and he looks mighty shifty.' And Eustace the Eunuch kinda darts his eyes toward one of the big mirrors and winks like he agrees with her, and I sorta peer out over the top of my page, and . . ."

She went on from there, spinning the tale out in minute detail, full of derision and spite toward Robby, with Mrs. Brickbosom and Eustace the Eunuch providing an occasional Greek chorus. Now she was approaching the climax: the scene where Rob popped the crucial question and she told him Yes, but only to fool him, so he'd get his hopes up and she could dash 'em by not showing. It was a cruel joke, one Jay probably wouldn't approve of, even when applied to his brother. But it was such a holler—and Jay was a stick-in-the-mud anyway.

(Now where had that last come from? It certainly didn't reflect *her* opinion.)

"So anyway, he said, 'Dal, my girl, would you do it?'"

"And . . . ?"

"And?"

A puzzled frown. "So what did you say when he asked you?"

"I said—" Dal paused. What *had* she said? For a moment her whole mind went empty.

"I said I wouldn't— No, that's wrong; I told him that I *would*—do it, I mean."

Jay turned pale. "You're kidding."

Another blank, a stabbing return of the earlier headache, the muddleheaded feeling. She crushed the cigarette between her fingers.

"Dal, you *are* kidding, aren't you?"

"Uh, actually, yes I am—kidding, that's it. I was kidding. I told him I would, but I'm not. Isn't that a riot?" (Sure it was, it was ridiculously funny. So why was Jay still frowning?)

"That was real shitty, Dal," he said finally. "I mean I understand perfectly, and it's certainly a real sort of justice —and believe me, part of me wants to be splitting my sides. But another part's telling me not to."

"But, Jay, why not?" (Why is he looking at me that way?)

"'Cause you compromised your honor to do it."

"He's a jerk; he shafted my friend."

"He shafted me, too; but I don't want to get down to his level. You lied to him, Dal."

She had, hadn't she? And that disturbed her. Maybe Jay was right. *Damn!* the headache stabbed again, sparks flashed behind her eyes. She couldn't think straight.

"But I really didn't lie, Jay," she finally managed.

(*Huh?* another part of herself asked. That wasn't what she'd intended.)

"Oh yeah? So what else do you want to call it?"

"Well, the truth of the matter is that I *do* want to do the play."

"You what?"

"I told him yes."

(Dammit, what was going on? Her tongue had answered

before her mind could formulate a more truthful reply. Well—that *was* the truth, literally, but not the truth she wanted. It was as if one part of her—the part that ruled her tongue, apparently—was bent on leading her to destruction, while the other part—the rational part—sat helplessly back and watched. She was acting like two people, she realized, and wondered if she had suddenly become schizo.) But her tongue still blundered onward. "I'm going to do it, Jay."

Jay's mouth popped open in stunned silence.

(No, Jay, don't listen to her—me—us!)

"You're sure about this?"

Dal nodded and stared at the floor. She could feel Jay's gaze burning into the top of her skull.

"Dal, look at me!"

She obeyed—and her old self (her *real* self) flinched. Jay's face was a mask of confusion and betrayal, but under it something colder and darker was fast taking shape. *God, what have I done, and why?* she asked herself; then began to rationalize as Jay's anger lit a spark of her own, and her mind merged once more with that other. He didn't own her, and he evidently didn't trust her either, if he was that worried about her working with Robby. But relationships were built on trust, and if Jay Madison chose not to trust her now, or—worse—put his own insecurities above her happiness, maybe she had taken up with the wrong guy after all.

Jay's mouth worked soundlessly, then: "Dal, I think we ought to talk about this—"

"There's nothing to talk about. You said yourself I shouldn't have lied. If I don't do it now, I *will* be a liar, and you wouldn't want that, would you?"

(No, no! What am I saying? They're my thoughts, but I'm putting them wrong.)

"You're turning my words around in on me."

"*You* said 'em."

"Dal, I—this isn't like you, Dal. First you do a complete about-face on Robby, and then it's—it's like you're *trying* to pick a fight." His eyes widened. "Hey, you're not, like, *on* something, are you?"

"Of *course* not!"

Her shout made Jay step backward. "Okay, okay—just wanted to make certain."

"Are you calling *me* a liar now?"

Jay stiffened but did not reply immediately. When he spoke again he looked much calmer, though it obviously cost him a great effort. "Okay, now look, are you *sure* you're okay? You look a little glazed around the eyes and all. I—"

"I'm *fine,* dammit! Just a little muddleheaded."

"More than a little, I'd say."

"I've got to go; I've got to get to rehearsal."

"You've got to *what?*"

"I'm gonna do it, Jay. Scarboro needs me, the department needs me, and Rob needs me."

"But you can't *stand* him, Dal!"

"Yes . . . I . . . can. . . ."

A chill raced over her. She wanted to scream. *No, Jay, I can't. I hate Rob, I hate the whole goddamn thing.*

But she couldn't. She was still here, still Dal. But something else was ruling her body. All she could see in her mind's eye now was that strange new fire in Rob's eyes that had so entranced her this morning.

She was walking, she discovered, fiddling in her purse for her keys. Jay was staring at her, so tense she feared he might shatter.

"I have to go," she heard herself repeating. "I've got to get out of here."

"Dal, don't do this. If you walk out that door I—I don't know what'll happen."

I don't have any intention *of walking out that door, Jay. I don't* want *to do the play.*

But instead, she found herself shouting, "I don't *care* what happens! I'm sick of hanging around with you! I never want to see you again!"

A glance at herself in a nearby mirror nearly made her

scream, for she saw her wild eyes—and saw that her own face had hardened into stone.

"Dal, I—"

She stumbled for the door, turned to close it gently—and found herself slamming it instead. But, she discovered as she pounded down the stairs, at least she could still cry. And did.

Jay stared at the door through which Dal had just departed. The force of her blow had set the walls rattling, and one of Myra's paintings had slipped its nail and crashed to the floor.

He drained his beer and slammed down the empty bottle in disgust.

What in the world had come over the girl? She'd seemed okay at first—a little agitated, maybe, or preoccupied, but then she often was, with academic problems and all. But as soon as she'd got started on her second Rob story, she'd seemed to lighten up. The whole business had had a sort of confessional air to it, and he knew she'd been sorely tempted.

But suddenly Dal's face had clouded, her eyes had seemed to glaze. And her tone had changed, had become slower and more incoherent than her usual quick-clipped style.

Maybe bro drugged her or something. Nah—it couldn't possibly work that way. But something was obviously wrong. The whole thing was just too unlike her.

Something *had* to be wrong.

"Dal!" he cried, and scrambled for the door. Maybe there was still time to stop her.

By the time he reached the sidewalk, Dal's Prelude was already accelerating through the traffic light at the bottom of the hill. It turned red behind her, but if he hurried . . .

He jumped into the Monarch and turned the key frantically. For a wonder it caught first try. He slammed it into Drive, and twisted the wheel savagely left—gunned the gas.

—And had gone scarcely thirty feet when he felt the

wheel jerk violently in his fingers and saw the right side of the car sag downward.

Damn it to hell. He got out and strode around to the passenger's side.

Both right side tires were as flat as piss on a board. And from the front one's sidewall still protruded the small dagger Scott had given Dahlia one Christmas—the one she always carried in her purse.

Reluctantly, Jay nursed the car back to its parking space just as Piper rumbled up on his newly repaired Harley.

Piper stared first at Jay, then at the car, then at Jay again. "Looks like I'm not the only one having a bad day," he noted.

"Not hardly," Jay grunted sullenly.

Piper raised a sympathetic eyebrow. "Oh, yeah?"

"Yeah," Jay nodded. "I . . . I think my lady just left me. And now this. And how was *your* day?"

"Not as bad as yours, I don't reckon," Piper whispered sadly. *"You* lost your marvelous lady; *I* just lost my crappy old job."

Chapter XIII: Fall on Me

Jay hadn't a clue what to do.

What he *wanted* to do, since there was no hope of catching up with Dal now both tires were goners, was go upstairs, have a good cry and get it over with, then get well and truly plastered. Except that wouldn't really attack the problem, which meant that—much as he hated the notion—it was time to set his brain working.

Except he was still too awash with adrenaline to think, so he stood on the sidewalk and fidgeted for a moment, then simply walked off and left Piper standing there with his mouth open.

Somehow he found himself a block away, pounding the pavement through the growing twilight of springtime Athens. He wandered "historic Cobbham" first, with its confusion of lifestyles, where restored Victorian cottages stood porch by portico with the genteel decay of still-in-the-family Greek-revival mansions; and decrepit Gothics subdivided into as many tiny apartments as there were itinerant musicians and artists to inhabit them filled up by interstitial spaces.

He still had no idea what to do. He tried to think logically, but it was damned hard. It hadn't really been a fight, more a discussion that got out of hand until there at the end, when Dal had started screaming about how she hated him. But that just couldn't be true. And she'd been acting *so* strangely, which made him wonder if maybe she wasn't having some kind of breakdown, in which case he should have notified somebody, except—what if she wasn't? What if she'd meant everything she said? Then having the cops or whoever out after her would be the last thing he needed if he was trying to repair things. Lordy Jesus, what a mess of confusion!

A car swished by too close and Jay looked up, surprised to find himself downtown. He let his legs take over, feeling the pulse and pop of his feet on the pavement keeping occasional time with the music creeping out of the various bars and clubs that honeycombed the peripheral streets like warrens for the strange mix of perpetual students, artists, and local characters who formed the heart of the Athens music scene.

He thought of going into one, maybe the Uptown Lounge or the 40 Watt Club, and just letting his consciousness be carried away by music and booze. But that might not be such a good idea; he'd already gotten blitzed once this week—last night after his and Dal's anniversary bash had gone to blazes. Two nights in a row wouldn't be cool at all—at least not if you were drinking alone.

Maybe with Scott, though. Scotto would listen to him and spot him a pitcher or so, and take care of him until tomorrow when it was more likely he would know what he wanted to do. He realized dimly that he had already sublimated much of the disagreement and was running on a pure, unfocused adrenaline high, the quest for *something to do* taking precedence over the actual situation.

In the meantime he needed company—and suddenly felt a twinge of guilt for the way he'd just treated Piper. What had his second-best buddy said? Something about being fired? Dammit, he should have listened, should have been an available ear. And knowing Piper (*did* anyone know Piper?), there was no telling *what* the boy would do. He hadn't seemed bothered by the whole thing, but one never quite knew what bothered him. Jay should have at least seen him safe into LaWanda's loving arms, though, before stomping off to feel sorry for himself. Except, come to think of it, LaWanda was working at one of her many part-time jobs tonight.

And it was too late to do anything about it anyway.

Jay glanced up and discovered that he was about as close to a particular *there* as he was likely to be that evening.

The building itself was not remarkable, just another example of the two or three story turn-of-the-century buildings with which downtown Athens was crammed. This one had especially large windows with fake stained glass borders a foot wide surrounding a nicely lettered logo (another one of Myra's commissions) which read in an Arabic-looking script:

TENNIS BIRD SHORTS

and beneath it:

BOOKS—USED AND (OCCASIONALLY) NEW; COMIC—AND
NOT SO MUCH SO
RECORDS, REGALIA, AND TOMMYROT
AND ONCE IN A WHILE SOME MOVIES
PROPRIETOR: E. G. HEAD
ENQUIRE WITHIN

Within was where Scott worked his second job.

Jay took a deep breath, pushed through the heavy door, and slumped inside.

The man himself was propped up behind the front counter, poring over yet another book on foraminifera. Beyond him, shelves and tables crammed with ragged volumes swept into a dusty, yellow-lit infinity, rising two levels in the back to provide a shaky gallery lined with yet more moldering tomes. Through a door in the far left corner lay a tiny room where the owner—a library expatriate who had finally decided to follow his own true calling—sometimes showed movies on Friday or Saturday nights. Somewhere in there was a kitchen where Scott brewed strange teas and LaWanda now and then made stranger sandwiches for both public and private consumption.

Just now, at seven-thirty, there was nobody in except Scott, who glanced up, closed his book, and laid it carefully aside. "Christ, roomie, what's up? You look like death on a soda cracker."

Jay shuffled over, plopped his elbows on the counter, and commenced to fiddling with a black Magic Marker. He did not meet Scott's gaze. "Well, Scotto, I don't *feel* that way yet, but I expect to before the evening's over."

Scott leaned back. "That bad, huh? Better tell Dr. Scotto, so he can talk you out of anything drastic."

Jay lifted his head and smiled weakly. "I think that was the idea."

Scott raised an eyebrow. "Does this problem have a name?"

Jay nodded and commenced drumming his fingers. "The wind they call Mariah; the problem I call the Fabulous Dahlia Cobb. No longer so fabulous at the moment."

Scott's mouth popped open. "Christ, man, you guys never fight!"

"I'm not certain we do now, actually. It was more like a series of statements and counter-statements and absolute declarations that just sort of got out of hand, and then . . . well, she walked out and I—I just walked and walked and wound up here."

Scott sighed and reached out to pat Jay on the shoulder. "This looks like it's gonna be a *long* one, kiddo. Tell you what: I've got a pot of some kinda weird brew the headman brought by boilin' to the dregs in the back, and there's still some of those almond chicken sandwiches the Witchwoman made; I can microwave a couple." He eyed the gathering darkness outside. "I ain't had nobody in here this evenin', anyway. I'll just close up the joint, turn off the front lights, and you can bop back to the head-shrinkin' couch and tell me all about it."

All of which came to pass.

"So," Scott said when Jay had finished, "what are you gonna do—or barrin' that, what would you *like* to do, given an optimum scenario?"

Jay threw up his hands in exasperation. "I dunno, Scotto. It just all seems so final. I mean she looked *really* hard, *really* unyielding. I've never seen her like that before. But you know, it was kinda funny the way she built into it—'cause she started off like it was all gonna end in a big laugh, like she'd led Rob on and was gonna yank the rug right at the end; only somehow the whole thing shifted and it was *me* who got the rug yanked. It was like watching a John Hughes film and having John Cryer come on in the final reel and carve up Molly Ringwald with a chain saw."

Scott scratched his chin. "Hmmm. That sure doesn't sound like our Dal."

"Tell me about it."

"You're sure she's not pissed at you or anything?"

"Not that I know of. It was business as usual, and then suddenly it just wasn't. It was like . . . I don't know. Like some real first-string hard-ass just walked in behind her eyes, and took over."

Scott leaned back and bit his thumb. "You're startin' to sound like Wannie."

Jay's brows shot up. "Now *there's* a thought: maybe a little south Georgia swamp magic'd set Miss Dahlia straight."

"If anybody could set Dal straight, it's Wannie."

"If. But it really was strange: almost like some kind of breakdown."

"Well, she has been under a lot of pressure with papers and all. Maybe she kinda stressed out."

Jay regarded him dubiously. "Maybe."

Scott took another sip of coffee. "But you still haven't answered my question: what're you gonna *do?*"

Jay shrugged. "Hell if I know. Part of me wants to go after her, pound on her door, beg, plead . . . And the other half wants to do something violent to Rob for asking her—and then give her a real good shaking and set her straight. And part of me's saying, 'She's probably as upset as you are, just get on home and wait for the phone to ring.'"

"Straight talk, roomie. Do you love her?"

Jay stared at the cup in his hand. "More than life, man. More than goddamn life."

Scott took a deep breath. "Well, you certainly sound convinced, but—well, I hate to say it, but sometimes it seems like you're more in love with bein' in love than you are with her."

Jay's head snapped up. "Would you like to explain that?"

"I mean—Christ, this is hard—but don't you think you, like, make her more a symbol than a woman sometimes?"

Jay started to get up, but Scott restrained him. "Just think about it, bro. That's all I'm asking."

"But why bring it up now?"

"'Cause if it's love that's hurtin' you, then maybe you should take a real long look at it, and see if it's the real thing and not its evil sister."

"By which you mean . . . ?"

"Not the fact, Jason; the reason. Isn't it possible you hit on Dal to get at Robby?"

"I saw her picture before I ever knew she knew Robby."

"Just covering the options."

"I *love* her, Scott! There's a big hole in my life when I'm not around her." He sank back with his head in his hands.

Scott slapped his fists on his knees decisively. "Well, then, I'd just sit on it. At least her motives seem honest:

career stuff and that's all. Hell, put yourself in her shoes. Wouldn't you do the same, or at least be tempted?"

"Yeah, I guess."

Scott stood up and stretched. "Right. So you've got to trust her. Your lady ain't gonna quit lovin' you all in a minute, Jay. I've known both of you too long for that. I've seen her eyes when she looks at you."

"So you think I—"

"I think you ought to sit tight for the next little while. She's smart; she'll start to think. Eventually she'll figure out that she kinda overreacted."

"She hurt me, Scott."

Scott reached over and ruffled Jay's hair. "And you've never been hurt by a woman?"

"You *know* the answer to that: she was my first—no, *is* my first. My first, my last, my one and only. World without end, amen."

"It's hard sometimes."

"Goddamn hard."

"Okay, so you feelin' better now?"

Jay nodded, reached up to squeeze Scott's hand.

"Well enough to go home? I really oughta reopen the joint for a couple more hours."

"Yeah, I guess." Jay started to stand, then hesitated. "Oh lord, Scotto," he whispered. "I forgot to tell you about Piper!"

Scott took a deep breath and bit his lip. "I think I'd better put on another kettle."

"You look magnificent," Rob told Dal as she emerged from the wood and canvas dressing room at his theater. "Good thing you and Erin are more or less the same size."

"Good things spandex makes us so," Dal shot back, casting an eye down the expanse of shimmery red leotard. She still had a headache and was more than a little bemused at suddenly finding herself engaged in high-level dress rehearsals in the wilds of Bogart on a Thursday evening. She seemed to remember a previous commitment, but somehow it wouldn't focus. She'd done okay in *Second Shepherd,* she thought; but now the new play was coming up. She'd only read the thing once—though where that had been, she wasn't sure. She stared down at the script. She had to cavort with the musicians some, do her big speech, then lead Mankind astray, tempt him into building his own kingdoms, until at the end St. George would come in and rescue poor Mankind and behead the Devil, which was her. Then there was a little more fooling around, and they'd all get up and sing that strange little song, and it'd be over.

"Okay, folks," Rob called. "Let's get the show on the road."

Dal ducked around behind the Hell mouth, awaiting her entrance. The musicians had already trouped onstage. She waited, listening, heard the drum beat that was her cue. Someone threw smoke bombs out of the gaudy Hell mouth, and she stepped through. This was her element; never mind that the only audience was Rob, she was doing this for herself. She stalked, slithered, skulked across the stage, strode to the front, crouched, leaned forward, hissed conspiratorially.

"'I am called Satan, I'm Lord of this World,
  I've more power in one finger than a king or an earl ...'"

She went on, the couplets unreeling themselves. She found herself barely glancing at the sheets in her hand.

"I would raise up my kingdom, in Alban of late ...'"

She could practically see it: Satan's kingdom—not the flaming red Hell of tradition, but a quiet place, all gnarled, twisted trees inhabited by strange, shining animals that looked vaguely familiar. Joy welled up in her as she went on. The words made her feel as powerful as Satan, and as they rolled off her tongue, it was as though she *knew* they had power.

No, my little one, a voice seemed to whisper. *The Power is yours, where the other one was lacking, but this is not the time. I must gather it for a little while yet, and hold off that which comes a little longer. Time there will be soon enough in which to loose it.*

But some of it had already gone wandering.

Piper still hadn't found the right place.

When Jay had left him standing dumbfounded on the sidewalk, he had stood perfectly still for a long moment, feeling slightly dazed, then had shrugged and gone inside. Maybe Jay hadn't really heard what he said, 'cause it wasn't like Black Jay to desert a buddy when he was down. But then, he considered, there were plenty of jobs in Athens, but only one Fabulous Dahlia Cobb.

He'd gone inside, searching for Wannie, but had recollected she was still at the dining hall, and had a midterm painting critique afterward—and a stint at Long John Silver's after that.

And nobody else was home, except their downstairs neighbor, Medium, whom he seemed to have roused from a nap when he knocked, and he'd decided, after the guy's groggy face had greeted him at the door, that it would have been just too much heavy karma to lay on somebody half asleep, especially somebody you didn't know real well.

So he had grabbed his Uillean pipes, hopped on his ancient Harley, and thundered westward out of town.

Before long he found what he wanted.

A dirt road turned left off the ratty pavement, aiming for a stand of woods a quarter of a mile ahead. He was pretty sure it was forest service land—probably Oconee National Forest, so there'd be no trouble with trespassing—or with being trespassed against. It was nearly dark, so he switched on the headlight, let it cut a bobbing path through fields of yellowish sage and splatter across the scaly trunks of pines.

Piper slowed the bike to a rough, puttering crawl along the rutted road, just fast enough to retain its balance.

Branches closed in overhead, and he continued on for a

ways, sometimes walking the cycle. Beyond the branches ragged patches of sky showed the first stars of blue evening among the dark green needles.

Then he broke through into twilight and found just what he was looking for: a middle-sized clearing completely surrounded by woods. A jumble of weeds, stones, and rusted metal in the center were all that remained of a burned-down house—except for the chimney, which jutted skyward like an impudent finger.

Piper set the kickstand and jogged forward to stare up at the tower of pitted brickwork.

"Yeah, man, I agree," he muttered, as he raised his right hand skyward and gave the heavens the finger. "Fuck you," he cried; then, fearful the Deity might have thought Himself addressed, added "Not *You*, Big Guy—but fuck the world anyway! Fuck the fucking world!"

When the world maintained its peace, Piper retrieved the pipes from the back of the bike, picked his way through the detritus of ancient domesticity, and set himself down on the hearth of the defunct dwelling.

He began to play. Slow stuff, first. He was still a little skittish of having somehow angered the gods with his outburst, so he didn't think it proper to immediately lay down a good, strong, ear-shattering chord, though he certainly felt like it.

Rather, he built into the music gradually, improvising around themes, mostly laments. He let himself go, put his pent-up sadness and frustration into the music, let tears run as they would. It was not for his job that he wept, but for what its loss signified: one more failed endeavor, one more misplaced ambition.

Ms. DeRenne's words still echoed in his mind. *"You had no authority to do that, Piper. And unauthorized duplication of rare material is simply not a thing we can overlook, especially of something as important as the Bowman-Smith Codex, not when someone like Monteagle complains. I'm afraid we're going to have to let you go."* And that was it, no apologies, no good-byes, no second chances, just that strange, distant expression on her face, those glazed eyes, as if she were not quite aware of what she was saying. And then the worst part: Robby Tolar lurking around outside, looking smug.

So here he was back to square one: degreeless, still, though he had credits toward six (music, psychology, art, agricultural engineering, ornamental horticulture, and Latin) and in one additional case (entomology) lacked only a thesis; jobless (he refused to count the number of *those* he'd lost); and, for the nonce, apparently without friends.

That was the bad thing: not having anybody to talk to. Jay had Dal, or—failing her—Scott or even him. He had the rest of them too, except, dammit, where were they when he needed them? He *did* need them, too, more than he let on, and that set him to blaming himself—for being so easygoing, so happy-go-lucky. It made him easy to underestimate. Everybody *liked* Piper, but did anybody really *know* him?

He didn't think so—but, he considered, he was probably his own worst enemy.

He paused and took a swig from the hip flask of Irish Mist he had stuck in the back pocket of his fatigues, let the heady vapors rise into his nose and tickle his throat with the heavy sweetness.

Then he started up again, trading sadness for anger note by note, substituting loud for soft, fast for slow, playing as wild and furious as his fingers would let him.

The tune became "King of the Fairies."

"King of the Fairies," or "King of Fools"?

This was the perfect reflection of his mood—indeed of his whole life: the exact synthesis of wild and strange and ordered, just like him; a song that constantly threatened to go out of control.

He closed his eyes, heard only the tune, wished he could just keep on like this forever, wished he were in some other place—a place of wide skies and high hills and dark forests; a place where a man could do nothing but play his music and never have to worry about working. On and on he played, faster and faster still . . .

Felt a brush of warmth against his face, a tickle of mint and pine in his nostrils.

Opened his eyes—

And immediately shut them again very tightly.

The music ended in a midnote, shadowed by a sour, trickle-down buzz from the drones.

This was not the same clearing he'd been in a very short time earlier.

True, he still sat within a ring of trees, but these trees were taller, with lacier branches fanned gray and silver against a sky of midnight blue. He blinked, rubbed his eyes, blinked again, squinting toward that preposterous new growth. It had a transparent quality to it, he thought, squinting harder, trying desperately to find something familiar—and almost crying out with joy as he caught a brief faded glimpse of the familiar pines shimmering amidst the shadows like a reflection in dark lowland water.

Cautiously, he lowered his gaze, saw that he still sat on stone, that the chimney still reared behind him.

But the chunks of metal roofing and derelict appliances were gone, replaced with a fiery red glow in the air where they had lain. The bottle-green grass that grew elsewhere, there appeared crisped and sere.

The entire square of foundation was absent.

But in its place—only maybe a little further out—was a sweeping arc of light.

Piper stood up, let his pipes fall to his side. There were people in that arc, many people, all bearing candles or lanterns. They were of all sizes, too, from very tall to amazingly short. He spun around, looked beside him, behind him.

They encircled him.

Not knowing what else to do, he sat down and waited.

The lights dimmed and brightened.

One man stepped from among the others and came to stand in front of Piper. He was very tall, with black hair to his shoulders and a black mustache that swept against the bare collarbones exposed by the deep vee neck of the long-sleeved, ground-length robe he wore. White fur accented the tawny gold velvet at hem and cuffs; a belt of heavy golden squares cinched it at the waist. Though bare chested beneath the robe, the man appeared to be wearing white hose and thigh-high white leather boots.

"You must be a mighty piper," he said, "to send your music through the World Walls and set my folk a-dancing."

Piper stared, wide-eyed.

"And you must be a very talented piper to play so well my people call me from my palace to listen."

Piper blushed and smiled uncertainly. He shifted his weight and fidgeted with the chanter.

The man's black brows lowered. "But you must also be a very *foolish* piper, or else a very brave one, to play that song in that manner in this country."

"Uh—why's that?" Piper croaked.

"For two reasons, mighty piper," the man replied. "Because it is a song of Power, else it could not have pierced the World Walls and brought you here—though it needs the Power of another to awaken. And because it happens to be about . . . someone I am very close to.

"And," the man continued, "I would hear you play it again, and another tune after, and then another. It may be a very long time before I tire of your piping. A very long time indeed."

Piper nodded very, very slowly.

"Play for me, James Morrison Murphy," the man whispered, as he folded himself down at Piper's feet. "Play as if Death waits at the music's ending."

Piper closed his eyes and lifted the chanter.

Chapter XIV: Maps and Legends

Rob couldn't sleep—but not for the usual reasons. Normally when he had trouble with insomnia it was from too much work or too much stress. Or because he was arguing with himself about his latest indiscretion—like why he treated his brother so badly (he knew, rationally, that none of what had happened between his parents had been Jay's fault), or why he felt compelled to prowl through other people's mail in search of scandal.

But those last two things, in particular, hadn't seemed of much consequence the last day or so. He felt much more confident now, much more sure of himself. And never had he felt so certain of his mission—which was to make the Scarboro show the best thing he had ever done. He tried to recollect when the change had come over him, but couldn't really place it. Nothing mattered anymore except the play. He'd made numerous small tweaks on it since acquiring

McLaren's draft, and many things that had at first seemed ambiguous were clearer. With such singleness of purpose, he had no time for minor inconveniences like guilt or remorse.

And Dal: oh, what a wonder! It was thinking about *her* that was keeping him up this evening. He was so tickled with her performance he could hardly stand it. She'd put on *Second Shepherd* like putting on familiar old clothes, given her character a lot of herself, and still taken his direction like a trouper.

And as Satan—Christ! Not only had she looked like a million bucks in the skintight red outfit (his one concession to convention; it was not, strictly speaking, medieval), but she'd played the role like it was written for her: from Gill, the shrewish housewife in *Second Shepherd,* to the Lord of the World, all in a costume change. Oh, she'd had to carry the script onstage, but he guessed it would be only a performance or two before that was unnecessary.

Of course, she hadn't had much to say to him otherwise; had spent most of her offstage time staring into space as if she were a thousand miles away, but he supposed that was to be expected. Not that it didn't worry him. He wasn't at all sure about the long-term effects of the hoodoo, but it didn't seem to matter anymore. What mattered was getting that first performance under his belt. After that, who cared?

God, it was gonna be great! The other actors were marvelous, and every obstacle seemed to solve itself as if by magic. Even the Hell mouth was working like a charm.

And in the meantime, Dal was in the palm of his hand. He'd play it cool, play it distant, just be real nice, real low-key, never mention Jay, and maybe he wouldn't have to use . . . whatever it was that let him control people.

Rob closed his eyes and flopped back on the unmade bed. Oh lord, Dahlia Cobb was gorgeous.

He began to conjure her in his mind's eye. Sometimes it helped him sleep, like relaxing his body a joint at a time as a cure for tension. Only instead of relaxing *his* feet, he

envisioned Dal's feet; not his calves, but hers. The same
for thighs, belly, breast, fingers, arms. The image became
clearer and clearer. He could almost see her: a slim shape
beneath white sheets. He knew she was naked there.

He wanted her, wanted her now, wanted her more than
he had ever wanted a woman.

The image became even sharper. He imagined himself
drawing back those sheets, touching her. Loving every part
of her—first with his eyes, then with his hands, his lips,
finally with his whole body.

He took a deep, shuddering breath; another...

Felt his eyes roll back in his head.

Felt—

Cold! He was freezing to death!

He opened his mouth to cry out, but the cold had already jerked away—

Opened his eyes and nearly cried out for another reason:
he was in Dal's bedroom!

She lay partly on her left side, knees drawn up together
like an infant. One arm was pulled close to her throat, the
other raised above her head and curled around it. Her hair
lay against her pillow like the wings of a raven; her eye-
lashes were black feathers on her cheek. Her lips were
slightly parted.

He started forward, the stopped himself, as realization
suddenly dawned. *How in the hell did I get here?*

Frowning, he inventoried his memories. He'd been unable to sleep, had been thinking of Dal, had achieved that
nice, floating, in-between state, wishing he was with her,
and—

And suddenly he *was* with her!

Except that it was impossible. It was teleportation or
magic—if they weren't the same thing. Magic, something
told him, but no more magic than controlling Monteagle or
Marlyn DeRenne or even Dahlia: simply a complete and
utter desire to achieve one particular thing.

Absolute desire.

Well...maybe. He still didn't want to believe in such

things. Except they evidently happened in spite of him.

Dal stirred, rolled onto her back, moaned slightly.

Oh shit! Rob thought, suddenly wondering what he would do if Dal were to awaken and find a partially aroused and totally naked Rob Tolar in her bedroom. His luck was good, but not that good.

She moaned again, put a fist against her eyes, twisted sensually.

Gotta get outta here!

He closed his eyes. *Lord, I wish I was home!*

Cold again. Cold like death everlasting . . . Then gone. Eyes open . . .

He was back in his own apartment.

Did you enjoy that, Robert?

His heart skipped a beat. It was that voice.

It was very well done, you know—for a first time.

"Who are you?" Rob shouted. "What the fuck are you doing in my—"

Pain filled his head, sent him reeling.

Impudent mortal boy! Then more gently, as the pain faded, *No, perhaps it is time you joined my dreaming. Watch, Robert Tolar, and listen, for this is the start of my story. . . .*

He was a tall man, slim and redheaded; and he stood in a round chamber, high ceilinged, made of stone.

At his feet Cathal the gryphon paced and purred and squawked as he always did when he was hungry. Wingless, like all males of his kind, his limbs were lightly armored with leathery plates, a feature absent from the pinioned females. Perhaps in compensation for the lack of wings, however, Cathal's hip and shoulder joints gave off pulses of light as he moved, and his elbows and knees did the same. Colin smiled, remembering the strange, frantic beauty of the elaborate mating dance his feathered and furred companion had performed when last a female gryphon had found their tower. The display had cloaked the creature in a cloud of glory and had lit up the whole land for half a hundred strides or more about.

The gryphon stuck its beaked head up to be petted, but Colin ignored it, glancing briefly out the north window of his great round tower. His *single* tower, where Alberon had fifteen—and walls and halls and arching, thin-stretched bridges in between, and that just his summer palace. His winter home, locked in its far northern mountain, was smaller, grimmer, at once *on* the land and *in* it, but in spite of that, no less magnificent.

Still this one tower was enough—for now. One day it would not be; for Colin mac Angus had ideas and ambition.

Meanwhile, he considered the view.

There was more land now than there had ever been, and the older parts were becoming more solid. *Tir-Gat*—the Stolen Country, Colin called his land in his own private version of the complex tongue of the Daoine Sidhe of Alban—Tir-Gat was coming along nicely.

Closest in was a band of forest, and immediately beyond, the crystal maze he had contrived as much for diversion as protection—for the walls shifted constantly, sometimes mirrored and sometimes not; one time roofed and others open, doors present one instant, then gone. Even Colin oftimes had trouble finding his way among the halls and chambers. And outside that maze was another of gold, and beyond that, one of silver. Farthest out, simple wood sufficed, then, perhaps a hundred arrow flights away, he had let the trees and bushes have it, though they grew in patterns that were not entirely random. Beyond the last line of forest, fields took over, where the pattern was seen only in the whorls of the grasses, in the looping tangle of their roots, perhaps in the winds that brushed them.

Then there was the first line of hills, though it had been necessary to fight both the land and the Tracks to construct them—that was when he was still ignorant of the Power the silver Tracks commanded. Had he not raised them up, his own tower would have been the center of his world and the highest point as well, as the Tracks built its hill ever taller from below. For a while he had enjoyed being able to gaze on all his holdings, but had soon found in that no mystery, so he had called up trees to veil some portions and carved hills to hide vaster sweeps of countryside so that he could imagine what birds and beasts and half-mad soulless things went there (all stolen from Alban, as were the thousands of gryphons that were his favorite thralls. Cathal alone had come of his own volition.) As far as his own kind—the Daoine Sidhe of Alban—Colin was alone in his fresh-built land.

He looked higher, toward the sky that was shading more to blue with every waking, and saw at the limits of his vision a gleam of self-lit silver that faded gradually into the line of gray that might have been moor or desert or ocean, and was at times one, sometimes another, and once in a while all three.

Or none.

He did not look out the other three windows, for he knew the view would be the same: the maze, the forest, the hills—and one of the four silver Tracks, running straight from tower to horizon, which cut Tir-Gat into quarters.

He sighed and flexed his fingers. It was time to begin, time once more to be a builder.

He climbed the spiraling stairs to the tower's roof, removed his loose robe of red and silver plaid, took his single dagger between his teeth, and started. . . .

There was a pool on the top of that tower. The wind blew constantly in that high place, wet and wild, and moisture condensed on the tall merlons and low embrasures and trickled along four runnels in the floor to a deep, circular depression in the center. From that, four other runnels carried thin streams outward once again, to disappear into channels set in the four stone sides.

Careful not to wet his hands, Colin lowered himself into the edge of the pool where it was knee deep, and drew the dagger. One stroke only he took: one quick flick of blade across a finger. He turned it over and watched with strangely distanced concentration as a single drop of fiery

He looked down. Blood was still dripping from his finger. A thin line of it had seeped from his wound and slid down the white curve of his arm.

By pure reflex, he thrust his whole hand into the pool.

He would have died then, had such a thing been simple for his kind. Power fled from him, seeping outward along the Tracks, and with it fled his life. Perception spun and shifted, his vision began to fail. He flailed outward, touched nothing; tried again, and struck the pool's stone border. Gasping for breath, he heaved himself from the pool, to lie wet and naked and nearly bloodless upon the stones atop his tower, while the winds howled about above him, grown suddenly cold and cruel.

He slept.

When he awoke the sun was shining. A green-plumed bird of a kind that was common thereabout set a grape against his lips and he ate it.

He rose, found his robe, put it on, gazed down the shaft of his tower and thought it was a bit taller, then felt momentarily guilty for stealing once more from Alberon.

But surely the King of Alban would not begrudge him this one pile of rough stone—especially when he had no intention of Alberon ever seeing it.

Yet beyond him, Power born of his blood but no longer his to master raged outward along the silver Track, taking this tree and that stone . . .

And at last a particular mountain.

Very interesting, Rob told him, *but how—*

Colin cut him off. *Sometimes I do not dream, Robert Tolar, but imagine. Yet here, where I am only memory, other memories abide as well, and those I can catch and examine and let go again like salmon in the quick streams of Alban. But sometimes, too, I keep those shadow shapes that leak from other heads; and sometimes I make them my own. And sometimes, even, I share them.*

* * *

Alberon was in his winter hall which suited both his mood and the season far better than the lofty spaces he used for summer court.

He found himself longing for summer, for any time when the seasons moved farther apart than usual: when winter and winter did not lie so close together. Those times Alberon could step from Alban into the World of Men and bring back some choice lad or damsel and show them summer in the midst of snow, and send them back with tales of the Faerie King's splendor.

But this was no such day. The planets twirled in contentious circles, and the suns spun not together in either World; the golden Tracks were weak and fickle, and the Walls between the Worlds had been thin for days—so thin, and for so many days, that for the first time in four hundred Years of Men frost glittered on the north fields of Faerie.

So Alberon sat alone, staring down the long file of low, spraddled arches that commenced their outward curve even with the floor and spanned three times further than they lifted. The windows to his left were narrow, the stones between plain or crudely worked or hung with grim tapestries of gray and black and white and tarnished silver. Indeed, the only color in the whole vast chamber was the blood in the battles those webs depicted, the cold blue of Alberon's eyes, and the hot golden wine in his chased silver goblet.

Soft booted, Alberon's feet scarcely hissed upon the rushes as he glided to the left and wedged himself into a window embrasure. Cold stone slapped hard against his back; his feet he propped on the wall opposite. Warming his hands in the steam of the wine, he gazed through half-frosted glass into his kingdom.

It had been long since he had looked out across his country in the early morning. Alban slept out there, wrapped in fog, as if the whole land had given up feasting and fighting and contriving wars in the Lands of Men, and had chosen this one day to lie fallow. It was the deadest part of the year.

Yet Alberon felt strangely alive, and decided it was time

for an accounting. He flattened his hand on the thick glass, oblivious to the tiny pains prickling at his fingers. The frost melted quickly away from his touch, and before long he could stare out into his dominion. His eyes grew wide, then blank, and at some point he ceased to use them.

Yet still he saw: saw the trees and their twigs and leaves and even the tiny hairs on those leaves where frost crystals glittered like stars. He saw beasts, felt their hot blood and their wildness.

And he saw the Sidhe: his folk, the high, strange folk of Alban. The tall, beautiful ones who slept naked amid furs and rich fabrics, or wore beast shape and plied the fields and rode the breezes. Other creatures, too, he saw that were not quite men nor yet any longer animals, but strange in-between things in the process of becoming.

And he saw the earth itself, saw gold glittering in hidden seams, felt the tickle of swift water across the land, sensed the shadows of clouds upon dry ground and the cold breath of wind on barren soil.

Something was amiss, though. The land seemed disturbed in many quarters. Connections that should have lain smooth between sand and stone were frayed and twisted, torn and not yet recovered. And those strange scars were everywhere: tiny scars that lay between things—grains of sand or pebbles, leaves and branches. But there were many greater scars as well. Trees sorrowed for their fellows; the roots of grasses searched for those with which they had been twined. And there, to the southwest, a mountain missed a mountain, its hidden streams screaming where half their beds had vanished, tree roots flailing helplessly in air, layered shelves of sandstone feeling numbly toward each other across a gulf that should not be.

Alberon's sightless eyes widened. He questioned the stones and rocks, the life upon them and within them. And finally he found a mouse that remembered how the Power of silver had brushed him, awakened him, and sent him scurrying in terror. That Power had come from the east.

Alberon quickly found it: a Track, yet unlike any he had

encountered, for where most Tracks only increased one's own motion through time, space, or the levels, and could only be followed, not directed; this one could be moved by a man's volition, as a breeze might turn a mortal man's windmill. And, he discovered, another Power had often touched it as well.

Alberon sent his thought first into the shallows, then into the deeper strength at the center of the Track, and allowed it to carry him onward.

At some point he knew he had left his realm. He had never seen this place before, that lay at once upon, beneath, and within his own Alban. It was a jumble and a maze, linkages not yet made firm in many places: water falling away to mist and never recondensing, stones burning away to powder. Yet in other places stones were growing onto stones, and roots were once more joining underground. Power was everywhere—*wild* Power—and the cries of the land uprooted from its ancient home. And there, to the left, was his mountain. Already its roots were merging with the plain around it: marble fusing to granite, and quartz to limestone and clay. Here a fossil fish head mated a leaf a million years older.

It was all wrong, a disharmony, a frightful assemblage of parts cut out and rudely thrown together in mockery of his own land, as a bare tree in winter is but a phantom of its summer glory.

There was life here—everywhere, but life twisted and filled with revulsion for its own imperfection. And there were minds alive with thought—though none of his folk would dream such dark dreams. Not even Fionna, his cousin Finvarra's half-sister, or Ailill, her dark-souled twin.

But there in the center one dreamed and now, Alberon knew, he also feared—for he had felt the Alban King's touch upon his borders.

Let him, Alberon thought. *Fear is the best cure for arrogance I know of.*

* * *

Colin had been discovered, his secret realm found out. Alberon's host stood poised at his borders, ready to invade —he could *feel* them out there, waiting.

The circle had not yet tightened; but it soon would—of that Colin was grimly certain. Alberon's thought had brushed his own already: in a red rage and hungry for blood and vengeance.

But even the Lord of the Daoine Sidhe, High King of Tir-Alban, could move only so fast with so many, and the golden Tracks were all but useless here.

Colin had time to prepare a welcome. He had thought once to flee, abandon Tir-Gat to its fortune, but he knew even then that the land itself would prevent him. He had sealed himself to it already with nothing less than his blood spilled by the ancient formula and fixed with the Words of Power. Now for better or worse he was king: King and Land, Land and King—soul of one soul forever.

Tir-Gat was a thing alive, and it was his child; he could not bear to imagine it suffering.

Perhaps if he was skillful, though, there might yet be time to prepare both himself and his country for the breaking of the bond between them. That way—possibly—he could save one or the other.

He took himself to the top of his tower, and Cathal the gryphon went with him. There he drew his knife, and with it cut the tips from all of his left-hand fingers, quickly calling sun fire to seal the wound and staunch the bleeding —for he had no time now to lie senseless and grow new ones.

Then he cut those fingertips into sections, and to each section gave a Word in a tongue of men, so that Alberon's Power might not find them.

Birds, he called to him, and they came, and other flying things as well. To each he gave a part of a digit, and set them winging to the borders of his kingdom. At the many points of his land, they found springs or wells or other waters and dropped their burdens there, and where those finger fragments fell they drank from those waters, which were in turn linked to his own Well of Power, and thus was his substance rejoined.

But other bits of body fell on dry ground, and drank from that, and grew and changed and put on bark and limbs and became oak trees and hollies and briars, and stretched their roots out through the soil until their tiniest hairs met and mated.

And the final piece, and the largest, he gave to Cathal, who refused to leave him.

He was ready, now—as ready as he could make himself. He took up his crown and scepter, and waited.

So it was that when Alberon's warriors broke his border, the trees were ready for them: biting at them with gnarled boles and tripping their horses with roots come quickly alive. Even the leaves grew dagger edges and ripped at the flesh of the soldiers.

Alberon, riding not quite in the van, saw all this and nodded, and plunged in himself and fought them as best he could, but did not look beyond their surface enchantment to find that which lay in their hearts and gave them Power —either Name or matter. Colin had bent his land to his will, and the silver Tracks as well, and Alberon's task was not easy.

Yet Colin would lose in the end, he knew already. His only hope now lay in the strength of his resistance. Alberon liked a good fight, he had heard, and tests of war skill of strange complexity—and that, at least, he could provide. Perhaps that would be his salvation; perhaps when Alberon finally took him, he would be enough impressed that his vengeance might be one degree lighter.

Alberon had met the creatures now, and was laying battle to the beasts Colin had forced to serve him: gryphons, mostly, or the strange bull beasts whose breath and excretia were flame. More than one of Alberon's force felt fire upon his flesh and abandoned his form for a season. Yet the bulk of the host were great lords, and they had Power of their own. They looked at the beasts and stilled them, cast their spears and set herds of horned monsters fleeing, shot their arrows and burned gryphons into ashes at their flying.

But mostly they fought with swords, and hewed limbs and lopped off heads and fed blood and meat and bone back to the soil that had birthed it—for that was proper in battle.

Colin could see them with his own eyes now: a glitter at the edge of his forest. Even the bushes were fighting, twigs creeping out to tangle legs both hooved and human. Yet ever the swords of Alban flashed, and ever vines broke and branches withered, and eventually they reached his inmost defenses.

Colin had hoped that the maze might defy them or at least turn them aside for a little, but Alberon drew his long-sword and leveled it before him, closed his eyes and pointed it precisely, and a section of maze fell away to powder.

Colin raised himself and looked down from his battlements upon the King of Alban who rode calmly toward him on a horse black as his sable armor. Dust welled up around that horse's hooves, and dust shimmered in the air behind them.

"You can come down now, Colin mac Angus," Alberon called from the foot of the tower.

"Not without you coming up to get me!"

"If that is the way you will have it, that I will abide. I grant you that much favor, King of the Stolen Country."

It was over.

Colin stepped back from the embrasure. There was but one thing more he could try.

Cathal looked up at him, and he looked back at Cathal, and the gryphon lay down on its side as if he had told it in words what would happen.

Colin tore open his golden robe and revealed the pale splendor of his chest; and with the knife he slashed through his breastbone and exposed his beating heart to the sky. And then he opened the gryphon's chest; the strong beast heart laid bare.

A series of cuts so quick that neither were bloodied, an intricate twisting of Power, and a moment later his own heart kept beat in Cathal's body, while the gryphon's thumped on in his.

One final thing he did to finish—which was to rip the scabs from his fingers and surrender his blood to the pool. Power flooded out of him, to find its way to the Tracks and twist free Tir-Gat's borders, set it to drift on its own, with no further links to Alban. But there was still plenty of life left in him when Alberon's warriors found him and led him away.

It had been enough, he thought, as they escorted him from his castle: Tir-Gat would yet survive.

Alberon might destroy his body, but Tir-Gat had his heart and most of his soul—in roots and waters and the breast of a young golden gryphon. His land had drunk deep of his flesh, and would soon be beyond Alberon's power. One day, perhaps, he would call it, one day he would once more be its master. He was planning that day already.

That day is . . . Beltaine? Rob asked him.
My dream has become anticipation.
And Robert Tolar awakened.

PART IV

Chapter XV: Welcome to the Occupation

(April 30)

Should I or shouldn't I? Jay was wondering.

He had paused in midstep on his way from Park Hall to Reed-Gillespie, and now stood twisted half around, with the hot sunshine bouncing silver novas off his mirror-shades. But what he saw through them was illumination of a far different sort: the former light of his life, the Fabulous Dahlia Cobb, for the nonce remarkably dimmer.

That was her all right, not thirty yards away, sitting on the top front step of the main library, still dressed in his totem color and reading *The Red and Black* as if nothing traumatic had happened the night before, while *he* stood on the sidewalk looking stupid and debating whether or not to go up to her and find out if she was okay; or if nothing else, figure out which way the land lay.

But he just wasn't sure he was up to it.

The previous night he had ignored both his own vow

and Scott's firm admonitions and had once more let his rational side relinquish control to its troublesome emotional twin—and had chugged an entire six-pack of beer as a consequence. And had *still* lain awake most of the night, alternately worrying about the breakup—if that was the right term—and being angry both at himself and Dal, and perhaps at the world in general. Throw in a morning spent getting his tires replaced, and it was no wonder he felt like crap today. And still he debated: should he or shouldn't he?

Dal shifted her position ever so slightly, stretched her legs in that innocently sensual manner he so loved. He felt his throat catch, found he had taken a step forward, then caught himself and reconsidered. Was he ready to dredge up the whole messy affair again so soon? Either she'd be glad to see him and things would be fine, or she wouldn't, and he would only be more hurt, at least in the short term; and he wasn't sure he could handle that.

But wasn't it worth the risk? He took a deep breath and started toward her.

Dal stood up and stretched again, tucked the newspaper under her arm, glanced around. Her gaze brushed him.

Jay felt a chill race over him.

Dal stared at him for a moment, then shook her head, as if she were trying to recall something. She took a step in his direction, then paused, spun sharply around, and marched back into the library.

Another chill, though Jay couldn't think why. Anger would have been a more reasonable response than the case of terminal weirds he was getting. It was that same feeling of somebody else walking in behind Dal's eyes and taking over.

She was gone now, and he maybe knew one tiny thing more about where things stood. But he didn't like it one bit better, and he was still puzzled.

Wearily, he turned on to the sidewalk that angled off to his left and slumped along beneath the old trees of north campus. *Best to go on with your own life,* he told himself. Now on to the next problem: another potentially explosive confrontation. He had decided to appeal directly to Marlyn DeRenne for permission to use the Bowman-Smith Codex —and perhaps to see if he could find out anything about what had caused her to fire Piper.

He hadn't seen his friend since the evening before, but that was scarcely remarkable. Still, when he got home, he'd noticed that Piper's bike was gone. It had been absent this morning, too, though that was hardly surprising, since Piper was well known as an early riser.

So why did Jay have such a strong sense of foreboding?

"Are you *sure* you've got to see her today?" Blondie asked him five minutes later, with an extravagant roll of his eyes. "She's been acting *so* strange for the last couple of days."

"'Fraid so. It's something I've been putting off, but I don't think I can any longer. Any idea when she'll be back from lunch?"

Blondie glanced at his watch. "Maybe five minutes?"

Jay nodded sullenly and rearranged himself on the maroon leather sofa. He still had no idea what he was going to say to Ms. DeRenne.

The silence stretched and thickened, and Jay found himself gazing into the reading room where an exhibit from the Bowman-Smith Collection had been mounted. He could see the sword from where he sat. Maybe he ought to—

"Hey, you live with Piper, don't you?" Blondie asked him suddenly. "In the same house, anyway?"

Jay nodded mutely.

"So how's he doing?" Blondie went on. "I mean how's he taking it—being fired so sudden-like and all?"

Jay shrugged. "I don't really know, I've only barely seen him. Don't know what it was about, even."

"Well, if you ask me it was damned unfair," Blondie confided. "I mean, sure the guy's a bit of a flake, but he's usually here on time and does his work okay. Polite and reliable and all that."

"Do I detect an impending *but?*"

Blondie shrugged in turn. "Dunno. It was just real strange. I mean, I was, like, just sitting here, and your brother—"

"*Half* brother," Jay corrected sharply.

Blondie glared at him. "So Rob Tolar came stomping in and demanded to see Ms. DeRenne. So I buzzed her, and she didn't want to see him 'cause none of us can stand him, but finally she did, and he started in on her about some Xeroxing Piper had done that he shouldn't have."

Jay felt a sudden pang of guilt. He had a very good idea what Xeroxing that had been. "You *saw* this?"

"Heard it. They started in before she even got to her office."

"Ah-ha."

"Yeah, but it was real funny, 'cause I knew she'd stand up for Piper—shoot, she *likes* Piper, and she *did* start off taking up for him, but then the door closed and I couldn't hear anymore, but when Rob came out, he looked like the cat that swallowed the canary, and a minute later it was all over. Saw Ms. DeRenne a little later and she looked like she'd been thwacked between the eyes with a sledgehammer."

Something clicked in Jay's mind, and an unexpected chill passed over him. Blondie's description sounded exactly like what he had noticed when Dal had walked out on him. And there now appeared to be a common thread: Robby Tolar.

Jay took a deep breath and continued. "So you say she started to stand up for Piper, then changed her mind?"

Blondie nodded. "It was real strange, a complete reversal. And she's been acting funny ever since. Like Piper's boss went in to talk to her, and came out all wild-eyed and said she went silent and closed on him. And when I asked her about what to do with Piper's last time card and stuff, she just turned off."

"Turned off? How?"

Blondie took a deep breath. "It was—it was just like

somebody else took control of her, like she went on auto-pilot or something. One minute she's all relaxed and friendly like normal, and the next minute she's like a puppet on a string."

Oh Jesus, Jay told himself, *this is just* too *strange.*

The swish of the front door jarred him from his reverie, followed by the *tap-tap-tap* of high heels on the flooring. He peered around an intervening column and saw Marlyn DeRenne heading toward the desk. In her black suit and purple silk shirt she looked magnificent.

"Any messages?" she asked Blondie.

He shook his head, then inclined it toward Jay. "Mr. Madison needs to see you."

As Jay stood up, Ms. DeRenne looked around. A shadow crossed her face, but she recovered and smiled brightly. "So what's up, Jay?"

"Uh, yeah," Jay began awkwardly, more uncertain than ever. "Well, what I wanted to talk to you about was the Bowman-Smith Codex," he managed. "I—" He stopped in midsentence.

For Marlyn DeRenne's face had turned pale. Her whole body stiffened, her eyes went glazed and blank. "What about it?" she said stiffly.

Jay swallowed. "Well, I was wondering what its status is now—as far as doing some work with it, I mean . . ."

The woman stared at him dully, and Jay had the uncanny feeling he was watching someone trying to translate his words into another language and back again. When she finally answered, her voice had acquired a draggy quality. "I'm . . . afraid that won't be possible. I . . . gave exclusive rights . . . to someone else."

"Monteagle?" Jay prompted, eyes narrowing with a suspicion he was not quite ready to face.

"No," Ms. DeRenne said. "To Robert Tolar. I . . . told him yesterday."

Jay stumbled down the steps in front of Reed-Gillespie, haunted by Marlyn DeRenne's look of stunned incomprehension. He had simply turned and bolted; had to go somewhere and think. Things were just getting too bizarre.

And speaking of bizarre, here came LaWanda, still wearing her I-Hop uniform, which—with dreadlocks—looked more than a little absurd.

The black girl broke into a run as she spotted Jay. When she finally reached him her eyes were wide.

"Jesus, Wannie, what's wrong? You look like death on a stick."

LaWanda flung an arm across the metal railing at the foot of the steps and sagged against it. Her dark eyes were wide, imploring. "It's Piper," she sobbed. "He never came home last night. I got in from the late shift and he wasn't there. The bike was gone, and so were his pipes. And he still wasn't back this mornin'. Myra hasn't seen him either; and I couldn't find Scott to ask."

"But that's no big deal," Jay replied, though he was suddenly afraid it might be. "I mean, he doesn't exactly keep regular hours."

"Yeah, but I've got a *feelin'* about this one. He's in trouble, I know he is. I was standin' there at work yesterday, and all of a sudden I *knew* somethin' was wrong. And when I came home, them vibes like to have knocked me over. I didn't sleep a wink last night."

"Oh jeez," Jay whispered, knowing how accurate La-Wanda's premonitions usually were.

"Too bad Barry Knight doesn't have a phone," he said, while he tried to get his thoughts in order. "You could've called out there and found out if he made it to rehearsal."

LaWanda nodded vigorously. "Tell me about it."

A thought struck Jay. "Wannie, did you *see* Piper yesterday afternoon?"

LaWanda shook her head. "What's that got to do with anything?"

"Piper got fired," Jay said softly. "Robby ratted on him about the copying he did for me."

"Fired?" LaWanda cried. "*Fired!*—and over a little thing like that! Shit fire! That boy never *can* keep a job."

"Yeah, well, that's true," Jay replied lamely, "but—gee, Wannie, I kinda screwed up, too; I mean—well, Dal and me had a . . . significant disagreement, and Piper came bopping up right after and said something about getting fired, but I was too concerned with Dal leaving to pay much attention. Guess I should have."

LaWanda's eyes were blazing. "You let Piper go off by himself when he was depressed?"

"Well, I wasn't exactly in a mood to play Sigmund Freud. He was home when I left, and had a rehearsal; I presumed he'd go to that. But, gee whiz, he didn't seem to be very bothered."

"Oh, but he would be," LaWanda mused sadly, "he would be. Piperman don't tell you guys that kinda thing, but he does me."

Jay put his arm around LaWanda and gave her a solid hug. "Shoot, girl, he probably just had one too many and stayed over at Knight's house."

"But what if he *didn't?* What if he's hurt?" LaWanda countered. "Rationalize all you want, I still think he's in trouble. My mojo says he's in trouble."

"You think you'd know if anything . . . *permanent* happened?"

"You bet your sweet patoot I'd know! A man comes in me, I got his power; that power gets cut off, you better believe I'd *know!*"

"But it's nothing like that," Jay inserted quickly. "Right?"

LaWanda shook her head. "No, but it still bothers me. Piper's just like a kid or somethin', Mr. Jay—got no sense, no *real* sense. He could've had a wreck, or somebody could've robbed him. . . ."

"More like he's run out of gas and doesn't have a quarter to call home on," Jay replied, trying to lighten the conversation. "Don't worry, Wannie; he'll come bopping in about three in the morning with his sneakers in rags and that silly grin on his face."

LaWanda slipped out of Jay's embrace and took a deep

breath. Some of the tension seemed to flow out of her. "Maybe I did fly off the handle just a little. Maybe I put too much faith in my mojo."

"Maybe so. You're sure he didn't leave a note or anything?"

"I'm sure, I'm bloody well sure. Reckon we oughta file a missin' person report?"

Jay shook his head. "I don't think we can this soon. I think we oughta sit tight, maybe try to catch up with some of the boys in the band and see if they've seen him. If Piper's not home by dinner, we start to worry. If he's not home by breakfast, we go to the cops, 'cause that'll mean he's reneged on playing at Scarboro, and we both know he'd never do that."

"Yeah, I guess you're right. Makes sense anyway, but lordy, I hate not knowin'."

"Yeah, tell me about it."

LaWanda's eyes narrowed. "Hey, you know you don't look too good yourself, Mr. Jason. Did you say somethin' 'bout a fight with Miss Dahlia?"

Jay nodded wearily, and told her.

"And somethin' else botherin' you too?"

"Dreams, Wannie, dreams."

LaWanda shook her head. "Them dreams is bad juju," she said, "Ver' bad. Ver', ver' bad."

Jay regarded her quietly for a moment, wanting desperately to comfort her, yet feeling an even more desperate desire to go off by himself and try to make sense of the deepening puzzle. If he could sort *that* mishmash out, maybe the rest would fall into place. Impulsively, he reached out and took LaWanda in a long, tight embrace. "Don't worry, girl, Piperman'll be okay. And so will I." He kissed her on the forehead.

"I hope so, Mr. Jason, I truly hope so."

"You okay?"

LaWanda shrugged. "Lotta strange things goin' on."

Jay nodded. "Too many."

He released her and headed for his office, his brain a-twirl.

Jay stared at the yellow legal pad in front of him. Its entire surface was a scrawl of names, comments, and arrows. Right at the top of the list it said Robby Tolar.

Jay was trying to come to terms with the accumulating strangeness item by item, so he asked himself the first question one more time.

What sort of strangeness involved Robby?

Well, to start with, he had spoken to both Dal and Marlyn DeRenne in the last couple of days, and in both cases they'd begun acting atypically soon after. That the results of those conversations had had adverse effects must also be considered—Piper losing his job and Dal walking out on him. But was Jay himself the common factor? Or was it some third alternative of which he was unaware? Hell, there might not even *be* a connection.

He looked back at the list. Dal's name was next: what was going on with Dal? He had already listed the fact of her conversation with Robby which had convinced her to put aside her misgivings and agree to work for him at Scarboro. But there was also the fact that she hadn't really seemed to want to, or rather didn't know *what* she wanted —that eerie sense of someone else being in control when she'd dropped the big one. So that was two things: Dal's sudden reversal of priorities, coupled with a strong sense of her not being herself.

And there was her story of being followed by something she was not certain was normal. She'd admitted to being a little bit buzzed beforehand and more than a little buzzed afterwards. But that didn't really make any difference. The simple fact that Dal had drunk a considerable quantity of vodka right after gave veracity to her story because she only did that when she was really upset. So whether or not she had *actually* seen something, she obviously *believed* she had. And the fact that she'd chosen not to tell him simply added another level of authenticity to her tale. Intelligent people didn't usually tell things that would get them ridiculed—even if they believed them.

So what did all this have in common? Exactly nothing that he could tell.

Now what about Scott and Myra? Had anything untoward happened to them? He drew a blank there, too. Either nothing had happened or they, like Dal, had elected not to speak of it.

And on to other small fry: Sparks? Nothing outré there, unless you counted his fixation with brownies, which Jay was certain was simply an affectation.

Dr. Monteagle? Nothing strange there either, except maybe the business about not getting Jay's letters and denying his calls. Hmmm. Maybe something *was* up, because Monteagle had at least a couple of things in common with some of the other problems, one of which was a peripheral acquaintance with Robby—and Dal and DeRenne.

And while he was thinking about the drama department, what about Dr. McLaren? She knew Dal, Robby, Sparks, and Monteagle, too. And she was dead. And hadn't he read somewhere she'd been working on the Bowman-Smith Codex when she'd died? But when had that happened? Jay tried to think. The funeral had been on Sunday, which meant . . . He remembered now; Dal had called Saturday afternoon to tell him. McLaren had died the night before, which was—Jay's hair stood briefly on end—the same night Dal claimed to have been stalked by something, in McLaren's neighborhood.

Okay, so much for that: some case for collective weirdness in the drama department. What about his other friends?

LaWanda seemed to be another case of nothing out of the ordinary, except by association with the possibly missing Piper. No, wait, that wasn't true—because she had also been along on the trip to the Faire that had ended so strangely. Jay wished his memory of that affair were clearer; more to the point, he wished he hadn't been stoned at the time—that none of them had been. He'd more or less attributed it to that after the fact, just as Dal had ascribed her weird occurrence to too much alky. But suppose something *had* happened?

He was beginning to get a headache.

Onward, now, to Piper, who had also been on that eerie drive. And there was the matter of his firing and subsequent sudden disappearance, except that Jay wondered if he should really count those, since they were so typical.

That left himself: what had happened to him lately that was out of the ordinary? Well, he'd seen strange reactions in Dal and Ms. DeRenne, and maybe in Monteagle. And, again, there'd been that weird trip back from the Faire.

And there were the dreams. He could still recall almost every detail from them, even to thoughts and feelings. They had begun the night of the hoot. The night of the Terrible Day when Robby had blown up his thesis.

Another strange thing had happened that day, too. He had found the manuscript—and the sword: the sword that had made him feel so marvelous. . . . Now that was interesting. And he had got a splinter from the blade in his finger, and then had dreamed about the Middle Ages.

Of course, he'd had *other* medieval stimuli that day: the Old Norse class, Dal's play, his own thesis, Sparks's T.H. White book. Discovering the manuscript, hearing medieval-type music, talking about the Renaissance fair . . .

He wrote them all down. Together they were a lot to ascribe solely to coincidence.

And then there were his own experiences: the book and the sword, the dreams, the ride out of the world. He had suppressed them all, refused to dwell on them. Why? Because he feared ridicule? Or because he feared the facts themselves?

The key must be in the dreams, if only he could go back to them and look for answers.

Well, why couldn't he try to dream? That was what Dal had suggested; maybe it was worth a shot.

He took a deep breath and tried to recall how the dreams had occurred before. He'd been asleep the first time, so that was no help. But the second time . . . He'd been in a semimeditative state. And he'd been staring at the sword Myra had given him. Maybe he should try that.

So he took another breath and stared at the blank page before him, let the rest of the world slide gradually out of focus as he tried to blank his mind, then conjure the image of a sword—the one he'd just seen in the library. And suddenly it was there before his eyes: narrow, dented blade and plain brass cross hilt; grip of wire-wound leather. He concentrated on the juncture of hilt and blade, narrowing his vision, seeing the blade not as a single strip of metal, but as folded layers of atoms.

For a moment he saw nothing. Part of him was afraid, wanted to withdraw; but a stronger part urged him onward.

His eyes rolled up—good, he was going under.

Then he attempted to zero in on Edward the smith. But that didn't work at all, because he realized suddenly that in his dreams he had always *been* Edward the smith, and thus he had no idea what that shadow-self *looked* like.

So he tried focusing on the boy instead. Harry was his name: white-blond hair; narrow, freckled face; gangly body already filling out across the chest and shoulders; the tattered blue jacket he always wore (how had he known that?). Then, so slowly Jay was hardly aware of it happening, the boy's face slowly took form before him, looked out at him, opened his mouth. . . .

"Where have you been?" the boy was asking urgently. He was shaking, and not from the bitter cold.

Edward the smith of Ripon looked down at the small figure on the threshold before him. He should have known: Harry was ever the lightest sleeper—and the lightest of foot as well. He was the smartest too, as quick in his head as he was with his feet and fingers.

"Where have you *been*, Father?"

Edward still gave back no answer, for he was gazing at his son with a strange new sadness, as if seeing the boy's proud carriage and clear blue eyes for the first time.

"Father?"

Edward reached for words, but they fled from him; grasped for memories, but they slipped away.

"Nowhere," he finally managed, though even that effort cost him. "I went nowhere beyond the dooryard."

He frowned. That was a lie, yet he had *meant* to say more. The memory was clear as yesterday's forging. Only when he looked for it, it eluded him, leaving a blankness murky as bog water.

"You were gone a long time, Father."

Edward felt suddenly frightened, though he did not know if it was for himself or for his child.

"And how do *you* know, boy?"

"I heard a knock, I saw you go to the door. But then . . . I guess I went to sleep." He hung his head.

"Then how do you know how long I was gone?"

"The heat woke me, and I crept to the door. The moon was at the top of the sky, and now it sits on the horizon. You were gone that long."

"I was walking."

"I looked all around the house. I could see everything; the air was very clear."

"Enough, boy. Get to bed."

"But, Father—"

Edward took a long, ragged breath. "I *can't* tell you, son."

"Why not?"

"Because . . . when I reach for words, they're not there. I can see pictures, see everything clear as day in my head . . . but when I would set my tongue to them, they vanish."

Harry's eyes brightened. "D' ye think it's *witchery?*"

Edward shook his head. "Maybe so, son; but if it is, the priests do not speak of it aright."

"But why did you take your sword?"

Edward looked down, saw that he still had the sword with him. That surprised him a little. The memories that he saw but could not speak of spun and twisted in his head, playing hidey games. His sword was part of them. He drew it from the scabbard, stared at it. Moonlight glittered off the plain blade, sparked on the brazen hilt. There was some dark discoloration along one side that he did not recall having seen before. He wet a finger and ran it along the surface, trying to rub away that new blemish—then swore as his fingertip came too near the gleaming edge. A tiny dark bead welled out on his skin and became a slow, bright trickle, first on his flesh, then on the metal. He did not notice the wound immediately, but when he did, merely stuck his finger in his mouth and continued with his polishing.

Harry's eyes grew very wide. "It *vanished,* Father."

"*What* vanished?"

"The blood! You cut yourself, and a drop of blood ran into the hilt on this side. But it didn't drip off, it just vanished. Just melted into the metal."

Edward's frown deepened. "Show me!"

"It'll hurt!"

"You're enough of a man to name me a liar; are you man enough to show me you're *not* one?"

Harry bit his lip and nodded grimly.

Edward handed the sword to the boy. Harry looked at it in the moonlight where he held it horizontal before him. His wrist wobbled slightly with its weight. He extended a tentative left hand, moved his finger along the edge, pressed harder...

Pain! Pain and *cold!*

He opened his eyes. The blood was still there. A thin runnel of it flowed from his finger down the steel and dripped to the frosted ground, nothing more.

Edward raised an eyebrow and looked at him with silent, amused admonishment, as he reclaimed the weapon. "Ready to go back to bed now, little curious one? The cock'll be crowin' none too distant, and I'm gettin' a chill standin' here on the doorstep."

Harry nodded sheepishly and shivered in spite of himself.

Edward opened the door and followed his son into the warmth of the house.

It *was* warm, too! Warm as summer—warm enough to sleep naked on top of the covers. Warm enough for anything.

Harry seemed unconcerned, or else he did not notice.

"Into bed with you now," Edward whispered.

"And with you!" Harry dared him back.

"I'll have my hand to you, young hellion!" But he was grinning when he said it. He aimed a slap at the boy's hesitant backside.

Harry evaded him, grinning even wider; and climbed back over the foot of the bed.

Edward found his own place beside Annie, but it was a long time before his eyes would stay closed. They kept sneaking open, constantly drawn back to the hilt of the sword he had laid on the chest beside him. He wondered why he had left it there instead of putting it back in its cupboard; wondered, too, why it was suddenly so warm in the cottage—especially since one of his irresponsible urchins had apparently let the fire go out. Or maybe it was simply that the cold wind had stopped blowing.

His only dream was of riding.

Jay Madison also dreamed.

He was no longer Edward of Ripon. But the dream sword still floated before his eyes. It had been so neat—so beautiful in its functional simplicity. He tried to retain the image as he found himself drifting into lighter realms of slumber.

His eyes popped open.

"I've seen that sword *before*," Jay announced with absolute conviction.

And it was true—for, at the precise moment between waking and sleeping when the mind is most open to possibilities, Jay had realized that the sword in the dream was the same as the sword at the library.

The sword was the bridge between the dreams and present reality.

It was more than he could believe, yet it seemed the only possibility. But where had the sword come from? It had been part of the Bowman-Smith Collection, but where had *that* come from? He remembered seeing the packing labels, but only noticing the country of origin, not the whole address. Maybe he could find out, though. His eyes scanned the room, came to rest on the pile of *Red and Black*s in his bookcase. He spun his chair around, grabbed the pile of dusty newsprint and dumped it on his desk.

A moment later he had found the article about the discovery of the Bowman-Smith Codex. He skimmed it frantically, then found the line he had been looking for: ". . . he suffered an unexpected heart attack and died at his rural home near Ripon, England."

Ripon, England.

Jay frowned, went over the facts once more. He had dreamed of Edward of Ripon. Edward of Ripon had owned a sword that still existed. That sword had come from Ripon—which meant that Ripon was almost certainly another element in the puzzle.

But what did Ripon have in common with the rest?

The play? But was the play itself special?

Well, Dal was involved with it now—a strangeness there, at least in the circumstances surrounding that involvement. But there was something else. . . .

He had it: he'd been reading it on the way back from Scarboro the day reality seemed to have gotten out of kilter.

But there was something else, too: Dr. McLaren. According to the paper, she'd been working on the manuscript when she'd died.

Therefore the play was almost certainly involved. But how? And there was still the matter of whether something had stalked Dal, and if so, what. And the problem of what had happened to Piper.

He had to go back to Reed-Gillespie, he decided, and take another look at the sword.

If he could still get there. It was 5:40 already and they closed at six. (Christ, how long had he been out, anyway?).

Then he'd go home and take a good, long look at his copy of the Bowman-Smith Codex.

Chapter XVI: West of the Fields

Scott felt more than a little self-conscious as his old VW Scirocco barreled along the dusty backroad west of Bogart. He was on his way to the pre-opening-day dry run of Scarboro Faire, and his cassette player was thumping out the one song uniquely appropriate to the occasion. Simon and Garfunkle's quasi-medieval ballad was a fine piece in its own right, but Scott felt just a wee bit naive playing the tune, much less enjoying it.

And to make matters worse, there was the getup he was wearing.

Myra had given it to him that morning when he'd ducked in to brief her on Jay and Dal's altercation right before he'd left. She'd made him put it on then and there.

It was a long-sleeved shirt of lightweight cambric, and it was made with neither seam nor needlework. It had taken Myra some doing, she admitted, and she'd had to decide exactly what constituted a seam but had finally succeeded, at least to her own satisfaction. A piece of fabric had been folded in half, then cut on a *T*. The raw edges had been folded under and fused down with interfacing, thereby solving the no-needlework restriction; and the edges under the arms and along the sides had been laced together with silk cord run through closely spaced grommets. It looked a little foolish, but fulfilled the letter of the law. And in the (fused on) pocket was a small pouch full of herbs which he knew beyond a shadow of a doubt were parsley, sage, rosemary, and thyme.

The whole situation, gifts and circumstances both, had altogether been quite befuddling—because, according to the same song, the making of such a shirt was a precondition of the conferring of true love. Was that Myra's roundabout way of announcing her interest and/or availability? Something told Scott that might just be the case—which was both good (someone he liked found him attractive) and bad (he wasn't sure he wanted a girlfriend just now, not when he was still on the—admittedly protracted—rebound). Had he somehow led Myra on? Was she reading his close friendship as a prelude to something more? Suddenly he felt very guilty, and as guilt often will do, one pang began to attract others.

Things *were* in kind of a mess back in Athens, and he was beginning to get the feeling he shouldn't have left so many of his friends with unresolved crises.

There was Jay's problem with Dal, for instance—what looked like their first serious rift, and Jay certainly could not be accused of being indifferent to it. Yet he had seemed strangely subdued this morning, almost as if nothing had happened. Was it disturbing his buddy more than he was letting on? Or had the illustrious Mr. Madison simply progressed to the denial stage?

Or maybe *Dal* had given in and had trashed the whole idea of performing at Scarboro. That much he should have an answer to in a couple of minutes.

Come to think of it, maybe that was why he had been so

eager to get underway this afternoon—because the answers to so many questions seemed to be tied up with
Scarboro.

According to Piper's orientation schedule, there would
be a final rehearsal on-site around four-thirty. So if Jay's
former lady was there, that'd tell him one thing, and point
the way for future relations with his roommate.

And if she *wasn't* present, that would mean another, and
one problem would more or less be solved.

And since Piper was supposed to be playing tomorrow
as well, Scott would find out then how losing his job was
affecting him. He began imagining the poor guy's explana-
tions to LaWanda, and laughed out loud. He'd passed
Wannie on the street on his way out of town, and she'd
been walking fast and furious toward the library. Maybe
she was gonna take matters into her own hands.

As for himself, well, it was gonna be good to get back
in the Creatively Anachronistic saddle again. This would
be his first time back with the SCA for an extended period
in well over a year. He wondered how many people he
would know. Probably not as many as he expected; there
were never as many old timers as one hoped for.

Yes sir, it was going to be interesting. How long would
it take him to bury Walter Scott Gresham the Third and
resurrect Bryan of Scotia? He smiled. *It* will *be fun. I* will
have a very good time.

He rounded a corner, and was suddenly engulfed by
sunshine. Before him was a newly graveled parking lot—
largely empty at the moment. Beyond that was a dark line
of mixed oak and pine; and a good way beyond those he
could barely make out the concrete gate towers that supported the arching sign that proclaimed SCARBORO FAIRE in
brilliant red letters. Colorful pennons flew from those
bogus battlements; and behind the plastered walls he could
dimly see towers, thatched roofs, and projecting half-
timber gables.

"Well," he said to nobody, "looks like this may just work out after all."

Once Scott finally found it, hanging around the SCA campsite at Scarboro proved to be like old home week. Everybody was there he had wanted to see: all his old friends and cronies, as well as many of the luminaries of the southeastern kingdom they called Meridies. The local royalty were present, for starters: the baron and baroness of both the groups in Atlanta and Athens, the South Downs and Bryn Madoc, respectively. Duke John the Mad Celt was there—the quintessential long-haired leaping gnome, and Master Edward of Glastonburh in one of his inevitable foolish hats. And naturally Thomas the Wordsmith was declaiming loudly to a group of bemused young folks, "I am the Wordsmith, hear me, hear my voice. . . ." Scott ignored the rest and concentrated on looking for more of the Athens crowd.

The Anachronists were still setting up, getting ready for their exhibits of the morrow: legitimate medieval crafts, displays of handmade costumes, armor, and jewelry—all as authentic as research and available resources could make them. And with the artifacts were piles of books showing how things *really* were back then.

"Hey, Scott Gresham!" someone hailed him, and he spun around to see Mad Tom Hundley, the lead singer of Just Thrid, trotting his way all shirtless and sweaty, with his black beard and hair all a-tangle, and his black eyes sparkling with mischief.

"So you decided to come," Tom panted. "Thomas the Hun, I am here," he added, extending a blackened hand—which he drew back apologetically as soon as he noticed. "Been doing a little smithing." Thomas nodded over his shoulder to a raised hearth from which smoke still issued.

"Been meaning to talk to you," he continued. "Meant to back at the party at your house but got distracted." He motioned to the rucksack full of rattan swords and other martial regalia Scott had piled behind him. "Didn't know you fought. Come to it, wasn't sure how involved you were with this deal."

"I'm not real active now."

"Oh," Thomas said. "But, hey—wanta armor up and have a go?"

Scott sighed. It'd been months since he'd fought anybody who knew what they were doing, and he was afraid he was pretty rusty. But Thomas the Hun was obviously aching for a serious round or two. Well, he had to get at it sooner or later.

"Just let me get garbed up."

"Meet you over at the tourney field?"

"Right," Scott said without much conviction. "Sure."

Well I'm even less the man than I thought I was, Scott told himself an hour later as he flopped down on a bench below a curve of whitewashed concrete wall. He leaned his head against the barrier and closed his eyes. Thomas had flat worn him out: half a dozen rounds and he'd been too tired to raise his shield to defend himself. He'd had no idea he was in such bad condition.

He'd followed his reintroduction to sword and shield combat with a quick shower in the garden hose and black plastic sheeting bathhouse that had been rigged up behind a stand of pines a little way off, and was now attired in a pair of gray sweatpants that weren't exactly medieval but were close enough to early period peasant garb to bum around in, and a short-sleeved blue tunic that wasn't strictly accurate either, yet was sufficiently arcane to attract curious stares from the many workmen still lurking about in odd corners.

Scott picked up the sword he'd brought along for repair; he'd intended to find a nice quiet place, strip off the old duct tape, then rewrap it, and maybe follow that with a quick nap before somebody dragged him off to a night of feasting and revelry. He pulled out a pocketknife and began slitting the thick encrustation of old tape, then paused, staring at the plain black hilt.

I wonder how Jay made out with Ms. DeRenne.

He made a few halfhearted stabs at the old tape, but quickly became pleasantly bored. It was just too nice here, too relaxing and mellow in this magical neitherworld that was half woods and half town. Quite without knowing it, Scott drifted off to sleep, only to come to himself sometime later. *Must be around five,* he decided, by the quality of light, the length of the shadows.

It took him a moment to realize there were sounds nearby. No, it wasn't just *sounds,* it was *music:* a lively, though rather simple, medieval tune rendered on penny whistles, lute, and drum.

Wearily he stood up and followed the melody around the line of wall and bulge of gate tower, to find himself staring down a long file of wooden benches at a stage. A sign nearby read THE MORRISMAN'S MEN, and in smaller letters beneath it: *Courtesy University of Georgia Department of Drama.*

As if he wouldn't have known as soon as he saw who was onstage.

It must be the new play. He'd glanced through Jay's copy of it a time or two, but had never found time to read it.

And now he wouldn't have to because Dal was onstage in her guise as the Devil. Watching her captivated him in an instant. God, that girl was good! Looking at her he could *believe* the Devil was a woman, because she embodied all the enticements a very powerful woman could command and all the power of a completely amoral man.

"'I am called Satan, I'm Lord of this World . . .'"

He could not take his eyes off her.

Thomas the Hun joined him. "She's sharp, isn't she?" Thomas muttered appreciatively, then: "Hey, wasn't she at the party? Ain't that your roommate's lady?"

"Not anymore," Scott grunted.

"She split or what?"

"Yeah," Scott grunted.

"Well, gonna split myself," Thomas said after an awkward pause. "Gotta go grab some dinner. You stayin' on-site?"

Scott shrugged noncommittally. "Yeah, I reckon."

"See you later, then?"

"Not if I see you first," Scott tossed back, relieved to see him go.

Not that he had anything against the guy. But moment by moment, as he watched Dal seducing the wayward Mankind into a desire for riches, leading him astray with the promise of Power, he found himself becoming angrier and angrier.

She had no right to treat Jay like she had. Oh, her acting was good, brilliant, even—but she had sold out to the enemy. What had Jay ever seen in her anyway but a way to get at Robby? (Not that Jay would admit it, of course.) And he wanted to *marry* her? Well, so much for that!

Of course if Rob hadn't led her into temptation . . .

"I hope you choke, Robby Tolar," Scott muttered, and stalked away.

St. George swung the sword, and the Devil's dummy head thumped to the floor. One of the musicians grabbed it and ran, whereupon the Devil chased clumsily after it—a bit of humor to defuse a gruesome image. The musicians followed, picking up their tune, chasing the poor Devil and kicking her in the rump.

Then the (still headless) Devil bumped into St. George and grabbed him by the neck and strangled him, so that he too collapsed in a heap, and there they both lay until the Doctor came on stage, complete with carpetbag of potions, and poured something in St. George's mouth which had him up and capering in no time. But while the Doctor was attending to poor, befuddled Mankind, the Devil was pouring the last of the potion down the hollow collar of her costume, and—presto—her head was restored, and she slinked away to deliver the last line: "'I am called Satan, I'm *still* Lord of this World...'"

Applause began, a smattering of appreciative claps from the assortment of stage crew and Faire workmen gathered about.

Rob grinned appreciatively and stood up as well, clapping vigorously. "Perfect!" he called. "Perfect! Couldn't be better. Hey—what say we all bop back to Athens, and I'll treat us all to beer and pizza?"

"Great!"

"Sure!"

"What about you, Dal?"

Dal did not reply, and Rob gazed at her intently. Her eyes were dead. Once her performance had ended, she had seemed to lose her fire, when she should be running on the same adrenaline high he was. Rob knew acting took a lot out of a person, but he'd thought Dal would be more resilient, even considering... what he knew. But a lifeless "Sure," was all the answer she gave him.

One of the musicians rushed up. "Did I do okay? I lost a button on my pants and they kept slipping..."

"You were perfect. Absolutely tremendous."

Perfect, a voice echoed in his mind. *You have served me very well, Rob Tolar.*

"I want to hit something," Scott snarled into the strip of forest he was jogging through. The applause was still echoing behind him, amplified by the flat surfaces that surrounded the theater. He was surprised that so few people could make so much noise; still, whatever else you might say about Rob, his productions were wonderful.

"Oh lordy, lordy, I wanta hit something."

He increased his pace, soon entered virgin forest. The ground began to dip slowly, becoming more marshy. Wisps of fog appeared here and there among the clumps of laurel and rhododendron. That was strange; it had been a warm, clear day. But the woods had their own rules sometimes— he knew that much from the time he'd spent hiking the lonesome trails of north Georgia and eastern Tennessee. After all, the forest had been here first.

The fog grew worse, momentarily obscuring his vision. He slowed, took a few steps, saw it turn thicker yet. He could barely see.

Two more steps, and he came into clear air. A glance up showed blue sky above him, but the fog still hung at his back, pale and menacing. He shrugged and continued onward, knowing that even if he became completely lost he had only a mile or two to go in any direction before he hit pavement, and after that he was home free.

The trail kinked abruptly to the right around a particularly large clump of laurel—and a tree loomed suddenly before him, right in the center of the trail. It struck him as odd that whoever had made the trail (he thought it might be part of an abandoned logging road) would have left an oak smack in the middle of it.

Not that it wasn't a fine tree. Nearly four feet thick its whole surface was whorled and twisted in a fantastic wartwork of knots and boles, even to the roots which rose waist high in a maze of knobs and bulges. Elaborate racks of mushrooms and shelf fungi obscured the furrowed bark in many places, and thick moss obscured other spots. It looked very old, very strange, and altogether quite intimidating.

An acorn fell from the leafy dimness to thwack Scott on the head.

"Watch it, tree," he grunted.

Another acorn found its mark on his nose.

"Watch it!"

A third and a fourth . . .

Scott shot a glare skyward, looking for a reckless squirrel or chipmunk, but saw nothing except a brilliant glitter of sky through a lacework of dark green leaves.

He started to go around it.

—Tripped.

Picked himself up and glared at the tree again.

"All right, bush; you asked for it!"

He drew back his sword and swung a mighty blow straight at the trunk.

The sword bounced back, sending pain shooting through his palm and into his wrist. Even with rattan, some things were too hard to thwack on.

Four acorns fell at once.

"Okay, that does it!"

Scott hit the tree, once, twice, again and again, leaving sticky silver smears across the bark, but doing no damage.

Something inside him snapped, and he began to rain blows on the unyielding wood, seeing the tree at once as a foe, as a symbol of all that stood in his way, and as a surrogate for Rob.

"Take that and that and that, Rob Tolar," he hollered, picturing each blow connecting with Rob's smug face. "Take that and that and that."

He aimed a particularly strong blow at one of the knobs that stuck out chest high.

Struck it . . .

But the sword did not rebound. Instead, it stuck there, stubbornly refusing to move. Scott let go in surprise. The sword stood straight out from the body of the tree as if super-glued to the wood.

He stepped forward, gazed curiously at the juncture.

—Just as a cleft snapped open in the trunk and dark branches thrust him in from behind.

Chapter XVII: I Believe

Jay stared through the heavy glass front of the display case in the rare book library's reading room that housed an exhibit from the Bowman-Smith Collection. On the lower shelf lay three plastic-encapsulated pages from the play. The book in which they had been hidden was not on display, Blondie had explained, because the spine and bindings had been too badly damaged when the book was dropped.

And on the top shelf, pillowed on a strip of black velvet, was the sword.

The blade had been withdrawn partway from the scabbard, and Jay knew as soon as he saw it that it was the same blade as in his dream. The brass and leather hilt was identical, down to the broken binding wire, and the quillons showed the smoothed-out places he remembered. He would have bet any amount of money, too, that there was a nick a hands breadth from the point.

He did not know whether to be thrilled or terrified. Had his earlier encounter with the sword merely *influenced* his dreams? Or—more frightening—had his first touch of the sword perhaps awakened some arcane psychic remnant which had found purchase in his dreams? Jay was not particularly superstitious, but anything as old as the Bowman-Smith sword simply *had* to carry a lot of emotional baggage with it—if you believed in such things.

It had certainly given him a start the one time he'd touched it—as if it remembered every one of those five hundred years, as if every hammer blow that had forged it, every slash and thrust that had been its use, still resonated in the layers of folded steel. Men had died on that blade, and according to all he had read about parapsychology, it was exactly such violent encounters that were the prime progenitors of psychic phenomena. If *anything* could give off vibes, it would certainly be a fourteenth-century broadsword.

Jay tried to conjure in his mind exactly how it had felt before, wondered again if the peculiar elation had been real or imaginary.

But the only way to test that was to actually *touch* the sword, and they wouldn't unlock the case and let him do that. It was too complicated to defuse the burglar alarm, they said.

So Jay was forced to stand and stare, knowing it was the sword in his dream, wondering what that meant. Wondering why he felt that it should mean anything, yet knowing of a certain that it did.

Well, if he couldn't get his hands on it, maybe he could try something else. He might look a little foolish, but the staff already knew he was one of Piper's friends and thus knew he was a bit of a flake. So what was there to worry about?

Jay glanced over his shoulder at Blondie who was sitting behind the kiosk at the side of the room. "Uh—don't get nervous or anything," he said, "but I'm gonna try to pick up some vibes off this sword. It probably won't work anyway."

Blondie nodded wearily, and Jay looked back at the weapon. It was interesting, he reflected, that his eyes kept being drawn particularly to the blade. He wondered if it was significant.

He took a deep breath and tried to duplicate the procedure he had just practiced in his office: to simply let his mind go blank, to see nothing except the juncture of blade and hilt, then not even that. He was afraid that he might have another vision right there; that the library staff might decide once and for all he was a kook and call the cops. But this was too important; he *had* to know more.

A sensation of falling . . . the room receding around him.

Edward, he called. *Edward of Ripon!*

The world spun, and all at once he found himself gazing at a middle-aged man with strong, craggy features, a ruddy complexion, blue eyes, and black beard and hair, the latter rough cut and shoulder long. The thickness of the man's neck hinted at a muscular physique, but none of his body was visible.

Their eyes met for a moment; a spark of recognition passed between them, and Jay knew that he was at last looking upon the face of Edward of Ripon. Their gazes locked, and Jay had the sudden impression that Edward was appraising him.

Then another face swam up from behind those startled blue eyes and replaced Edward's homey, human visage with one that was too pale and too narrow of chin, too slanted of eye and brow and cheekbone to belong to the mortal world, though Jay had seen something like it in his first two dreams. And *those* eyes bored into his soul; recognition once again leapt between them—to be replaced with uncertainty, then with rage.

You are not the one!

The words exploded in Jay's mind like a thunderstorm. He gasped, blinked, and staggered backward, but managed to brace himself against the back of a sofa. A bearded man who had been plowing through manuscripts at a nearby table was somehow there beside him, holding him upright.

"You *okay?*" Blondie called nervously, eyes wide with sudden concern.

Jay shook his head and dragged his eyes back into focus. His head hurt abominably, his heart was beating fit to burst. "Jesus, oh Jesus," was all he could gasp.

"Jesus, oh Jesus," Jay was still panting two minutes later as he darted across South Thomas Street and continued at a solid run across the north perimeter parking lot, oblivious to the rush hour traffic. He was unable to stop the chills that were pouring over him, unable to slow the frantic throbbing of his heart, the pounding of his legs, as an overload of adrenaline sent him flying in near-blind panic.

Something had reached out to him from the sword; something that was in—*no, be rational, guy*—was *associated* with the sword. Then something else had interrupted—had spoken to him. Or had there even *been* words? Whatever it was had been comprised of equal parts anger and hatred.

Hadn't it?

It wasn't like he'd been real relaxed lately. Progress on the thesis was going slowly; Sparks had been working him far too hard—and add the blessed dreams and Dal's little bombshell, and mix well with one of Piper's caprices that had LaWanda all stirred up . . . well, that was *more* than enough to keep a guy off balance.

Except that he *had* heard those words and seen those faces. There *was* something to that sword, something altogether beyond his experience. And the play wasn't exactly typical either. And for the first time he asked the question no one seemed to have considered: *why had the play been hidden?*

Thoroughly winded, he paused and looked around, surprised to find himself nearly at O'Malley's. A cold wind whipped in from the north, and Jay's chills redoubled—redoubled when he should by rights have been sweating like a pig. He stood still for a moment, too numb to move, too numb to think; allowed his gaze to drift toward the Oconee River.

Something moved there, white and tenuous.

Fog.

A final shudder wracked him. Fog was creeping into the riverbed below O'Malley's.

Fog on a late April evening, when it had been sunny earlier?

Even as he watched, the white tendrils thickened.

It was well after six when Jay finally got home, and the sudden recurrence of fog at the foot of Hancock Hill hadn't helped any, had almost completed weirding him out when he'd found himself driving into the murky stuff. Unable to see beyond his hood ornament, he'd narrowly missed a badly parked car. And he was trying very hard not to consider that this was something else that wasn't normal.

Reality, it seemed, was reordering itself about once every two minutes.

Jay padded barefoot into the kitchen and put two slices of leftover pizza in the microwave to warm, hoping the enforced routine would help calm him. While he waited, he stared at the Scarboro Faire poster push-pinned to the wall. It was strange the way the Faire had become a nexus that had snared so many of his friends.

The timer buzzed, and he removed the hot slices, grabbed a couple of paper towels to serve as napkins, snagged a beer, and sauntered back into the living room. After setting the pizza down on the footlocker that served as an end table, he trotted off to the bedroom to retrieve his copy of the Bowman-Smith Codex.

A moment later, he took a healthy swig of suds, leaned back in the deep-pillowed comfort of his papa-san chair, and began to read.

Halfway through he realized he had no idea what he'd

read, so he took another swig and started over. His lack of sleep the night before had caught up with him. Maybe if he read aloud . . .

He cleared his throat, and hesitated. He'd been doing that when he and Piper and LaWanda had had their . . . occurrence. Oh well, might as well duplicate circumstances as closely as he could. What did he have to lose?

" 'I am called Satan, I'm Lord of this World . . . ' " he began. " 'I've more power in one finger than a king or an early . . . ' " He tried to relax, to let the words flow naturally, without forcing rhyme or rhythm.

As he continued, his voice assumed a greater degree of authority, quickly becoming stronger and more melodious. Somewhere along the way his accent shifted slightly, picked up a lilt that was not his own. It sounded vaguely British at first, then began to take on overtones of Scots or Irish. Whatever it was, it only added to the power of the words, as the recitation gained in strength and resonance. *God,* he thought, *I sound good.*

And he felt marvelous, powerful, as if each word poured new strength into him. Unconsciously he stood, suddenly aware of the whole world around him glittering with new clarity. Somewhere there was music, familiar music. He barely glanced at the page as his voice thundered on.

And then his heart skipped a beat, and his body tensed in sudden alarm; he could feel his muscles straining, suddenly pulling against each other so fiercely he knew that if they did not stop he would rip apart. Pain filled him, as muscle and tendon tightened further. His heart thumped fit to explode. His lungs were fire. He'd felt queasy before but nothing like this. Yet he could not stop, did not want to, wanted to continue hearing the pure beauty of his voice driving forth those words, though it cost him his life.

An agony clamped on his heart.

" 'I am called Satan, I'm *still* Lord of this World.' "

And with that the play ended.

—To be followed by a scream, long and anguished, as

the agony exploded away from him, leaving him empty. He had just time to suck in a long, blessed breath—

The sudden dull silence of the cozy living room was split by a noise like thunder. A force—wind or pure sound, he didn't know which—slammed Jay back in his chair. His eyes stretched wide, but he clamped them closed again, not believing what now lay beyond them, not daring to gaze once more upon that impossible slit of *nothingness* that halved the room from floor to ceiling: the slit at the center of which he had barely glimpsed a mind-boggling vista of dark forests and purple mountains and strangely familiar green birds.

The rumble and the wind ended abruptly. He heard the bedroom door slam. There was a heavy thump, and Jay opened his eyes again.

Piper was slumped on the carpet like a lifeless puppet, but his eyes were open, and his lips were moving. "They made me play for them, man," he gasped, making feeble clutching motions in Jay's direction. "They *made* me!"

Before he knew it Jay was kneeling by his friend's side. "*Who . . . who* made you play for them? Come on, man, tell me." Then, "Shit, Piper, where the hell did you *come* from?"

Piper tried to smile. "I think you said it. I think I just got out of Hell."

Jay leaned back on his heels. "Oh, no! Don't lay *that* kind of crap on me, not when you just popped here out of thin air. You *didn't* just pop out of air, did you? Tell me you didn't just pop out of the air!"

"I . . . Jay? *Is* that you?"

Jay laid a hand on Piper's chest. His heart was thumping as wildly as Jay's. He started to help him up, but Piper stopped him.

"I just wanta lie here a minute, Jason. The world's still spinning— Say, 're my pipes okay?" He began patting the floor around him as if searching for something.

Jay saw them lying a little way behind him in a tangle of black fabric and dark wood. "Yeah, they're fine."

"Good, I was scared I'd lost 'em."

Jay helped Piper to a sitting position, still on the floor but leaning against the sofa. He took a deep breath. "Okay, Piperman, you wanta tell me what happened?"

Piper shook his head. "No way. No fuckin' way."

"Wanta tell me why no way?"

"You'd think I'm crazy."

Jay hugged him. "I *already* think that, bro, but then I think I am too."

Piper smiled weakly, but remained silent.

Jay shook him. "I've *got* to know, Piper. It's not like I'm *used* to claps of thunder in my house and people popping into my living room out of nowhere."

Piper clutched at Jay's shirtfront. Tears brimmed in his eyes. He was shaking.

Jay held him there for a moment until the shuddering subsided, then helped him onto the couch.

"Okay, look, Piper, I'm gonna go get—"

"—Myra?"

Jay looked up to see her standing in the doorway, topknot awry, arms folded. "I should hope so. What the hell's going on up here? Something explode or what?" Her gaze fell on Piper. "Oh my God!" she cried as she rushed forward and stared at the boy.

Piper focused bleary eyes on her and smiled crookedly. "Oh, hi, Myra, how's it goin'?" His eyelids dropped. In a moment he was snoring.

"What do you *mean* 'how's it going'? Where the *hell* have you been? Don't you know your lady's been worried sick about you?"

"Wanta call her?" Jay suggested.

Myra shook her head. "She's due home any minute, was gonna do some posing for me later on. But that doesn't answer my question."

Jay looked up, wide-eyed. "I . . . I think something abnormal's happened."

Her eyes narrowed. "*Abnormal?* Like what?"

"Like that noise you heard a couple of minutes ago."

"Yeah, sure." She looked away.

"Would you like to know what that noise *was?*" Jay persisted.

Myra raised an eyebrow. "I'll let you tell me."

"That was Piper arriving."

"*Arriving!*" Myra sputtered. "Jay Madison, what are you *talking* about?"

Jay shrugged. "I'm not sure, Myra. I was reading that copy of the Bowman-Smith Codex Piper did for me, and then it got real weird all of a sudden, first like I couldn't stop, then like I was about to explode. And then I finished, and screamed, and *bang*, there was that noise and I was staring right into a—I don't know. It looked like a—like a hole in the air in the middle of the room. And in the middle of that hole was—it was like another country, then suddenly the hole was gone and there was Piper."

Myra looked at him askance. "You're *not* serious."

"Well, I kinda wish I wasn't, but the fact is Piper's here, and scared to death by something. *I* didn't let him in, I'm pretty sure he didn't let *himself* in, and it's pretty obvious *you* didn't let him in."

"So he just zapped here from Mars?"

"That's what I was getting ready to find out when you came in."

Jay did not wait for Myra's reply before he rejoined his friend on the couch. Piper appeared to be conscious once more, so Jay handed him his beer, which he took greedily. Myra went into the kitchen and returned with a bottle for herself and a replacement for Jay.

Jay put his arm around Piper's shoulders and hugged him gently. "Okay, Piperman, ready to tell us what happened?"

Piper buried his face in his hands. "Oh Lord, man, it was so awful! So beautiful and so weird, but so bloody fuckin' *awful!*"

"*What* was, Piper?"

Piper swallowed, leaned back, and began. "Well, like

you know I was in kinda bad shape when I—what day is it, man?"

"What do you *mean,* 'what day'?" Myra asked.

"It's Friday, Piper," Jay said, shooting the girl a warning glance. "April thirtieth."

Piper's face brightened. "Well, that's a relief! I've only been gone a day. Bet Wannie's pissed."

"Worried's more like it, but get on with your story."

"Oh, right . . . Anyway, I rode out into the country, out past the mall. Nearly in Bogart. I wasn't really paying 'tention. I was upset, you unnerstand."

"Right."

"So anyway, I found this nice little clearing back in the woods, and I started crankin' up the old pipes, 'cause I couldn't find anybody to talk to and I thought I'd just let the music sing to the trees and the night sky, or something. I do that when I get down. Anyway, I started up on 'King of the Fairies,' and was really cooking when suddenly I felt cold, and then everything *changed.* Well, not everything. I was still standing in the middle of the woods, but it wasn't our woods no more, and then this bunch of lights came and circled around me, and it turned out to be people, and I met their head honcho, and he told me to play for them."

"People? What kinda people?"

"The *little* people, Jason. Elves, fairies, whatever. Except their leader. He was a big guy. Tall as Scott—thinner, though. Told me he was their king."

"Their king?"

"The king of the—of the fairies, I guess. Well—he didn't actually say that, but he sure implied the hell out of it."

"Oh, come on, Piperman. Give me a break!"

"I *am* giving you a break, man, just by telling you, 'cause believe me, if I'd had a chance to pop back here by myself, I would have. And I'd have thought long and hard and never said a word to anybody. You guys caught me off guard."

"Okay, so what'd you do?"

"Nothing, really. I played for them. They danced, and I played, and they brought me food and stuff to drink—wine, I think. And I just never got tired. Best damn playing I ever did, too; and you know what? I could have gone on forever, I think. Until—"

"Until what?"

"Well, it was sorta like a storm—no, more like bein' *inside* and hearin' a storm comin' up all of a sudden *outside* or something, except that the wind really did start gettin' up. And that kinda reminded me of that storm you and me and Wannie sat through, and that put me to wishing I was home even worse than ever, so then I remembered something the tall guy said about 'King of the Fairies' being magic and all, and started up on it again. And—*bang, thud, swoosh*—I'm back here. And all of a sudden I realized they'd had me. They'd *had* me, man, under complete control. It was awful. Bloody, fuckin' awful."

"But you don't know what brought you back?"

Piper shook his head.

"Could it have been this head honcho guy or something?"

"Don't think so. He'd left by then—not that it made any difference!"

Jay's eyes narrowed. "What was that you just said? Something about the tall guy telling you the song was magic?"

"Oh yeah, right. Said I was a brave piper to play 'King of the Fairies' there because—let's see, how'd he put it? 'It is a song of power, else it could not have pierced the World Walls and brought you here—though it needs the power of another to awaken. . . .'" Piper's features brightened with surprise. "Jeez, I can't believe I remembered that."

Jay regarded his buddy curiously. "Are you sure the line was 'It needs the power of another to awaken?'"

Piper nodded.

A chill raced down Jay's spine. If that meant what he thought it did . . .

"Okay, Piperman," he managed finally. "You look whipped; how 'bout you just relax here a little while."

"Oh, I am, I'm so tired." He was instantly out again.

"So," Myra said. "What d'ya think?"

"I think something pretty goddamn bad's happened to Piper."

"But you don't believe all that bullshit about—about the other world, do you?"

Jay shrugged, almost certain that he *did* believe. "Why not? Folklore's full of tales of people carried off to visit the fairies."

"And you think . . . ?"

"As far as that goes, I don't know what to think. All I know's what I found out from reading the early stuff and from a few real recent things. Except for basic fairy lore, which I learned from playing around in the *Secret Common-Wealth*."

"Oh lord."

"Yeah, this is weird shit."

Myra cocked her head as a wild scrabbling and thumping came from the bedroom. "What's that noise?"

"Guess I'd better go check." Jay levered himself off the floor.

Myra followed him. "You guys don't have a *bird*, do you?"

Jay paused at the door. "No, why?"

"I think I hear one flying around in there. Listen! There it is again, louder!" Then, when they had entered the bedroom and Jay had turned on the light: "Oh, Jay, look—over by the window!"

Frantically beating itself against the glass pane was the greenest bird Jay had ever seen.

"Now where'd *that* come from, I wonder—*Oh no!*"

The bird had knocked itself out. It tumbled to the floor and lay still. Its neck was broken.

Myra picked up the tiny limp body. "Poor little thing."

"What kind of bird *is* it?" Jay asked, as he followed her

back into the living room, though he had a sick feeling he already knew.

Myra looked at him with wide eyes and whispered, "Jason—I don't think there's a bird on this *planet* like this one. It doesn't have any legs—and doesn't look like it ever had any!"

"You're kidding!"

She held it out. Jay looked at it—and gasped. What Myra had said was true: the bird's belly was as smooth as a feathered egg.

"Myra," he whispered, as he probed the feathers with a finger, "I think you're right. It must have flown through as soon as the slit opened and been trapped in the bedroom when the door slammed."

"She is," came Piper's shaky voice from the couch. "It's like I been trying to tell you. It's *not* from this planet—nor even from this world."

"What d'you mean?"

"It's a bird from *there,* one of *their* birds. There were a lot of 'em. You know—"

"My *God!*" Myra's scream interrupted him.

Jay was beside her in an instant. "What?"

"Look at it!"

Jay stared at the small green form in Myra's open palm, and felt his heart skip a beat. It was becoming transparent, fading away, as if it had never been. In an instant it was gone.

Myra wiped her hand on her thigh. "I didn't see that. Tell me I didn't see that!"

"But you did, Myra. And I think I've seen one of those birds before, too."

"Yeah, I know," Piper said. "We saw one when you and me and Wannie got lost in the woods that time."

"Oh lord, Piper, you're right! And you know what I was doing when we got lost?"

"What do you mean?"

"I was reading that play, aloud. Same as I was just before you . . . appeared."

Myra frowned. "Come on, Jay, this is too much. Get real."

"You got a *better* idea?"

"You really think reading that play summoned this bird?"

"No," Jay replied, "I think reading that play—I don't know—opens some kind of gate between the *worlds* or something, which that bird, and Piper, came through! Maybe me and Piper and Wannie went through it the other way."

Myra's brow wrinkled thoughtfully. "Well, is there any way to prove it? Could you do it again?"

Jay shuddered, remembering how close to death he felt he had come the last time he had read it. Yet he felt strangely invigorated now, as though the whole experience had left him stronger. What had Piper said? "It needs the power of another to awaken?" Did that mean that he, skinny Jay Madison, had some kind of power, perhaps power that had itself just awakened? For that matter what *was* power? Was it the same as magic? Was *that* what had caused the dreams? Facilitated his communion with the sword? Caused him and his friends to drive out of the world?

But if he had power, maybe other people did as well. Was *that* what Robby had used to influence Dal and De-Renne, and maybe even Monteagle?

Or the late California McLaren, who had died of a heart attack right out of the blue?

Oh, Jesus!

"Jay?" Myra prompted.

Jay took a long, shuddering breath as another piece of puzzle fell tentatively into place, revealing yet more of the terrifying picture.

"I . . . I don't think it'd be too cool to read it again just now," he managed finally, his eyes growing wider, "'cause you know something, Myra Jane? McLaren was supposed to have been working on that play when she died, and— Jesus! Suppose . . . suppose she did what I did: read the whole thing aloud—and something happened like what happened here. God knows I felt it almost killed me; suppose it *did* kill her! Maybe she wasn't strong enough, or . . . or maybe she saw something like I saw and it scared her to death. Hell, suppose something came *through* and killed her!"

Myra bit her lip in consternation. "But that doesn't make *sense;* that play's been read lots of times. They're rehearsing it at the Faire after all. And what about when they're learning lines? Something can't happen every time."

"Why not? Do you imagine anybody's keeping track? All I know's that something weird happens when you read that play—or maybe only when the right person reads it— someone with power or whatever."

He thought of Dal's tale of being stalked, and shivered. Maybe McLaren's reading *had* released something. . . .

"Oh my God," he cried. "Dal could be in serious trouble."

Chapter XVIII: King of Birds

"Any luck?" Myra asked from the sofa, as Jay grimaced in frustration and dropped the receiver back on the cradle.

"No," he replied ominously, "and that's bad."

"But if Dal had a late rehearsal they might have gone out to eat afterwards."

Jay shook his head. "No, something's wrong. I *know* it."

"Yeah, but *how* do you know?"

"'Cause Dal's phone rang and rang."

"So, she's not there. That's all that means."

"No, you don't understand," Jay said as calmly as he could, "she's got that answering machine, and phones in every room. If she's there, she answers, period. If she's not there or doesn't want to be bothered, she leaves the machine on. Look, could you keep an eye on Piper? I think I'd better get over there."

"But Jay..."

"I'm going *over,* Myra. She may be pissed at me, but that doesn't mean I don't still love her. If she's in trouble, I've gotta know!"

He grabbed his jacket and stormed out the door, keys already jingling in his hand.

In the two hours since Jay had last been out, the fog had grown much thicker. Milledge Avenue was totally closed in, and South Lumpkin Street was even worse. And when he finally turned left down the steeper slope of Welch Place nearly thirty minutes after leaving home, visibility was reduced to zero. He found himself forced to creep along with the windows down and once had to open the door so he could see the pavement.

At last he braked the Monarch to a stop in the parking lot in front of Dal's building. He was here now, and suddenly didn't know what to do next. He glanced up the sloping hill to Dal's apartment, could barely make out brighter places in the fog that might be the security lights, the two dim squares that could mark Dal's living room windows.

Steeling himself, he stepped out. The fog reached out to engulf him, probing him with chill, damp tendrils. Had he not known he was in Athens, he might have been anywhere—or nowhere. Cautiously he made his way up the paved slope. A shape loomed into view to the right, which proved to be the red Toyota MR2 that belonged to Dal's downstairs neighbor. The fog was thinner there.

And there was Dal's Prelude, in another thin place only three feet to the left.

Which meant she should be home, too.

He made it to her door. Lights glimmered fitfully through the haze from the windows of the floor above, but her curtains were drawn and he could discern no shapes behind them. He hesitated there, then bounded up the two steps and knocked forcefully.

He heard sounds inside: a sort of scuffling. Somebody

was coming. He knocked again. "Dal?" he called softly, then louder. "Dal. Dal? It's me, Jay. Are you all right? You don't have to let me in; we don't even have to talk, but I need to know if you're okay."

More scuffling sounds. A thick, padded thump that didn't sound encouraging at all.

"Dal?" He was pounding on the door now.

"Jay . . . Is that . . . you?"

It was Dal's voice, all right, but it sounded weak, uncertain.

More thudding, followed by a rustling sound, the thump of feet on the stairs. Then a whispered "Oh my God!" And silence.

"Dal?" Jay rattled the knob. The door was locked. He twisted harder, set his shoulder against the thick wood and pushed, then realized to his chagrin that he had a key. Dal had given him one long ago, but he so rarely had reason to go by her apartment when she wasn't there he'd forgotten it.

He unlocked the door and cautiously pushed it open.

—And came face to face with horror.

It was standing halfway up the steep stairs that led from the tiny entry vestibule up to the vaulted living room; golden eagle's head large as his own, slitted yellow eyes, talons big as a dinner plate. A tan-gold length of low-slung leonine body sprawling up the steps behind.

And Dal at the top of those stairs, clad in her fuzzy white bathrobe, traces of greasepaint still visible on her face. Her mouth hung open slightly; her eyes looked dull and lifeless.

"Dal!" Jay screamed before the gryphon began to stretch those talons toward him, even as its cruel, hooked beak gaped open.

Beyond it, he glimpsed Dal's blank-eyed stare—then backed away and slammed the door behind him, his mind awash with terror and confusion as he ran down the parking lot. He wanted to get in the car and drive away—*anywhere*.

But he didn't.

Jay Madison, he railed, *you are a coward and an idiot.*
He risked a glance back toward the apartment, saw nothing
but the streaming fog. Reluctantly, he squared his
shoulders and started back up the hill.

A fragmentary plan began to emerge. He would scoot
around back to where Dal's railed deck was, then shinny
up the corner posts from the apartment underneath and look
in through the glass doors that opened on the living room.
From there maybe he could get some kind of handle on the
situation.

He skirted around a bank of low hedges to the back side
of the building until he could look up at Dal's apartment. A
moment only it took him to climb up the cast iron post that
led to the deck, a moment more to clamber over the railing.

Finally faced with the doors, he hesitated. There was no
use trying to move it; Dal kept a stick in the tracks. And he
was not prepared to break the glass.

He crept closer to the door, grateful for his black jeans
and T-shirt, which might render him less visible. The
drapes were drawn, of course. But they were not very
thick, and a gap showed in the center where they didn't
quite meet. He peeped in there.

The room was illuminated by a single lamp. Dal sat on
the raised hearth before the fireplace, staring into space.

And at her feet was the creature he had seen.

He gazed at it, captivated. It was a gryphon, all right—
and real. He could see its feline sides rising and falling
gently, the slow tensing and untensing of its claws—catlike in back, an eagle's head and legs in front. Its eyes
were nearly closed.

Jay looked closer—and bumped his head against the
glass.

The gryphon was on its feet in an instant, turning its
beaked face toward him.

Jay backed away in horror, then stumbled on a deck
chair and staggered backward. Thus it was that he saw the
beast claw the curtain aside to glare out at him. Their eyes

met. Beyond it he could see Dal, still sitting, still staring.

The gryphon was staring, too. Right at Jay. The whole world was going yellow. . . .

He clamped his eyelids shut.

Open them, a voice seemed to sound—yet not in his ears. *Open them, mortal.*

No! Jay thought in desperation.

OPEN THEM.

No.

Yes! Yes! Yes!

Every word-thought was a blast of pain in his brain. Jay gasped.

Another blast, and another.

His eyelids popped open.

The beast was still before him, right on the other side of the glass door. It had raised its left talon, and was carefully incising a pattern into the glass.

Jay watched, spellbound, as the design grew, took on a life of its own, coiled outward to frame the whole doorway, then began to assume three dimensions and stretch through the glass toward him. Lights began to flicker along those lines, following the great spirals first outward, then back to the center.

Quite against his will, Jay started forward, then tripped and toppled sideways, arms flailing.

He grabbed the iron porch railing—and almost cried out as the lights in the pattern flickered and vanished.

The gryphon glared at him but took no other action.

Jay's mind whirled. What had happened? What had he done that had broken off the attack?

Suddenly he knew: iron. Cold iron was supposed to be proof against the things of Faerie. Maybe if he could just break off a piece of railing or find some other piece of iron, he could—

You could, the mind-voice affirmed. *But long before you could reach me, your lady would be dead with my beak in her throat and her own blood feeding me Power. So you see, mortal, if you value her life, you have no choice but to leave us.*

Jay started forward again.

The gryphon opened its beak in warning. A flick of black tongue lashed out, a splatter of spittle struck the glass and sent small tendrils of vapor rising there.

Jay stared at the creature in horror. His heart flip-flopped, his gorge was rising.

"I'll be back, though," he screamed helplessly, as he vaulted over the railing. "By God, I swear I will!"

But what will I do when I come? he added, as he hit the ground and rolled, then gasped as a pain shot up his ankle. Grunting in agony, he managed to regain his feet and stagger a few yards, then half limped, half hopped back through the parking lot.

Mind-words followed him as he went, a derisive chant in his brain: *Fool's blood, fool's blood, fool's blood.* There was the car now, in its own fogless space.

Fool's blood, fool's blood, fool's blood . . .

Somehow he made it, jerked the door open, fell inside.

Fool's blood, fool's blood, fool's—

He slammed the door and the taunts cut off abruptly.

Jay wanted to kill, wanted to take a sword and stab and stab until that sleek feline body, that awful feathered head were awash with gore. He could imagine himself doing it, too. Could see himself, sword in hand, holding off the gryphon. The image was becoming more concrete by the instant. Was he on the verge of yet another waking dream?

But the vision lingered, and he found himself staring at his outstretched hand, imagining a sword clutched there.

And the sword he imagined was the one from his dreams—the one in the library.

"Oh Jesus," he cried, "let that be the way! Let my guess be the right one!"

He unclutched his hand and cranked the car. In the windows of Dal's apartment behind him, the fitful lamplight had vanished.

* * *

Jay sat at the Lumpkin-Milledge traffic light and fumed. He couldn't call the police for help, of course. After all, what would he tell them? That his girlfriend was being held captive by a telepathic eagle-headed lion who liked to draw Celtic interlaces on glass with its claws?

Sparks, then? Would the Elf forsake his foolishness about brownies long enough to listen to him objectively? Probably not. Then he remembered that Sparks was out of town—again.

The light turned green.

Jay found himself once more turning down Milledge, heading home through the fog at the same nerve-racking creep. Myra and Piper might have some suggestions. It was all he could think of. He tried to remain calm as cars loomed out at him from the grayness. Once he almost struck a jogger who veered into the street right in his path. The finger the guy shot him reminded him once more of the sword. It all had to be connected, if only he could find the secret. The creature, Dal, the play, the sword, the dreams: all were somehow part of one pattern. "'The play's the thing,'" he found himself repeating, "'wherein I'll catch the conscience of the king.'"

"We've *got* to go to the library, Piper," Jay pleaded, still a little breathless from his dash up the stairs a moment before. "We've absolutely *got* to. I've got to get hold of that sword."

Piper shook his head. "No way! *I'm* staying here with my lady." He gazed beseechingly up at the recently arrived LaWanda, who stood imperiously behind him, looking by turns relieved, confused, and for the moment as though she might like to skin Jay Madison alive.

"Library's closed," she said flatly. "You'd have to break in, and no way am I lettin' Piper outta my sight for something like *that*—not now!"

Jay was finding it hard to control himself, given what he'd just seen at Dal's. "Look, Wannie," he gritted, "I *know* it's closed—hell, it's been closed for hours. But I've got to get in there. Dal's in terrible danger, and the sword may be my only weapon."

"Yeah, but why does it have to be *that* sword? If Dal's in trouble, wouldn't any sword do? For that matter, what do you need a sword for at all? Why not just call the cops?"

Jay shot her a withering glare. "'Cause *that* sword just may be magic."

LaWanda's eyes flashed. "Bullshit, boy. You ain't takin' my Piperman off nowhere."

"He tell you anything about where he was, Wannie? He give you the tale of J. Morry Murphy and the King of the Fairies?"

"He did," LaWanda said flatly. "Only difference is that *I* think he's sick—*you* believe him."

"Which makes *me* sick, huh?" Jay snorted.

"Or crazy."

Jay ignored her and took a deep, slow breath, forcing himself to become calmer. He flopped down beside Piper. "Looks like you're doing better, anyway," he managed. "How you feelin', guy?"

"Fine, my buddy, just fine," Piper replied. "Only thing is: my memories are, like, fading. I can barely remember—"

"No!" Jay cried. "Don't let 'em go—they may be useful."

Myra stared at him appraisingly. "Well, I don't know what else is wrong with you, Jason, but you *look* like—"

"Like I've just seen a ghost? Yeah, well, it was worse than that, Myra."

"Crazy man," Wannie told her.

Myra shook her head. "No, I don't think so. Something *did* scare him, you can see it in his eyes."

"Then he better start talkin' sense."

"I *am* talking sense," Jay shot back. "Except that it's the sense of another reality." He took another deep breath, clapped his hands on his knees. "Okay, look: there's *something* funny going on here; we all agree with that, right?

Myra, you saw the bird; Wannie, you'll agree that something weird happened after we'd been to Scarboro that time—getting lost when we shouldn't, and that weird storm and all?"

LaWanda nodded slowly. "Okay, go on. . . ."

"Well, I'd been reading the play that time, right?"

"Yeah, but Myra already told me your theory about that."

"But you'll agree that was strange, okay?"

"Yeah, it was strange. Got my mojo up, that's for sure."

"Okay, and I was reading the play when Piper reappeared, right?"

"I'll take your word for it."

"So, okay. But Myra'll at least attest to the fact that there was one godawful noise when Piper appeared."

Myra nodded reluctantly. "Yeah, but I still say that's *stretching* it. I keep telling you: there *can't* have been a manifestation *every* time somebody reads it aloud. They've been rehearsing the thing for almost a month now."

"Yeah, but looks like at least some of the time, when anybody who's *not* associated with the official production reads it—reads it aloud, anyway—something happens."

"I think you're stretching it there, too," LaWanda noted.

"Okay, maybe I am, but you'll at least admit you got a feeling when Piper vanished, right? You *said* you did, anyway."

"Yeah, okay."

"But that's not part of the pattern," Myra pointed out.

Jay looked puzzled. "No, not exactly, or at least I haven't figured out where it comes in yet. But he was close to Bogart, right? And Dal said she had to go to rehearsal, which would probably have been over just about the time he disappeared."

"—Which I still don't believe in," Myra inserted.

Jay ignored her. "Yeah, but suppose what the man told him was true: Suppose 'King of the Fairies' is magic, and suppose it does need the power—magic or whatever—of another to awaken. Where would that power come from? *I* wasn't reading it then, so what does that leave? Maybe the play? Maybe Piper was near enough to Scarboro for a rehearsal to exert some influence. How does your juju feel about that, Wannie? About Piper's story, I mean? Do *you* think he's lying? Shoot, all you gotta do is look at him to know *something* happened!"

LaWanda's eyes were suddenly huge. "I don't know, boys and girls, I don't *know* nothin'. But I got a feelin'— just a *feelin'*, mind you, that Jay may be right."

"Got your mojo working?"

"My mojo don't work all the time. Can't force the mojo."

"But what difference does that make, anyway?" Myra wanted to know. "And what's any of this got to do with the sword?"

"Because I *still* haven't had a chance to tell you guys what happened to me at Dal's." He paused. "Shit! I haven't told you any of this have I? You don't know about Ms. DeRenne, or my third vision, or about when I looked at the sword this afternoon. Well, folks, you better sit down, 'cause this is gonna take some *serious* believing."

"We're listenin', white boy."

"Okay. Well, it all started this afternoon—"

"So when you touched the iron railing, that ended it?" Myra asked when Jay had finished.

Jay nodded. "Yeah, and the—the telepathy or whatever it was stopped when I got in the car—the *steel* car, mind you. And steel's supposed to be proof against the fairies."

"Whew," LaWanda sighed. "That's the craziest story I *ever* heard anybody tell."

"Yeah, but do you believe me? Based on what you've seen, what you've felt, do you believe me?"

"Jay," LaWanda began, "I'm...I'm not saying I believe you, but now I think about it a bunch of things *have* seemed kinda funny lately, includin' them dreams of yours. So, since you said it happened when you read the play, maybe you should do that again. See what happens."

Jay felt a shiver roll down his spine. "Oh no! I'm not gonna risk that again!"

"But Jay," Myra said reasonably, "it's the only way to prove your case, looks like to me."

"Beyond simply trusting me? I mean look, ladies, I know I've got a tendency to flip out a little, once in a while, but not this time. And I have *got* to get into the library. I can't waste any more time."

"You're not still serious about that, are you?"

Jay drew himself up very straight. "Certainly I am, whether you guys come along or not. Piperman, you got any idea how to get in? I mean presuming you wanted to break in, could you?"

Piper shook his head, "No way, man! I'm in enough trouble already. I'm not going out again, not with *them* maybe out there. —Where you need to get to, anyway?"

"Rare Book Room."

"Oh lord, Jason, they've got security out the *wazoo* over there."

"But you know all about it, right?"

"Some of it. Don't know how much. I've still got my card, though."

"Your card?"

Piper nodded. "Security card."

"But that'll set off an alarm or something, won't it?"

"Yeah," Piper said, "but I know a way around the secured places."

"So you've *gotta* help me."

"Then what're you gonna do?" Myra asked. "You can't—"

"I'll go," Piper interrupted. "I think I know a way to get in."

LaWanda's sharp inhale sounded like a hiss, but Jay eyed him hopefully. "Sure you're up to it? I'm willing to try it alone, if you'll tell me what to do."

"What I had in mind," Piper replied, "you can't *do*

without me. Words and music, man: your words, my music."

"Huh?"

"Well, like, I've been figurin', man. Tryin' to find out how I got home. And the best I can decide, you were readin' the play, I was playin' 'King of the Fairies'—and wishin'."

Jay eyes him with a mixture of doubt and horror. "So you think if I were to read the play, while you played 'King of the Fairies' . . ."

"And I wished real hard to be in the library . . ."

"We'd wind up there? Come on, Piperman."

"No, man, it's worth a try, 'cause believe me. *I* don't doubt you; I *know* there's another world."

Five minutes later they were ready. Piper sat in the middle of the sofa with his Uillean pipes tucked under his arm, while Jay stood behind him with one hand on his shoulder and the play in the other. Myra and LaWanda flanked him, both with flashlights in hand. Each girl grasped one of Jay's arms.

"Ready?" Piper asked.

Jay nodded, took a deep breath, and began: "'I am called Satan, I'm Lord of this World . . .'"

And Piper closed his eyes and slowly started to play.

"'I've more power in one finger than a king or an earl . . .'" Jay continued. His words droned on, as the music buzzed in his brain. It was hard to concentrate: the words, the music, his desire for haste, for *any* solution; his fervent wish that Piper's wild notion was right.

"'See that land yonder? That land is mine.

And see you that creature, that gryphon so fine? . . .'"

The music picked up speed, and Jay too read faster, feeling the Power warming within him—but not like before, not filling him up, not twisting his body into agony, but entering somewhere, then flowing out once more.

Words on a page, like tadpoles in a pond, words swimming before his eyes, his tongue a tangle of current around them.

And then cold and darkness. A screaming in his ears—
two screams.

Music trickling down to a dull buzz, and then gone.

"'I'm still Lord of this World.'"

Gray walls and carpet beneath his feet.

"It worked," he whispered, then: "Oh my God!"

The sword was gone. The velvet where it had lain
looked undisturbed, but there was no sign of the weapon.

Nor was there any trace of Myra or LaWanda. Piper
alone was with him.

"Oh no!" he moaned, then looked hopelessly at Piper.
"Any idea where it might be?"

Piper shook his head. "Not like them to move things
around in cases like that."

"Then where is it?"

Piper reached down and removed something from the
carpet. "This look familiar?"

Jay studied it for a moment. "Yeah," he sighed, "that's
Robby's tigereye key fob. Mom gave it to him for
Christmas."

Chapter XIX: Song for a Future Generation

Rob stood in Dal's darkened living room staring at the sword in his hand. Cathal the gryphon rubbed against him, but he evinced no surprise. It all made perfect sense now; the plan was nigh to fruition. He cast his mind back a couple of hours, remembering . . .

It is time, Robert Tolar.

Rob jerked himself awake. What time *was* it, he wondered, rubbing his eyes. A glance at his watch showed eight o'clock. On the tube *Entertainment Tonight* was just ending.

Now *that* was peculiar. It was awfully early for him to be dozing off in his own living room on a Friday night. He frowned. His head was a muddle, a dull blur between pulses of pain. Surely he hadn't had *that* much to drink after rehearsal. He tried to remember. He recalled driving back, keeping one eye in the mirror for Dal following in the Prelude, then sitting around in DaVinci's drinking san-

284

gria and eating pizza and giant cookies and cheese soup. But beyond that was a blank. He didn't remember paying the bill or leaving or anything, much less getting home. He seemed to recollect planning something with Dal, but . . .

It is time to begin, Robert Tolar.

Those words pounding in his head again, insinuating themselves between the pulses of his headache. A part of him was frightened by them. But another part cherished every word they spoke.

Rob nodded dully, stood up, and strode mechanically to the center of the living room. *What am I doing?* a part of him asked.

He closed his eyes, tried to banish the headache, the clouds of muddle. Of *course* nothing was wrong. It was simply time, that was all. Time right now.

Abruptly, the muddle was gone. Rob felt wonderful. Strength had flooded into him, and he felt ready to take on the world.

You need the sword.

The sword . . . ?

You saw it two days ago in the library. Search your memories; I will show you.

Rob closed his eyes again, let himself float like he had that time he had found himself in Dal's apartment. An image came into his mind, and quickly clarified. The hilt, just so . . . the scabbard like this . . . the blade . . .

It was hard to focus on the blade, so he confirmed his efforts to effecting a minute vision of the hilt.

Now, want *it!*

Rob discovered that he *did* want it: wanted it more than anything in the world. He found himself imagining how it would feel to curl his hand around that wire-wound leather, the exact amount of pull on his forearm it would take to heft it—

Cold and a sensation of falling . . .

Rob opened his eyes and found himself in a chamber illuminated only by single security lights at either end. It was the reading room of the rare book library.

The place was dead quiet, but he had a feeling of being watched. Everything was the same as it was in the daytime, except for the gloom, and the relatively brighter blinking of tiny lights on normally unobtrusive security devices.

But ahead of him a third light, a pale fluorescent, illuminated the glass case where lay the sword.

He reached toward it, then noticed the alarm wires that traced the edges.

Take it.

I can't.

Take it!

There are alarms. I'll get caught.

Take it, I tell you!

There's glass in the way.

There is only glass because you believe *there is glass.*

Come again?

Believe there is no glass and there will be no glass.

How?

Close your eyes . . .

Rob did.

Stretch out your hand.

Rob raised his right hand and cautiously extended it forward.

Now imagine nothing except the hilt. Nothing between you and the metal. Reach for the hilt. Grab it. Take it!

Rob closed his eyes more tightly. He pictured his hand reaching out, not for the sword on the square of black velvet in a glass case, but toward the sword laid on a wooden shelf in some medieval building. He stretched his hand further, his whole mind focused on maintaining the image of his hand closing on the hilt.

His fingers brushed something.

He took a ragged breath, touched it again: Leather wound with wire.

He had done it! He started to open his eyes. . . .

No! Not yet! Your power is still young. Do not test it!

Rob nodded and very slowly withdrew his hand. He

stepped backward, once, twice, thrice. Not until he had taken five full steps did he dare open his eyes.

He still held the sword; it glittered in the gray light, vibrating ever so slightly.

Beyond him was the glass case. The transparent panes were unmarked.

Shift your grip.

Rob hesitated, puzzled.

Shift your grip, foolish mortal!

Rob did, and felt his palm close on the snag of broken binding wire. A fine, clear pain slid into his palm. —And dizziness took him. His knees buckled. The sounds in his head became a chorus of joyous, hysterical laughter.

The last thing he remembered was slow-motion falling —and the certainty that every cell of his body was aflame.

Colin was cold, as he had never been cold in his own land, standing there in Alberon's winter hall. Tapestries stirred upon frost-rimed wall as storms raged in the Lands of Men that lay below Alban, and in the nameless, empty land that lay next above it—and broke through the Walls to chill the king of the Daoine Sidhe at his judgment.

But colder still was Alberon's face. The light of a thousand candles that should have washed That One's flesh with gold, should have laid fire in the hollows of cheeks and eyesockets: all that light, it did nothing.

For Alberon was pale as Death in a land of the Deathless. Dressed in a white velvet robe and a fur cloak of the same empty color, only the rage in the depths of his chill blue eyes gave him the look of the living.

To either side stood the lords and ladies of Alban, likewise all in white, though gray and silver, lavender, pink, and palest blue shadowed here and there as jewels upon their bodies.

Colin drew himself up to his full height. He alone wore color of any force: a robe of green velvet furred at hem and wrist and collar with the thick winter pelt of a rare golden enfield. The fur was the color of his hair; the robe made to mirror his eyes.

Alberon thrust aside the sword of state that lay athwart the high arms of his throne, and stood. His face was grim.

"Usurper!"

"My lord—" Colin began.

Alberon cut him off. "Do you *deny* my accusation? All here know of it. They have only to look to the east, to where a mountain no longer stands, for proof of your treason. The mighty have only to listen as stone cries out to stone and hears no answer—as beasts search for mates and vanished children. My land has been pillaged, Colin mac Angus. It has been stripped away by a third in countless places. Again, I ask: do you deny it?"

"I deny *nothing*, Alberon."

Alberon's eyes narrowed. "You *name* me? Do you thus claim yourself as my equal? Would you set up your land as rival to my own? I call you fool, thief, and traitor."

"Perhaps you are not fit to rule so fair a kingdom."

"Perhaps you are not fit to wear so fair a *body*," Alberon stormed back at him.

"What? Die? —By which I assume you mean forever? Why should I? Only of my own will may I sever the Silver Cord, and as I am sure you are aware, I choose not to."

Alberon's gaze grew colder. "I will have no more of this. You are guilty, Colin mac Angus; all who stand here now know it—and you have not said us nay. Any other crime I could perhaps ignore, but this alone I may not forgive. You must therefore abide my judgment: the Death of *Iron*."

Colin's face blanched whiter than Alberon's garments. "You would not dare!"

"I have already located a headsman." Then, looking higher, "Guards, we shall wait no longer!"

"No!" Colin screamed, but already he was thinking.

The Death of Iron, Alberon had said, yet even that could be outlasted—if one had strength to do it, could stand the blighting of soul as well as body. And his soul was not all where Alberon expected.

Hands seized his upper arms but he scarcely felt them, any more than he felt a thousand minds clamp down upon his Power and smother his magic.

The thick silver doors at the end of the hall swung open. A burst of cold air snapped in, harsh as a whip. Snowflakes glittered in the air: a first in Faerie.

Somehow he was outside, his hands bound behind him with chains of silver alloyed with iron: bound there by two mortals in Alberon's service.

Before him was the block. Beyond it, the King of Alban.

"You should feel honored, Colin mac Angus. I have brought your soul-cutter from the Lands of Men. A swordsman, he is. No common axe shall free *your* soul. One clean stroke of steel and over."

Colin felt himself shiver. He thought of his poor kingdom, lost now, its border sealed by his own blood, with no one there to love it, no one to watch over the gryphons.

Alberon's tall silhouette passed from view, and another shape stood before him. There was glamour at work there; the mortal man saw, yet did not see. Thoughts took form in his mind but were drowned again as quickly, as Power picked away at his memory. He could not see the man's face, for it was hidden by a hood of black velvet, but his chest was a mass of muscles greater than any of Faerie-kind; the legs below seemed thick as tree trunks.

Then Colin saw the sword: iron, of a certain, glittering in the pale Faerie sunlight. But the hilt . . . the hilt was not made of the cursed, never-cooling metal! Bound with leather it was, but underneath was brass washed with gold. It was the man's own sword, he knew, brought with him from the Lands of Men. A plan began to take substance.

"Kneel!" Alberon's voice rang out.

He knelt mechanically, shook his robe back from his shoulders, held his head proudly upright.

The mortal moved to one side.

He waited.

Something hot touched his bare nape, sending a tremor down his spine.

There was a swish in the air, a dull smack . . .

Pain—like fire . . .

He heard the sound of his own head falling.

But his soul was already free, fleeing the fire—denying it for a moment—as it rode with his own smoking blood to the hilt of a mortal's weapon, then became one with the brass.

The one place no one would look for him.

His strength failed, then, and he gave himself over to fire and pain.

In Alban someone was raising his severed head. Smoke would already be coiling from his corpse as most of his Power left it. Soon his body would fade and vanish.

But Colin's soul-of-souls was still alive. Wounded, imprisoned in a sword hilt by his own desperate will—but nevertheless able to function, to do one final thing before he yielded to madness: read the mortal's mind.

It was as he thought: Alberon had bound his tongue and was already blurring his memories. Perhaps to protect his realm, perhaps from some sense of mercy, the lord of Alban did not mean his headsman either to speak or to remember. For how *could* a mortal mind stand its own bleak world once it had gazed on the splendor of Faerie?

Colin, however, thought differently. With the last of his Power he touched the mortal's mind, noting how Alberon was already returning him home—with an unsuspected guest in his sword hilt. Even now the man's thought paths were shifting—denying, reshaping.

Still, though Alberon might drown that poor mortal's memories, Colin could put a drain in the basin. As time passed, Edward the smith, late of Ripon, *would* remember —every detail that had happened. In dreams they would come to him, and of dreams, he was free to tell others.

Colin thought that might be useful, but to insure it cost the last of his Power.

For a long, long time, all was madness and pain.

Sometimes he awakened, touched the World of Men, and at one of those times set a Watcher.

But then pain sucked him back again, until he learned how to flee to the place of his dreaming.

Most often he dreamed of his dying.

He relived it constantly: the cold, the trial, Alberon's face before his own. Fear racing down his spine. Despair turned to triumph, then to horror.

And he remembered the pain of iron.

Until something touched his Power once more.

And Colin in the sword hilt awakened.

Robert Tolar also awakened. Colin's memories were fresh in his mind—terrible memories of hatred and fear, and of dying. He took a deep breath and levered himself off the floor, thrust the sword in his belt.

Home? he thought to that unseen other.

Home—for now.

Rob thought *home*.

Cold, a falling sensation . . .

. . . Warmth, and the feel of rich carpeting under his feet.

He opened his eyes.

Well done, Robert Tolar. Now we have only a little more waiting—and one more important errand.

And in the lobby of the Reed-Gillespie Rare Book Library a smoke detector and a motion sensor also waited, as they had done for the last several years. They blinked on unceasingly. As if nothing had transpired to disturb them.

So that was the way of it, Rob thought, as Cathal continued to rub him. A part of him knew he should be terrified.

But he was not—because he knew that other mind now,

or else the Angel of Death did, for that was the aspect it favored: the part that hated his brother for what their mother had done when he knew there was no rational reason for such animosity. The part that thought it would be neat to have Dal, even against her will, though he knew such an act would only be a foul shadow of pleasure: blind rut—but sometimes blind rut was sufficient.

She was before him, even now, sitting silently on the hearth where he had found her a moment before when Colin had sent him there. *A final errand,* that one had said. *Another test of your Power—if such a thing happens to please you. For it is there now, awake; you can use it. It will take you to the lady, if you would have it so. You can even steal her away, if that is your decision.*

But where?

Any place you have been, there you may travel, you have only to imagine it—to desire *it. Even if you have not been, you can still go there, if someone you know is present already. You can go to a place or a person. Even a thing—as you did when you freed the sword.*

And I can take Dal with me? Rob thought, remembering his single trip to Los Angeles as a child.

Perhaps, when you are stronger, you will even be able to make your own *places.*

When I am stronger?

You will be stronger tomorrow, as strong as I can make you—and I will be free.

Will I still have Power?

Some. That which I gave to you will return to me, but perhaps by then your own will have awakened.

I have Power?

All mortal men have Power, though they deny it. Yours is . . . adequate.

How do you know this?

It is obvious. Now look to the object of your desire. Think on where you would take her.

Rob opened his eyes—or became aware of seeing once

more. Somehow he had come to stand behind Dal. His fingers rested on her shoulders.

Close your eyes and see where you would go.

Rob did.

—Cold and a falling sensation . . .

Rob opened his eyes again, and frowned.

For he thought he heard Colin laughing.

Chapter XX: Letter Never Sent

Jay stared at the empty display case and wrinkled his brow in despair; his shoulders slumped. "I just don't know what to do, Piper. I've flat run out of ideas."

"Yeah." Piper was sympathetic, though he kept shifting his weight nervously from foot to foot. "But, like, don't you think we ought to go look for the ladies?"

A sigh. "Yeah, I guess you're—"

A frantic tapping echoed through the empty chamber.

Piper started. "Shit! What's that?"

"Huh—Oh!" Jay whipped around, scanned the gloom.

The tapping again, louder—from the opposite side of the room. He started forward.

A set of glass doors confronted him, and silhouetted against the gray murkiness of the other side were Myra and LaWanda.

They pointed at the doors and gestured inquiringly.

"It's locked," Piper called.

"You got a key?" Myra mouthed.

Piper grinned, fumbled in his wallet, and quickly produced a plastic oblong like a credit card, only thicker. He ran it through a slot to the right of the door and waited. The sound of metal bolts popping open echoed loudly in the silence. "We're in luck," he whispered. "They haven't deactivated my card."

"But won't this cause some alarm to go off somewhere? All we need's the cops to come swarming in."

Piper pointed to the ceiling where a pair of cream colored wires disappeared into tiny holes. "See that broken wire? This one's screwed up. Developed a mind of its own the day before I left and they still haven't fixed it. Thank the lord for bureaucracy."

Jay pulled open the door.

"Oh lordy, lordy!" LaWanda gushed, rushing to embrace Piper. "Man, when we appeared in that office, I thought I was a goner."

"What office?" Jay asked sharply.

Myra pointed back over her shoulder. "DeRenne's, I think."

Jay looked puzzled. "But why would you end up there?"

"Search me, white boy. This is all new shit. Any luck with the sword?" LaWanda asked.

Jay shook his head sadly. "No, zip. It's gone. Stolen, it appears"—he held out the key fob—"by my brother."

LaWanda heaved an exasperated sigh. "Wish I knew what the hell was goin' on."

Myra regarded her levelly. "You *do* realize what just happened, don't you?"

"Huh?"

"Jay just worked some magic."

Had LaWanda not been holding onto Piper she would have fallen. "Lord liftin' Jesus, you're right. I was so worried about findin' the boys I forgot."

Myra shook her head. "You didn't forget, Wannie, you

blanked. I did too, for a minute. What just happened couldn't have—but it did."

"So how come we got separated?"

Myra shrugged. "Any ideas, Jay?"

Jay shrugged in turn. "Hell if I know."

Piper looked puzzled. "Well, me and Jason were wishing to find the sword—what were *you* wishing for?"

Myra glared at him. "Why, the same thing, of course; weren't you, Wannie?"

"Sure I was." She paused, frowning. "Or maybe not. That's what I was *supposed* to be wishin' for, but what I think I really wanted was to find out what the hell's goin' on. That's what my *heart* was hopin' for."

Myra pursed her lips thoughtfully. "Maybe I was too," she said slowly. "The guys obviously believed more strongly than we did; and I don't think there's any reason to doubt that Jay really wanted to get to the library."

"I thought he wanted to get the sword," LaWanda interrupted. "Why didn't he wind up where *it* is?"

"But he thought it was in the library," Piper said, "and so did I."

"Well," Myra said, "if we use your logic, Wannie must have landed in the office because the solution to the problem is somewhere in there."

Jay looked at Piper. "Okay, guy, how 'bout it: what's in DeRenne's office that might be relevant?"

"The book!" Piper cried. "Of course. The book where the play was hidden is in the vault!"

"In DeRenne's office?"

Piper nodded.

LaWanda and Myra exchanged glances. "Good thing we didn't wind up inside!"

Jay looked at Piper. "You know the vault combination?"

"No, but I know where to find it."

Piper spun the dial, and the last tumbler clicked into place. He gave the heavy handle a twist, and the massive door swung smoothly open. "Know what you're looking for?" he asked.

"I hope so, but you were there too; you ought to know what it looks like."

Illuminated by an automatic light, the interior of the vault was maybe six feet square. To the left and right stood shelves of moldering volumes and a few Hollinger boxes full of manuscripts. A copper cylinder housed the Confederate Constitution. On a lower shelf rested a tattered Spanish *graduale* from the early sixteenth century.

And lying flat on the top range next to its thinner twin was the new *Civitate Dei*.

"Anywhere we can check this out without setting off alarms or being seen?" Jay asked as he slid it down.

Piper nodded to his right. "There's a table in the office next door; windows were bricked up years ago."

"Good job."

Jay carried the book to the adjoining room and examined it by the light of the desk lamp. The back cover had not been reglued, and Jay wondered how the secret hollow there had escaped detection all those years, since the wood was obviously a laminate and far too thick to be typical.

But what about the other cover? He flipped the book over and studied it.

The front was as thick as the back had been—which meant it was probably a laminate as well. A closer examination verified that, and showed a definite crack between the layers.

"Hey, I think I'm onto something," he cried, "if I can find something to prise with."

"This do?" Myra asked, as she snagged an elaborate dagger-shaped letter opener from the desk.

Jay nodded and began working it around the juncture of the two layers until, with a sound like ripping paper, they split apart, revealing a small packet of manuscript apparently torn from some longer work. It took him a second to realize that the spiky, close-spaced writing was English.

"Don't tell me you can *read* that hen scratchin'," La-Wanda sniffed.

Jay ignored her and stared at the first sheet. "As a matter of fact, I can—sort of. Let's see: 'To whomever should read this, know that I am William Smith, of Ripon; son of Edward, whose father was Thomas, the son of Harry, the son of Edward, called the smith.'" Jay's voice suddenly quieted to a near whisper. "Oh my God, folks, do you know what this means? *I* was Edward the smith, of Ripon. This guy was one of his descendants!"

"Heavy man," Piper whispered. "Heavy-duty heavy."

But Jay was too busy reading to reply.

"'I write this in the thirteenth year of the reign of our sovereign King Henry, the eighth of that name. It is a thing I have come to believe, that I am not to be much longer in this world, but whether it be God's will or my own folly which sends me to judgment, I know not. I have written an unholy thing, and now I am sore afraid for my soul, and for this reason, propose to set forth the tale of how I came to be in such sorry state, though I have no leisure for setting out this narrative in its proper order, so I must, perforce, include such journal entries as I have made and pray that he who may chance to read them will know why I felt I must preserve this work of mine, that I have included here in the back of this volume, and hope that the good words between may stand as proof that I bore no ill will in its writing, and may God have mercy on my soul.'"

"Sounds like a confession," Myra noted.

Jay picked up the next leaf and cleared his throat. "'It was a fair day today, and there came to me men of the guild of tanners who, having heard that I was somewhat accomplished in the dramatic arts, desired that I scribe them a play for the May festival ...'"

Jay skipped through a long section filled with an elaborate discussion of monies paid, then picked up again.

"'I find myself wondering what would make a fit subject for this play I have promised. No one will want to see Noah and the Flood or the Tower of Babel, nor will they wish to hear sermons on the evils of this world. Yet perhaps there *is* a tale I might use, that my father used to tell, of how his father three times back one time slew the Devil —though I suppose I must combine it with Scripture to please my patrons. I still have the sword that was said to have done it.' "

The next page was dated a week later.

" 'I have been writing for five days, and the work grows long for such a little thing as a play. The notion is simple enough, merely my father's tale cast in to allegory of Man, St. George, and the Devil. Yet as I wrote, I was constantly in mind of the sword, and at times it was if *it* were telling me what to write, or how to set the phrases. I fear it is the Devil's hand that writes through mine. Perhaps it is an ill thing to make such jests of That One as my mummer contains.' "

"More on the sword, huh?" Myra muttered. "This doesn't make a bit of sense."

Jay picked up the next scrap of paper.

" 'A thing passing strange happened today. I had just gone into the tavern when a stranger called me to him. He was dark-haired, very fair of visage, tall and strongly built; and his clothes were very rich and strangely cut, as if he were from another country. He asked me about the play that I was writing, but I told him I had taken an oath not to speak of it (which was a lie), for something about him made me fear him. That man then grew wroth and said that I should put an end to it immediately, that there was a devil in me who was writing through my fingers, and that if my work were performed, it would cause a land of demons to break through into our world and thus destroy it, and his own land as well, though he would not say where that lay. There was a tower of demons at the center, he added, from which would spring forth silver scythes of destruction. And I rebuked him, then, and called him a fool and told him to begone or I would have his tongue on the floor, and his ears lying beside them. Yet even as he departed the tavern, that man spoke again, and said a curious thing: "I have asked you rightly, and you have denied me. Now it is my will that shall be done, and by my laws!" I was sore afraid at that, though why I cannot say. I asked those about me who that man was, then, and an ancient man from Scotland told me he had seen that black man once, and that his name was Alberon and that he was a devil of that land. But he would say no more.'

"Jesus!" Jay whispered. "Maybe he's the king of the Scottish fairies."

"Any more about him in there?"

Jay flipped through several pages that contained only a random mention of work on the play and additional money paid, then shook his head. "No, but listen to this.

" 'I write this in the middle of the night, for I cannot sleep. I have dreamt of the sword, though it does not speak to me now, except to torment me. In my dream I saw the Devil slain with it, only *I* was the Devil, and it was God who had denied me my right to be ruler of this world and I hated him for it. Perhaps I should abandon the play. I only pray these blasphemies will not be held against me. . . .'

"And then this . . .

" 'I have dreamt again, and this time it was my twice great-grandfather who spoke to me, and what he told me, I can scarce believe. He said *two* spirits inhabit the sword— one in the hilt, and that one a demon called Colin; and another in the blade, which is my grandfather's own soul that is set to watch over the other, which does not know of his presence, the blade being of iron where my grandfather is, and the hilt of brass, where is the demon who cannot abide the touch of iron; which the old women speak of as proof against spirits. He said a great battle rages between these two, for Colin stole a whole kingdom from Alberon, who yet had him slain for it; and my grandfather himself was the slayer. But when Alberon went to reclaim his land, he found it sealed against him and by this knew that some part of Colin still lived. He sought out my grandfather, then, and found that Colin had tampered with the wards Alberon had left on my grandfather's memory, and was exceedingly wroth, but had already begun to plan.

" 'Nothing happened for a long while, then, but several years later, when my grandfather was crippled by a hammer blow, Alberon came to him again, told him the whole tale, and offered him a bargain: life as a cripple or to die quickly and then to watch over Colin, since only were that one to live again could Alberon both reclaim his country and put an end to his enemy. The story my grandfather found a hard thing to believe, though his own memory said otherwise, and he at first refused the bargain. But when Alberon told him how Colin had caused the sword to slay two of his dearest kinsmen and had tormented his youngest son to madness with dreams, he had no other choice, for he had seen these things and wondered at them and at last agreed to the bargain. Alberon slew him, then, and trapped his soul, and put it in the sword's iron blade where the two would be always together, though Colin would not know it—and there my grandfather's soul remains and watches and uses the powers that now belong to it in its immortal form, and should Colin do those things which would effect his own resurrection, my grandfather is to enlist such aid as he might, and wait until Colin's land begins stirring and slay him before he can take the life of another. For in order for Colin to sustain himself the sword hilt must taste blood; and for the land to return to Colin's power, it must have a life. Only by destroying Colin before his land returns may my grandfather find rest at last.

" 'Oh, what have I done? What evil have I been tempted to set forth upon the earth? It is my play that will summon this demon's country, and now it is too late to stop it, for I have this day delivered it to my patrons.'

"And a day or so later:

" 'The priest was here today, and exceedingly wroth. He said my play was a blasphemy, and that it would not be performed, and that I should do a heavy penance as well. He made me watch as my manuscript was burned (though I have kept a copy). . . .'

"Then:

"'Alberon came to me last night in my own home, and told me to hide the copy of the work I had retained, for Colin might once again be able to use it at a more auspicious time when perhaps he could be defeated without risk to Alberon's country, though he seemed to hold no care for our own. I have been ill lately, and I fear some contagion is upon me, and ever the sword haunts me and I feel Colin's mind prodding at me. I have a fever and my bowels are in flux. I have not eaten for days. . . .

"'I am much weaker. Tomorrow I will write my will and set my affairs in order. To my son I will leave the book that it may give him some comfort. As for my secret, it will die with me. I pray I have strength tomorrow for what is at hand. . . .'"

The four of them stood looking at each other for a long moment.

"Is there more?" LaWanda asked finally.

Jay shook his head. "That's all. That stuff at the beginning must have been the apology he was talking about."

"Okay, but what about the sword?" Myra asked. "That part lost me completely."

"I can see that," Jay said. "But the way I caught it was that there're two souls in it: one called Colin, who's in the hilt and is evil and basically immortal, maybe even one of the fairies—I think he was the one Edward executed. And the other one's more or less good and mortal—originally. I think he's Edward himself—the guy I dreamed of being. At least the bits and pieces seem to fit, like the business about being a smith and all, and the stuff with the sword drinking blood." He paused, looked at his finger curiously. "In fact, maybe it was 'cause I got that sword splinter in my finger that Edward was able to make contact. The dreams started right after that, anyway."

"But what if your blood reached the hilt?"

Jay shuddered. "Good thing it didn't!"

"You sure?"

"Positive. There wasn't that much."

"Yeah, but then why would *Robby* take the sword? He didn't even know about it, as far as I know."

"Hmmm . . . Yeah, that's a problem—except whether or not Rob knew about it before, he evidently does now. Judging by what the manuscript said, I bet Colin's somehow taken him over—'cause he's apparently got some kind of power over people's minds he didn't have before."

"Give me a break, Jay," Myra sighed. "You really expect me to believe all this?"

"My God, woman, what does it take to convince you? You saw the bird; Piper's been to the otherworld; I've had visions—had one while I was reading that friggin' manuscript."

"Jay, I—"

Jay stood up suddenly. "Enough of this. We've got to figure out some way to stop the play!"

"What about those other things?" Myra persisted. "Why doesn't it manifest every time?"

"Who knows?" Jay shrugged. "No, wait, remember that part about blood? Maybe Colin doesn't have enough Power yet to fully use the play; maybe he's having to hoard it. Or maybe there's another factor we're missing."

"Like what?" LaWanda wondered.

"Won't find out standing around here," Jay replied decisively. "Piper, reshelve that and let's boogie." He paused, glanced at the journal entries. "I think we'd better bring these with us, though. Might want to use them for reference." He gathered them up with the copy of the play.

"Whatever you say." Piper stashed the book and slammed the vault door behind him. "So what're we gonna—"

"*First* we check up on my lady."

LaWanda stared at him in exasperation. "And how're we gonna do that?"

Jay grinned at her. "Why, the same way we got in here. Only this time we focus on Dahlia."

"But what about that monster you mentioned?"

"Okay, we go back to the house first and arm ourselves, *then* we travel."

LaWanda's mouth twitched sourly. "I've got a feelin' I may regret this."

PART V

Chapter XXI: You Can't Get There from Here

(May 1)

Rob surveyed the cozy round chamber he had been assigned inside the top floor of his theater's lefthand gate tower. The space had to be there for looks anyway; so it was logical for the Scarboro people to provide quarters for people who might need to be on-site a lot. He even had a security pass—not that he'd needed it tonight. This evening, he'd traveled another way—one he was beginning to find particularly attractive.

He'd been working on the place a couple of weeks now; and his little home away from home was finally beginning to look habitable—though the bare block walls were in need of paint, and the exposed beams of the conical ceiling were shockingly shoddy. Still, it was a pretty neat little sanctum.

In one quadrant a pair of hooks and a footlocker vied for space with the door that let onto the battlements, and thence down a ladder to the ground where the public toilet was. The next section to the left (the one with the window) was taken up by a desk improvised from boards and two-by-fours and flanked by a pair of folding director's chairs. Directly opposite the door a microwave oven and a tiny refrigerator shared a K-Mart wall unit with a cassette player and a small TV; and the remaining quarter was given over to the bed. Draped on either side with cheap flowered material in a semblance of medieval style, the narrow twin's dominant ornament was none other than the Fabulous Dahlia Cobb herself—though anyone else might have considered the fantastic eagle-headed beast asleep on the Oriental rug in the middle of the room to be of greater interest.

Rob's interest, however, was on Dal. Asleep, as he had chosen for her to be since he had brought her here, she lay curled upon the bed's black fake-fur coverlet. Another fur covered her—real, this time, and also black, which Cathal had brought from somewhere. Moonlight shimmered across low-lying fog outside to provide the room's sole illumination, setting off Dal's pale skin to perfection against the dark furs.

Slumped in one of the director's chairs, Rob had only the vaguest notion what time it was—or of anything else except that he now possessed the one thing in the whole world he most desired. In a moment he would awaken her and let Colin dance among her memories, burying ever deeper those that pertained to Jay, strengthening those new ones he had asked the Faerie mage to give her of their years together.

He stood up, skinned out of his T-shirt and brown cords, and reached for the quasimedieval robe he had borrowed from the costume shop. He would greet Dal as her knight in shining armor—or as a prince in his royal nightshirt, at any event. He leaned closer, bent over her sleeping form, kissed her pale cheek gently. Began to reach out his thought to awaken her.

No! Colin's voice rang sharply in his head. *I have no*

more time for meddling with the dreams of mortals, much less for reshaping memories, I have done enough of that for you. I have a kingdom about to be reborn, now, and you have a play to oversee. Are you certain all is in readiness? You have the sword at hand?

Rob glanced toward the blade and frowned. He ignored Colin's question. *But I want her. I have waited so long. Things are exactly as I would have them!*

I nevertheless command you to wait.

It was you who had me bring her here.

Where she would be safe.

It would help me relax.

I can do that for you much more quickly.

No.

Go to your bed, I command you!

My bed is taken.

Then lie beside her, for that is what you had planned. Perhaps your dreams will be—stimulating.

Old fool.

Young idiot. Sit or sleep, it does not matter; I have other things to look to. I will return to you on the morrow.

G'night. "Partypooper," Rob added, aloud. But he would do what he could, anyway. He flung the robe aside and crawled naked under the fur coverlet beside Dal. With one hand cupped around her breast, he slept.

" 'I'm still Lord of this World.' "

Jay's last words hung in the air, and then the air vanished.

Cold and dark: cold and dark and falling . . .

Too long!

Something was wrong. Jay had finished the play right on cue: just as Piper brought "King of the Fairies" to an end. The world had shifted; the cold had clamped upon them, and with it had come a darkness that transcended black. But where before almost no time had elapsed between the conclusion of the ritual and their arrival at the library, this time it was different. Now the cold gnawed at him like hungry wolves, the darkness threatened him with madness, and Piper's last note echoed in his head like distant thunder. Jay tried to focus on one word: home.

But home was a long time in coming, and meanwhile the cold persisted, crept into him, froze his bones. His eyes were open, yet he could not see, could not feel, except his left hand on Piper's shoulder, his right that held the manuscripts, and Myra's and LaWanda's grips upon his arms.

And always the cold.

A voice screamed suddenly, full of terror: "Jay! Where—" He felt the hands ripped away, the world spinning. Up was not, and down had vanished; right and left were gone.

Myra was gone too, and LaWanda. Their hands were clamped hard around his upper arms one moment, then simply absent.

"*Jay!*" That scream again—distant.

Panic filled him. He forgot everything, forgot Piper, flailed outward, felt fingers close on icy nothingness— brushed a hand. Grabbed at it—missed. Grabbed again.

"*Jay!*"—even fainter now, and now so were the pipes.

"*Jay!*"

He closed his eyes—closed them and *wished;* reached, touched flesh. Grabbed—*got;* wished harder, found the other. Still heard the fading echo of the pipes. And wished for all he was worth. . . .

Light—and warmth, and soft carpeting . . .

He opened his eyes—and could barely make out a darkened room.

Breaths hissed around him, and he glanced about, saw Piper still before him, LaWanda to his right clutching the two of them, his own hand twined in Myra's.

Jay squinted into the gloom, recognized the couch, the chair, the painting to the left of the fireplace. He took a deep breath. "Oh, shit," he groaned, "we're at Dal's!"

He stiffened suddenly, felt his breath catch as he spun around in place, eyes probing the shadows. "She's not here—not in this room—and neither is the gryphon. But it may still be around." He glanced at the stair, sank automatically into a wary crouch. "You folks better boogie! I'll check out things here."

"The hell you say," LaWanda gritted. "We're in this together, now. We stay with you."

Piper was still gazing around. "Jay's right; she's not in here. We better, like, search and destroy."

"But how did we get *here?*" Myra wondered. "We were supposed to be focusing on home."

"The magic must have picked up underlying desires again," Jay said quickly. "That's probably how we nearly lost each other. But—" He froze in his tracks. "Oh God, no!"

"Huh? What's wrong?" That was LaWanda.

"I've lost 'em, Wannie," he moaned, "the play and the journal, I mean. It was when I thought you two had vanished and I grabbed for you—I guess I dropped them."

"Oh no," Piper wailed. "And that means no more magic."

"Unless Jay can remember some of it," Myra pointed out, "or he's got another copy."

Jay shook his head. "Neither, really. And to tell the truth, I'm not sure I'd be up to doing it much more, anyway, 'cause it sure takes it out of a guy."

Armed with kitchen knives, they searched—but found no sign of either Dal or the gryphon.

"Well, I'd guess Dal's with Rob, that he's taken her who knows where—his place, maybe, or else to the Faire." Jay was grim.

"We can check that easily enough; his place is on the way home."

"But how're we gettin' there?" Piper asked.

"Dal's car, if it's here," Jay said. "I know where she keeps her spare keys."

Ten minutes later LaWanda sprinted across the Rebelwood Villa parking lot and rejoined them. They'd assigned her the task of reconnoitering Rob's apartment, first because she was black and would thus run less chance of being seen from inside if she looked in the windows; and because Rob didn't know her as well as the others and might not recognize her if he did see her. Jay shifted the Prelude into Drive as she climbed in behind him.

"Any luck?"

LaWanda shook her head. "'Vette's there, but no lights in the apartment, 'cept a little one in the middle hall. Checked the windows, too, but didn't see nobody; even screwed up my nerve and knocked on the door, but no answer. I'd bet you any odds they ain't there."

"So what do we do?" Piper asked.

"That seems obvious," Jay replied heavily. "We go to Scarboro Faire and try to stop them."

"You're absolutely certain they're there?" Myra inquired. "Hell, Jay, they could be anywhere."

"Yeah, you're right. But I don't have any better ideas, and they're bound to wind up there eventually. One thing, though: I think we ought to leave right now."

"Oh come *on,*" Myra groaned. "It's the middle of the night!"

"Yep: the middle of the night on May Eve. One of the nights when according to folklore the walls between the worlds grow thin—just like Halloween. And by the way, have you noticed something odd about this fog?"

"Just that it"—Myra's eyes grew wide—"just that it doesn't aggregate around cars! *Moving cars,* yes, but parked cars . . ."

"And what're cars made of?"

"Iron—well, steel actually."

"Oh, Christ," Piper whispered. "So you think this fog's—"

"I don't think it's natural."

"I *know* it ain't natural," LaWanda said.

"When's the Faire open, anyway?" Myra asked.

"Nine, I think."

"And what time are the plays?"

"One and four," Piper volunteered. "No, wait, not today. Rob had a fit until they gave him a special premier at ten. And the Bowman-Smith play won't start till after that—according to the program they sent me."

"So we've got plenty of time to rest and gear up."

"Myra, I hate to tell you this," Jay said, "but if I have to just sit and wait, I'll go crazy. Hell, I'll probably start off by myself."

"Yeah, you probably would. And if the fog's this bad in the morning . . ."

"But that's still hours away, bro."

"Could *you* sleep, Piper, knowing Dal may be in danger?"

"And besides," LaWanda added, "we can't just walk in in the middle of the play and say, 'scuse me, but we've come to take away your leadin' lady—oh, and by the way, can we have that fine lookin' sword, too?"

Jay chuckled in spite of himself. "You're right, there. So we've got to sneak in early. And Scott'll help—if we can just get him to *believe* us."

Jay went on decisively, "Let's go back to our place and pick up some stuff. Scott's got a couple of pretty good swords and Wannie's got that neat little machete." He paused and looked at her. "You don't happen to know any good juju for this, do you?"

"Nope, this is *way* beyond my juju. I'll be takin' notes, though, let me tell you!"

"Okay, then: home, and some coffee and a snack. Let's see: it's twelve forty-five now. Give us a half hour to get home, a half hour to get our act together there, and another hour to get to Bogart in this mess. That leaves us a little over seven hours to come up with a battle plan. And I really don't think we can do anything until we get inside the Faire, anyway."

"And when we find Rob?"

"I don't know," Jay said. "Maybe the best thing would just be to knock him out."

"Yeah, but the play'd still go on."

"Maybe not—if we get Dal out of there. She's got the central part; they can't go on without her. Probably ought to catch her at the last minute, though. If she doesn't show on time, Rob'll know something's up."

"Lord, what a mess," Piper sighed.

"Look at it this way, gang: twenty-four hours from now it'll all be over."

Cathal the gryphon was restless. He paced the inner edge of the narrow rampart outside the mortal's quarters, reached the end, turned, and retraced his steps. Being a magical creature in a nonmagical land made him nervous, for he had ever to be on guard against the iron that was everywhere. A nail here, a scrap of metal there, more than enough in the mortal's chamber to make it uncomfortably warm. Several times he had stepped on something and felt fire shooting up his leg. A little he could manage, as a mortal could flirt with a candle flame and not be burned, but a large amount could consume him utterly. With so much iron about, he wondered what would happen when Master's realm broke through. He knew so little of Master's plan, except that he would stay in this World only a little while. What would happen to man's World when Tir-Gat came did not matter.

But in the meantime Cathal was nervous and impatient. It would not be long now before he could go back to his mountain and sleep, only rousing himself now and then to gaze afar at the twisting vistas of Tir-Gat or visit Colin in his tower. Perhaps one of the winged females would even find him. Such a coupling there would be! He felt Power surge within him, at that; and leapt from the rampart— landed soundlessly upon the ground. A flicker of light showed at his joints where the force of movement set them sparking.

He could *feel* Tir-Gat waiting around him—hiding in the shadows, its radiance barely shaded from this World. It was almost, at this juncture between the halves of the year, as if both Worlds existed in one space, the more so because of the low-lying fog Master had made him summon to help ease the merging. Every tree now had its shadow twin, every bird its double. A single oak became a grove in Tir-Gat; a flake of crystal was a glittering spar long as his body. It was a wondrous feeling: breathing at once the wind of this world and of another. *This* breeze smelled of men and their cooking and the bitter scent of iron, but *that* breeze brought with it the cinnamon odor of wyvern's wings and of virgin woods and unworked stone.

But iron yet burned through: a nail upon the ground dispersing the fog in a tiny shell around it, glowing with a dull red light as its Power fought with that of the fog.

Cathal began to pace the grounds, hugging the darkness. Around him the Faire slept. Trees stood sentinel. Banners and pennons twitched in an early morning wind. A few people snored in the SCA compound; a lone security guard paced the grounds, but he was easy to avoid. It was almost like his first home had been; almost like those parts of Alban that lay farthest from Alberon's palace—*almost* as the Lands of Men had been when last he had seen them six hundred years before. That had been a place of colors and smells, clearer than this world now held. He wondered if it was because of the iron. Oh, they had long used that metal in the Lands of Men. But now it was *everywhere*.

He was glad Master's realm would soon return. Then they could leave this place. He started back to the tower, dreaming of the land he might construct someday, if Master showed him how. He would call it The Land Without Iron.

"Jesus," muttered LaWanda. "Can you see anything at all, Miss Myra?"

"Not really," Myra replied, shaking her head. She peered out the windshield of her gray Nissan pickup at the encircling fog. "I'm mostly going by the feel of the right side of the road—which is fine, as long as there're no curbs or anything."

"Which there was just back there," Piper added from the crossways jumpseat in the back. "Or so it felt like."

"Yeah, well, I couldn't help that."

"Want me to open the door?" LaWanda suggested.

Myra puffed her cheeks in consternation, then nodded. "Guess you better."

LaWanda checked her seat belt and eased the door open. "You're okay, I reckon, just keep easin' along."

"Where *are* we, anyway?" Piper asked.

Myra frowned. "We passed the mall a couple of minutes ago. Must be 'bout out to 78."

"Yeah," said LaWanda, then: *"Lookout girl!"*

Myra jammed on the brakes, sending coffee sloshing into Jay's lap. "What is it?"

"Uh—nothing, I don't reckon, hit a patch of construction's all. Road turned to dirt and freaked me out."

"Construction?" Jay cried. "I was just out this way day before yesterday. I didn't see any construction."

"Not even a water main?"

"Nope, not a thing."

"Oh, crap," Piper moaned. "We're lost!"

"We *can't* be lost. We're on the friggin' main road to Bogart, driving on the right hand side of the road. There aren't any turns."

"Well," LaWanda said finally, "since we're just *sittin'* here, I'm gonna check it out." She undid her seat belt and hopped out, leaving the door open. She had gone scarcely three feet before her shape disappeared into the fog.

A minute passed. Jay busied himself watching the fog burn away from the truck. By the time LaWanda had returned, there was a clear patch two feet wide all around it. Not that it helped much.

LaWanda climbed into the cab and slammed the door. Her eyes were huge beneath her black bandana.

Myra raised an eyebrow. "So spill it."

"We in the woods, lady. We in the goddamn *woods*."

"We can't be!" Jay moaned.

"Well, we are. Wanta look for yourself?"

Jay slid the back window open and stared out into the fog. He thought he could make out the looming shapes of trees close by.

"Guess I'll try to back out," Myra said.

"You ain't gonna back out of *here*," LaWanda replied.

"What do you mean? I just now ran off the pavement."

"Yeah, Miss Myra, but ain't no pavement back there. Ain't *nothin'* but woods and a piddly little dirt road. I know, 'cause I walked twenty paces forward and twenty paces back. Ain't no pavement back there, and ain't never *been* none."

"Forward it is, then," Myra sighed. She put the truck in gear and began easing forward.

Five feet, ten feet. Twenty—possibly. The truck coughed, sputtered, began to backfire and clatter viciously. And finally quit.

Myra switched off the ignition and lights, turned the ignition key and ground the starter till it hurt to hear, all the while pumping the accelerator for all it was worth. Nothing worked. The car was dead as a doornail.

Chapter XXII: We Walk

(May Day)

Scarboro Faire awakened into a dense morning mist that seemed uncannily resistant to the sunlight Thomas the Hun could see burnishing the tops of the nearby pines. A hint of blue promised a beautiful day, if only the confounded fog would disperse.

Thomas stared groggily about for a moment, trying to recall where the john was. The fog confused him. He frowned, looked to his left. Maybe that way? He started toward the compound gate and stumbled over something lying close beside it. Glancing down he saw the shield that Scott fellow—no, what was it? Bryan of Scotia? had brought with him yesterday. His gear was piled beside it, damp with condensation. Now that he thought of it, he hadn't seen him since the previous evening. Bryan was an old Athens member who had gone inactive and was trying to feel his way back in. Maybe he'd intended to leave his gear and come back today; or maybe he'd simply forgotten something. Hadn't he made some remark about wanting to go back to Athens and get another sword? Thomas scratched his head, and pushed through the gate.

Outside, the Faire was coming alive. Fires were being lit to burn charcoal for the quasi-medieval food Scarboro would serve: grilled chicken and turkey legs, steaks on a stick, corn on the cob; hot cider and cold beer and mulled wine. Here a potter was testing his wheel; there a red-haired woman was hanging a purple banner which bore the signs of the zodiac in gold. The wooden sign beside her tent read: MADAME WENDI—KNOWS ALL, SEES ALL—FORTUNES FORETOLD.

He was in the main commercial part now, the people were everywhere, unlocking doors, loading pottery and glassware, pewter or leather goods, onto shelves and tables; It really did look authentic—the Renaissance crossed with Woodstock. Many of the artisans, he suspected, had never truly forsaken their ancient hippiedom, and had been glad to trade tie-dye for doublets and patched blue jeans for spandex tights.

A low, shingled building loomed ahead. LORDS, it proclaimed in Gothic type, and Thomas entered. Indoor plumbing was the thing he would miss most if these were the real Middle Ages, he decided, as he entered a stall.

A sudden rustling made him look up. A bird had flown in through the space between the top of the walls and the beamed roof. He stared at it. Surely no bird in Georgia was *that* green. The bird swooped over to the top of the wooden partition to his left, brushed a wing against a protruding nail—and shrieked. As it flew away, Thomas hoped it was just a trick of light that made him think the bird's wingtips had been trailing threads of vapor. But he *knew* he smelled burning feathers.

Rob didn't know whether it was the sunshine glaring into his eyes, Cathal's feathers tickling his exposed bare foot, or Colin's prodding in his mind that awakened him.

He yawned and rolled away from the sun; drew the foot back under the cover. But he could not so easily escape Colin.

Awake, mortal. Morning is nigh spent and I have let you rest, but you may rest no longer.

Go 'way, man. Let me sleep.

No!

The command was a pain that exploded in Rob's brain and sent shrapnel through his body, as though every cell had taken fire, as though every nerve conducted slow, burning lightning. He would have screamed, but found his throat locked. Then, as quickly as it had come, the pain subsided.

"What time is it?" he gasped shakily, staring at Dal asleep beside him. Her face was peaceful, calm—too calm, for it bore a heavy, mindless slackness.

Time is a thing men have invented in their efforts to command their world, Colin informed him. *But it is not a thing to be measured, it simply is. There is a right time and a wrong time for acting. The stars and planets, the sun and moon, they bend and focus the Power of the universe. When the focus is correct, it is time; when it is wrong, only ill can come of any action.*

And now?

The focus is nearly perfect. The suns align in three Worlds at once, and the moons on five planes rise together. The Words have only to be spoken, and my land will answer and be free.

The gryphon padded back into the room from the battlements, put off the glamor he had assumed so that mortal men might not see him.

Trouble, Master. Someone knows of our plan. I felt their thought in the ether. Even now they are approaching.

But did you not shroud the Lands of Men with fog to fool the eye, to weaken the will?

I did, my lord, but still some came creeping. The fog cannot fight the sun forever. Already it fades in places.

Do they come here?

They try, but Tir-Gat awakens around them. Perhaps the maze will prevent them.

Perhaps you should help it.

I shall, my master. It will be my joy.

You heard what my servant told me, Colin said when Cathal had departed.

A threat approaches?

Aye, and I know not its nature, though I suspect. Are you ready? Are you strong enough?

I . . . am.

You had best be, for if you fail me . . .

What?

What you imagine Hell to be, would be but the faintest shadow.

I will not fail.

Jay tripped on the root and staggered, stole a glance over his shoulder and wished he hadn't.

There *should* have been a trail back there: a rearward continuation of the rutted, marshy path down which they had been plodding single file for what seemed like forever.

But behind was only a gray-green-white froth of dripping laurel leaves, ragged mist, and tangled branches all mixed with wicked briars, and beyond that a ghostly loom of impossibly tall trees. And the worst thing, the *worst* thing was that the root he had just tripped over was slowly dragging itself into the shaggy cover of an immense stand of maidenhair ferns.

Jay suppressed a shudder and jogged on ahead, suddenly fearful of losing sight of Myra's blonde topknot nodding along in front of him. He tightened his grip on one of Scott's swords, wishing he knew what time it was. They'd gone from having a huge window of opportunity to maybe none, all because of the frigging fog, the frigging forest, the frigging—

He caught Myra glancing at her watch and giggled. He'd been doing that too—fruitlessly. Because ten minutes after they had collected their weapons and abandoned the

truck, the LCD on his new watch had begun to switch on
and off at random. A moment later it had stopped entirely,
frozen, like his old one, at 18:88. Myra had looked at her
expensive Elgin and seen the hands spinning wildly.

"God*damn*!" LaWanda snarled from the front of the line
where she was striding along swinging her machete. "If
we're in Georgia at all, I'd be real surprised."

"Yeah, the air's weird here," Piper acknowledged.
"Thicker, or somethin'."

"Maybe it's like the Amazon," Myra suggested, "so
much photosynthesis going on there's literally more oxy-
gen."

"More methane, too," LaWanda grumbled. "Smell of
decay every time I step down. And, lordy, the stink those
briars make when you cut 'em."

"Yeah," Jay said, glancing at a jagged slash in a ruddy
stem. "And this stuff in 'em looks more like blood than
sap. Wonder if it tastes—"

"Don't you dare!" LaWanda commanded.

They walked on in silence, following an increasingly
crooked path that was by turns wide and narrow, clear and
obscure, firm and soggy. But always when Jay looked
back, the road behind them was gone, the sky a different
color, the sun in a different place. Once he was certain he
saw not the sun but the moon.

Jay was grateful for the need to walk quickly, the constant necessity to step over logs or push a branch aside or
climb a bank, because all those things ate up the adrenaline
that was flooding his system as fast as he could burn it.
When LaWanda spoke again, it was as though her words
came from some great distance.

"Huh?" he found himself asking.

"I said the trail just stops," LaWanda repeated, sounding
angry and frustrated.

Jay shook his head and shouldered up beside her. They
had just followed a fairly wide swath of mossy path between two immense gray and lichened boulders that towered twice their heights, then been turned sharp right

immediately beyond. But now, ahead, was a tangle of laurel so tall and thickly laced with briars that it was absolutely impenetrable.

"Can you cut through?" Jay asked.

LaWanda's eyes grew large. "Cut through that? Those thorns'd cut *me* to ribbons 'fore I got two feet!"

"Well, we can't go *back!*"

"No," Myra agreed, "we can't. But what about burning through or something?"

Jay stared at the sorry sword in his hand. One of Scott's replicas from above the fireplace, the edge was dull, and he doubted there was very much temper, but it was made of steel and might be proof against things of Faerie. Tentatively Jay extended his blade, touched it first against a laurel leaf and saw no damage, slid it against the trunk of a nearby pine and perceived no effect. Then scraped it along the side of the huge rock to his left—and saw the stone glow red, crack, and flake away.

"Maybe there *is* a way!" he exclaimed. "Maybe if we go at it with steel!" He set the blade to one of the briars—and noted for the first time that the slick surface smoked at that touch: smoked, and parted, and floated away into nothingness.

Of course! It had probably been happening all the time —but in the mist and darkness they hadn't been able to tell fog from steam from smoke.

But how did the real leaves get mixed in?

He thought he had an answer to that, too: Colin's country wasn't supposed to manifest entirely until the play was performed. So what was happening must be that the real world and Colin's were shifting in and out—that they were in both at once, though Colin's must be stronger, otherwise they'd see more houses and cars.

"All right!" LaWanda cried, shaking him from his reverie. "Between my machete and your sword, we ought to be able to do a job on these boogers! Tell you what, we'll try a couple of feet, and if that doesn't go, we'll try something else."

"Sounds good," Jay nodded, and attacked the leafy barrier. LaWanda followed suit. The air hissed with the sound of their blades as the flora of two worlds flew in fragments around them.

"Good deal," Jay shouted suddenly, for his blade had slashed into empty air.

LaWanda joined him as Myra and Piper crowded up behind.

Jay pushed through the remaining fringe of vegetation and stood upon a wide, clear path running to either side between tall walls of mixed briar, fern, and an unknown plant somewhere between hedge and ivy. The laurel seemed to have vanished, though rocks still loomed here and there behind the walls. Five yards to their right was an opening in the opposite wall.

LaWanda trotted over there, looked inside. "Oh my God!" She cried. "Would you look at *that!*"

The archway opened atop a low hill overlooking a wide valley completely filled with mist. But beneath that tenuous white layer he could make out the curves and angles of a vast sprawling maze, the nearest dull silver walls of which bent right up to the hedge on either side, not five feet away.

But what almost took Jay's breath was what he saw rising clear and dark above that vapor: a vast stone tower at least three miles off. He couldn't even guess at how tall it was.

"We've finally got something to aim by," Myra told them. "Remember what the manuscript said about the land of demons? There was another line somewhere around there about Colin's tower being in the center of that land."

"And silver scythes of destruction—don't forget them," Piper added.

Jay ignored him. "So?"

"So if he causes it to manifest, wouldn't it be logical for him to be in the center?" Myra said.

Jay looked at her doubtfully. "I'm not sure. But," he

added, "you've followed my hunches, I guess it's time I followed yours."

Dal stood at the tower window combing her hair and looking out at the world. Fog was still everywhere, defying the sun, but at least it seemed to be mostly ground fog now. The tops of trees stuck out above it, as did the roofs and pinnacles of various buildings. And of course most of the flags rose above it in a panoply of blazing, sunlit color.

Directly below her was the theater. The fog was less pervasive there, she was relieved to note, though the odd tendril still gave a hint of strangeness to the wedge-shaped area. She wondered where Rob was; he'd been gone when she'd awakened. Funny how she couldn't seem to re- member much about the last few days. The rehearsal had gone well, and there'd been sangria and cheese soup at DaVinci's, then—nothing. She must have had more to drink than she thought. Oh, she recalled following Rob home—no, wait, since *she* was here, *he* must have driven her here—to his wizard's tower, his magical fastness. Bless him, too; to have let her sleep when he could have . . .

Maybe he *had?* She shook her head. No, it wouldn't be like him to take advantage of her when she was drunk. She wondered where her hangover was, too, 'cause if she'd had enough to utterly obliterate the night before, it should be manifested now as a horrendous headache. Yet she felt light and energetic, as if she could float out the window. Humming to herself, she put on a bathrobe and went downstairs to wash her hair.

As she ran a sinkful of water, she tried to recall the tune that was prologue to the Bowman-Smith play. But every time she got started, it seemed to shift into that real fast number one of Rob's—no, one of *Jay's*—friends had once played. What was it called? "King of the Fairies"? She shrugged. That part of her life was now over. And as for Jay Madison, she wondered what she had ever seen in him besides a foolish grin, nice buns, and a large dash of boyish naivete. Rob had so much more than that: fire and mystery and ambition, to name a few. She continued humming and was not surprised to find it echoed by a brace of bright green birds that flew about her head.

"I feel like Rhiannon," she whispered. Outside she could hear a cryer ringing a hand bell and calling out "Nine o'clock, the Faire's officially open, and all's well."

Dal smiled. All *was* very well.

The maze had shifted subtly, from walls that looked suspiciously like tarnished silver to the walls of gold between which Jay's company had been traveling for roughly the last thirty minutes.

And it was shifting again. The golden walls now bore patterns: interlaced designs of loops and spirals which until very recently had been carved into the stone or metal, but which now seemed to be increasingly composed of inlaid crystal. And as Jay and his friends pressed onward, the spirals became more complex, the layerings of glass and mirror more pervasive, until they realized that the whole maze had become glass: glass and mirror and faceted crystal. Easy enough to get out of—or so they thought until Myra aimed a blow at one of the walls and was rewarded with a sore hand, a dulled machete, and no damage.

Jay studied the point of impact carefully, but saw only the merest trace of melting. He laid his own blade against that shining surface and saw the glass ooze back—but the progress was too slow to be of any service. And so they continued, making poorer time now, because the ground had become glass as well and was difficult to stand on, and reality was becoming harder and harder to focus. There were walls that were transparent, and walls that were mirrors—or even the two layered together; and the same was true for the floors and roofs. And the angles had become strange as well: acute, then obtuse, then acute once more; and sometimes walls that had been opaque became transparent or vanished altogether, and at other times the opposite was true. And the openings seemed to come and go at their own caprice, so that retracing their steps was impossible.

Fortunately there was the shaft of the tower looming taller and clearer ahead of them: seen at this moment, obscured the next, as walls rose and fell, roofs cleared and silvered around them. Or as it was hidden by the omnipresent fog spinning in and out of openings that appeared and vanished without any apparent logic or reason. And always, now, were the shadows that hid in the fog: shapes that could not be discerned by direct observation but that showed out of the corner of one's eye, or as reflections, or even as true shadows. Jay thought they looked like trees, or—sometimes—like cars or buildings. He was certain he was seeing that part of his own world which lay within this other place, and thought that whatever boundary separated the two must be thinner there, because another thing he had started to notice was that the further along they got, the more there were tiny patches of fire on the ground or within the walls. Once Jay bent down and saw that one of the patches had at its heart a common steel tuna fish can. Only here it was transfigured, held a sort of inner glow as if it were red-hot and where it touched this eerie world, a tiny hole was burned: the glass floor giving way to a patch of asphalt pavement big as his hand.

Jay told the others of his discovery, and they too began to notice that the maze had worn thin in any number of places. Once they came to a place where the steel frame of a building waged unceasing war with the shifting walls. Heat flared at the points of that juncture, and fragments of glass melted away to puddle and reform elsewhere.

In another place, the glass and mirrors gave way almost entirely to a spot of his own world in which sat, amid a field of broom sedge, the derelict rusty corpse of a 1965 Pontiac Catalina. Sunlight streamed down on it from nowhere, striking bright glints off its pitted chrome.

"What I think is happening," Jay volunteered, mostly to ease his nerves, "is that Colin's country is manifesting itself atop our own, but so close that where there's iron in our world it just can't take full form. Apparently iron never loses its heat here, even if it feels cool to us. It's sort of like laying a sheet of ice on top of a hot stove: the burners melt through in places."

"Neat theory," Myra panted. "Problem is that the further we go from town, the less steel there is in our world, and the more woods. And the Faire's entirely in the woods. Only the odd nail would cause a problem, and I'm not sure iron in such small amounts has much effect."

"So we must be getting close," Jay said hopefully. "Because the tower keeps getting bigger every time we see it. Besides, the only shadows we're seeing now are trees. And the iron inclusions are the sort you'd expect to find scattered about the countryside, not in town."

"Maybe, but judging by the last time we saw the tower, I'd say we've still got at least two miles."

"I *feel* like we're gettin' close, though," LaWanda volunteered. She passed a long wall of alternating horizontal stripes of mirror and transparent sections, and turned right through an opening that suddenly appeared.

—And screamed.

Jay dashed through the opening close on her heels, and came face-to-face with that which he had hoped never to see again.

The gryphon was there, down the new corridor to the right: not fifty feet beyond LaWanda's wary machete. The beast was crouching already; muscles rippled across its haunches. Its feathered ears twitched. And beams of light flickered from the armored joints on its legs.

"Jesus Christ!" Myra breathed as she brought herself up short behind Jay.

LaWanda assumed a guarded crouch that Jay recognized as an unorthodox but apparently serviceable combination of some Japanese martial art, fencing, and SCA combat. The main thing was that she was very deliberately keeping the blade prominently displayed between herself and the monster. Jay wanted badly to join her, but the corridor was too narrow. And if he tried to ease her aside and take her place, the beast would surely take advantage of the distraction.

"Wannie," Jay whispered desperately. "See if you can back out."

"Uh, Jay," Piper muttered from behind him. "She can't back out, and neither can we." For the opening through which they had entered was now a long corridor ending in a solid plate of mirror.

"Shit," Myra groaned.

No one breathed for a moment. Jay was aware only of a desperate need to do *something*—anything. He looked around frantically. Glass sparked and glittered on all sides —except straight in front where LaWanda held off the gryphon. He took a breath and whispered, "Edge to the right, Wannie, I'll try to join you on the other side. Maybe with two of us there holding iron that thing'll think twice before attacking."

"No, Mr. Jason," LaWanda muttered. "Ain't no room for more'n one. I'll hold it off, 'cause ain't no way it can get me unless I get it."

"Wannie, no!" That was Piper.

The gryphon's muscles tensed. It eased its talons half a step toward them.

LaWanda tensed as well, and crouched even lower.

"No! Wannie!" Piper darted forward—but slipped on the slick surface and skidded sideways straight into Jay's feet, unbalancing him. Myra grabbed for him. Piper's flailing hand brushed LaWanda's foot. She screamed, staggered—

Myra fell forward onto her hands and knees.

The gryphon leaped.

LaWanda ducked just as Jay toppled toward the wall at his left.

—And passed through it.

For the wall which seconds before had been solid now showed an opening. Unable to maintain his balance on the slick floor, Piper followed Jay; and Myra, unable to stop herself, slid through as well. Jay saw the gryphon sail over his head, just brushing LaWanda's left shoulder as it passed. The machete shrieked by in the creature's wake, but did not connect.

"*Now,* Wannie!" Jay screamed.

But it was too late, for the air behind them was thickening, first becoming cloudy, then acquiring a mirror finish as the wall re-formed.

The last thing Jay saw was LaWanda's look of horror as that barrier rose between them—and the look of greater horror as she glanced over her shoulder and saw the gryphon once more turn and crouch.

Chapter XXIII: Shaking Through

"Look, it's nothing personal," Rob said as calmly as he could to the indignant young man who stood before him, legs wide braced and fingers fisted in a perfect study of defiant tension. Chest to chest, they faced each other in the rough non-privacy of the men's dressing room at the Morrisman's Men.

"Nothing personal, hell!" the young man spat. "You may be the director, but it's *my* part. If you think you're gonna take over Saint George on this kind of notice, you're crazy."

Rob's eyes flashed dangerously, but he forced himself to remain calm. "Yeah, I may be crazy, a little—but *look,* Dave, it's only for this one performance. The idea only came to me last night; it'd be my tribute to McLaren, kind of."

"Your tribute to yourself, more likely," Dave shot back.

Rob glared at him. "One more word, and you're off permanently!"

"You shit!"

Rob had been afraid it would come to this. He preferred not to use Power, because it only complicated things. Once you started fooling with people's minds, you set up a domino effect: one change led to another, and pretty soon you had to do a shitload of work to cover your ass—if you didn't want a lot of people doing more thinking (more *puzzled* thinking) than was good for you. Puzzlement often led to the asking of questions that had no logical answers. Dal was enough of a problem, he thought, trying not to think of Monteagle and DeRenne. Besides, he might need the energy later.

"Okay, Dave, now listen."

Enough of this! Master him and be done. I have no patience with such fools.

He will ask questions—

It will not matter.

Why not?

You ask too many questions. Do it!

And Rob did: simply reached toward Dave Menshew's mind (or was that Colin forcing his way? he couldn't tell anymore), reached, stabbed through, and darkened certain parts, blurred others, altered others still.

Dave blinked, started as if he had suddenly awakened. "Huh? Oh, yeah, sure you can take over St. George—assuming the costume'll fit."

"It will," Rob replied confidently, patting the sword that hung at his side. "I'm certain there'll be no problem."

Somebody elbowed Thomas the Hun in the side just as someone else jostled into him from behind, threatening to upset the pewter tankard of beer he was trying to juggle while he fished in his pouch for the fifty-cent admission to the premier performance at the Morrisman's Men. Miraculously he saved himself and slid two quarters to the blonde wench behind the ticket window in the base of the tower to the right of the entrance. He could not resist a long, appreciative look down the considerable decolletage of the peasant blouse she was stuffed into beneath her front-laced bodice. She noticed him noticing and slipped him a coy wink along with his ticket. "Maybe," she whispered. "See me later, darlin'."

Wondering if she really meant it or was simply playing the tart for the locals, Thomas made his way inside and found a place on one of the split log benches halfway toward the front. An upward glance showed him a splatter of sky—finally; the morning fog seemed largely to have dissipated. It looked like the day might be a real scorcher. Ah, well, that'd just give him one more excuse to down a few. He took a sip of the stuff in his mug and savored it curiously.

The place was filling up. A white-haired man in Bermuda shorts sat down to his left, and a young-looking woman with a small daughter in tow joined him to the right. After much puffing and grunting around those already seated, a skinny, fortyish man and his thirtyish wife and preteen son found places right in front of them. The woman, at least, was a classic example of a certain type of rural Georgian: solidly plump, and wearing the inevitable hideous summer uniform of sleeveless polyester pullover blouse and bright, skintight shorts, all of which showed too much of a bulging figure. By contrast, the nine-or-so-year-old boy she had in tow was a study in high-tech elegance: white Reeboks, black parachute pants, and sleeveless gray canvas vest over a black T-shirt. The kid's spiky haircut with tail was the finishing touch. Generation gap for certain.

The woman to Thomas's right apparently recognized the older woman and reached forward to poke her brawny bare shoulder. "Hey Erline! How're you doin'!"

The older woman twisted around. "Lordy, Sue, am I glad to see you," she intoned nasally. "I tell you what, I thought we weren't a-gonna make it here, what with the damned fog an' all. They was a place or two we couldn't see squat."

"Yeah, I know," Sue replied. "I had to roll down the window to even see the damned road. And"—she bent closer—"let me tell you somethin' else, and if you tell it I swear I'll deny it afore God, but I *seen* somethin' on my way here. *Somethin'* run across the road ahead of us, and I swear it looked like one of them dragons you see on television. Had to of been thirty feet long. Amy saw it too, didn't you hon?"

"Sho did!" the child volunteered loudly.

"You're kiddin'!"

"Swear on the Bible."

"Yeah, well I'll tell *you* somethin', then," Erline confided. "You'd of told me that yesterday, I'd of said you'uz pullin' my leg, but me and the old man was just a-rollin' along as pretty as you please, and all of a sudden, the road got rough, and it was like we'd just run off the main highway and was in the woods or somethin', and the car started buckin' and skippin', but then we ran out of it, an' the car smoothed out, and I swear to God, I looked back and saw a solid wall of trees, and when I looked back again, there wasn't nothin' there but good old U.S. 78 for two–three miles. And I told Marvin, I said—"

Marvin smacked Erline smartly on the thigh. "Better hush, woman, I think they're startin'."

Thomas took another sip of beer and looked up. A tallish young man in parti-color red and white tights, burgundy doublet, and gold flop hat complete with green ostrich plume had walked onstage. He wore a particularly attractive and authentic-looking sword stuffed jauntily in his belt. Thomas thought he looked familiar, but couldn't place him.

The man smiled and bowed very low. A smattering of applause erupted, and the man extended his arms for quiet. "Ladies and gentlemen," he intoned. "Lords and ladies, welcome to the first production at the Morrisman's Men ever to grace God's green earth. I know you are anxious to see the show, so I will provide the smallest of introductions and leave it to those you have paid to see." He took a deep breath. "Today's show will consist of three major parts. First a classic piece of medieval drama called the *Second Shepherd's Play*. That will be followed by a short example of what is called a Robin Hood play, and *that* by our crowning achievement: the first presentation in nearly five hundred years of a work currently known only as the Bowman-Smith Codex, though I like to call it *The Lord of This World*. If you would like to know more, please see the program. For now, I bid you—enjoy!"

"Did he say *Kotex?*" Marvin wanted to know, but Erline shushed him.

The man bowed, the applause began, and two bandy-legged shepherds wandered on from stage right playing drums.

"Wannie! Oh my God, no!" Jay screamed, smashing his sword's pommel against the unyielding barrier that had sealed them off from LaWanda. The steel simply bounced off the glass, which showed no damage; and even when he laid the sword against the shiny surface, it only hissed and glowed dully and melted far too slowly to be of any service.

Piper and Myra joined him there, both of them more than half hysterical.

"Wannie! Wannie!"

"Dammit—stuff won't break—"

"Oh, shit, man!"

Then faint but clear a voice came to them over the high walls: "Cool it, guys, I'm fine!"

"But what about the gryphon?" Jay called.

"It ain't movin'—and I ain't either!"

"Wannie, can you—?"

"I'm backin' up." A pause—and a dull scrambling, a thud, then a silence.

"Wannie!"

Another pause. Then: "It's okay, guys. Another wall formed just as it leaped, and—oh God!"

"Wannie! What is it?"

"This thing's roofin' over; it's—"

"Wannie!"

But it was no use.

Myra's face was a mask of despair. "Jay, is she . . . ?"

"I . . . I don't think so. That section just closed in, and we can't hear her now. We know the gryphon missed her, and she's a bright girl. She'll be okay." He did not sound convinced.

"I've gotta be *sure*," Piper wailed. He ran off down the corridor, sliding his hand along the mirror wall to his right.

"Piper!"

A moment later, he was back. He shook his head sadly. "Mirrors all the way, and no doorways as far as I can see. I guess it's best we move on."

"Piper—"

"No, it's okay. Like you said, Jason, she's a big girl, she can take care of herself."

Jay knew the effort it must be taking him to maintain any semblance of control at all. "I'm the only one who's really gotta go on," he said. "You guys wanta stay here and . . . and see if you can help?"

Piper laid a hand on Jay's shoulder. "Dal's Wannie's friend, too, Jay; she'd want us to go on without her."

Myra looked at him appraisingly, but tears were misted in her eyes. "Okay, Jay. Left or right?"

Jay pointed right. "That way, I reckon. Gotta keep goin', otherwise we'll all lose hope."

They plodded onward for maybe another five minutes. All the while the mirror walls to either side continued unbroken except for subtle changes in the inlaid designs. They had to be even more careful about their footing, though, because the glass flooring was slowly arching in the middle, presenting a curved surface which forced them constantly toward the walls.

"You hear something?" Myra asked. She had been walking along the left-hand side with one hand to the glass. "Hey, and feel this!"

Jay swapped sides and laid his hand against the slick surface—and felt a vibration. At the same time, he caught the noise. "It sounds like a train."

"It's gettin' louder," Myra noted.

"Yeah," Jay agreed. "And—oh my God! Look!"

The mirrored wall before them grew cloudy, then opaque, then began to thin and melt away into the air. The vibration became a rumbling which got louder as a hole formed in the glass. And as that opening grew larger, Jay found himself staring through the walls of fairy glass at the iron wheels of a freight train thundering by not two feet from his nose.

"Oh my God!" Myra cried, as the hole spread her way. "It's like—like the train's melting its way into this world."

"Which maybe explains why the car gave out rather than carving a hole in the Otherworld," Jay said. "I think a car—a moving car—simply doesn't overlap any one place long enough to do any lasting damage. But a train... a train's big and long and got a *lot* of metal in it, and it occupies the same place for a long time, so to speak. Maybe this one's long enough to burn through completely."

"Wait a minute," Myra interrupted. "If there's a train, there must be tracks. So maybe—"

"Maybe if we can get on the tracks before this wall closes we can use them to get back to Scarboro!"

"Worth a shot," Piper said. "All we've gotta do is wait for the train to go by, and jump."

It proved to be a very long train, maybe several hundred cars, and the longer it passed, the more the glass faded around them. The wall straight ahead had dissolved completely, and the floor was vanishing as well, giving way to the gray and pink granite chips that were a common roadbed in this part of Georgia. They were almost back in their own world. Almost—for behind them sheets of glass and mirror still rose far above their heads, reflecting at times the passing rumble of boxcars and flats, and at times the tangle of light and distortion that had characterized them before.

Finally the last car thundered by.

"And... *now!*" Jay yelled as he grabbed his friends and vaulted into what he hoped was his own world.

They stood on creosoted wood and hot steel, and the sky above them was the bright blue of early May in middle Georgia, while the wind brought with it a scent of diesel fuel and metal. The fog was gone except for odd tatters caught in a grove of pines across the tracks. Jay glanced over his shoulder, expecting to see the ominous icy glitter of the maze, but it too had vanished.

"Maybe," he said slowly, "we can't get back now. Any idea where we are?"

Myra studied the terrain. The tracks stretched straight to left and right amid a scraggly landscape of open fields, scraps of pine woods like that opposite them, and a couple of run-down mobile homes. A shallow ditch and a half-dozen yards of grassy right-of-way where all that separated them from a highway along which cars were whizzing as if another world did not lurk at one remove all around. "I'd guess we're a mile or so past Bogart," she said after a moment. "I think I see a Scarboro Faire sign over there."

Jay followed her gaze, so filled with relief he could hardly stand it. "Anybody for hitchhiking?"

"*You* guys stay here," Myra ordered as she undid the top three buttons on her shirt. She pranced boldly to the road-side, and stuck out her thumb.

Not ten seconds later a brand new GMC pickup skidded to a halt beyond her. "We need some help," Myra told the driver, a shirtless and dark-tanned boy of about seventeen. "Me and a couple of friends need a ride to Scarboro Faire. We're part of the show and our car broke down and we're late. One of 'em's got a sword, but they're friendly."

"Sure thing, lady," the boy called, as Myra motioned Jay and Piper forward. "Hell, I worked on the damn thing after school all winter. Might as well see how it turned out."

"What time is it?" Myra asked casually.

"Little after ten."

"How fast will this thing go?"

The boy grinned. "How fast you *need* to go, lady?"

"All she'll do," Myra told him, as he left twin streaks behind him.

* * *

Thomas the Hun was practically rolling in the aisle with laughter. One of the shepherds (Mak, he thought it was) had stolen a (stuffed) sheep and was trying to figure out where to hide it. Dahlia Cobb was on stage as Gill, Mak's shrewish wife—shrewish, but still not so willful as to ignore a possible opportunity. She grabbed the lamb from Mak's clutching fingers and headed toward the simple bedstead to the right of the stage.

"A good trick have I spied, since thou ken none," she cackled. "Here shall we him hide till they be gone—In my cradle abide—let me alone, and I shall lie beside in childbed, and groan."

To which Mak replied, "You think so?—I mean, 'Thou red?' And I shall say thou was light of a male child this night." Dal climbed under the covers and commenced moaning loudly.

Thomas doubled over with laughter.

The GMC stopped practically at the inner gate to Scarboro. Myra reached over to give the young driver a good solid smack on his cheek and call a quick thanks.

"No problem, lady," the boy called back, blushing, as Myra climbed out and met Jay and Piper who had already vaulted down from the bed where they'd been riding.

Jay found himself running, with Myra and Piper pounding along behind. They had entered the woods again—the real woods this time—and were weaving in and out among the more slow moving attendees on their way to the main gate.

So intent was he on making time that he almost thudded through the gate without stopping to pay. As it was, he had to pause and fumble in his pockets, then wait for Myra and Piper to arrive to sort out the finances. Tickets finally in hand, they entered Scarboro Faire.

Jay wished he had time to look around, because it really was like being in the Middle Ages. The atmosphere was right, the buildings acceptable.

"God, this is neat," he said in spite of himself.

Myra poked him. "What do we do now?"

Jay jumped. "Oh jeez . . ."

He stared around at the multitude, then nodded decisively. "Okay, Myra, you see if you can find Scott 'cause I think we may need him, and Piper and me'll go to the theater and scope that out—see if we can find Dal, or—God forbid—Robby. You can meet us there."

Myra nodded, "Gotcha."

"Okay," Jay replied. "Come on, Piper, let's boogie."

A radical change had taken place in *The Second Shepherd's Play*. After a good fifteen minutes of slapstick and farce, the action had taken a serious turn as the shepherds metamorphosed from larcenous medieval peasants to those very shepherds who were keeping watch in their fields the night the Christ Child was born.

"Hail, sovereign Savior, for thou hast us sought! Hail! noble child and flower, that all things has wrought!" one of them was saying as Jay brought himself to a stop right outside the entrance. Piper tumbled into him from behind.

"Jesus, Piper, watch it!"

"Sorry, man. I was just wondering about Wannie."

Jay reached out and hugged him impulsively. "Yeah, I know. But she'll be all right—she's got iron with her, and her own good sense. If anybody could come out of that, Wannie could."

"Yeah," Piper replied. *"If* anybody could."

"You okay?"

"Much as I can be." Piper straightened, squared his shoulders, tried to grin, but his eyes misted as they met Jay's. "So what do we do now, *Kemo-sabe?*"

Jay started to answer, and froze. What *were* they going to do? He was so near, he thought; at least they weren't doing the Bowman-Smith play yet. But how *did* one rescue a lady? How *was* one supposed to stop someone—or some*thing* like Colin?

Piper was looking at him expectantly. A single tear had

sneaked out of the corner of his right eye and was curling
down his cheek.

"Uh, yeah," Jay said finally. "I guess—I guess you'd
better look for Rob, while I try to find Dal."

"And then?"

Jay threw up his hands. *"I* don't know. He'll probably
have the sword with him—I would—so you'll have to be
careful whatever you do. Best I can say is delay him however you can. Try to get him away from the theater. Hell
—brain him with a board if you have to. The important
thing's to keep him from using the sword. If it draws
blood, God help us."

Piper hesitated.

"You up for it?" Jay asked.

Piper nodded.

Jay stuck out his hand and Piper slapped it. "Just think
about Wannie, Piper. Think about LaWanda."

"Always and forever," Piper replied as Jay darted away
to the left. He took a deep breath and started toward the
ticket window.

Myra watched as Jay and Piper melted into the throng,
then jogged determinedly away along the opposite side, to
double their chances of meeting Scott. She passed a potter,
then a woman selling intricate leather vests of every color
and material including purple snakeskin. There was a bunch
of stuff she wanted to look at, stuff that would go great in a
painting—when she had time. Somehow her jog became a
slow trot. A food vendor caught her eye, then a juggler
spinning apples and oranges above his head, three well-
coifed women standing beside a leering young man in purple
velvet doublet while a red-haired wench photographed them.

But no Scott.

Faster now, giving each booth a fast check, each face a
quick survey, often spinning to inspect a face more closely,
but never losing the rhythm of her feet.

She reached the middle of the Faire, and saw ahead of her
the Anachronists' compound: a small enclosure circled by a

split rail fence. Colorful shields hung along it, and above, before an arc of striped pavilions, a veritable forest of pennons and banners flew. She stopped at the first table she came to, behind which stood a man whose long brown hair flowed from beneath a brass circlet to well past his shoulders.

"And how can I help you, pretty lady?" he asked. "Duke Sir John the Mad Celt at your service."

"I'm looking for Scott," Myra gasped. "Scott Gresham."

Duke John frowned. "He one of us?"

"Uh, yeah. Used to be. Was supposed to have come last night."

"You don't happen to know his Society name, do you?"

Myra shook her head. "Sorry, can't remember—no, wait—" She pointed to a roundel of brightly painted plywood. "That's his shield, I've seen it over their mantel."

Duke John scratched his jaw and called over his shoulder to a small attractive lady who was engaged in a piece of intricate embroidery at a small table right behind him. "Hey Rhonda, you know whose shield that is—the sable and gules?"

"Oh—that's what's his name? Bryan? Yeah: Bryan of Scotia."

"Is he here?" Myra asked. "Have you seen him?"

"Not today. Last I saw him was late yesterday afternoon. He was sitting over by the theater, and then it looked like he got mad and stalked off."

"Which way?"

Rhonda pointed with her free hand. "Toward the woods, I think, past the Morrisman."

"And you haven't seen him today at all?"

"No," Rhonda replied. "And now I think of it, Thomas the Hun was wondering why he never came by last night."

"Uh—was it foggy out here last night? Real foggy?"

"You got it. Came up right before sundown."

"You know," Rhonda added thoughtfully, "come to think of it, the last time I saw Bryan he was walking into a patch of fog."

"Thanks," Myra managed to croak, as she headed toward the forest.

Machete poised before her, LaWanda slipped quickly around another archway.

A fast glance left, then right. Good, the coast was clear. Which way now? She glanced toward the opposite wall—lower than many—and saw looming to the right above it the tower, closer than it had ever been. Dark stone it looked like, and crenelated on top.

Okay, then, we go right.

Thirty paces covered, ever at guard. No openings to either side, no archways, nothing coming up behind. She allowed herself to relax a little.

Actually, she considered, things weren't nearly as bad as they'd been a couple of minutes earlier, when all that confusion behind her had resulted in her friends vanishing before her eyes. She'd thought she was a goner—the thing had leaped right at her, but she'd managed to dodge and only take a light rake across her left shoulder from one of the talons. The important thing was that the creature had landed poorly and had taken a moment to turn around. The wall had formed and saved her ass, and she'd been able to get word to her friends that she was okay before the top glazed over. Now if she could make tracks, she might yet catch up with them. She might even—

It was back, slinking through an archway thirty yards ahead. If she could just make it to that last opening, maybe—

She slid a foot behind her and struck glass; risked a glance over her shoulder. A wall of mirror had risen silently behind her.

No choice, then. She crouched.

The gryphon crept closer, staring.

Seconds crept by like centuries; confrontation became standoff.

Ten feet separated them. Ten feet between a slender young black woman with her hair in dreadlocks beneath a black bandana and her feet bare as the day God made her because she had decided to kick off her shoes for better traction on the glassy floor; and a creature that looked like it belonged on a flag somewhere—three or four feet high at the shoulder (about where the lion part ended), who knew how long from the feathered tip of its furred tail to the sharp golden beak that gaped wide and those glittering yellow eyes and those incongruous feathered ears that looked so strangely out of place on the colossal eagle head.

Sleep!

What was that? Had she heard it, or had it been in her head?

Sleep, dark one. And dream.

Crap! It was trying to distract her, to frighten her—but she wouldn't let it.

Sleep, those buzzing words insisted. *Sleep—dream—close your eyes!*

She felt her lids start to droop—fading, fading . . . But that would be disastrous. (*Keep one eye open at all times, girl!*) So she closed the right one, rested it for a tiny moment, and tried to focus for an instant on the iron blade in her hand.

It was working, too; or at least it was maintaining the status quo. But she didn't know how much longer she could resist.

Sleep.

She blinked. Somehow the gryphon was closer.

Sleep, it insisted. *Dream of warmth and darkness.*

The other talon slowly creeping, the eyes never leaving hers. *Sleep, pretty one, and dream—*

Chapter XXIV: Through with You

Oh, Wannie, Wannie, I hope you're okay, Piper told himself as he wove expertly through the crowd outside the Morrisman's Men. He meant to go inside, *would* go—as soon as he scoped things out a little more here. It wouldn't do to let Jay down by being hasty.

So he ignored the ticket window and headed for the entrance intent on doing a little spying.

A high wooden gate with rough-hewn points along its upper surface spanned the space between the two concrete towers, effectively cutting off the view from anyone who chose not to pay the admission. Now that the show was actually in progress, a small door set in one side of that barrier was the only point of ingress.

As nonchalantly as he could, Piper made his way toward the section furthest from the ticket window. Once there, he leaned against the boards and set his eye to one of the vertical gaps, hoping to determine if Rob was in the audience.

Rapidly he scanned each row and aisle . . . No luck. He would just have to break his last dollar.

One final hasty scan, and he made his way to the ticket window. "I was wonderin' when you'd make up your mind, darlin'," the buxom lass said, smiling, her phony cockney accent sounding a cut or two above the Scarboro norm. "Was 'fraid I'd have to call the constable an' have you put to the gallows. Thought you was a peepin' Tom or somethin'."

Piper tried to act unconcerned. "I was just seein' if it was worth me pennies, love," he told her. "And, hey, is it okay to go in while the show's in progress?"

The wench smiled. "It's near half over. Myself, I'd suggest you try the next one if you want to get the full effect."

Piper shook his head. "Can't—folks I came with gotta leave early. Uh, look, a friend of mine's in here, and I'd really like to see her; it's, like, *important*."

The girl eyed Piper levelly. "Okay, luv," she sighed. "Twenty-five pence for half the show, but don't tell nobody I told you."

Piper grinned and handed her his dollar.

"I can't resist brown eyes and curly dark hair," she explained as she returned his change.

"Me neither," Piper told her sadly, and left.

A moment later he eased open the small side door and entered the Morrisman's Men. Rob wasn't along the periphery, so Piper skirted to the right, making for one of the few empty places over in the front corner. His eyes moved constantly, checking faces, noting profiles. No luck. He was almost to his chosen seat: still no Robby. Maybe closer to the stage, maybe in the front row . . .

—Red about the legs, burgundy about the body, and gold about the hat, and then it was too late—because the figure who stepped out of the fabric-draped archway next to the stage had slammed into him with enough force to send him sprawling on his backside.

"Hey, watch it," Piper mumbled, glaring up at the dark shape who was already muttering apologies and extending a hand to help him up. The man's cow-flop hat cast his face into shadow, and it was not until Piper had regained his feet that he saw whom he had run into.

"Oh my God—!"

"Hardly." Rob Tolar grinned.

Piper's heart skipped a beat. "Uh, how's it goin', Robby?"

What are you doing here?

Did he *have* to shout like that? Piper wondered, then found himself wondering whether he had heard the words with his ears at all. Christ; what was he gonna do?

Look at me, Murphy! the inner voice commanded. Piper's breath caught, the muscles at the back of his neck tightened against his will, forcing his face to tilt upward.

Look at me!

Somehow Piper was staring straight into Rob's eyes.

What are you doing *here?* Rob demanded again.

"I'm supposed to be here," Piper managed to whisper. "I'm—I'm performing."

He's lying! Not Rob's thought, and chills raced over Piper's body. *He is a spy—a sneak,* that other continued. *He was looking for you.*

"So!" Rob whispered. "And why might that be?"

Piper's eyes widened. "Nothin', man. Just checkin' things out like I told you."

"Liar!"

Liar! And as that second accusation exploded in Piper's mind, he felt his knees start to buckle. Only Rob's iron grip supported him.

Tell the truth! two minds screamed as one.

Piper did not want to answer, did not want to give these terrible people the information they desired.

But to his horror he felt his throat loosen, his lips open. "Jay," he whispered hopelessly. "Jay's looking for Dal. He's gonna stop you."

Rob's eyes bored into his, and Piper saw the whole

world go first blue, then red, then black. He was distantly
aware of his legs crumpling beneath him, far less aware of
Rob helping him to a seat on the ground by the concrete
wall; then he lost himself in dreams of demons.

"Just leave him alone," Rob told the concerned man
who had come up beside him. "Guy just got a little light-
headed, and when I ran into him—blammo—sent him
over the edge. But don't worry, I'm gonna go get help."

It's all okay, he added, and watched with considerable
satisfaction as the man nodded stiffly and resumed his seat.
With Colin's help, Rob cast a small glamor to ensure that
anyone who chanced to glance that way would see only a
worn-looking fellow dozing in the shade, elbows resting on
bent knees, head flopped comfortably forward.

Then he ducked under the archway—and ran.

Myra was trying hard not to lose hope. She'd had no
trouble at all finding the trail the Anachronist lady had
mentioned, and had been rewarded shortly thereafter by
what she thought were Scott's footprints in the soft earth at
its upper end.

So she had followed the trail and had soon discovered
two more sets about a hundred yards further on, and a little
way beyond that a grommet she recognized from having set
ten like it along the neck slit of one of Scott's tunics. But
the thing that disturbed her was that though the prints all
led into the forest, none came out again.

Of course he could simply have exited some other way
—hell, he could have decided he wanted to leave with no
one noticing, skirted around through the woods, emerged
at the parking lot, and gone from there.

Myra suddenly wished she'd had the presence of mind
to look for his car when they'd come in—except, of
course, they'd had no reason to suspect he was missing.

And now she was deep into the forest and rapidly becoming frightened. She had hoped, at first, to keep the roar
of the Faire within range of her hearing, but that had been

impossible. She'd resigned herself to keeping one eye firmly on the trail, one on her shadow beneath her, and one on the sun halfway up the sky. Particularly on the sun, because though she preferred not to think about it, she was aware of the tricks that bright star had been pulling while she and Jay and Piper and poor, lost Wannie had been wandering around in places that had no business being where they were, much less acting like they did.

Sighing her exasperation, she pounded on down the path, establishing a steady jog that covered ground quickly but still gave a reasonable chance of noticing whatever signs there might be.

Unfortunately, she did not notice that the trees had suddenly become denser and taller than typical Georgia pines nor that the fog between those dark and shaggy trunks was slowly encircling her.

—Not until it touched her.

She screamed, felt a chill run down her back. That nebulous, twisting tendril was too cold to be natural. She froze, stared at the ground, realized to her horror that the fog was pooling, flowing ahead of her around the trees and down the trail.

She ran, then, with a deadly cold whiteness all around her—and suddenly no path before her to mark the way.

Lower your weapon! Lower your weapon! The words were a thunder of pain in LaWanda's head.

Yet she resisted, though each syllable cut through her skull like a bullet.

No! she thought back, though she wasn't certain when she had learned how. She had simply known.

Die!Die!Die!Die!Die!

The barrage intensified, and LaWanda started back in spite of herself, but regained her composure the instant she saw a tightening of muscle on the creature's shoulder.

DIE!DIE!DIE!DIE!DIE!—in a steam of agony.

LaWanda swallowed, suddenly aware of the sweat popping out all over her as she tried for all she was worth to

ignore the assault and at the same time not to lower her
guard.

DIE!DIE!DIE!DIE!DIE!DIE!D—

The attack ended. The pain vanished so quickly she
gasped.

And at the exact moment her attention faltered, the gryphon leapt—suddenly jerked around in thin air—and fled.

LaWanda backed away reflexively, wondering what
would have happened had her adversary not suddenly acted
so strangely. She tried to see what had become of it, but all
she could make out was a speeding golden shape a thousand times reflected before it rounded a distant corner and
disappeared.

Jay could tell by the abrupt cessation of applause that
the Robin Hood play had started. It would be followed by a
short musical interlude and the Bowman-Smith play would
come after.

Which meant he had about ten minutes to find Dal and
somehow—*somehow*—keep her from going through with
the thing. He supposed what he ought to do was get her out
of the way, then go after Robby, though what would happen at that point he had no idea. He still had his sword,
though much good it would do against a real one like Edward's, even if Rob didn't know how to use it.

Meanwhile, he crouched by the back edge of the Morrisman's left-hand wall and listened. Straight ahead was a
stand of pines, and beyond them the line of wooden fencing that marked the site's outer boundary on that side. The
fog was still lurking around back here, too, though it had
burned away in most other places.

And right at his feet were the half-dozen steps that led
up to the wings— into the women's dressing room, he
assumed from the symbol painted on the door.

Better get on with it, kid . . .

He took a deep breath and started climbing.

The door proved to be a sheet of plywood with cheap

hinges and a wooden knob; he simply pushed it open and slipped inside.

Inside was a sort of vestibule screened from the dressing room beyond by a sheet of cheap red fabric nailed to two-by-two framing. He didn't hear Dal's voice among the others whispering hoarsely on the other side of the divider, but to be sure he crept quietly to the curtain and squatted down to peer around it.

He saw mostly legs. Then, as he raised his eyes, the bodies above them: three in brilliant red demon outfits, several more in various stages of undress, and a harried-looking pair in jeans and Scarboro Faire T-shirts who were probably costume or makeup assistants. A chubbier girl with a sheaf of paper in her hand was doubtless a script coach, and the skinny kid in cutoffs was bound to be the prop mistress.

Dal wasn't anywhere to be seen, which meant she was almost certainly onstage—probably as Maid Marian.

"Ready, Anne?" one of the devil girls whispered.

Her taller friend nodded. "Hey, break a leg, huh?"

They giggled nervously.

Jay waited until a rumble of applause signaled the end of Robin Hood, then stood and gave three smart raps on the two-by-two that held the fabric partition.

The property girl poked her blonde head around the corner. Her face was dark as thunder.

Jay smiled apologetically. "I—I thought I'd drop by and wish Dal well."

The girl blinked in surprise and recognition. "Oh, gee—I didn't know you guys were back together. I thought—well—" She blushed. "Sorry. Come on in, everybody's decent." She stuck her head around to make certain. "No, wait; everybody's *not* decent. I forgot about Lannie."

Lannie, Jay remembered, was one of Dal's friends who would be playing Seductive Maiden in the Bowman-Smith play.

"Hold on a sec," the girl added. "There's Dal now, I'll

get her. You can't talk too long, though, 'cause she's gotta change *real* quick. Besides, you've gotta give yourself time to get back out there to see it."

Jay tried to look as though the fiction was true, and waited.

The ensuing dozen seconds were the longest in his life.

A strange silence filled the dressing room.

Then footsteps were coming toward the partition, and Jay was looking that way, anticipating.

What would he say?

Maybe a simple, "Dal, I love you."

A cloaked figured turned the corner.

Jay had only time to take in red hose and a burgundy doublet and a gold- and green-plumed hat and to wonder why Dal was suddenly so tall and wide shouldered—before three feet of fourteenth-century steel flashed out at him, slid neatly between two ribs, and buried itself in his body.

"You!" he had time to whisper, as white agony filled him.

"Us!" he had time to hear in gleeful reply, as Rob's arms grabbed him, dragged him to the outer door, and pushed him through before Jay could even see the blankness behind his eyes.

For a moment laughter echoed in his skull, then reality narrowed to the sound of his heartbeat growing slower and slower.

And of the passing of day into night.

Chapter XXV: Feeling Gravity's Pull

As she ran, Myra Buchanan felt the cold close on her. Her side was agony, and her feet had almost lost their feeling in the chill of surrounding fog. Her hip hurt, too, where she had fallen—a long skid down a bank she had not expected, and thank God nothing had broken. She had been on her feet at once, though, and rushing onward.

Pound, pound, pound: the sound of her footfalls, strangely distant. She felt the grinding of overstressed knees, the awful tightening of her chest as lungs demanded more air than she could provide.

The only point of comfort was the warmth of the dagger she had set in her hand when she started. She wasn't even certain where she'd got it, though it might have been one of Scott's. All she knew was that it had a satisfying heft and a sharp blade.

It *was* warm, too. And when she shifted it to her other

hand it left a pleasant tingle, and the more she noticed it, the more that warmth increased and flowed throughout her body and gave her strength.

Cold iron, Jay had called it, but iron was hot. It was a thing Faerie could not withstand. But this new power was different: the power to warm the soul.

Or was it the iron? Maybe she had some power of her own, born simply of strength of will. Perhaps if she *thought* warm she would *be* warm: desire had worked before, both for Jay and Piper.

Not breaking stride, she tried to imagine each movement generating a tiny pulse of heat, each exhaled breath spreading warmth upon her face.

It was working! She continued until she was toasty, then noticed for the first time that the fog was drawing away a little. She slowed, then, saw no increased threat, dared a full stop, waited, and eventually found herself at the center of an unstable sphere of clear air—facing a huge oak tree, so cracked and knobbed and fungied she could hardly believe it was part of any nature.

A scrap of color caught her eye, and she stepped closer. From one of those fissures hung a six-inch triangle of bright blue fabric—exactly like the tunic she had re-hemmed for Scott not three days before.

"Scott!" she shouted, slamming the dagger's hilt against the trunk. "Oh God, Scott, can you hear me? Are you okay?"

No response.

Myra stared first at the tree, then at nine inches of high-carbon steel in her hand.

—And stabbed the blade into the twisted surface.

A downward slash, and the blade struck a recalcitrant nodule and would not come free.

It was a terrible mistake. It had looked so simple, had worked like a charm the few other times she had tried it. But now, with the blade lodged firmly in the black bark, she knew she had expected too much—or too little.

For the oak was burning: flame creeping outward in a

slow line from the cut. The center was already glowing red, and smoke was curling back in a pale, thin line above it.

But Scott was yet a prisoner—and still alive, she thought because the tag-end of tunic had started to bunch and twitch, as if he were pulling against it.

Or writhing in agony.

"Scott!" she screamed again, pounding the bark once more. "Oh, please, Scott, answer me!"

Though she could not herself feel the heat of iron, the flames it brought forth in the Faerie wood were certainly real, because she could feel them. And likewise the smoke, which made her cough when the fey wind swirled it in her direction. And Scott was on the inside: closer to both.

Frowning, she gripped the hilt with both hands, set her foot against the gnarled bole, and tugged with all her might.

The blade jerked free, sending her tumbling backward, but she was up again before the impact had time to register, and carving away frantically, two feet to the left of the first cut. More flame and more smoke, as the blue flag of tunic twisted even more violently and the odor of charring cotton filled the air.

Until a few moments before, the one thing in the world that had given Scott any comfort was that the oak which had ensnared him was rotten in its core, so there was a sort of narrow chimney above him which let in a trickle of air. Unfortunately, it also let in the cold and the damp and a smattering of insects. He could feel them now, crawling all over his body, and he could not move to prevent them: the tree held him that solidly. Its rough wood gouged in from every angle, prisoning his arms, pressing tight along his legs, restricting his chest so that he could only take shallow slow breaths. He could swallow, a little, and move one eye upward to see a narrow oval of sunlight slowly creeping across the dark wood four inches in front of his nose. If he tried very hard, he could twist his upper body a couple of inches, but that was all.

He had long since stopped worrying about his hunger, or the agony in his bladder he had not been able to resist. These things no longer concerned him, because earlier he had become aware that the sticky dampness in which he stood had soaked through his shoes and started to work on his skin. His feet were burning now, burning and itching and he could do nothing at all to stop either. It was exactly as if he stood in a pool of mild but corrosive acid.

Thump!

What was that?

Thump, thump, scrape.

"I'm in *here!*" he had time to shout before the wood started to tighten.

"Help!" he tried again, weakly. "It's—"

He could move his ribs no longer, could take in barely enough air to get by.

And to make matters worse, it was suddenly becoming warmer. His right thigh and hip were hot already, and geting hotter by the moment. *Too* hot! A tiny gasp—all he could manage—and that new air brought with it the odor of smoke. A second brought more, and his arm and whole right leg were suddenly in agony. He put all his energy into one last frantic twist, but to no avail. What was going on? Was the fucking tree on fire?

"God*damn!*"—grunted, as the agony spread to his hand.

The pressure loosened the merest fraction.

He gave it all he had, twisted for all he was worth. . . .

Gasped, as the pressure suddenly lessened further; again as he felt a tug on his tunic.

And fell backward into clear air and the shaking arms of Myra Jane Buchanan.

"I must look like death on a stick," he croaked, and fainted.

Myra could not believe that her desperate efforts had succeeded. Yet here was Scott: completely befouled with wood crud; raw, shredded skin on his feet and ankles where something had dissolved his boots right off him; blistered burns visible through the foot-long chars on the back of his right arm, hip, and thigh. And he smelled terrible.

She dragged him as far from the blazing tree as she could, and stretched him out on the ground.

A leather wineskin slung at Scott's side was miraculously still full. When his eyes opened again a moment later, she offered him as much as he could manage without choking, then took a long swallow herself. To her surprise it was not wine but Gatorade.

"You okay?" she asked, when his eyes had cleared a little.

Scott nodded stiffly. "I hurt like hell all over, but I don't think there's anything wrong a good meal, a hot bath, and a generous slatherin' of burn goo won't cure."

"Can you walk?"

He flexed his legs experimentally. "Oh yeah. I'll have to go slow though."

"Good," Myra said, nodding over her shoulder. " 'Cause I think we'd better."

The oak was in full flame now: trunk and roots and branches, and those flames were already spreading.

Scott levered himself up. "I see what you mean."

Myra wrapped an arm around his waist, while he flopped one across her shoulders, and together they stumbled away. The heat was dispersing the fog, and already the trail was clearer.

Soon Scott had let her go, and limped along on his own, though she knew that effort cost him. She risked a glance behind her, saw a wall of flickering gold and red, then looked ahead again, to see the trail dart up a short, steep hill crowned with a line of dark trees, beyond which showed a brightening of the air that was not born of flame.

"Hurry, Scott," she cried, tugging at his hand. "I think there may be a clearing."

They redoubled their efforts, going as fast as they could, struggling up the hill. They shouldered between two trees and dashed from forest earth onto something both colder and softer.

"Jesus Christ," Myra exclaimed.

The woods had simply ended, trunks and limbs alike sliced cleanly away in a long straight line. Dust pooled about their feet—sawdust, mostly, inches thick and shimmering with gold and silver in their wake as they ran further into—into what? A highway maybe? It was like one: a long flat strip smashed laser straight through the forest—and the maze too, apparently. Opposite them, perhaps a hundred feet away, the forest resumed; to the right this strange clear space disappeared into fog once more, though Myra could see the glitter of glass and mirrors fifty yards up from where they had blundered through.

And to the left, no more than a half mile away, stood the tower. Tall it reared, dark against a lavender sky.

Shrouded in sulfurous smoke and flickering strobe light flames, the Fabulous Dahlia Cobb was counting backward from twenty, taking a deep breath through her mouth each time and exhaling it slowly through her nose. It was like the Tom Petty song said; the waiting was the hardest part. And no matter how many times she took the stage, how many performances, how many standing ovations, her first public appearance in a new role always did the same thing to her. Oh, she *looked* calm and composed (people had said) but inside all was chaos and turmoil.

She stole a glance through the gauze curtain behind the Hell mouth and surveyed the audience. A good crowd, anyway; nobody seemed to have left after the Robin Hood play, and the musicians were doing just dandy. One more tune, then she was on. Unconsciously, she smoothed a slender, black-nailed hand over the sleek red spandex of her costume. Rob had told her how terrific she looked right before she'd taken her place—but then, he was always telling her that. It was one of the nice things about him, one of the reasons she loved him. In fact, it had been just such a compliment that had made her accept his first offer of dinner and drinks and the 40-Watt Club after—when was it? A week ago? Jay never did stuff like that, the cheapskate. She wondered again what she had ever seen in him, then frowned, feeling the edge of a headache.

It had been such a nice dinner, too, she thought, trying to recall the particulars. They had gone—where? She couldn't remember. Martell's maybe? She shook her head. Nerves must be worse than she imagined. Back to business, girl.

But still the memory nagged. Something was still not right: her mind had been playing tricks on her lately—tying her up in knots. She'd even mentioned it to Rob a little while ago, but he'd only grimaced and told her it was typical stage fright exacerbated by the fact that she'd had to sign on at such short notice. But Rob had needed her, Rob had—

"Twenty seconds, Dal," someone whispered. She nodded, and took an even deeper breath than usual.

Five. I am not nervous. I have done this hundreds of times. The musicians started the tune that was her cue. The brawny demon lads began to scoot the Hell mouth forward. Dal straightened her shoulders and went with them.

Four. I know my lines, I know my cues, I look magnificent.

A smattering of *oohs* and *aahs*. The jet of flame leaped out right on time, scorching a hapless musician. Uproarious laughter. Dal arched her back, curled and extended each finger in sequence.

Three. I am *the Devil, and the Devil is me; evil is what I live for.*

More flame, more smoke, the smell of rotten eggs. The whistle player was now the only one playing, his tune becoming even more complex. The prompter was giving her the hold/five-second signal.

Two. There is nothing in the world I want more than to see man forsake God and be my servant.

The fans behind the smoke machine came on. Red and yellow lights flashed beyond the veil of painted gauze. A kettledrum began to rumble.

One. And man I will betray!

She pushed the curtain aside and stepped from the mouth of Hell.

Then, step by careful, tiptoed step, crept toward the poor musician—raised her pitchfork—and stabbed him in the backside.

As the audience roared with laughter she chased him frantically around the stage. One lap, two laps—*God, it was good to make people laugh!*

The musician made it to safety—barely.

The stage was hers.

(And good to scare the crap out of them as well.) She drew herself up to her full height and strutted sensuously toward the edge, paused, surveyed the audience appraisingly, then narrowed her eyes and looked straight at a gaping teenage boy.

" '*I am called Satan, I'm Lord of this World,*' " she hissed at him alone.

As the suns of *three* Worlds coincided.

Rob stood in the wings and watched and waited. It was all going perfectly. The musicians had done their work, the audience was primed. And Dal, not even a minute on the stage, already had the audience in the palm of her hand. He waited for the familiar opening lines—*and found he could not hear them!*

For with her first syllable, an impossible chill clamped around his heart and froze his blood and made his lungs feel like they would shatter if he even dared to breathe. Then that awful cold was replaced by heat so intolerable it was as if all the frozen cells of his body had melted and were boiling away into vapor. He stared at his hand, expecting to see steam pouring from every pore, but nothing greeted his eyes except smooth skin, neatly trimmed nails, and a dusting of wiry black hair.

Agony once more ripped through him.

Colin, what is it? he cried.

No answer. There was nothing subtle about the Faerie

mage now, as he smashed through Rob's memories, swept
aside emotions, and set his senses flaming.

No! Get out! Rob screamed, as he felt fire flash down
his optic nerve, saw his vision go out of focus, and knew
that Colin looked out there.

*Why, what is the matter, Robert? I'm doing exactly as I
told you.*

Rob gasped for breath, but those gasps came at Colin's
discretion. His heart thumped the beat of a panicked drummer. Colin was forcing himself into Rob's entire body, filling him, making him feel as though the space between his
very atoms was suddenly crammed to overflowing, like hot
metal poured in a mold. He tried to scream but could not.
Neither his tongue nor his throat would obey him. Colin
was now his master.

Rob could only stare in amazement. Colin had evidently
done something to his eyes—stretched them, *changed*
them, and done likewise to all of his senses. For now Rob
could see things that he knew he should not be seeing, feel
things, hear things, *sense* things—*know* things he should
not know.

Yet he knew them . . .

Knew fog had clamped down all over middle Georgia in
a cold, dense whiteness that sprang from clear air and
smothered vision like a soggy blanket. And somehow he
was one with that fog; whatever touched it touched him.
He *felt* it when cars raced blindly into silent white curtains
with no lights on, then shot off the road or smashed head-
on into traffic . . .

And he *felt* the horror, as air traffic controllers at the
world's busiest airport in nearby Atlanta blinked in baffle-
ment when clear runways suddenly became invisible, then
heard them shouting frantic orders as radar screens exploded with dots and sparkles, while a Delta 747 from
Memphis tried to abort its landing, failed, took a freeway
overpass with it, and cartwheeled onward, burning . . .

And he *saw* an oak tree rise up in the middle of Athena
Carpet Mills two miles away, then collapse again in cinders

when its branches tried to twist aside the steel rafters; and he *felt* the heat of that burning . . .

Saw mountains shimmer and flash as they fought to take form to the north; *heard* the crash of thunder that smashed half the windows in Gainesville . . .

Saw students at the University of Georgia stare in amazement at the trunks of trees that exploded into being all over campus, tore buildings asunder—and vanished before a solid wall of wind . . .

Saw and *heard* a magnificently winged female gryphon screaming from the top of the IBM Tower in Atlanta and another answering from atop General Lee's head at Stone Mountain, and a third picking up the cry forty miles away in the center of Sanford Stadium where five hundred feet of scaled and fanged horror was oozing into being around the second level, hungry for the hot blood of mortals . . .

Rob saw all these things and more, saw and felt and heard them—and was disgusted. But Colin laughed, gloating as Tir-Gat ghosted into existence in the Lands of Men —ghosted and flickered and melted away once more. For the words were not yet finished that would free both land and him, nor had the Other One arrived whom he needed to complete his resurrection. Even then, it would take until the suns broke apart at nightfall for all to be concluded.

Colin could have watched forever, at once sorry for the chaos he had summoned, yet glorying in the Power it implied. A world—a whole world was his, coming to life as he watched.

Piper wasn't certain whether it was sound or cold or simply weird vibes that awakened him after Rob had hoodooed him. But part of him had been aware that when Dal came onstage and started talking, something had *changed*. Then had come a flood of cold that poured over him like one of those frigid patches you sometimes found while swimming, only this one had gone right to the bone, then had tickled his heart and made it twitch before it had finally passed.

But it had evidently twitched some nearby hearts and *not* gone on, because a fat woman was lying on the ground scarcely ten feet away, gasping. Somebody was mumbling about heart attack, and somebody else was talking about pacemakers, but they were all putting out vibes that felt mighty like panic.

As a matter of fact, Piper had never felt such vibes before: not in one of Wannie's trances, not when Myra'd hypnotized him, not even from that bodacious amethyst crystal Jay had brought him from Hiawassee—

Jay!

Oh Christ, Piper thought. *I gotta go warn Mr. Jason.*

"Christ, oh Christ," he repeated as he scrambled to his feet and ran for the fog-filled gate.

Colin had relaxed a fraction; and Rob Tolar once more was waiting—though now he had a hole in his memory.

The play was coming along nicely, even with the chaos that had broken out here and there. The Faire medical people seemed to have that pretty well in hand, though; they had already taken away the woman who had collapsed.

And of course Dal was doing famously. She almost had Mankind in her grasp. He had resisted money and power and now Satan was offering him sex—overtly in the form of three scantily clad ladies the Lord of this World had caused to appear through the miracle of smoke bombs and trapdoors, but also covertly in her own gliding movements, seductive glances, and provocative twitches. And poor Mankind—a thatch-haired, open-faced Gary Carmichael in patched blue tights and ragged gray tunic—was having a hard time resisting. Indeed, the bogus phallus beneath his costume was *not* resisting, and the audience was practically beside itself as they watched it push the skirt of his tunic further and further out as the actor squeezed the concealed bulb apparatus that activated it. In a moment one of the damsels would drop a strategically placed (but still G-rated) veil, and he would lunge for her.

Then it would be time for his entrance: Rob Tolar as St.

George, resplendent in shimmering (plastic) mail and the white surcoat bearing the traditional red cross. His costume was authentic, right down to the sword beneath his hand.

But Colin was seeing things, too; watching the worlds align beneath the fog. He could already sense the silver Tracks spinning about in search of substance, could half make out his mountains and valleys and his poor, shattered maze. His tower was taking form, too—exactly where he stood. Too bad the humans could not see it.

Nor, for the moment, could Rob, because Colin had to allow his slave control enough to play his part until all parts were ended. In the meantime he watched and waited, and saw the shadows grow solid around him. And wondered what was keeping the Other.

Piper felt his way around the curve of gate tower and struck off in the direction he had last seen Jay heading. The fog was back, weaving all around him like a living thing, so dense he could scarcely see his feet. And wherever it clumped in patches he started seeing shadows, like things were sort of hiding in there until they could finish taking form. He suddenly had no desire to ever see fog again.

But he wanted very badly to see Jay.

The wall abruptly ended, cut off so suddenly that his hand skidded into space and threw him off balance. He lurched forward, snagged his foot on something soft but substantial, and sprawled hard onto his face.

His breath was knocked out of him for a moment, and the most fascinating lights and glitters swam briefly before his eyes. But eventually sense returned, and he sat up and felt behind him. Whatever he had tripped over was too big and gooshy to be a normal obstacle.

His fingers brushed something. Hair stood up all over his body. Suddenly he was afraid to look back. His sweat was colder than the surrounding fog.

Come on, Murphy, you might as well get it over with.

And with that he twisted his head around and came face-to-face with Jay Madison.

"Jason, my man!" he cried joyfully, "what're you doing back here . . ."

But even as the words left his lips, his throat locked and his heart gave a little twitch. Jay's eyes were wide open and staring at absolutely nothing, and there was a large stain across the front of his T-shirt and a puddle of sticky red blood all around him.

Sweet Christ, no! Piper breathed, not realizing until his left hand touched flesh that he had even sent it questing.

Something broke, then. "Jay?" he whispered, then louder "Jay! Answer me!" Then, "Oh God, bro, answer me, answer me! Not you too, it can't be! I love you, man, you can't leave me, can't leave your buddy Piper!"

But Jay never moved.

Though it cost him more than anything he had ever done —except, perhaps, abandoning LaWanda—Piper reached out and closed Jay's eyes. "Rob did this, didn't he, man?" he sobbed. "Oh Christ, man, I'll get even, I'll kill that fucking son of a bitch for you. But shit, I can't leave you here, gotta find some help, gotta get you taken care of."

He started to rise, but sat back down again. It just wouldn't do to leave his friend alone and cold in the fog, not Jay who loved sunlight and summer and sunbathing in the nude by the side of the river.

No, it simply wouldn't be right.

Suddenly he had an idea: he would give his almost-brother his own personal send-off. He fished around in the inside pocket of his vest and found what he was looking for.

Even in the fog it glittered a little, and as he looked at it, the white vapor seemed to draw back from it a fraction. It was his old, cheap penny whistle, the one he never went anywhere without. He smiled wanly, brought it to his lips, and kissed it gently. "This one's for you, bro—and maybe you too, Wannie," he whispered, not even trying to blink away tears as he began to play.

The song was a slow, mournful version of "King of the Fairies."

Chapter XXVI: Finest Work Song

A corner turned, fog swept aside, and Cathal ran ever onward—though not in pursuit of the mortal. She had eluded him once already, which galled him, but what sport he might have gained from resuming their sparring match had faded from importance when Master's Call had started. It was growing stronger by the moment, too, and that was all that mattered. Someone was speaking the Words that called Tir-Gat into being, yet alone they were not sufficient. Master needed *him*. Needed him now. He had to hurry.

Mirrors flashed by, showing his golden reflection a thousand times over, but he ignored them, turned another corner, plunged once more into shifting white shadow as mirror walls rose behind him. All he knew were the Words, the chill of the glass beneath his feet, and the fact that in spite of having summoned that fog, he was lost in it—but getting nearer.

The creature was closing, though LaWanda still could not see it. But she could hear its breathing and the swishing of the air at its passing. Frantically she sought escape, a place to hide. Zip. There were no openings nearby, the glass was too slick to climb, and she could not count on capricious walls to save her again.

This was it, then. She took a deep breath, pressed herself against the wall, and waited, machete poised for one final deadly slash if only she got the chance.

Closer and closer—the claws and the breaths and the wind-swishing all. She glanced that way, saw a flickering glimmer in the fog that could only be the beams of light emitted by the creature's joints.

She tensed, saw the beast itself, a darker shape amid the swirls . . . Out of the mist and rushing down upon her . . .

Just a little longer; hold . . . hold . . . NOW!

LaWanda leapt, machete flashing.

The gryphon swerved, shouldered her aside—and ran *past* her.

She slashed anyway—once, twice. Touched nothing; saw only a few drifting feathers.

And paused for a moment, listening, not daring to hope, though she could already hear its footsteps fading.

Not returning.

Twice that had happened! Twice it had had her and blown it! *Thank you, Jesus!*

Still not quite believing what had happened, LaWanda dusted herself off and continued on her way—the opposite direction from the gryphon. The corridor bent sharp left a hundred paces further on, disclosing a series of archways. She chose one at random, and had not gone twenty yards down the ensuing hallway before the walls vanished abruptly from either side, and she stepped into an open space ankle deep in gold and silver sand mingled with sawdust.

The fog was much thinner there; she could see for yards all around. The sky was brighter, too, and there was wind —and the smell of burning.

She glanced around, saw a flicker of red a fair way off to her left, and felt the merest brush of heat against her face.

And then that warm wind twitched the fog aside, and she saw the tower looming straight ahead, dark and threatening.

As the fog parted further, she caught a clearer glimpse of the road (if that's what it was). Arrow straight it ran, aimed directly toward that edifice. And not fifty yards away were Scott and Myra.

"Wait up!" she shouted, and started running.

Myra whirled around. "Oh my God, Wannie!" she cried, and was running herself as LaWanda dashed through a tendril of mist and leapt toward her with a grin on her face as wide as the world—a grin that reflected back a million times in the dust of mirrors below them.

Suddenly they were together. Myra's face broke into a grin that was at least as wide as LaWanda's, and they clasped each other in an embrace Myra thought would never end.

"Hey, take it easy, girl," LaWanda gasped when Myra finally released her. "Hey, it's okay, I'm fine, but I think we oughta boogie, 'cause you-know-what's still hangin' around somewhere."

But Myra was not quite ready to move on. "Wannie, Wannie, Wannie," she kept repeating: "Oh, thank God, thank God!"

LaWanda smiled. "Never mind, girl, we both know there was nothin' you could do to help; and besides, you had another problem to deal with. Shoot, I had a good time back in there with that kitty-bird."

"Liar!" Myra chuckled.

"Only about the last part. But seriously, we oughta get movin'. I see you found your main man."

Myra's face colored at the reference. Scott was still where she had left him: hanging back discreetly like the gentleman he was, and looking thoroughly bewildered.

He raised an eyebrow. "Like to tell me what the hell's been goin' on?"

Myra sheathed her dagger, slipped an arm around his waist, and started for the tower. "Yeah," she said. "It's like this . . ."

Rob was on stage now, facing Dal, with Gary Carmichael between them.

—Except that it was St. George contending with Satan for control of Mankind's soul. They glared at each other, the two of them relishing the confrontation, Satan hissing and posturing, and St. George imperious and bold.

"You call yourself the master of men," St. George snapped, "But you're nothing but piss in a potful of sin."

"You think you're a warrior, a fighter, a knight!" Satan gave him back, "But you're less than a flea or a fly or a mite!"

"I've the power of goodness, I fight in God's name; and I'll swear on my sword, and my strength, and my fame."

"Your fame is a fraud, your strength is a joke, and as for your sword, why it's just rotten oak!"

And as St. George glared ineffectually at her, Satan went on: "And I'll now take this man, for his soul I have won; and defy you, the Father, and his sniveling Son!" And here Satan took Mankind in hand and strutted defiantly toward the Hell mouth.

Whereupon St. George could stand no more, drew his sword, and ran after the Lord of Evil. He caught her, of course, though not without resistance, and tore Mankind screaming from her grip, then poked the blade into the small of her back. With his other hand, he produced a rope with which he bound her hands together before her.

Then, to hearty applause, he spun her around in place

several times, and as the poor confused Devil attempted to stagger away, led her to an executioner's block which had miraculously appeared in the center of the stage. He thrust her down behind it and strode around in front, reveling in his power (and conveniently blocking the view while Dal loosened her hands and maneuvered a dummy head into position from under her voluminous cloak). Jesus, it was nice, Rob thought, to stand in front of all those people and know you looked like he did: it was an image for kids to take home and remember. Maybe it would even make some of *them* become actors.

Satan kicked and thrashed.

St. George flashed his teeth and wiggled his eyebrows at the audience confidentially as he ran a finger along the edge of his sword. It cut him, but he did not let that show, nor did he notice how the blood ran down the blade, nor how the hilt greedily absorbed it.

With a flourish of robes and a flash of blade he strode around to stand beside the cowering Satan who had now replaced her head with a papier-mâché copy while Dal drew her own head down beneath the high collar of the cloak. Again he grinned at the audience, really camping it up.

Satan shuddered violently.

St. George raised the sword, then lowered it and tested it against Satan's neck. Once more he wiggled an eyebrow, then repeated the sequence twice more.

The next blow would be the real one. He raised the sword chest high . . . shoulder high . . . over his head . . .

—Shifted his grip, jammed the broken hilt wire into his palm.

Suddenly the gates of memory that he had locked (or that had been locked against him) broke open. Suddenly he knew: Colin's dreams, his wishes, his plans. He was Colin mac Angus; Robert Tolar was nothing. And *he*, not the cowering Satan, was Lord of this World. Blood was all he needed now to summon Tir-Gat and make his form corporeal—blood, and the help of that Other.

For a moment he savored the weight of the sword, then started to swing it downward.

Not toward the dummy neck but toward the real one.

Though Piper did not know it, the Power released by the ongoing play coupled with his music—that old, strange tune out of Faerie—had taken him a little outside time.

Not that it would have bothered him had he known; all that mattered now was that the music continue. Too much had happened lately, first to him, and then to Wannie, and now to his buddy, Jason; and he just couldn't stand it any longer. So he sat on the chill damp ground with the fog a white blanket about him and poor Jason's head pillowed in his lap. This way he could both play and look at Jason's face, and the tears that were falling from his eyes in a regular torrent would fall on Jason's face too, and that would be good karma: a personal kind of water-sharing straight out of *Stranger in a Strange Land* or *Dune*.

Don't be dead, Jason; oh please, Jason, don't be dead. The words circled round and round through Piper's mind in a litany that wove in and out of the melody. He supposed he really should notify somebody, but somehow the music demanded he continue, that he tootle his way through round after round. He was doing variations, now; and the tempo had picked up and achieved a sort of wildness that was far more mad than sprightly.

You're losin' it man, and it's showin' in the music.

Yet on and on he played, with Jason's blood and his own nimble brown fingers on the penny whistle the only color in all the white world.

Jay was floating in silver radiance as peace wove itself about him, and calm slid smooth fingers around the point of pain that centered in his chest. It was so pleasant, so wonderful. He wondered if he was dead. Whatever it was, he liked it.

Then three things happened.

The first was that music came into the place where he

was and danced and twitched like a wind among dry leaves, and where it moved, it brought memory of life: of things loved and desired, of joys yet untasted—and urgent tasks yet undone.

The second thing was that the pain in his chest shifted by degrees to a point of heat which slowly trickled through his nerves and muscles to enfold his faltering heart where it suddenly exploded into fire.

It was terrible! He couldn't stand it, couldn't stand the agony; he had to escape, had to—

Thump.

The first strong stoke brought more pain than he could imagine. But the second followed so quickly with even more, and the third and fourth so easily transcended even that that he thought he had surely been consigned to eternal damnation. Yet by the tenth beat the pain had lessened, and by the twentieth it had ceased to trouble him, as warmth began to travel throughout his body, awakening each part first with flaming agony, then with relief—and finally with an ecstasy that was almost sexual.

The third thing that happened was that he became aware of a voice speaking to him inside his head. *I am with you, now,* that voice told him, *and it grieves me that you had to suffer so upon our joining.*

Edward? Jay thought.

Aye, Edward the smith, of Ripon.

I think I am dying.

Were you dying we could not speak. Beyond hope your friend's music has healed you. Now, Awaken, for Colin's country is forming. Can you not feel it?

So we've gotta hurry.

Aye, but Tir-Gat must come closer still.

At the expense of our *country?*

If need be. I made an oath, a foolish one perhaps, but I would not be forsworn. That is the price of hate.

You hate my brother?

I hate the one who controls him, the one who would have had you slain.

But—

*Whenever I doubt I recall how Colin tormented my fam-
ily: my child that he twisted with dreams; his children and
their children after who kept the tale alive of their old
father who had slain the Devil.*

How do you know this?

*Some I witnessed, some Alberon told me. He revealed
the future to me as I lay wasting, and told me what I must
do to prevent it. But things went awry, and more than
awry, and I waited long and long before you touched me
and I reawakened. That bond may have saved you; for
when your brother stabbed you, I left the blade and came
into you. By then but one hope remained, which was that I
might give you strength enough to return and complete my
wyrd. I have helped you; now you must repay me.*

How?

First awaken.

I am awake.

You are not; you simply dream it. Breathe.

I am breathing.

Not enough to sustain you.

I have forgotten how.

Breathe!

It hurts too much.

You have known more pain than that already.

But that was not my doing.

*Breathe, damn you, or be damned! Send me to oblivion,
send your lady into shadows. He will drink her life, you
know, drink her dry to her very soul because of Power that
is in her blood. She will not come here. You will never see
her more on either side!*

No, that wasn't possible, he *had* to see her again, *had* to
love her one more time. He remembered the sound of her
voice, his joy in the way she looked; remembered the way
her lips tasted and the way she could be comfortable and
homey one moment and wild and free the next, remembered that wry way she had of telling stories. Why, there

was the one about the time she had caught Piper and La-Wanda . . .

Somehow he was laughing—first in his head, then he felt his diaphragm tighten, his lungs start to push against his ribs.

Agony ripped through him, but reflex took over and he inhaled. His first gasp started nothing. The second tasted blood.

The third brought the scent of cooking meat, pine trees, and flowers.

Jay opened his eyes, and looked up at Piper, who sat above him, still playing his whistle.

"Piperman?" he giggled. "I'm back!"

Something wet splashed onto his face, and he blinked. When he opened his eyes again, Piper was looking at him.

"Then I got what I wished for," Piper told him. "And you have got to get movin'; I think there's still time to save her."

Jay dragged himself to his feet, though his body was a mass of scrapes and bruises that protested with every movement. Piper helped him with one hand, while the other somehow kept the beat of the music.

For a moment Jay simply stood there, rubbing his arms in wonder, feeling the firm muscles beneath his hands, the thumping miracle of pulse once more sending fiery blood pumping through his veins to awaken his body and sweep the last of the cobwebs from his brain.

Hurry, Edward told him. *I will lend you as much strength as I dare.*

Even so warned, the shock was beyond anything Jay had ever experienced: energy flooded into him, obliterating pain and banishing fatigue. And with it came a sharpening of the senses, a further clearing of the mind—and better than all these, the joyous return of that almost mystical elation that had filled him when he first touched the Bowman-Smith sword. He had never felt more alive, never more certain of himself or his mission.

Squaring his shoulders, Jay leapt up the steps, opened the dressing room door—and ran.

One moment Jay was shouldering through a shabby, cluttered room full of costumed, protesting women, and the next he was pounding across the vast emptiness of a stage that was completely bare except for a gaping Hell mouth at back left and, in the center, a sword-wielding Rob towering over a kneeling Dal.

But as he ran, the focus of his world widened, his senses stretched thin and taut. Time felt strangely attenuated, and he had plenty of leisure to note the amount of give in the thick plywood flooring and the matching flex in his joints that compensated for each heavy footfall; and to hear that wood creak and feel the air thin as mouths popped open in surprise and inhaled as one when the crowd realized someone had intruded into the action who did not belong there. A thousand human eyes rounded in amazement—and a thousand more glittered in the fog that was quickly ghosting in from outside to hide the audience.

Jay saw as if in slow motion the sword descending toward Dal's neck. In spite of everything he would be too late to save her.

Three feet to impact, two feet . . .

One . . .

At the last possible instant the sword twisted aside and struck off the dummy head.

A slow gasp crested through the audience, and a few laughed or applauded, but by then Rob was raising the sword again and turning around so that Jay could read his features: a quick shifting of confusion and surprise and anger, all touched with a trace of betrayal, as if part of that anger was directed inward. Words echoed in Jay's mind, though he knew they were not meant for him.

Coward! Betrayer! Weakling! Fool!

You betrayed me, asshole. You almost made me kill her! You were a fool to trust me!

Rob paused in mid turn, his body suddenly frozen, and

Jay knew that two minds were contending inside him. Then Jay's body stiffened, and another mind smashed through his thoughts and seized control of his muscles. He felt his legs tense, his arms stretch wide as a leap sent him flying straight toward that blade which before had nearly killed him.

Only this time he was faster, this time Edward was in control, and before Robby could move to impale him, the two of them crashed together and slammed to the floor. Then Jay was wrapping his arms around Rob, while his brother stuggled to extricate the sword which had become trapped beneath him.

It was awful, Jay thought, to know one's body was entirely out of control, to inflict pain and feel pain, yet not be able to stop it. But the worst thing was Edward. Edward was insane, now, or so far enraged as to make no difference. Jay could feel the man's emotions: feel five hundred years of hatred gain focus and take aim at Robby. Suddenly Jay was very sorry for his brother if something similar had been happening to him.

Somehow Jay got Rob's arms pinned and was pounding his forearm across his brother's wrist, numbing the nerves so that Rob's fingers finally loosened their grip on the hilt.

Jay yanked it free—and felt an unearthly chill as Power jolted through him like an electric shock.

Then Edward took complete control, and before Rob could recover, was driving the sword straight toward Rob's heart.

Rob twisted aside, but not far enough. The sword buried itself in the flesh above the ribs. Rob gasped and thrust Jay away, then grabbed the blade as Jay tried to wrench it loose for another blow.

Jay tugged at the sword, but Rob would not let go. Inch by inch he dragged his bloody hand along the metal.

—And abruptly clamped it down upon Jay's.

Jay heard screams from the audience, saw people rushing in from the wings and Dal dragging herself to her feet as Piper thundered across the boards behind him.

And then everything disappeared, and he found himself thrust into a world comprised entirely of thoughts and emotions. Rob was there: confused and in agony yet still arrogant: and so was he, indignant at having his body usurped against his will and relieved that Dal had survived one crisis, although horrified at what had happened; and Edward was there with his rage already subsiding into re-gret—until it flare to life again because Colin's thoughts had flared to brighter life as well. Jay reached toward the twisted brilliance that was the Faerie mage—brushed the surface of his thought—and cried out as Colin's anger stabbed into him like a dagger, found something and dragged it free before Jay even knew what it was.

What . . . ?

I have found what I need in your memories, mortal boy, Colin told him triumphantly. *You thought to defeat me, but you have blundered into your own doom.*

No! Edward shouted, enraged.

Jay echoed that aloud. For his vision had returned, just in time to see Rob's eyes open wide in terror as his body began to blur and reform.

Then Rob's eyes were gone: it was Colin who looked out of his face, and Colin who drew on the pure Power that was his in the body and blood of Rob Tolar to send him tumbling, sword still in hand, into Piper.

Jay scrambled to his feet as Rob also rose, but by then Rob had grabbed Dal and was making signs in the air.

"Jay—" Piper called.

He felt Piper's hands clamp his shoulders and had just time for one final desperate stab before the fog entombed them.

And then the whole world turned over.

Chapter XXVII: It's the End of the World as We Know It (and I Feel Fine)

Jay only had time to see that there was hard stone under his feet and a circle of battlements waist high around him and to get a sense that he was suddenly high in the air beneath a sky that was all the wrong color, before Rob was once more upon him.

His last frantic stab had apparently pierced only fabric, but the blade was still ensnared, so there was no good way to meet his brother's abrupt leap forward. He tried to dodge sideways, but the parapet was hard to the right and some kind of pool was to the left; and in the instant before he could choose the lesser evil, Rob's left hand slammed down on his outstretched wrist, just as his right grabbed for the sword. Jay suddenly found himself facing an adversary who was not only larger than he, but also armed and possibly both possessed and crazy.

Jay jumped back, narrowly avoiding a lightning thrust.

He was distantly aware of Piper scurrying out of the way, of Dal looking pale and shaky at Robby's back.

A flip of Rob's fingers, and Piper flew backward into the wall, then slumped down on the stone pavement.

Rob smiled wickedly—or what looked sort of like Rob, for he was growing taller and thinner, and his eyes showed a flicker of emerald above cheekbones that were now more prominent. His hair was getting longer, too, and turning red. And he still had the sword and was still advancing— taking his time now, toying with Jay, backing him ever closer to the pool.

Jay was frankly amazed his brother could even stand. Yet the blood had already stopped flowing from his wound, and there was no trace of awkwardness in his movements as he took another step. Then a worse realization dawned: his brother could read his thoughts—which meant he could foresee Jay's every move and be there ahead of him to block it.

Why doesn't he just zap me and get it over with? Jay wondered.

Because this way provides more pleasure!

Jay swallowed hopelessly, feeling naked and alone on the top of this terrible tower. His fingers slapped desperately at his hips, searching in vain for the dagger he had stashed there earlier; wishing he had the sword he had lifted from Scott's collection; wondering how he had been such a fool to forget it back at the Morrisman.

Rob stepped closer, the point glittering with death.

Another step back, another, a feint to the right, then left, hoping against hope the move was too quick for Rob to anticipate.

Brief success.

The sword whistled; Jay ducked, shot his left hand out and down to flip an handful of water into Robby's face.

The back slash did not connect.

How did I do that?

I acted while you waited, Edward told him.

"Jason—here!" Piper's cry was weak but the message was clear.

A sideways glance, just long enough to see Scott's sword leave Piper's hand and skitter across the flagstones. Jay leapt that way, dodged another blow, then rolled, as Rob's sword whistled past his thigh. His hand brushed metal, and he closed his fingers around the hilt.

"Go get 'im," he heard Piper call as he continued his roll. Robby leapt to engage him. Jay was still down, but a quick kick at his brother's legs sent him staggering. Good, Colin didn't know that kind of fighting. Another kick, another roll, and Jay was on his feet and whipping the sword down in a sudden blaze of sun fire as he turned sideways to present a smaller target. Parity was achieved again, sort of.

Jay tried to steal a glance past his adversary to Dal, who had somehow stumbled to the opposite side of the tower. "Piper—see to Dal!"

Then there was no time for words, because Rob was moving quicker than Jay could follow—drawing back and to the left to avoid the pool, angling his right side forward, blade inscribing quick-spun circles in the cool damp air.

Jay's eyes widened, but then Edward took charge once more and forced his body into a defensive stance he did not exactly know but which felt familiar from his backyard SCA bouts with Scott.

Rob's blade flashed down, but Jay raised his own to block it. Another fell, and another. Jay suddenly had his hands full simply trying to stay alive. Edward was in control now, and he sensed that his co-walker was a master swordsman, yet that fact gave him little comfort. Blows were aimed right but fell short, parries were met, but a fraction late. Jay realized, to his dismay, that his efforts were increasingly becoming defensive.

"So, Edward of Ripon," Colin cried. "You have the skill, but not the body to use it. How does it feel to infest such a pitiful weakling?" And with that he lunged forward, narrowly missing Jay's face.

Jay staggered, but turned it into an elegant backpedal

hat bought him distance and allowed him to see, beyond Rob, that Piper was slowly making his way toward them. "No, Piper, see to Dal!" he shouted again.

"See to Dal," Rob mimicked—or was it Colin? "Always your lady, isn't it? Always the true knight—except that you never were a knight, Edward the smith! And now you have failed! All those years of planning come to naught because of a mortal's weakness."

Stop fighting me! Edward snapped. *That's the problem! You're resisting just enough to make my work impossible. Give yourself over, and quickly!*

But . . .

Do it!

And Jay did. To his amazement he simply let go and let his body relax. New strength awakened as Edward settled into full control.

The attack came suddenly—not Rob's this time, but his. Jay darted forward, sword up one moment, down the next; forcing Rob to leap back to retain his balance.

Another flurry of blows, and Jay's sword opened Rob's other side, and a moment later ripped his right arm.

They had worked their way nearly to the opposite side of the tower, always skirting the pool that glimmered darkly in the middle; and Jay had almost forced Rob against the crenelated wall. Too close to Dal, though, and getting closer. One of their engagements had cut off Piper's advance, and he'd been forced to head back around the other way. Now if he'd just get Rob away from Dal while he was weakening, maybe he could finish him off.

Rob *was* weakening, too: his responses were clearly slowing, and though he now looked almost entirely like— *Colin*, Jay supposed—he fought no better than he had before.

Jay lunged suddenly, and Rob lunged as well—sideways, so that Jay's weapon missed him.

But Rob's next blow did not come flashing toward him. Rather, to Jay's horror, it whistled to his right and stabbed straight toward Dal. "Power I will have," Rob shouted. "Human blood thick with Power!"

Jay tried to block that thrust but tripped on a flagstone and fell. He saw Piper rushing forward from the other side, but he was already too late Rob's sword sank into Dal's shoulder and remained for a long, agonizing instant.

"Dal!" Jay screamed.

Her eyes went round as realization blazed into them. She stared at Rob—and in one quick series of fluid moves yanked the blade from her shoulder, lunged past it into Rob's startled arms, and smashed him in the nose with her fist.

Rob's mouth dropped open, and before Jay knew what was happening, Rob hurled Dal aside—and flung himself into the pool.

"What the—?" Piper began.

Jay twisted around and saw Rob's body lying facedown in the reddening water. Blood was pouring from his wounds faster than Jay could imagine, flowing out of the merest scratches more quickly than a human heart could pump it. It was flowing out of the pool, too; already finding its way into four channels set in the paving, and from them disappearing over the sides of the tower.

It would seem Tir-Gat has finally had its fill of Colin mac Angus, Edward told him. *The pool will suck him dry in a moment.*

Horror gripped Jay's heart. *But that means he'll—die! That was the point of all this.*

But . . . he's my brother!

An arm curled around Jay's shoulders, pulling him gently back. "Uh, Jason, my man," Piper said, squatting beside him, "I think it's over—I—"

"No!" Jay shouted and threw himself into the pool, slogging out through knee-deep water to grab Rob's floating form. He struggled to turn him over, to bring his brother's face into the air. Blood blinded him and water; he dropped the sword. The dark smell of death was everywhere. He struggled backward, slipped—fell.

Water closed over him.

Yet it was more than water, for something else was in it—something he recognized.

Colin's thought smashed into his brain. Jay opened his mouth to scream; felt his mouth fill up. Closed it, flailed wildly, felt his hands slip free of Robby. Colin was inside his head, locked in a threeway battle for control.

Let him go, mortal, I am stronger.

Not while he lives, I made a vow.

To Alberon? The one who imprisoned you?

The one who told me the truth!

What do you know, foolish mortal?

I know that I am stronger. My body could outlast yours; and I'm just as stubborn as you are.

But what of your mind? Where is your Power?

Had I no strength of will, I would be mad. Your kind knows immortality, mine does not. The fact that I still am makes me stronger.

But you are mad!

Edward ignored him.

Mad, I say!

It was a strange sensation, Jay thought: playing host to warring spirits in one's head. But he was not prepared for the attack when it came. It seemed his whole body had exploded, and every nerve ran raw with lightning. *Colin,* he somehow knew: Colin was trying to force out Edward the smith.

Pain, it is, then. Do you know pain, Edward?

I have felt my share.

For half a thousand years? Pain unceasing?

Silence.

Then Colin's fiendish chuckle. *But can the boy stand it? With both of us against you, you will vanish.*

Silence.

Suddenly Jay was on fire—no, he was freezing—no, he was being flayed. He felt hot knives driven into his eyes, felt salt poured on skinless muscles and opened nerves. Felt his balls smashed between two hammers. . . .

It is only pain, Edward shouted. *It is not real. Fight it, fight it with me.*

Jay could not. Pincers clamped his nails and jerked them out.

Fight it!

Acid dripped over his eyes.

Fight!

Supersonics ruptured his eardrums.

I—

Fight or die!

Jay gathered his will and resisted, as silver needles bored through his teeth.

Colin, you lie! And with that thought the pain lessened.

Edward was there with him, urging him on, helping him, pouring out his own strength of will.

I'll give you hammers and needles and knives! Jay focused his pain—and slammed it all back at the mage.

Suddenly Colin simply *wasn't.*

Jay gasped his relief—and breathed water, coughed and floundered. Jerked his head above the surface.

The agony was gone. Colin had vanished.

Hands closed on his shoulder. He opened his eyes.

Piper was standing there, knee-deep in water, and Dal was stumbling forward, clutching her injured shoulder.

"No, Dal!" Jay shouted. "Stay back!"

She stopped at the pool's edge, confused.

"It'll *kill* you, drink you as dry as that sword! I've got to get Robby out; I think he may still be alive!"

Jay glanced at Piper then. "Hey, give me a hand here."

Piper nodded, and together they snagged Rob's limp body under the armpits and heaved him up onto the bloody flagstones.

Jason, Edward warned, *I am not certain . . .*

Not now!

Dal was beside him, but Jay had no time for her just then. He was staring at Robby lying pale and slack on the paving. His brother had his own face and body back now, but he wasn't breathing, and his wide-open eyes looked dead. His wounds bled only a tiny trickle.

Feeling his own eyes suddenly fill with tears, Jay reached over to close his brother's.

And felt the merest brush of breath against his palm.

"Oh my God!" he shouted. "He's not dead, he's not dead!" Quickly Jay jabbed his fingers into Rob's throat to clear the airway, pinched his brother's nostrils with his other hand, then bent over and pressed their mouths together. A long, slow inhale through the nostrils, and an exhale through the mouth. Then the same thing over and over.

Eventually Rob shuddered, and Jay dared open his eyes.

Rob flinched, pulled away. But he was breathing on his own now, though he was still not fully conscious.

Jay looked up at Piper. "How 'bout it, guy; think he'll make it?"

Piper nodded. "Yeah, man. But hey, I'll watch out here; *you* ought to look to your lady. I wouldn't be surprised if she didn't start goin' into shock."

In an instant Jay was on his feet and by Dal's side. "Sorry about that," he began, "but I gotta deal with things as they fall. I—" He paused, noting how pale she was, how her pupils had slowly begun to shift size. He put his arm around her, then jerked it back abruptly, staring at his reddened palm.

"Good God, girl!" he cried. "We gotta do something about this wound!"

Dal nodded numbly as Jay peeled back the red spandex from her shoulder.

Blessedly, the slash was not as bad as it had looked. Jay ripped a long strip from the fabric, made a pad, and bound the wound. Finally he dared look at Dal's face.

She was pale and groggy, still distant. But as he watched, her lips twitched and her lashes fluttered; her skin took on more color. It was as though a veil had lifted. She blinked at him, unbelieving. "Jay? *Jay?* Is that you? I'm—" Her cheeks paled again as she glanced around, her eyes gone wide and staring. "Where *are* we, Jay? What's going on? All I remember's Rob asking me to be in the play, and then— Oh, shit, where'd I get this costume?"

Jay rolled his eyes. "A long story, Dal."

Her breath caught. She was staring at Robby's sprawling body. "He's at the bottom of it, isn't he?"

Jay nodded slowly. "Yeah, and . . . I don't quite know how to tell you this—but we're not in Georgia anymore."

Dal's gaze swept around the parapet, the dome of lavender sky—now flawed by a thick cloud of smoke in one quarter. "I think," she said slowly, "I'd better sit down for a minute."

Jay led her back to the stone wall and helped her ease down there. He put his arm around her, then glanced over at Piper who was ministering to Rob's wounds. "How is he?"

"Hard to tell, but I think he'll pull through now. Wounds've stopped bleeding, anyway. He's out again but still breathing."

Dal was shivering, and not from the cold. Jay held her tighter. "It's okay," he whispered. "I'd be scared shitless too."

She looked up at him. "But how did I *get* here? For that matter where *is* here?"

"Well," Jay began, wondering where to begin. "Do you remember that sword over in the library? Well, it—"

The slap of feet running on stone interrupted him and grew quickly louder as he listened. He reached for his sword and leapt up.

Jay crept over to the single turret that rose above the walls, where he noticed for the first time the head of a narrow curving staircase. As he steeled himself and peered down, a black-clad figure rounded the curving wall and bounded into the clear light, followed by another and another. The last one was clearly limping.

"Wannie!" Jay cried. "Myra! Scott! Thank God!"

Scott grinned. "How're you guys?" He paused, noted Dal and Rob, then frowned doubtfully. "They okay?"

"Dal'll make it. As for Robby, who knows? But Colin's destroyed: Robby more or less killed him."

Myra looked incredulous. "You're kidding!"

"Who's Colin?" Scott wanted to know.

"The guy in the sword," LaWanda hissed.

Jay laughed and shook his head. "Rob and me were fighting, and then all of a sudden he switched tactics and wounded Dal. But something about his face changed when he saw he really had hurt her. I think the real Robby won through then, and I think that Robby—the *real* Robby— knew from having Colin inside him that the only way to destroy him was by leaping into that pool and letting it drain him dry. He, you know, kinda reasserted himself then and did the right thing. Almost killed himself to save Dal."

"Surely you jest," Scott snorted.

"No, really, I saw his face."

"But—"

LaWanda walked right up to Piper, looked him up and down, and glowered. "And just what have you been up to, James Morrison Murphy? How did you get here, and how the hell are we gonna get back home?"

Piper shrugged. "I dunno. Got a *bunch* of things to think about." He hesitated. "And one thing is for us to get the sword outta the pool there 'fore it boils it dry—guess I oughta return the damned thing to the library. Gonna be *real* interesting to explain."

"I'm not even gonna ask," Scott muttered.

Jay raised an eyebrow. "I wouldn't either."

Piper dismissed them with a shrug and waded into the water, one section of which was indeed boiling—from the heat of the iron, Jay assumed. Piper felt around on the bottom for a moment, then stood up, flourishing the blade. A trickle of blood oozed from the hilt and across his fingers.

But the eyes that looked out of his face were not Piper's.

* * *

LaWanda was the first to notice, but by then it was already too late. Piper's whole face was ablaze with anger and hate, and as she watched his body was stretching, his muscles starting to swell and twitch and change. Before she knew what was happening, he had leveled the sword straight at her and started forward.

Fortunately, her body took over and put her once more on guard.

"So, Nubian bitch," Piper spat, "would you set yourself against me? Your blood will do very nicely—so much Power there." And with that he lunged.

LaWanda sidestepped—straight into Scott who was backing away to the right. She recovered fast, straightened, and stood her ground. That couldn't be Piper, it just couldn't; it had to be that magical fellow. "Fight it, Piper, fight it!" she shouted.

"Jay, do something!" Myra and Dal screamed as one.

Suddenly Piper attacked. His sword smashed into the machete LaWanda raised only just in time—and almost broke it. She gasped, feeling the pain quiver up her arm as she tried to hold her ground. This was impossible: that was Piper she faced—Piper whom she loved, Piper who made such wonderful music, whether with his pipes or his whistle or his body. She *couldn't* kill him—

Yet he was certainly trying to kill her! "Piper," she bellowed again, "fight it—fight back!"

Something moved to her right; and she saw Jay leaping to her aid from that direction, sword at ready; and then Myra was slipping in from the left, dagger glittering wickedly in her hand, with Scott right behind her with his rattan SCA sword. She took a deep breath and advanced, saw Piper swallow and step back toward the pool. Jay moved forward, and then Myra. Slowly they began to encircle him.

Piper took another backward step—and skipped sideways, maneuvering himself away from the perilous well.

Myra feinted toward him, and he laughed derisively and slashed her, drawing a long line of blood from the back of her forearm. Jay saw the opening and lunged for Piper's unprotected left side, but he was too quick, and too quick again for the uncertain machete blow LaWanda aimed at his thigh.

"Can't do it, can you?" Piper taunted. "Can't kill your scrawny lover! But he can kill you! All of you!"

LaWanda started to taunt back, then paused. She had heard something: a whisper of sound from the stairs, a distant scrabbling. She wanted to look that way but dared not let her eyes leave Piper.

But Piper *did* glance in that direction—from pure reflex; and LaWanda made her move, slashing high and low and high again: bringing blood from hip and shoulder.

Piper lashed out in a flurry of blows, pressing her back, as she saw her friends fall back beside her.

A red sweep of fabric swished through the air toward Piper's head, struck him in the face, and wrapped and blinded. Too late he raised his hands to ward off the clinging satin. LaWanda risked a glance sideways and saw Dal whipping her cloak around like a matador. This was her chance, then: now or never, and might God have mercy on her soul. She struck at Piper's chest, but his struggles took him away from her. And then something else moved to her left.

Master, I come! The words crashed into her mind like music played too loud, and the gryphon was upon them: rushing through the turret's archway, beak and talons outstretched, leaping . . .

Master, I will save you!

Myra flung her dagger—and swore vividly when it missed.

Scott batted at it with his sword, but an absent sweep of foreleg knocked him aside and into Jay.

LaWanda slashed out at Piper, but he ripped the fabric free and thrust out his blade to parry—

Just as the gryphon reared up to intercept LaWanda's blow with dagger talons. The machete slammed into its shoulder, and it screamed—but by then Piper's wildly swinging weapon had found purchase in its exposed chest. Before he could stop himself, the sword had sunk in almost to the hilt.

Two screams split the air, then. The first was something between a roar and a bestial squawk, long and shrill and agonizing. The other was a man's voice, crying out in horror and dismay as the gryphon careened onward and tumbled into the pool. It remained there, half in, half out—not moving.

LaWanda stared at her lover. He looked slack and empty, as if all hope had gone out of him. And beside him lay the gryphon, bright blood feeding the water around it, its eyes already glazed and dim as its blood pumped out around the blade.

"You bitch," Piper screamed. Their eyes met, thoughts swam back into her mind. She could feel something probing at her, seeking control.

Scott ran in from her right, grabbed Piper under the armpits and dragged him away, though he fought on ineffectually while she simply stood and gaped.

A touch on her hand made her look down.

"'Scuse me, but I need to borrow this." Jay took the machete from her numb fingers and before she knew it had leapt atop the gryphon's corpse and started hacking at its chest where it rose above the water near the pool's edge— exposing finally the silent, shattered heart still impaled by the blade of Piper's sword.

"Gross," he grunted.

For the iron was already burning away the gryphon's flesh, and the creature's blood was dissolving the metal.

"And double gross," Jay added, his face contorting in disgust as he clamped his hand around it and tugged.

LaWanda saw his jaw clench as he slashed the heart free with her blade, and clench again as he threw the awful fragment, sword and all, into the center of the pool. It floated there for an instant, bleeding freely, then began to vanish, as though the waters had commenced to absorb it. In a moment both heart and sword were gone.

A rattling gasp made her look to the right.

Piper hung limply in Scott's arms. His chest was rising and falling slowly. But the look on his face was peaceful.

Jay laid an arm across LaWanda's shoulders and drew her close. "He's okay, now: Colin's gone. I don't think he was strong enough to truly manifest in Piper's body. The only real part that survived was his heart, which was in the gryphon; and now that part's gone as well. Ain't nothin' left of Colin but ripples in the water."

"But didn't they think that before?" Myra asked. "Didn't he fool even the King of the Fairies?"

Jay nodded. "Yeah, but Alberon wasn't watching closely enough then. Colin's—Edward calls it his Silver Cord—snapped; his spirit vanished—only there was part of him still alive elsewhere, and a part of him hiding in the sword hilt where no one would have thought to look because the sword itself was iron. Both parts had to die before it was over."

"But how did you know about the heart?" Myra persisted.

"Edward told me that, too—though *he* didn't find it out until it was almost too late. He felt that something wasn't right, and sent his mind questing—he could do that, since he didn't have to concentrate quite so hard on keeping me alive. Colin let the guard down on his memory, and Edward—pounced."

LaWanda eyed him dubiously. "You sure about all this?"

I am certain! Edward told Jay, though LaWanda also heard him. The thoughts sounded weak and distant.

Edward! Jay thought. *What's wrong? You sound strange.*

I am leaving, Jason. My task is ended. By this you will know I have succeeded.

But Edward . . .

My thanks to you, Jason Madison, on behalf of myself and my kindred. I will give the last of my strength to heal your wounded.

And he was gone.

"Good job, Dal," Myra hollered suddenly. "Hell, good job everybody!"

Jay felt arms go around him. He blinked, looked down to see Dal gazing at him, obviously trying to make a good show of it, though her eyes looked wide and frightened. She still held the shimmering cloak in her hands, though the edges were stained with blood and water. When he returned her embrace, she was shaking. He suppressed a desire to pick her up, whirl her around, tell her how proud he was of her for the part she had played in their victory. But he dared not, she was still so scared she was trembling. *And with good reason*. Everything had hit her at once, not by slow degrees like the rest of them.

Dal looked at the gryphon and shuddered. "I've seen that thing before," she whispered. "I don't know where, but it was terrible—it kept looking at me as if it would like to eat me."

Jay stroked her hair. "Yeah, well, you did your part in the end. Way to go, girl!" He bent down to kiss her cheek.

—And lurched sideways as the whole tower suddenly shifted. He caught Scott with his flailing free hand and braced against him.

Water splashed from the pool, soaking his feet. He looked down, saw the well, the four runnels that led outward from it. And saw that they now ran red. He shuddered, then noticed something else. "Sorry again, Dal," he said, patting her hand. "Gotta take care of my bro."

For Rob's eyelids were stirring.

Jay started toward him, just as another quake threw him on his bottom.

"How is he?" Jay asked, when he finally got there.

Myra shook her head. "Comes and goes. He's like someone who's had a bad dream. Keeps almost coming to, then relapsing. I'll tell you one thing, though: he's lucky to be alive."

A third quake, the worst yet. The pavement heaved and

tilted. A section of parapet broke loose and fell away. The whole world rumbled like thunder.

Another: and darkness with it this time, and wind and lightning.

Rob's eyes finally opened, and this time they stayed. Jay held his breath, momentarily afraid they might be Colin's, even though it was Rob's face that now looked up at him.

Rob's gaze met Jay's and held it. Something new sparked there: a hint of resignation maybe, or was it simply gratitude?

Jay waited, breathless. A hand found his, the grip weak and shaking. He dared look down, saw Robby's fingers fumbling for his own. Jay smiled and took his brother's hand.

"Thanks, man," Rob whispered. "And, hey, Jason . . . I'm sorry."

Jay found his eyes misting. "No problem."

"I'm sorry most of all about Dahlia."

Jay nodded silently, shot a glance toward Dal who was looking on nearby, her face a mask of uncertainty. He started to reply, but another quake wracked the tower.

"We have *got* to get out of here," Scott cried. "Can Tolar travel?"

"Can you?" Myra asked him.

Rob tried to heave himself up but fell back, obviously exhausted. "'Fraid not. I'm just too light-headed."

Scott bit his lip, glanced at LaWanda and Piper. "You guys wanta help me?"

"Sure thing," LaWanda said, getting up. Then, when Piper tried to join her: "Not *you*, boy. You been through too much, I'm a helluva lot stronger."

Myra shot a glance up at Scott. "Yeah, and not you, either. Remember your tootsies?"

Scott sighed. "Yeah—though I'm feeling better already. Whatever Edward did must be working. Jay, you take care of Dal. The rest of us'll guide Robby. You ladies sure you can manage?"

LaWanda nodded. "You got it." She joined Myra beside Rob, levered him to his feet, wrapped their arms around him. He could stand—shakily.

"Okay, Mr. Tolar, just about a million steps, and then it's over. Think you can make it?"

Rob nodded.

The tower heaved and shook once more. Near-darkness whipped down upon them, lightning flashed and flickered. A bolt struck the turret not ten feet from them, turning the whole world briefly white, as splinters of stone splattered outward. One struck Jay in the thigh, but his shriek was drowned by the thunder.

He leapt to his feet, reached for Dal, and staggered forward. Somehow he found himself leaning on the parapet gazing out across Colin's country. A fissure wide as his hand cracked the stone beside him, but he ignored it, lost in the vision.

It was there, just as he had imagined: Tir-Gat, the Stolen Country. The tower, the moat, the circles of maze and forest—the long line of sand drift where Alberon's magic had blasted through—all lay spread before him. And beyond were the forests, the hills; at the limits of vision, the no-color of the earth/sky demarcation. Not very far away a vast forest fire was burning.

And there was something else out there, too: lines of silver like the radiating spokes of a wheel of which the tower was hub. They glittered in the troubled air, like mercury before a wind—and then they altered. Blood flowed into them from the tower, the merest trickle at first, which produced only a faint pinkening. But slowly the color gained force, and as it did, the lines began to spin counterclockwise.

As he watched, the Tracks slid across the land, and fog rose before them. And where they passed, other land showed through in patches: green land and a jumble of buildings he thought looked like Scarboro.

"Jay, come on!" That was Scott from the turret's entrance. Myra and LaWanda were already descending, with Robby between them.

"Come *on*, Jay!" That was Dal, dragging at his arm.

Jay paused for one final instant, for something was moving out there besides the silver Tracks. He strained his eyes: dark spots were coalescing out of the fog, emerging from the sheltering forest, creeping from the walls of the maze. Light sparked and flickered from their joints.

Avian shrieks echoed overhead, and he looked up, saw the glowering clouds of black and purple lit with lightning —and saw shapes diving down from them. Vast, winged shapes they were, with bodies like lions and the wings, heads, and talons of eagles. There were hundreds.

Another downward glance. The tower was surrounded, now—surrounded by beasts like those above except that they were wingless.

Jay pushed Dal ahead of him, ran for the turret.

The first gryphon landed, the second, then another.

In an instant they had ringed the top of the shattered tower.

Jay hesitated, caught up with wonder.

For one by one those beasts were bowing: lowering their heads and raising one foreclaw in honor.

Words echoed in his head: *Hail, Jay Madison, you have freed us. Hail, Jay Madison, Friend of Gryphons.*

Jay froze, dumbfounded.

An ominous shake rocked the tower. The surrounding beasts shifted nervously. Another section of wall sheared free and slid out of sight; the gryphon who'd sat on it remained there at a hover.

The tower shook again.

Jay took a deep breath and bowed in turn, extended his sword in salute. "If I have done you a service, I am honored."

The honor is ours, a hundred mind-voices thundered.

Jay smiled wanly, glanced at Dal. "Yeah, thanks—but we've, you know, kinda got to get moving."

No words followed, but Jay got a general feeling of assent, of approval and well-being.

Dal looked at him incredulously, as he followed her into the turret and onto the stairs.

Walls of limestone and marble curved around them. But cracks were everywhere: a spiderwebbing limned across walls, floors, and ceilings. One step, two steps; ten, twenty. Always a curve of walls, Dal right in front of him, moving as fast as she could.

With a shriek the wall to the left buckled outward. Jay rushed on, arm raised above his head to ward off fragments of mortar that fell from the ceiling.

Downward at a steady staccato half run, while the walls snapped, groaned, and shattered; and the steps beneath their feet bucked and tilted.

Abruptly it stopped.

Downward still, half out of breath, with agony poking him in the side and fatigue turning his muscles to jelly.

Another tremor halfway down, and another two levels from the bottom.

An archway loomed before him, and he followed Dal out into a high-vaulted chamber.

They were all there: LaWanda and Myra with a half-conscious Robby between them. Piper stood beside them, trying to take over for Wannie, while Scott leaned nearby his wounds already healing.

"Come on, now!" Jay called. "Why're we waiting?"

Myra nodded mutely, her breaths coming long and ragged.

A higher doorway stood before them, and they paused there, looking out into fog and chaos. The male gryphons had vanished.

A Track scythed by, leveling more of Colin's country. Fog followed it—and when it cleared again, they saw plywood flooring and the faces of people.

"Thank God," Dahlia whispered, as they looked out into their own world.

Chapter XVIII: Perfect Circle

Jay took another swig of Scarboro's dark beer and continued to stare foolishly at Dal. He could practically feel his eyes begin to twinkle.

Dal took a sip from her own mug and set it down on the round wooden table between them. Her eyes never left his. She looked tired beyond belief, though her wound had healed—legacy of Edward's promise. She still seemed a little distant, but she caught Jay's smirk and returned it.

Jay could feel a giggle fit coming on, and felt no urge whatever to suppress it. He needed a good solid dose of foolishness to put paid to the recent chaos.

And talk about chaos . . . In spite of their stained and tattered appearance, the other folk packed into Scarboro's Sword and Shield pub gave Jay and his friends no notice. There was too much else to talk about, things hinted at by the sodden shoulders, muddy sneakers, and plastered hair that marked many of the patrons as veterans of the recent weather wars. And there was the ragged gap in a corner of the ceiling from which a handsome pine branch protruded.

Still, business seemed almost back to normal at the Sword and Shield; and Jay hoped likewise with him and Dal.

Scott (also feeling much better) elbowed him in the ribs. "Penny for your thoughts, Mr. Madison."

Jay wrenched his gaze from the Fabulous Miss Cobb and regarded his roommate. "Penny won't do it this time, my man. These puppies are worth at least a quarter."

"More than that if they're what I think they are." La-Wanda chuckled. "Probably strictly X rated."

Jay felt his cheeks starting to burn and took a quick sip in vain hope of concealing it.

Myra exchanged sideways glances with Dal. "See, I told you red was his color."

Dal's eyes brightened and in spite of herself, she giggled.

Jay caught her eye and had no choice but to do likewise.

Scott, who had been distracted by a buxom barmaid, was slow on the uptake, but by the time realization sneaked up on him it was too late: caught with a swallow of beer half up and half down, he sputtered. His face turned even redder than Jay's, and a trickle of dark brew trickled from the edges of his mouth.

Myra poked him in the solar plexus.

The resulting explosion was world-class in both dispersal and distance. As the numbers hastily scribbled on napkins proclaimed, it was pronounced a perfect 10.

Perhaps attempting to salvage his dignity, Scott changed the subject. "Wonder if these folks know what happened."

Myra inclined her head toward the bar, where, after being pressed into duty for local weather reports, a large boom box was once more playing Fairport Convention. "Probably not," she said, "probably just what we heard the weatherman talking about when we came in: a hellacious fog plops down out of nowhere all over north Georgia—

which he *claims* has something to do with freak temperature inversions, though you could tell he didn't believe it. Then the weather just flat goes crazy."

"Yeah," added a new voice. "And I hear a little twister did in good old UGA well and proper. Took out about half the trees in north campus—and threw them at the rare book library, apparently. Got an entire oak right through the reading room, so I hear."

Jay looked around and saw Thomas the Hun standing there in dry medieval costume though his dark hair was still plastered to his skull. "Yeah, we heard something about that," he began. "I—"

"Want to join us?" Scott interrupted, scooting his chair closer to Myra to make room, but Thomas shook his head.

"Got a demo in a couple of minutes, just bopped in to pick up some brew." He caught sight of Dal and did a double take. "Hey, weren't you in that play? How'd it end? Fog and rain just got so bad I had to boogie."

Dal shook her head hesitantly. "Fine, actually. Hope you enjoyed it."

Thomas paused. "Oh yeah—what I saw was great, though I didn't understand that business with the fight. Hope I can catch the whole thing tomorrow."

"*Sure* you won't join us?" Scott insisted.

"'Fraid not. But you guys take care. We'll see you later."

"Not if I see you first," Scott called to Thomas's departing back.

"There'll be a new verse in the song, just for that," Thomas replied wickedly. "Something with foraminifera, curling irons, and an intimate part of *your* anatomy."

Scott steepled his brows in resignation.

Jay flopped an arm across his shoulder. "Just not your day, lad, is it?"

"So old Reed-Gillespie took some damage, huh?" Myra said thoughtfully. "Well, *that's* interesting—almost too co-incidental."

"Unless with all the magic residue in the Bowman-

Smith Codex, like called to like or something," Jay mused. "Anyway it was fortunate, considering we lost the sword. All we can do now is hope there was enough damage to cover our tracks."

"Good thing *our* house is okay," Piper added.

"Good thing Myra had sense enough to call Small and find out."

"Wish we could find out about Dal's place, though," Myra said. "I still haven't been able to get hold of anybody on that end of town."

Dal frowned, her face suddenly serious. "Right now I could care less," she said flatly. "Right now the last thing I care about's what's going on back in Athens." She relaxed a little. "I'm so glad just to be—just to *be,* I guess, I can't stand it. Have you guys got any idea what it's like to have a slice taken right out of your life?" She shuddered. "And that's not even counting waking up in some other place and finding out it really is some *other* place."

Jay reached out and took her trembling hand. "Yeah, but you made it. We're all together again, and the world's getting back to normal."

"But it'll never be normal, Jay," Dal said shakily. "It's like living your whole life in black and white, then discovering color."

"Gonna take some getting used to, that's for sure," Myra agreed.

"I still can't believe Robby didn't press charges," La-Wanda said, unexpectedly.

"Yeah, *tell* me about it." Jay cast his mind back a hour or so, remembering.

They'd found themselves back on the stage just as the last drops of what had obviously been a torrential downpour were splatting down—and apparently in the wake of an especially virulent bolt of lightning. The audience— what remained of it—was milling about holding their programs or bits of clothing over their heads, muttering uneasily and eyeing the stage with considerable suspicion.

Closer in, a trio of Scarboro security guards in red and gold livery were already sprinting toward them.

Then something marvelous had happened. In spite of his weakness, his obvious pallor, Rob had taken charge, had banished the guards with promise of an explanation later, and then he and Dal had somehow gotten through the remaining few lines of the play. As soon as the applause ended, Rob had staggered backstage and collapsed. Jay knew: he had been there—his shoulders firmly prisoned by the unyielding ham hands of two of the guards. There had been one critical moment of panic before Rob came to: a moment in which Jay very much feared his brother's wounds, coupled with his time in the well and his subsequent exertions really had pushed him past hope of recovery. And after Rob had come to again, there'd been another gut-twisting jolt when they'd asked him if he wanted to press charges.

But wonder of wonders, Rob had said, "What for? The guy *is* my brother, after all. And he *was* motivated."

They had gone on for a while, the guards obviously disappointed, but Robby had been as adamant as a person at the point of exhaustion could be. At a suggestion of a charge of disturbing the peace, it was he who pointed out that the peace had already been disturbed considerably by the capricious weather; and the assault-with-a-deadly-weapon suggestion came to naught because no weapon could be produced except a cheap stage sword Robby swore he had never let go of.

The guard had snorted and stared at Dal who stood nearby looking worried, still in her Devil costume, before speaking once more to Robby. "So you say you drove Mr. Madison here half crazy 'cause you made off with his woman?" A pause. "She go with you of her own volition?"

"False pretenses," Rob had added quickly. "I put one over on her."

Yeah, and on these folks, too, Jay had thought. *Still the same old Robby.*

Except, he had suddenly known, it wasn't—not anymore. Rob had been there at the battle between Edward and Colin that had raged inside Jay's head. They'd all been together then; and with their minds laid bare by that battle, Jay guessed Rob had found out some things. They'd both seen each other's souls naked. And what they had seen there had scared them. They were too much alike, at least in their centers: both too proud, too vain, too self-centered. It had taken magic to prove it, though, and now they'd both do better.

Rob had already shown signs of that. Finally satisfied that the guards would give them no further grief, he had allowed himself the luxury of passing out again—apparently there were limits to Edward's power. As far as Jay knew, he was at Saint Mary's Hospital by now. Jay had wanted to go along, but Rob had come to one final time just as they were climbing into the ambulance, and had insisted in no uncertain terms that the one who really needed attention to was Dahlia. "I've got holes in my body," Rob had told him. "She's got holes in her whole blessed mind. We both know which are more important."

And with that Jay could not argue.

"Jay?" LaWanda's words broke into this reverie. "Hey, man, you plumb phased out there."

Jay shook his head, realizing he *had* almost gone to sleep. "Yeah, well I have been up for—what is it? Almost thirty hours straight."

"Yeah, tell me about it." LaWanda sighed. "But look— me and Piperman're gonna go see if we can locate his band. They're not scheduled till three, and there may still be time to throw something together. Wanta come?"

Jay stole a glance at Dal and shook his head. "I reckon I'll just hang around for a while with my lady. Tell you what: you find out and let us know. If there's music, we'll be there."

Myra grabbed Scott by the arm. "Yeah! Hey, come on, Scotto, let's go with 'em."

"One more beer," Scott muttered.

Myra squeezed harder, darting her eyes meaningfully back and forth between Jay and Dal. *"Now,* Scott!"

Reluctantly Scott stood up and made his way with the others toward the door.

Jay found he could not take his eyes off Dal; he was so incredibly glad to have her back. And she was evidently glad to *be* back, though she looked bone tired, and he knew there would be long evenings filling in the gaps in her memory.

He took a deep breath and twined his fingers around hers. "I . . . just want to say one thing now and get it over with: I've been a jerk, a real son-of-a-bitching selfish jerk."

"Oh for heaven's sake, Jason, you have not."

Jay shook his head. "Oh yes I have, and the fact that you don't remember part of it doesn't make it any better."

He heard Dal's breathing catch, took a sip of beer to steel himself. "Look, it's like this . . ."

He told her: the whole thing, starting from the time she'd arrived in his living room when he'd thought she was gonna tell him about putting one over on Robby; ending with finding her on stage dressed as the Devil.

"But I wasn't myself through any of it; you know that, Jay. It was Colin and Robby controlling me!"

"Yeah, but I *was* myself. *I* got mad. *I* didn't want you to do what was good for you, even granted that I did try to talk about it. But I didn't try hard enough. And when you left—I didn't go after you, and I should have. You'd slashed my tires but I could have got another one or got Piper to take me on his bike. I could have gone to your house instead of going off to feel sorry for myself. I knew something was wrong, Dal, but I didn't follow up on it. No civilized person does that to his lady."

"Sometimes civilization's hard to maintain, especially when you start playing around with emotions."

"Yeah, but I should have trusted you. I should have made you go after that part in the first place, even before Robby asked you—listen to me: *made you go after it,* like I had control over you. I should have known that what's good for you would be good for me."

"But, Jay, I wasn't straight with you either. When Robby first asked me, I didn't tell you, 'cause I was afraid of what it might do to you just then. I doubted you, just like you doubted me."

"I guess."

"Feel better?"

Jay shrugged. "Confession is good for the soul, I reckon."

Dal laughed suddenly, joyously, her eyes sparkling. "First time I've ever been to confession in the middle of a blessed bar!"

"Pub, my dear; this is officially a pub. And I doubt if anybody's blessed it."

"But Scott baptised it really good."

"True."

"And speaking of which . . ."

Scott and Myra rejoined them. "Hey, you guys still at it?" Scott asked, grinning. "Piper caught up with the band. They're on at three."

Jay glanced at his watch—fruitlessly.

Myra saw him. "It's two-thirty-four now."

Jay looked at Dal, who mouthed a silent *yes.* "I just hope one thing, though."

Scott looked puzzled. "And what's that?"

"Please God, don't let him play 'King of the Fairies.'"

"I doubt he will," put in Myra. "But you know that new piece they've been working on? The reel?"

Jay nodded.

"He's found a name for it."

"Oh yeah?"

"Yeah—he's gonna call it 'Bane of the Gryphon King.'"

Jay rolled his eyes. "I believe," he said to Dahlia, "that I am going to have to speak to young master Piper."

"I think," Dahlia told him, smiling, "that might be a very good idea."

Epilogue

It was nearly sunset when Dr. Peter Girvan Sparks returned from Atlanta. The fog had been terrible for most of the morning, and though it had miraculously lifted around one o'clock, by then his good spirits had been utterly sullied. The conference had been a disaster, too: the dullest bunch of papers he'd ever heard—when they weren't absolute nonsense.

He stuffed his Nissan Maxima into Park, got out, bounded up the steps, and unlocked the door. Where were the kids, he wondered—and the wife? He shrugged. Oh yeah—they'd said something about going to that Renaissance fair out in Bogart. Well, they should be back soon, 'cause he thought it closed around eight. He kicked off his shoes in the living room, padded into the kitchen, snagged a beer from the fridge, glanced at the glass doors that led out onto his deck. And frowned.

Something was amiss.

He slid the heavy glass aside and looked down.

The dish of cream he had left there was empty. *Damned cat*, he thought—or else one of his students pulling pranks again. Then something caught his attention: a shot of small, dark spots beside the saucer. He knelt and looked more closely, eyes widening in disbelief. For beside the empty dish of cream were the tiny prints of bare human feet no more than an inch long and perfect in every detail.

And lying inside the saucer was something that glittered and sparkled and shot fire in a thousand colors. He reached down and picked it up. It was a diamond the size of a walnut.

TOM DEITZ grew up in Young Harris, Georgia, a tiny college town not far from the North Carolina line, which has as its main virtues two libraries and a helluva view any way you look—both of which were major influences on two of his main interests: writing and art. He moved to Athens, Georgia, in the early 1970s to pursue bachelors and masters degrees at the University of Georgia, and has been there ever since—probably because it really *is* a place of inspired craziness where you really *can* always find somebody weirder than you are. His particular interests include architecture, the Middle Ages (he is a member of the Society for Creative Anachronism), and cars.

Mr. Deitz has written two other novels for Avon Books, *Windmaster's Bane* and *Fireshaper's Doom,* both contemporary Celtic fantasies set in his native north Georgia mountains. Now a full-time writer, he still has access to two libraries (though rather larger ones), and has a view of a junglelike backyard.